W9-CLC-333

THE FALL

A 'COMMITMENT' NOVEL

NIA FORRESTER

WITHDRAWN
No longer the property of the
Boston Public Library.
Sale of this material benefits the Library.

STILETTO PRESS

This is a work of fiction. Names, characters, places, and incidents are the product of the author's imagination or are used fictitiously. Any resemblance to actual events or persons, living or dead, is entirely coincidental.

All rights reserved. No part of this book may be reproduced, transmitted, downloaded, distributed, stored in or introduced into any information storage and retrieval system, in any form or by any means, whether electronic or mechanical, without express permission of the author, except by a reviewer who may quote brief passages for review purposes.

Copyright © 2016 Stiletto Press, LLC
All rights reserved.
2nd Edition

ISBN: 9798691727320

For Tammy Jackson.
One day, I hope to be as good at this thing as you seem to believe
I am.
In sisterhood,
N.

ONE

NEW MILLENNIALS AND BOSS-BITCHES

GOD. HE WAS YOUNG. HE WAS SO YOUNG.

Lorna rolled over and out of the bed, squinting as she did. Stepping on the heel of one of the stupid pumps she'd bought only for the conference, she had to swallow the shriek that would no doubt have awoken her bedmate. With any luck, she would get into the shower and when she was done, he would be gone.

Those three glasses of wine at the mixer made her vulnerable to bad judgment, and the result was presently snoring softly, snuggled beneath the sheets. She should have gone to his room instead, but it was only at the very last moment when he walked her to her door that she decided to invite him in.

A graduate student. A student! He said he was "almost thirty" when she asked his age on the elevator ride up to her room. *Almost thirty*. It reminded Lorna of when her daughter Riley was younger, and eager to grow up. Particularly when she was twelve and pining for the label "teenager" she said whenever anyone asked, '*I'm* almost *thirteen*.' And now, Lorna had slept with a man so eager to escape the dreaded twenties and be considered a real adult that he actually said out loud, the words *'I'm almost thirty,'* hoping to impress a woman fifteen years his senior. It was ridiculous.

No, it was she *who was ridiculous.*

Something about her lectures at these conferences always seemed to attract young men like this one—eager to prove their manhood by bedding and satisfying the feminist theoretician. Because if you could get a woman like that and *please* her, then your masculinity was unquestionable. Very rarely did Lorna give any of them an opportunity to take their shot. She was uninterested in young men, and these days only marginally amused by the ones closer to her age.

But this conference had been particularly tough. There were "new feminists" all over the agenda. Young women who proudly proclaimed their feminism while wearing scarlet lipstick, platform heels and statement jewelry; who sneered at the old guard like herself, and insisted that it was *Beyoncé* who had revolutionized what it meant to be an empowered woman, that she had reinvented it, making it permissible for feminists to wear short skirts, shave their armpits, and shamelessly proclaim their intention to snare and keep a man.

It was increasingly exhausting trying to argue with these strident baby-feminists, none of them with any knowledge of the historical context, most of them brandishing the word just for its shock value. One of them this time around had actually had the audacity to suggest that "feminist" or "womanist" should be done away with entirely in favor of the more modern moniker "boss-bitch". Upon hearing that little pronouncement, Lorna laughed out loud, which only made the baby-feminist angrier, more strident and accusatory.

The panel discussion devolved very quickly after that, with Lorna finally telling her what she *really* thought of her, which was that her ideas were "embryonic, devoid of original thought and riddled with pop-cultural drivel." And then of course, they had argued, giving credence to one of the worst stereotypes about women—that they could not be trusted to congregate in groups larger than three without it turning into a catfight. By the time the session was over, Lorna had a headache the size of Texas and needed a drink. Badly. Instead of going back to her room to nurse the headache, she opted for the reception where there were drinks aplenty to be had.

And that was how the "almost thirty" graduate student had befallen her.

"Are you planning to go to any of today's workshops?"

Lorna froze at the sound of his voice and turned, facing him full-on. Perhaps the sight of her naked forty-something-year-old body would be enough to send him packing.

But on the contrary, his eyes brightened with appreciation. She wished she didn't care, but the admiration of men for her appearance still gave her a thrill. She enjoyed that they thought she was "sexy" and had "the body of a woman at least ten years younger." Both of those things had been said to her by men she slept with in the past year, and she cataloged them, even while pretending she hadn't. But they were useful remarks to take out and recall on a bad day. The truth was, she had the body of a well-preserved forty-something-year-old who was prone to some excesses, but food *not* being among them. So, she remained a comfortable size eight, with reasonably well-toned arms and legs, and only the slightest softness about her waist.

"I hadn't planned on it," she said, still facing him, but now raking her fingers through her unkempt hair.

"So maybe we can hang out," he said. "I'm pretty much done as well, and my flight doesn't leave until four."

Hang out?

"Oh, I would love to," Lorna lied. "But I have family in the city. And plans to see them just as soon as I can get myself together here."

At least that part was true. She was going to see Riley this morning and spend the entire day with her and her grandson. If she could bear the entire day. Cullen was in what child psychologists call the "age of denial" where everything was "no". Always, no. It was tiresome. Mother Nature sure knew what she was doing when she made babies cute—and Cullen undeniably was—because most of the time they were little assholes.

"That's too bad," the graduate student said. "I would have liked to ..."

"I know," Lorna said, cutting him off and beginning to back into the bathroom. "But this was ... nice."

His smile slipped a little at that, perhaps because with her tepid choice of words, it finally sunk in that whatever interest she had in him was spent in those sheets the night before.

"So, I guess I'll just ..." He sat up and Lorna averted her eyes at the sight of his bare chest.

Last night she'd kissed that chest, sucked the nipples, bitten them and raked her fingers across them. But now, she didn't even want to look.

"I have to jump in the shower, or I'll be late," she said, hoping she sounded apologetic.

"Yeah, yeah, no worries. I hope you have a good visit with your family."

"Yes. Thank you. And safe travels." She ducked into the bathroom and shut the door behind her, leaning against it, hoping he wouldn't lift her wallet or anything on his way out.

Opposite her, the mildly alarmed and very disheveled reflection of a middle-aged woman stared back at her. Lorna took a deep breath.

"Stupid, stupid, *stupid*," she muttered under her breath.

"THAT'S *HILARIOUS!*" Riley put a hand on her very pregnant belly, laughing as she settled in the chair opposite Lorna's. "So, did you let her have it?"

"I did," Lorna said, her tone regretful. "I shouldn't have, but I did."

"Why shouldn't you have?" Riley asked. "You've never backed down from a fight before."

"Yeah, I know. But it wasn't a noble fight. I don't like the optics of it. Me picking on the newbies. And who the hell am *I* anyway? Maybe they're on to something with this boss-bitch stuff."

Riley laughed. "Yeah, right. You must be really tired. What about your other session? How was that received?"

"So-so. There's nothing like seeing your life's work become obsolete. The room was half-empty and only a few questions at the end. Feminism in the traditional sense is very much out of vogue."

"Don't start sounding maudlin, Lorna." Riley reached out and touched her hand, squeezing it briefly. "Your work has been an incredible contribution to the cause of women's rights. You know that."

"I do know that. But maybe now it's time for me to be set out to pasture. Make way for the new millennial boss-bitches."

"Yeah, ahm ... no, I don't think so. And by the way, they're not '*new* millennials', they're just millennials."

"See what I mean? I'm a dinosaur."

"What's going on with you?" Riley sat up, more alert now. "I've never heard you sound so down on yourself before. Is it the birthday?"

Ah, yes, the birthday. She had been trying to avoid thinking about it. She was turning forty-six in two weeks. Inching ever closer to fifty. While she had never imagined herself as one of those people who threw themselves a Half-Century Birthday Blowout, she also didn't think she would dread the coming of that milestone like Armageddon.

"I don't know. Maybe," Lorna admitted, shrugging. "More than that, I think it might be the work. Sometimes I wonder if there's anything else to learn, to teach, to ... say about this subject. Do you ever wonder that about your work?"

Riley smiled sadly and shook her head. "Not really. But, I mean, I write about race. And race relations is at a really pivotal point right now so, it's different."

"Yes, I suppose it is."

"Mom, you're going to be fine. It's almost summer and you'll start writing again and before you know it, the ideas will be coming faster than you can get them down on paper. And women's rights, it's like any other issue—with ebbs and flows."

"Maybe I'll write something for your journal," Lorna suggested.

"*Would* you?"

Lorna laughed. "Why are you sounding so surprised? You have a journal, and I write. Doesn't it make sense that at some point I would contribute something? To my child's ... child?"

Riley shook her head. "I guess. But what are you always telling me? That you're *Lorna-Fucking-Terry*? I guess I started believing you were too much of a big deal for my little rag."

"Stop it."

"I mean it. I would love it if you wrote something for me. On any subject you want. Although it would be great if you tried to step out of your comfort zone a little and made it about something other than womanism. I'd love to get a Lorna Terry exclusive on, I don't know, immigration, or criminal justice. Something a little different for you."

Lorna leaned back into the plush, comfortable sofa, marveling at the elegance of her daughter's life.

Married to a performer, living on the Upper West Side in a luxury apartment building, and hobnobbing with the literary intelligentsia. It was certainly not the life Lorna had envisioned her having.

Riley, she thought, would have married some dreadlocked hipster, an expat from the Mediterranean who loved Bob Marley and smoked weed every day. They would have traveled the world and had babies she carried in a sling on her back while hiking through Central America. She would have written four or five books before she was thirty, and they all would have been brilliant.

But the life her daughter had now fulfilled her. She was doing what she wanted to do, with a man she loved to distraction, and who against all odds loved her back just as much. And Lorna was happy for them, and loved them both. But sometimes, like now, she felt like a visitor in her own child's life. Someone passing through who was always invited to stay, but who—everyone knew—never would. She felt like a remnant, in Riley's life and, increasingly, in her own. Even her work, which had always been a source of solace, was being taken over by younger women in fake eyelashes and Louboutins, claiming her territory as their own.

"Oh, I may be able to do that," Lorna said lazily. "Throw together a few words on the prison industrial complex, or something."

She was tired. Her night with the graduate student had resulted in only a few hours of sleep, and most of them fitful, with an unfamiliar body next to her. She was tired enough to spend the night here in Manhattan, even though she was pining for her own bed after two nights in the city. Hotel beds were almost too comfortable. They lacked all of the idiosyncrasies—the dips and dents—of one's own familiar sleeping place.

She should probably stay anyway since her grandson was napping and she hadn't spent any time with him at all. And she did want to see Shawn, her soulful, brooding son-in-law who was always a good bet for a few intellectually stimulating conversations.

"So, did I tell you Shawn and I chose a name for the baby?" Riley asked, rubbing her stomach again.

"No. What did you decide?"

They were having a girl this time, much to their delight. Lorna recalled Riley's rhapsodic description of the ultrasound when she and Shawn learned of the absence of a penis. After this one, there would be others. They were the kind of couple that needed corporeal evidence of their devotion. Lorna's money was on them having four.

"Cassidy." And when Lorna made a face, "I know. It sounds so ... fairy-princess-like, but Shawn picked it. He thinks it sounds adorable. And traditional."

Lorna rolled her eyes. Her son-in-law had been raised by his grandmother, never truly known his father and had a mother on drugs who ducked in and out of his life until she finally disappeared altogether. With Riley, Shawn believed he'd found the person with whom to create the ideal, storybook family. Lorna hadn't the heart to tell either of them that in her experience, there was no such thing, no matter how ideal the love on which that fantasy was based.

"So how's ... Cassidy doing?" Lorna sat forward and extended a hand, placing it on the fullest part of her daughter's distended abdomen.

"She's amazing. Is it weird that I already know what her personality is?" Riley placed a hand atop Lorna's. "When I was pregnant with Cullen he was like a little jumping bean, kicking and twisting all day long. And with Cass, I'm always poking myself in the stomach to make sure she's still with me. She's quieter, moves less. And when she does, it's just … different."

Smiling, Lorna pulled her hand away and leaned back again. "Cass? She already has a nickname, huh?"

"That, and a very old-fashioned middle name."

Lorna looked up at that. "Please don't tell me you're going to saddle that poor child with 'Lorna' as a middle name."

"Shawn insisted."

Tell him he's got lousy taste in names. Cassidy Lorna Gardner?"

Riley laughed. "It's what he wants."

"And Lord knows, you have to give the man what he wants," Lorna said dryly.

"Right. Like you're not the biggest sucker for Shawn there is," Riley said pushing herself up from the sofa with some effort.

Watching her waddle toward the kitchen, Lorna recalled her own pregnancy. Eons ago, it now seemed. Her situation had been very different from her daughter's.

"You want some tea?" Riley asked over her shoulder.

"Don't you have anything stronger?"

"Like what? A fifth of gin? It's not even noon. You're having some chamomile, just like a normal grandmother would."

"Oh, shut up," Lorna said.

TWO

FORTY-SIX

Who would've thought? That forty-six would be so much harder than forty-five?

Lorna leaned into the mirror, getting as close as the barrier of the sink would allow, and plucked the latest offending gray from her temple. She was still able to get rid of them by plucking, so that was something at least. Nevertheless, it was a shock to realize she cared. Always believing herself to be the kind of woman who shunned the ridiculous notion that women lost their luster with age, she was both annoyed and embarrassed to find that she cared about aging. She cared a great deal.

The man in her bed—the second this month—should be proof enough that she was still attractive, that she could have a lover if she chose, whenever she chose. Her inner thighs had begun to ache though, from all the energetic activity the previous evening. She couldn't even remember how many places and how often they did it. But she remembered well enough both of them eventually collapsing into her bed, still tipsy and giggly like the undergrads she taught.

Taking him home with her had been partly out of desire

and partly some pathetic need to prove to herself that she still could. Evidence enough that even she wasn't immune from the vanities that most women possessed. And also, Lorna liked that his name was Malcolm.

She couldn't help but think the letter 'X' whenever she heard that name spoken. But this Malcolm was Professor Malcolm T. Mitchell. Thirty-seven and having just been made a full professor in the English Department, he was Cambridge-educated and had been stolen from Yale, which had been courting him ever since he wrote a book that was almost uniformly labeled "brilliant" by the large contingent of literary snobs that hung around colleges and universities.

Lorna had first heard of him when his book was reviewed by *The Times*. It was about a young Black man from an under-privileged background with athletic talent who is courted and pursued by scouts from a young age and goes to college on a basketball scholarship. When he arrives at the school of his choice—the thinly disguised Duke University—he stuns his coaches and professors when they discover he is a math genius. Basketball is to him no more than an amusement and he all along wanted to be a mathematician, but knew that in that aspiration he would not have been taken seriously.

Lorna found the premise of the book amusing, but didn't believe that it was honest. Today, young Black men were as likely to be taken seriously as mathematicians as anyone else if their grades proved their talent.

Of course, last night at the faculty mixer, she hadn't said anything of the sort to Malcolm T. Mitchell. Instead, she'd nursed her glass of cheap red wine and watched him from across the room. He was surrounded by the English Department Maidens. Lorna called them that in her head—the female professors who were the cornerstones of the English Department, Professors Scott and Green, and then Professor Rogers who was definitely no maiden though Lorna lumped her in with them anyway.

Scott was Black, and so much was made of the fact that her specialty was the Classics—Shakespeare, Chaucer and the like. She had a long, single braid that she wore down the middle of her back, every strand of hair very severely restrained. Lorna knew that Professor Scott disapproved of her because of the way her lips tightened whenever they spoke, and because she couldn't seem to keep her eyes off the little flower tattoo on Lorna's ankle that she'd gotten in a fit of poor judgment several years ago.

Scott was divorced, and there was never any hint that she dated anyone. Lorna's gaydar told her that Scott was likely a very repressed lesbian who would live a life of celibacy unless she met some woman who was bold enough to overcome her defenses and turn her out.

Green was a slender woman, maybe about forty or so. She had reddish-brown hair and pretty amber eyes, and tended to blink excitedly when she spoke. She wore long skirts and poufy blouses, and was also divorced, but with three small children in tow. Lorna and Green had clashed often because Green fancied herself a feminist as well, and seemed to need to prove to Lorna, the feminist theorist, that she was more feminist than even she. It was tiresome speaking to Green and having endless debates about what Simone de Beauvoir's 'The Second Sex' really meant. Something told Lorna that Green would throw it all over and become a housewife if the right man came along who didn't mind taking her on with her three snot-nosed kids.

And then there was Rogers. When they'd first met, Lorna made the mistake of thinking she and Rogers could be friends. About thirty-five, the woman was quite stunning. A long neck, Venus de Milo proportions and with the subtle, graceful movements of a dancer. She had jet-black hair and a dark olive complexion, wearing very little make-up, just enough to accentuate her large, dark brown eyes. Her mouth was full, sexy. She seemed completely comfortable with herself.

Rogers' focus was on Modern Literature and her classes were wildly popular because the boys thought she was hot and all the girls had girl-crushes on her and tried to adopt her mannerisms. And it didn't hurt that she had an entire lecture series that studied the works of popular fiction authors like Candace Bushnell, who wrote the 'Sex and the City' books. Lorna thought it might be interesting to study the feminist perspective in those works but Rogers had rebuffed every overture.

Later, as she observed her, Lorna figured out why. Rogers, quite simply, hated other women. She viewed every other woman as an annoyance and only managed to tolerate Scott and Green because she had to for the sake of her career. When men were around, particularly men with power, Rogers blossomed like a midnight rose, exerting the full extent of her charms in their direction.

Lorna had watched her on many occasions with a dispassionate, academic interest, thinking, *Wow, she is* really *good at this.* There was probably not a man alive that Rogers could not get into bed if she set her mind to it.

So, last evening, Lorna had been watching the English Department Maidens surround Malcolm T. Mitchell, thinking that they had found their fourth cornerstone. Rogers was practically hanging on his arm, obviously attracted to him, and wanting him to be attracted to her.

From the back, Malcolm T. Mitchell was impressive—broad shoulders, square back, and impeccable posture. Wearing washed-out blue jeans and loafers, he seemed to have pulled on the sport coat as an afterthought, or a nod to the fact that he was in the hallowed halls of Gilchrist College. Lorna liked the sight of his ass in those jeans, and the hint of strong thighs. His hair was cut low, and he wore glasses. She wondered whether he needed them. Even from behind, she could sense that the English Department Maidens were just barely managing to hold his interest.

Had it not been the evening before her forty-sixth birthday, Lorna might not have decided to approach them. Had she not been feeling weepy about the fact that she was getting older, and embarrassed that she was feeling weepy, she would have finished her wine and gone home. But instead she'd emptied her glass and decided to go rescue the new wünderkind of the English Department, the new jewel in Gilchrist College's crown.

When she touched him on his shoulder, he turned right away, almost as though relieved. Rogers shot her a look of undisguised annoyance.

Professor Mitchell, Lorna said, extending a hand. *I've been waiting with bated breath to meet you.*

He smiled. He was handsome, in the manner of a man who when younger was not so handsome and now is quite perplexed that women seem to like him.

Good to meet you. You are ...?

Professor Lorna Terry, she said. *Women's Studies.*

His back straightened at that. Lorna was not without ego when it came to her professional reputation, and so it pleased her that he seemed to recognize the name.

Oh yes, he said. *Your son-in-law is that rap star.*

For a moment, she thought he was serious and then from the twinkle in his eye and twitch around his mouth realized he was teasing her.

Yes, she said. *Guilty as charged.*

Well, Professor Mitchell said. *He's very ...*

Lorna held up a finger.

Tread carefully, she warned. *I'm very protective of him and if you say a single negative word, I'll be forced to snub you from here on out.*

I was only going to say that he's very talented, Malcolm T. Mitchell assured her.

As are you, Lorna said. *Or so I hear.*

So, you haven't read my book? Malcolm T. Mitchell asked. He didn't sound insulted, as many stuffy academic types might.

Not a single word, Lorna said.

Rogers was growing visibly restless. She recognized verbal foreplay when she heard it.

Malcolm T. Mitchell smiled again.

And so, it began.

"YOU PLAN on leaving me alone in here all morning, or is this a ploy to get me to leave?"

His voice calling from the next room interrupted her thoughts and Lorna put the tweezers back in its place in the medicine cabinet.

"Not at all. Can I interest you in breakfast?" she called back to him, reaching for her toothbrush and putting on toothpaste.

"Yes. You can."

The door had opened and he was right behind her, shirtless and pant-less, underwear-less, and naked as a jaybird. Without his glasses he was sexy, like Clark Kent turned into Superman. His skin was smooth except for the stubble beginning on his jaw.

Lorna finished brushing her teeth though she was distracted by him pressing against her, leaning over her shoulder, rinsing his mouth, grabbing the toothpaste, using his fingers as a toothbrush.

"Should we eat at the campus café?" he asked, his mouth full and frothy.

"Only if you're not opposed to rumors," Lorna said. "It is only eight a.m. on a Saturday morning after all."

"Are you worried about your reputation?" he asked, grinning through the foam.

"No," Lorna said seriously. "I'm worried about yours."

She did a final rinse and went back out into the bedroom.

She hadn't planned for him to be here beyond dawn, but what the hell? She had no better ideas other than to mope about her impending old age.

"What does that mean?" he asked as he emerged from the bathroom.

"You know ... 'another one bites the dust', that sort of thing," Lorna said, beginning to strip the bed. They'd made quite a mess of it. In more ways than one.

"Ah. So you have lots of conquests do you?"

"What's 'lots'?"

Malcolm smiled. "Wow. That many."

Lorna looked at him, meeting his gaze evenly. "I enjoy men."

"Is this where I'm supposed to run?" he asked. "Or make an excuse and skulk away because my masculinity is threatened by your superior experience?"

Lorna straightened her back. "Well, not superior, but possibly more extensive. And are you?"

"Am I what?"

"Threatened."

Before he could answer, the phone rang. Lorna made no move to answer it but both she and Malcolm looked over at the phone next to her bed.

"Wait," he said, "is that an actual, physical answering machine?"

Lorna smiled. The phone rang twice more and then she heard Riley's voice.

"Will you pick up? Pick up! I know you're there. I know you're there. Okay, maybe you're in the shower. Shawn and I wondered whether you might want us to come up for dinner and you could see your grandson. Call us back. Happy birthday, old lady."

Malcolm T. Mitchell looked at her and smiled. He smiled a lot, this one. "I got more information from that message than I might have learned from you in weeks. It's your birthday and you have a grandson. What's his name? And how old are you today?"

"His name is Cullen, and it's impolite to ask a woman her age."

"Cullen is a great name. And with any other woman perhaps it would be rude. But not you."

"Why? Don't I deserve the same ...?"

"Let's cut the shit, Lorna. You're not like other women. How old are you?"

"Forty-six." She hated that it was difficult to say it. And that she wondered whether he might think she was too old for him. But even if she was, it didn't matter.

"Happy birthday," he said. "We should celebrate."

"Should we?"

"Yes. We should. Birthdays are important."

"Maybe I'll celebrate later with my daughter and her family." Lorna shrugged. She turned back to her task of stripping the bed.

"Maybe you will," Malcolm said, and he was right behind her. "But I thought we might celebrate right here, now ..." Hands on her hips, he was moving her back even closer to the bed. "And then we'll take a long shower together, and go eat at the campus café so you can ruin my reputation."

Lorna turned to face him, let her head fall back, and looked up into his warm, brown eyes. He'd been a good lover and would be good company for a while. He kissed her, his hands falling to her ass. Lorna smiled against his lips.

Forty-six, she thought, *might not be so bad after all.*

———

THE BEST TIME of year on the Gilchrist campus for Lorna was just after Commencement Weekend. She rarely attended the ceremony itself unless there was a particular student of hers she wanted to see walk across the stage and it had been several years since that last happened. Now, they all seemed interchangeable, even those for whom she served as a thesis advisor. In the fall, she would have two advisees, neither of whom she had taught before; at least not that she recalled. Their thesis proposals had been assigned to her for review among several others, and she chose them randomly from the pile of other uninspired offerings.

Now, standing at her kitchen window, looking out across her somewhat overgrown backyard, she wondered at her recent general lack of inspiration. In years past, she would already have had several ideas scribbled in various notebooks, and be chomping at the bit, eager to begin writing. But this year, nothing. Maybe, as Riley had suggested, it was the birthday. She didn't recall being this shaken by turning forty-five. On the contrary, last year she had been bursting with youthful enthusiasm and congratulated herself for feeling— and on some days, even looking—like a woman just over thirty.

Maybe forty-six was the other side of the crest, and the

decline would now begin. Her own personal commencement—the commencement of old age.

"Stop feeling sorry for yourself," she muttered.

That was another troubling development. She had begun speaking out loud to herself. The silence in her house was sometimes oppressive, and more and more, Lorna found herself longing for the sound of another human voice. So much so, she had gone and bought a television, a forty-two-inch monstrosity that looked incongruous among the books in her sitting room, and which she now sometimes kept on just as background noise, though she rarely if ever watched it. This morning it was silent, so the house felt like a tomb.

Determined not to give in to the doldrums, Lorna turned away from the window and went to the sunroom to get her sneakers. Putting them on at her kitchen table, she decided to take the long walk to campus and then around the perimeter which was marked by a two-foot high red brick wall on the far edges, a discreet line of demarcation between the exclusive college and the mostly working-class town. All told, the walk was about five miles, and at the end of it, Lorna had no doubt she would be too tired to obsess too much about anything other than the pace of her steps and of her breaths.

The campus was almost, though not quite deserted. A smattering of students remained, moving furniture and suitcases out of buildings, yelling at each other from windows on the upper floors of the dorms. Gilchrist College, formed in the 1800s, was once a college for the daughters of upper-crust New Yorkers who wanted to keep their children near enough to the city for the all-important coming-out balls and social season.

Located conveniently close to West Point, dozens of "Gilchrist girls" of yore had been fortunate to meet their husbands at socials hosted by the esteemed military academy. Back then, many Knickerbocker families had sent several generations to Gilchrist until the sixties when it became one of the first exclusive colleges to openly court Jews and Blacks, and in 1969, men as well.

Today, Gilchrist was a liberal bastion that attracted young people from the country's prominent progressive, artsy families, many of them with significant wealth, though much newer wealth than that of the student body in the 1950s and prior. The children of several well-known movie stars, writers, visual artists and performers were likely to be matriculated at the college on any given year.

Lorna had grown accustomed to the slight pause after many of her students told her their name, as they waited for her to recognize its significance. In most cases, the pause was wasted on her, since she was woefully ignorant of most of the goings-on and the players in popular culture. And in some ways, that ignorance had served her well, earning her the reputation for being an impartial judge of her students' coursework, no matter their pedigree.

After the first mile, when Lorna was growing slightly winded, she slowed her pace and turned her attention to the main building of the campus, the castle-like edifice covered in ivy and with an enormous, hundred-year old front door, complete with brass knocker. And as luck would have it, at just that moment, she saw Malcolm T. Mitchell emerge.

Wearing jeans and a driving coat with hiking boots, he looked almost as young as the undergraduates he would be teaching come fall, and had a slightly bowlegged pimp-walking gait that was very attractive. Even from a distance, he was someone she would have noticed, someone whom she would have wanted to know. That is, if she hadn't already ... known him quite thoroughly less than a week earlier.

With him was the persistent Professor Rogers, her dark hair loose about her shoulders, and whipping up in a sudden breeze.

She was walking very close at Malcolm T. Mitchell's side, and laughing at something he said. Or just laughing in general because she probably knew full well that she was quite beautiful when she did.

Hoping to avoid them and the inevitable meaningless small talk that would follow, Lorna abruptly changed course, ducking between two parked cars and glancing back over her shoulder to make sure she hadn't been spotted. In doing so, she collided with someone who yelped, and a pile of books fell to the gravel-covered ground between them.

"I'm so sorry," Lorna said, kneeling to help retrieve them.

"Professor Terry!"

Lorna looked up. The young woman whose books she had knocked to the ground bore an expression of recognition on her pretty face, but Lorna could not place her.

"Fallon," she said. She extended a hand. "Fallon Wright."

There was that pause.

"I audited one of your classes last year. My sophomore year. Remember? I came to your office and ..."

"Oh yes, yes." Lorna smiled and nodded though she didn't recall any such thing. "Nice to see you again, Fallon."

"And you're my thesis advisor in the fall."

This made Lorna pay more attention. "Oh?"

"Yes. I'm writing about Susan Sontag? You approved my topic?"

"Ah, yes."

This Lorna did remember. One of the many uninspired topics she had reviewed, this one was an examination of Susan Sontag as a social critic whose Achilles Heel was her inability to be *self*-critical. Hardly an original idea, but it would be interesting to see how it was dealt with by an undergraduate research paper.

"I'm really looking forward to working with you," Fallon

said as they both stood and Lorna stacked her books back onto the pile in her arms.

"So you're on campus this summer?" Lorna asked, out of politeness.

"Yes, I thought I'd get a head-start. And I have a part-time job in the library, so ..."

"Well, wonderful. Maybe we'll run into each other again. If not, have a good summer, Fallon." Lorna moved around her, pretending not to notice that the girl had opened her mouth as though planning to say more.

"Yes ... ahm, thank you."

Lorna moved quickly out of the vicinity not daring to look behind her in case Professors Rogers and Mitchell were still lurking about.

The rest of her walk was uneventful, and when she finally made it back home, Lorna was exhausted, exhilarated, and looking forward to a warm shower. There were two messages on her answering machine. One from Riley and another from one of the Deans, requesting a meeting in his office at her "earliest convenience.". Such was the nature of her life—there was Riley and her family, and then there was work. Very little remained to fill the spaces in between. How was it that she hadn't noticed that before now? How was it that what had once seemed to be more than enough had now begun to feel so inadequate?

Shoving those questions to the back of her mind, Lorna shed all her clothes and surrendered her aching body to the warm massage of her shower.

THREE

PUSSY POWER

"You can't possibly have thought that would be appropriate for us to publish in the course catalog, Lorna."

"On the contrary, Steven, that's precisely what I thought. Otherwise I wouldn't have sent it over."

Sitting behind his large mahogany desk, crawling with paper, some of it yellowed with age, much of it in piles that threatened to avalanche onto the Berber-carpeted floor, Steven Hunt looked every inch the stuffy college administrator, with a little Ichabod Crane thrown in. He was about six-five, but stooped a little, and ducked his head slightly when he entered and exited a room so one might get the impression he was freakishly tall. He had probably been one of those kids who sprung up fast around the time he was fifteen, and had gotten so used to thinking of himself as ungainly, that it became a self-fulfilling prophesy.

Lorna was sitting across his desk, and struggling to maintain focus. She always got distracted in this office, because Steven had floor-to-ceiling bookcases behind him with hundreds of books lining them, some of them tattered with age and over-use, and others brand new and clearly never read. It was always much more diverting to scan the titles than it was to attend to whatever conversation she had been summoned to have with the lanky Dean of Social Studies.

"So you honestly believed that we would include among our course offerings a class titled ..." He looked down. *"'Fifty Shades: Post-Feminist Backlash or Twenty-First Century Pussy Power?'* You *honestly* thought that?"

Lorna shrugged. "You were the one who said we were under pressure to make our department's courses more ... I think the word you used was 'alluring' to the undergrads."

"Alluring. Not provocative and, and definitely not *prurient.*"

"Is it the use of the word 'pussy' you object to?"

Steven gave a brief laugh. "Yeah. For starters. And then the reference to that book that had women masturbating during their lunch breaks. That didn't help either. We're teaching sociology, not ..."

"Exactly. So I think it'd be interesting to explore why women were masturbating to the idea of a 'romance' that featured a man who insisted on dominating the woman in question and having her subsume her entire identity in order to ..."

"You read it?" Steven looked scandalized.

"Of course. How could I not? It was only being talked about everywhere you looked. My curiosity *forced* me to. And believe me, there's *lots* of material there for feminists to talk about."

"Okay, okay. I can concede that much. If ..."

"There's always an 'if' with you," Lorna said, shaking her head.

"It's my job. So, as I was saying. You can keep 'Fifty Shades' as long as you lose the word 'pussy'."

"Pussy power is a concept, Steven. Not just a casual use of

coarse language. It doesn't work if you substitute it with 'vagina'. Trust me on this."

Leaning back into his leather chair, Steven folded his arms and took a deep breath. Finally, he shook his head.

"I'm going to have to insist that you consider other titles for the course, Lorna. And we don't have time for you to dick me around. I need the new title by tomorrow COB."

"*Dick* you around? I wonder would that be an appropriate course heading. Something with the word 'dick' in it. '*See Dick Run: Patriarchal Fear of the Feminine Form on the Modern American Campus.*' Something like that perhaps?"

Lorna watched as Steven's shoulders sagged and his eyes went flat and expressionless.

She was fully aware that it was only by virtue of their thirteen-year friendship that she was able to get away with this kind of insubordination. That, and the fact that they'd had a brief affair about seven years earlier. Back then, he hadn't yet met the woman who would become his wife, and if memory served, he'd used the word 'pussy' himself quite liberally at one time.

But he had moved on and was now married to a pretty girl with a pleasant smile who wore lots of LL Bean, and dressed their toddlers the same way. She was much too young for him and looked as vacant as an abandoned lot, but who was Lorna to judge?

"I have another appointment, Professor Terry, I'll look for email from you later."

"I'm *Professor Terry* now. Okay. I guess you mean business."

Steven leaned forward and made a steeple with his fingers, waiting. When he looked at her like this, he reminded her of John Houseman on that old series 'Paper Chase', staring inscrutably at his law students, his displeasure felt rather than seen.

"No later than tomorrow, close of business. Please."

"That's hardly giving me enough time to come up with something 'alluring', Steven."

"Well, you took a week to make this appointment to meet so you have only yourself to blame. So ... tomorrow. Please."

Steven's '*pleases*' were deadly. And they basically signified that he was no longer asking, but pulling rank and telling her what to do.

"Tomorrow, close of business," Lorna confirmed, feeling suddenly weary.

Steven opened his mouth as though to say something else but a knock interrupted him. Both he and Lorna turned and looked toward the door.

"Ah!" Steven stood, his face brightening. "Malcolm. Come in, come in."

Lorna stood as well, taking a moment to compose her features before turning to smile a greeting at Malcolm T. Mitchell. Seeing that it was she, he smiled as well.

"Lorna. Wow. I was beginning to wonder whether you still worked at Gilchrist. Or maybe whether you unexpectedly went on sabbatical."

After their night together, they had a very pleasant morning and then a late breakfast. He was interesting, and handsomer every time she saw him. And her colleague, albeit from another department. Lorna had long learned her lesson about making conquests on the small college campus. After a while it all became a little too close for comfort.

Steven was a case in point. She never knew what to make of his wife's relentless niceness. Was she completely ignorant of the fact that Lorna had once slept with her husband, and the niceness was genuine? Or was Lorna simply being killed with kindness and then later verbally hatcheted to death when the Hunts returned to their marital bed? It was too uncomfortable trying to decide which was true, so the solution was to simply avoid pissing in her own pond. Lorna had successfully avoided that for quite some time until Malcolm T. Mitchell and the evening before her birthday.

"Why? Have you been trying to reach me?" Lorna asked innocently.

Malcolm smiled again, his expression saying, '*are you kidding me?*' But out loud, he said, "I tried a couple times, yes."

"I'm terrible about checking my messages," Lorna shrugged.

Gathering up her bag, she slung it over her shoulder and moved from the space between the desk and chair. But Malcolm was blocking her path out of the office and looked disinclined to stand aside. Behind her, she could feel Steven watching the exchange between them.

"So then I wouldn't want to leave it to chance and let you walk out of here without making firm plans."

This one was *bold*. He didn't seem to care that they had an audience. That alone teased out the beginnings of the smile Lorna was determined to suppress.

"What plans would you like to make, Professor Mitchell?"

"A meal. Some conversation. Tonight."

Behind her, Steven cleared his throat. "Should I give you two some privacy?"

Malcolm T. Mitchell laughed. "I don't think so. I know exactly where to find Lorna. If she'll just give me a time, I think we can move on to the real purpose of my coming here."

Feeling her face grow warm, Lorna was aghast. She couldn't recall the last time a man—or anyone for that matter—made her blush. If they were alone, she might cut him down a peg or two, but what would be the point in making a scene in front of Steven and feeding the gossip mill?

"Six should work," she said, taking a step toward him.

He didn't budge. *Arrogant, insufferable man.* Was he going to make her *shove* her way out of the room or what?

They were less than a foot apart, and he was looking down at her with those molten chocolate eyes clearly visible behind those glasses, which for all she knew were just to make him look more ... professor-like. Involuntarily, her nostrils flared at his scent. It reminded her of that night, and of the sex—frenzied, rigorous, almost rough ...

"Good," he said, his voice quieter, and deeper. This time he was speaking very pointedly only to her. "See you then."

And after couple beats more, he stood aside and let her pass.

She felt his eyes on her as she walked away.

"SO, what was the disappearing act about?"

"Good evening to you, too." Lorna stood aside and admitted Malcolm T. Mitchell into her home.

"Good evening. Now what was it about?"

Wearing a powder-blue long-sleeved linen shirt and beige linen pants, he looked like he'd shaved just before coming over. He also looked like something Lorna might want to eat for dinner.

It was always easier to have the kiss-off conversation if one didn't still just want to kiss the man in question. But it couldn't be helped. It would be more difficult to say the words with conviction, but they had to be said: *it was just a one-time thing, Malcolm.* And this one time, out of considera- tion for his ego, she might go easy on him. In her experience, the arrogant ones were the most fragile when it came to rejection.

Shutting the door, Lorna turned to face him, and for a moment was taken aback to find him so close on her heels. She looked up at him, a question in her eyes and Malcolm smirked, then before she knew what was happening, her back was pressed against the door and he had her pinned.

"I'm waiting," he said.

For a moment, Lorna was confused and then gradually she felt her ire rise. That, and her excitement. It had been years since a man had handled her in this way—these days none of them dared. Her work came with all kinds of assumptions, not the least of which was that she wouldn't stand for a man simply acting like ... a man. On the contrary, she loved it.

Malcolm T. Mitchell had either figured that out about her, or he didn't care. It was that second possibility that irritated her. Who did he think he was? Who did he think *she* was? Scarlett-fucking-O'Hara to his Rhett Butler?

Putting her hands up, she shoved against his chest. It was rock-hard. She remembered that now; that beneath the urbane, collegiate exterior, Malcolm had the physique of a man who paid careful and almost meticulous attention to his body—not an ounce of extra fat anywhere. She recalled running the flat of her palms across his chest and down his stomach, and the way his eyes darkened, both warning and inviting her as she moved lower.

"What exactly are you waiting for?" she asked, stalling.

"An explanation. We had a great night. And then you pull some sophomoric little ..."

"Sophomoric?"

"Yes. Immature. Juvenile. *Young.* All those things."

This was where she should tell him off, push him off, and ask him to leave. But she didn't want to. And playing coy wasn't her thing. She wanted him, and what she wanted, she generally went after with gusto. Why should this moment be any different? Afterwards, she would tell him ... she would tell him ... afterwards ...

"And I guess you think the way to win me over is to come to my house and offend me."

"Are you offended?"

Lorna couldn't help but smile.

She shook her head slowly as his face came closer. And just as his lips made contact with hers, she closed her eyes. He nipped her lower lip and pulled it in, sucking it lightly before dipping his tongue in for a brief taste. She remembered this as well; that he was an exemplary kisser. Good enough to almost make her forget that there could be even greater pleasures than kissing. Lorna pressed in closer for more and felt his smile at her response.

One point to Malcolm T. Mitchell.

"You're going to return my calls," he said against her lips.

Lorna wasn't sure whether it was a question or a directive. She had a sneaking suspicion it was the latter, but she didn't care. At least not at the moment.

She nodded slowly and he deepened the kiss, his hands coming up to capture her wrists and move her hands from where they were still between them, pressed against his chest. Relieved of that barrier, he came closer and soon the only thing she could feel between them was what felt like a rod of granite at his groin. God bless his young soul, he was ready at the drop of a hat.

Smiling, Lorna pried one hand loose and reached down between them, feeling him. Malcolm groaned and pulled back abruptly, though their lips maintained contact. Capturing her wrist once again, he held it far away from the point of contention.

Lorna smiled, just as his lips traveled down her jaw and to her neck. She tilted her head to the side to make way for him.

One point to Lorna Terry.

She didn't want him to get the impression he could have the upper hand after barging into her meeting, and then into her home. A tie she could accept, but he couldn't have the upper hand.

"Let's go eat," Malcolm said, pulling away suddenly.

Blinking, Lorna almost gasped in frustration. *What the hell ...?*

"I'm on to you," he said smirking.

Then he reached behind her and opened her door, standing aside so she would exit before him.

He drove them to the Harbor Inn in his Range Rover, as yuppie-like a vehicle as Lorna might have expected from the young professor. Harbor Inn was a small place set right on the banks of the Hudson; it was family-owned and simply decorated, serving fairly decent seafood, and excellent steaks. It was the place where parents of Gilchrist students took their collegians when they came to visit, or for a nice graduation dinner.

On any given evening during the semester, there might be a few students at the restaurant on what they thought was a nice, grown-up date, but rarely did faculty go there. Probably because they wanted to avoid the students. But it was late spring, so there was little risk of running into anyone they knew, or might wind up teaching. Summer students rarely had the means to dine at places like Harbor Inn.

The hostess, an attractive girl with dark hair and startlingly blue eyes guided them to a table that overlooked the waters of the Hudson, and its craggy shores. Lorna loved this part of the country and missed it whenever she was gone too long. In just a few short months, the Hudson River Valley would transform, and become a golden landscape so breathtaking that people would drive from all over the tri-state area just to witness it. Since most of her conferences occurred in the spring and summer, Lorna was fortunate not to have missed this awesome display by Mother Nature in many years.

Their waitress surfaced with menus and rattled off the specials, and recommended wines when Malcolm inquired about a good pinot grigio. He chose one without asking Lorna what she wanted to drink, but she let it pass. The cool evening air, and the memory of their kiss in her foyer had her feeling docile and not inclined to argue.

"I was warned about you," Malcolm said when they were alone again.

"Oh, I have no doubt you were," Lorna said.

"I was warned that you're very difficult to get to know. And that you throw up barriers—usually intellectual ones—against people who try."

What was there to say to that? It was true, after all.

"I guess after hearing that, I was expecting something a little more sophisticated than the good old-fashioned refusal to return phone calls," he continued.

"Well, then next time I'll be sure to reject you in a much more sophisticated manner than refusing to return your phone calls."

Malcolm didn't smile as she would have expected he might. Instead he fixed that penetrative stare of his directly on her.

"*Are* you rejecting me?" he asked.

"Depends on what you're offering," Lorna returned. "I can be a friend and a colleague. A ... mentor, or ..."

At that Malcolm did smile. "What makes you think I need a mentor?"

"You're new to academia, you're young ..."

Malcolm smirked. "So that's how you plan to play this? I'm too young for you?"

"How old are you?"

"Thirty-eight. Somehow I doubt I'm the youngest man you've ever been involved with."

For a moment Lorna's memory flashed back to that graduate student from Ohio. She couldn't recall his name, and that caused her a moment of something akin to shame. She was way too old to be picking up anonymous lovers. Her twenties and thirties were riddled with that kind of behavior and nothing good had come of it other than a brief, but misguided sense of sexual liberation.

"I don't know whether to be insulted by that comment," she said, feeling nothing of the sort.

Their waitress returned with water and with a young man who opened a bottle of wine, poured the first glass and waited for Malcolm to sample and approve it. He nodded his assent, both their glasses were filled and then their servers departed.

"Of course I didn't mean to insult you ..." he began.

"Well, that's a relief."

"Lorna. *Stop*."

The forcefulness of his tone gave her pause. She felt almost chastened.

"I'm not interested in verbally jousting with you. I'm interested in getting to know you. And ..." Then he shrugged. "The jousting, of all kinds, can come later."

Sighing, Lorna picked up her wineglass and took a sip, enjoying the sharp, fruity taste on the back of her tongue. It was a good choice, though she hadn't been consulted.

"So tell me about yourself, Malcolm T. Mitchell," she said when she put her glass back down. "What brings you to Gilchrist when your writing career is so clearly about to take off? Teaching is what a writer does at the end of his career, not the beginning."

Turned out he was looking to become a writer-in-residence

somewhere, but teaching full-time wound up being a better bet since he had recently gotten divorced and needed the income. He had two girls—one thirteen and the other nine, who lived with his ex-wife, Charlotte, in the city.

Both he and Charlotte were attorneys but apparently, while she had taken to their chosen profession like a fish to water, he loathed it, and had written his book on weekends and late at night when his household was asleep. Around the time he grew more serious about his writing, and getting published, Charlotte grew more disenchanted with their marriage.

"And the rest is history," Lorna finished for him.

"I hope not. I hope the rest is actually just the beginning."

He emptied his wineglass and set it aside, as though he had satisfied some internal quota for how much he intended to drink.

Little things like that made Lorna think he was probably very disciplined, possibly even structured in his life. If she was right, she needn't worry about rebuffing him. Men like that could never tolerate the messy, jazz-like cadence of her life for very long. She woke at different times each morning, sometimes writing late into the night, sometimes before first light. She sometimes smoked, and then for a year or two, she quit.

She could be almost maniacally social at times—having dinner parties, brunches and wine tastings in her garden—and then at others, lived like a recluse. Her life was disorderly, its only constants being her work; and Riley, Shawn and her grandson. Everything else was temporary and disposable, most especially the men who passed in and out.

"I plan to read your book," she said. "I bought it shortly after we, ahm, met."

"You'll have to tell me what you think of it."

"What do *you* think of it?"

"Of my own book?" His eyebrows lifted.

"Yes. Do you feel as brilliant as they say you are?"

"No," he said with a laugh. "Never."

He had scampi with wild rice and Lorna ordered the sea bass, thinking all the while about her daughter who would have scolded her for choosing something that wasn't sustainable. She often heard Riley in her head, as though she was the parent, and Lorna the child. Her daughter was sometimes unnervingly mature for her age.

"So I'm interested in hearing who thinks I throw up barriers for people who want to get to know me," Lorna said, once their meal was underway.

"Professor Hunt, for one. He was very entertained by us when we were in his office this afternoon. Spent the first half hour of our meeting singing your praises."

"Telling you I throw up barriers doesn't sound like praise to me."

"He also said that every conversation with you makes him feel like the class dunce. That you're witty, sharp and have lots of barbs. That it only makes sense that you would be a feminist because you're probably right in your assessment that no man could ever live up to you."

Lorna took a bite of her fish. "Steven should know better. Being a feminist is in no way a retaliatory thing. It shouldn't just be defined in relation to men. Just like being Black is more than simply the absence of whiteness."

Malcolm grinned. "You should know," he said leaning in and lowering his voice. "Whenever you talk like that, it makes my dick hard."

LORNA HAD ALREADY DECIDED she would sleep with him by the time they got back to her house and was mentally taking stock of how she'd left her bedroom and bathroom. He had stayed the night last time, and she wouldn't mind if he did again. Last time they talked over breakfast and she wasn't the slightest bit bored. Dinner had been fun tonight as well, and when he used the word "dick" she got wet immediately, reminded of the occasion when she made the acquaintance of said dick.

As she recalled, he was circumcised and smooth as stone. And once fully tumescent, the tips of her fingers barely touched when she grasped him in her hand. She had taken him in her mouth and loved his slightly salty taste, and the vaguely musky man-scent. She could almost taste him now as they walked up the path toward her front door. And once they were inside, she would.

Reaching down into her bag, Lorna fumbled inside, trying to locate her keys. It had barely been dark when they left for dinner, so she hadn't switched on the outside lights, and now, under the eaves at her front door, it was almost pitch-black. Just over her shoulder, she felt Malcolm's solid presence, waiting. Then, just as her fingers touched the cold metal of the keys tucked into a corner of her bag, she felt his hands, warm on her shoulders.

Turning her to face him, Malcolm kissed her before she even knew what was coming. Her bag fell to the flagstone path and he backed her against the wall in the portico, just next to the front door. Lorna scarcely had a moment to react before his tongue was forcing its way past her lips, demanding that hers come out to play.

Malcolm T. Mitchell's kisses were insistent and assertive, turning off Lorna's rational mind and activating everything that made her a woman, responding to a man who knew all the right steps in the mating dance. Lorna's arms went up and around his neck and Malcolm shifted, his knee parting hers as he moved closer. The pressure against her clitoris made her breath catch for a split second, and she tore her lips away from his.

"Are you really going to dry-hump me right here at my front door?" she asked.

"I think we both know you're far from dry right now," Malcolm said.

Lorna chuckled against his lips and nipped the lower one with her teeth, which he returned by putting one of his large hands at the back of her neck, holding her in place so he could kiss her properly, thoroughly. Occasionally, he moved his knee, but mostly he kept it still where it was, his thigh a steady and firm pressure that made Lorna want to grind herself against it.

Oh he knew *exactly* what he was doing, because before long, that was precisely what she did, her hips moving slightly up and down while they kissed. Malcolm's free hand, which had been braced against the wall above their heads finally came down and between them. Moving his thigh, he reached for the stretchy waistband of Lorna's long skirt.

"Oh, *no* you don't."

In one split second of lucidity, she realized that if he touched her skin-to-skin, they might very well wind up screwing right there in her entryway. Stooping to retrieve her bag, she momentarily encountered the jutting protuberance in Malcolm's jeans. She looked up at him and found that he was looking down at her. They both laughed and Lorna stood, bag and keys in hand.

"Let's go in," she said, hearing the breathy impatience in her own voice.

"Ahm, I don't think so."

Freezing, with the keys in the lock, she tried to figure out what she may have missed. Unless she was mistaken, when they left off moments ago, he was literally trying to get into her panties. And now he didn't even want to come in?

"You don't think so?" She opened the door and reached in, flipping on the light.

Malcolm squinted for a moment, his handsome square-jawed face grimacing against the brightness before he adjusted. Lorna felt his restraint, she just couldn't for the life of her figure out why he thought it was necessary to exercise it. She had practically forfeited the entire game—they were going to sleep together tonight, and for as many nights as they both wanted, from here on out. *Why couldn't the man just be a gracious winner and accept his prize?*

"I've got to get back."

Lorna stared at him disbelieving. "Back to what?"

"Course descriptions. I haven't finished mine."

"Oh shit." Lorna recalled that she'd promised Steven a reworked title for her own as well.

But who the hell cared? That was an hour's work at most. He could come in and still have his course descriptions finalized before dawn, if he set his mind to it. And she was so horny, she thought she might explode. Hell, *he* was so horny he might explode, if that bulge in his pants was any indication.

"But look," Malcolm said. "You like chamber music?"

"Hate it," Lorna said, almost spitefully.

"Good, so maybe you'll be interested in the reggae festival in Peekskill. Third World, Damien Marley, Burning Spear. I'll come get you tomorrow at one."

Lorna stared at him, trying to formulate an answer, and Malcolm leaned in to kiss her one last time quickly on the lips before turning and heading back down the path to his car.

Lorna slammed the door and leaned against it.

Pussy power, her foot. Now where the hell had she left that damn vibrator?

FOUR

THE PIPER HAS TO BE PAID

"Change of plans. I may need you to come get them tonight instead of tomorrow."

Malcolm took a deep breath and ran a hand over his head. "I thought we were done with all that, Char. That we were agreeing to make plans and stick to them."

"Malcolm, it's out of my control. You know how it is when there's a big new client. It's all hands on deck. Particularly if those hands want to make partner."

Malcolm bit back the snide response that rose to his lips.

Just because he'd never cared about things like that didn't give him the right to denigrate Charlotte's ambitions. And Lord knew, his creative aspirations were about as ridiculous to her as her corporate ones were to him.

"What time are we talking about?"

"As soon as you can get here? I'm not leaving the office until late tonight, so I can tell Elisa to have them packed and to expect you at whatever time you say."

Elisa was Charlotte's mother's helper—the woman who packed Malcolm's kids' lunches, got them ready for school, made them do their homework, and on at least two nights a week cooked them dinner and ate with them. Most of the time it seemed to Malcolm that Charlotte was the one helping Elisa raise their kids, rather than the other way around.

"So if I have them tonight, how will they get to school in the morning?"

"Shit!" Charlotte said. "I hadn't thought of that. I keep forgetting that you live all the way up there in that godforsaken little town. Then how about you come here? Spend the night and take them to school. I'll be in at some point. And Elisa gets in at six a.m. so she'll have all the school stuff prepped and all you'll have to do is walk them in, and if you don't stay in the city all day, she'll pick them up."

"And you need me to have them tomorrow night still as well?"

"If you could, yes."

The original plan would have had him getting his kids in the city around seven p.m. on Friday night. He would have spent the afternoon with Lorna at the reggae festival, dropped her off and then headed straight for Charlotte's to pick them up. But if he spent tonight—Thursday night—in the city, he would have to come back upstate for his afternoon plans, then head back to the city again. That was a lot of driving.

Of course, he could cancel his plans with Lorna and simply stay in the city until Friday and take his kids back upstate with him as soon as they got out of school. No. The driving was probably worth it. It had taken far too long to reconnect with the prickly Professor Terry, and no way was he risking her slipping from his grasp and disappearing on him once again.

"I'll come tonight, but I have to leave right after they go to school tomorrow. Then I'll be back to get them later."

"Whatever works for you," Charlotte said, sounding rushed. "So I can tell Elisa to expect you? What time?"

"Nine ought to be fine."

"Thank you," Charlotte said, sounding relieved. "Normally, I would just have her stay over, but this time she couldn't. I really appreciate it, Mal. I mean it."

"Yeah, anytime."

Being there for his daughters, Piper and Hayley was never an inconvenience, but the way Charlotte failed to plan for things like this was. She knew the nature of her job, and she also knew he wasn't exactly a stone's throw away. Why she couldn't make contingency plans was beyond him. Her sister lived in New Jersey, and her parents had a seasonal home on the North Shore of Long Island, so it stood to reason that she could put them on notice to help out when she had emergencies, but since Malcolm moved upstate, she never had. Calls like this were almost a weekly occurrence now.

"And I don't know," Charlotte said. "Maybe we should talk about you moving back. To the city, I mean. Do you honestly need to live where the college is? You have a couple of courses that you're going to teach, but ..."

"That's out of the question, Charlotte. I can't be a full member of the faculty if I'm rushing to catch a train out of town the minute my classes end. Not to mention, I'm going to have office hours, and ..."

"Okay, okay. I just thought I'd throw it out there," she said sounding bored. "Anyhow, let me call Elisa so she'll expect you."

"Yeah. Thanks."

Malcolm checked the time once they'd hung up. It was already a little past eight. He could get to Charlotte's place in Brooklyn in an hour or so. The girls should be asleep by then, or at least ready for bed. He didn't know their routines any longer, since he hadn't lived with them under the same roof in more than a year, but with any luck he'd get to spend a little time catching up on their lives.

Charlotte was a good mother in her way, but there was no doubt he'd been the nurturer between the two of them. She was the drill sergeant, making sure everyone's teeth had been brushed, hair combed, permission slips from school signed. He was the hugger, the kisser, the keeper of secrets. And with Piper turning fourteen soon, there would be more secrets. Malcolm worried about not being there to hear them.

In that tony and exclusive school where the girls were enrolled, the secrets—and the concerns—were far different than anything Malcolm had faced growing up. Piper was already hearing about so-called 'pill parties' and classmates who snorted Oxy. A girl she knew had been taken by her parents to get an abortion, and another cut herself on her thighs, where the wounds were easily concealed until a teacher spotted them in gym class.

Malcolm knew there was no way to protect his kids one hundred percent from the ills of their privilege but he sure as hell intended to be the first line of defense. So when Charlotte's absences grew longer, he was going to do his damnedest to make sure there was at least one parent present. Even if it meant an unplanned drive into the city on a Thursday night.

Grabbing his keys, he headed back to the car and once he started the engine, checked the gas gauge to make sure he had enough fuel for the journey. There was no telling where he might encounter a back-up on the way in, and he didn't want to have to stop until he was in Brooklyn and parking outside Charlotte's brownstone.

Plugging in his phone so it wouldn't lose its charge, he considered making a call, wondering whether she would answer this time. She'd never given him her number and the only reason he had it was that he'd checked the faculty contact list in her department. Everyone's home and cell numbers were listed for the benefit of their colleagues, though the list was confidential to students.

Malcolm had just backed out of the driveway of his small, college-owned house when the first ring sounded in the confines of his car. He waited through a second and then a third, fully expecting that he would be sent to voicemail; so her voice was a surprise. It was smoky, smooth and sounded like that of someone who had not too long ago woken up. But that was the way Lorna Terry sounded all the time, and it just about drove him crazy.

"I wondered whether you might want to keep me company for a little bit," he said.

"Who *is* this?"

Her humor. That was another thing he liked about her. It was biting and sometimes caustic, not for the feint of heart. He could only imagine the number of men whose balls shriveled when faced with a woman like her.

"You answered."

"I think I recall having been *ordered* to do so."

"I was bluffing," Malcolm said.

On the other end of the line, Lorna sighed. "I'll remember that the next time you order me to do something."

"You never would do anything you didn't want to do anyway."

"Oh, I don't know. I can occasionally be coerced."

"I don't believe it," he said. "When was the last time anyone ever coerced you into anything?"

"Just this afternoon. Steven insisted I change the title of one of my courses. You walked in on the tail-end of the coercion as a matter of fact."

"Is that why you looked so put-out and annoyed? I thought that was because of me."

"You're vastly overestimating the effect you have on my moods, Malcolm," she said.

He smiled. Another zinger. A man would have to bring his 'A' game every single time with her, for sure.

Malcolm heard sounds like her moving around crockery, perhaps washing dishes, or grabbing a mug for coffee? He was curious about her life, and what she did to occupy it. Did she read in the evenings? Drink a glass of wine? Watch trashy television and drink flowery teas? Did she write, or entertain lovers? Everything about Lorna Terry intrigued him from the moment they'd met, and for a while he was proud of himself for having ensnared someone so fascinating, until his unreturned calls forced him to admit that it was she who had ensnared him.

"So what was the title of the course you were coerced into changing?"

When she told him, Malcolm spluttered into unexpected laughter. On the other end of the line, Lorna laughed with him.

"I don't think it's that shocking," she said finally, a smile still in her voice. "I mean, do you know what young people are up these days?"

"No, I *don't* know. Do you?"

"Well, no, but ..."

"It can't be much worse than what went on in the sixties."

"I know you're an English professor, but your math is terrible. I have no idea what went on in the sixties. I was born when all that was over—Kennedy had been shot, Dr. King was gone—and I missed the whole free-love party."

He was beginning to think the whole age thing was more of a soft spot for her than she was acknowledging even to herself.

"I didn't mean you'd experienced it, Lorna. Just that there's nothing new under the sun."

"Well, men's squeamishness about women co-opting their vocabulary to refer to *our* sex is definitely not new. So I guess I should have known that the word 'pussy' would have Steven clutching his pearls."

God, he could talk to her all night. He hadn't been kidding when he said what he had at dinner. She made his dick hard, just because of her intellect alone. And that there was all the rest of it? Well, that just made the whole package infinitely more appealing.

"So have you come up with anything? Anything other than 'pussy power' I mean."

"No," Lorna said sourly. "I think my brain is rejecting the exercise entirely. It's refusing to help me. Maybe you can help me think of something."

"No ma'am. I'm staying well clear of this one."

"Oh I didn't peg you as a coward, Malcolm T. Mitchell."

"I'm not. I just steer clear of coming up with, or using clever names for women's anatomy,"

"That's not what I remember," Lorna said.

Malcolm felt a twitch at his crotch, but said nothing.

"And speaking of cowardice. Why are you talking to me on the phone and not here with me in the flesh?"

The way she said the word '*flesh*' positively dripped with sex. If he wasn't careful, this woman would have him whipped, quick and in a hurry.

"I'm not about to let you use me for my body, Professor Terry," he said, trying to keep the tone light.

"So what would you *like* me to use you for?"

"Well, I don't want to be too hasty on the body thing. You can use that at will. But I want to be more than that. And I have an instinct about you."

"Really? What's that?"

She was practically purring now, and Malcolm felt himself developing what felt like an honest-to-goodness woody. Just from talking to her.

"My instinct tells me that you're a woman who doesn't value anything that comes too easily."

"Trust me. You're far from easy," she said. "I don't think I've ever had to work this hard to get laid a second time by a man I've already slept with once."

Malcolm laughed again. "I don't know what to do with you."

"Yes you do. You're just too frightened to do it."

"Hey. Not frightened. Cautious," he chided. "I want us to get to know each other better. Is that so terrible?"

"Not at all. In fact I look forward to it. But there's no reason we can't do that and sleep together too."

"You're being too agreeable. I think you're messin' with me."

"Not at all. So come over. I'll leave the door open for you."

For a split second, Malcolm shut his eyes. *Christ, he wished he could.*

"Can't tonight. On my way to the city to see my girls."

"Oh. Another time then."

Lorna sounded as though it made no difference to her one way or another. If it was the last thing he did, he was going to make this woman beg for him.

"Tomorrow," he said.

"Well ..." She let the word drag out. "Tomorrow's tricky for me."

"You didn't say anything about it being tricky when I mentioned it earlier. What's tricky about it?"

Down boy. You're the one who's begging right now.

"I told you, Steven wants ..."

"Bullshit," Malcolm said. "I'm coming for you at one, just like I said."

"Malcolm ..."

"G'night, Lorna. I'd better go. This is a weird spot for cell service."

"Malcolm ..."

He hung up on her and waited. If she called back, then she was serious about canceling. Malcolm counted to ten very slowly but his phone didn't ring.

Twenty. Thirty seconds. A minute.

The phone remained silent.

———————

ELISA OPENED the door and Malcolm was assailed by the sounds of high-pitched shrieking. Recognizing the voice of his older daughter, Piper, he looked wildly around trying to figure out where in the house she was before realizing that Elisa was perfectly calm.

"What the hell is going on?" he asked.

Elisa shrugged. "Her mother suspended her cellphone service. There were some text messages ..."

A cold hand wrapped around Malcolm's heart. "What kind of text messages?"

Elisa shrugged. "You have to ask Mrs. Mitchell. I don' know. And Mr. Mitchell? I'm so sorry, but I have to go. I have a ..."

"Okay, of course. I've got it from here. And you're in tomorrow, right? Six a.m.?"

"Yes. I'll be here." Elisa nodded and reached for the door handle, only glancing back once before ducking out the door and heading down the steps and to the sidewalk below.

Malcolm wasn't certain, but when she looked back, he thought the expression on her face might be one of relief.

Locking the door behind him, he turned to head upstairs. The shrieking had stopped, but he was quite sure the crisis that precipitated it was still a live one. At the top of the stairs on the landing, his younger daughter, Hayley, was sitting cross-legged and waiting.

"Hi Daddy," she said matter-of-factly. "Piper's having a meltdown."

"I heard. What happened?"

"Her phone got turned off. Mom saw some messages between her and this boy from her school. He's sixteen. His name is Deonte."

"*Sixteen?*" Malcolm said, ascending the stairs much faster now. "Where is she?"

Hayley nodded, indicating the door to Piper's room, which was firmly shut.

Hayley looked much more like him than Piper did, with a clay-toned complexion and light-brown eyes, the color of milk chocolate. Her hair was reddish-brown; that part she had gotten from Charlotte's side of the family. Piper was all Charlotte, through-and-through—slender and graceful, high-strung and difficult. And now that she was hitting puberty, the tantrums were more frequent, and harder to control with just a stern talking-to.

Shoving open the bedroom door to his older daughter's room, Malcolm found her sitting on the edge of her bed, staring defiantly down at the rug and picking at the pink coverlet. Her hair was in a single braid that rested on her shoulder. For about the millionth time, he wondered at how beautiful she was, and worried that this one, this kid would be the one who would break his heart.

"What's with all the screaming?" he asked, trying to keep his voice stern.

"I was talking to Mom," Piper said as though that alone offered an explanation. "She turned off my phone because I was texting with *my* friend, and she totally *violated* my privacy by ..."

"You don't have any privacy, Piper," Malcolm said, cutting to the chase.

He went deeper into her room and took a seat at the desk where she did her homework. The desk upon which sat a two-thousand-dollar piece of computer equipment. Was it any wonder kids these days turned out to be such brats with luxuries like these?

"But Daddy ..."

"You're a kid. Thirteen is not old enough to have rights of privacy. At least not while your mother and I pay for your food, shelter, clothing and everything else you need. You get privacy once you can afford it. And right now you can't."

Piper's lower lip wobbled, but Malcolm forced himself to hold strong.

"Who is this Deonte kid? What's his last name?"

Piper hesitated and he gave her a warning look.

"Deonte Simmons."

"How old is Deonte?"

"He's sixteen, but ..."

"That's too old for you to be hanging out with him. Or having private conversations. Gimme your phone." He extended his hand.

"Daddy ..."

"The phone, Piper."

Piper whipped an iPhone 5 from beneath her thigh, reluctantly handing it over.

Malcolm looked at the face and asked her for the password, which she supplied. Now, there were tears rolling down her face.

Looking through the text messages, Malcolm found the ones from Deonte, which Piper had listed as "Deo." They were mostly harmless, but in the last two weeks had become more flirtatious, with lots of 'you're cute' messages being passed back and forth, and finally, leaning toward the more provocative with Deo asking whether she wore bikinis or one-piece bathing suits, and saying he was sure she would look "hot" in a bikini.

"See?" Piper whined. "It's nothing. She so totally overreacted. I hate her."

"She didn't overreact, Pipe. She did the right thing. It's not appropriate for an older boy—or any boy—to be making comments about your body, or asking you personal questions about your body. And it's definitely not cool for you to respond to those questions."

"But what if he *likes* me?" Piper whined, her voice beginning to increase in volume once again.

"I don't give a crap, Piper!" Malcolm said losing his patience.

He resented that Charlotte wasn't here to help deal with this in person. And he was too tired from the drive to play good cop to Charlotte's bad, tonight. And hell, this wasn't a good-cop-bad-cop scenario; this called for both of them to draw a hard line and hold it, no matter how much shrieking Piper did.

"Well then I hate you too!" Piper screamed.

Her words stung like a slap across the face but Malcolm absorbed the blow and stood.

"I'm keeping this," he said, holding up the phone. "You're not getting it back. Not for a long, long time."

Piper's continued shrieks followed him out of the room.

A WARM HAND on his forehead woke him and Malcolm sat up, startled. It was Charlotte and she was apparently just getting in. Dressed in a pale blue suit skirt, the jacket in hand, she looked very tired. Charlotte was a beautiful woman. When he met her, Malcolm remembered thinking the word 'thoroughbred'.

She had strong, sturdy features, well-muscled limbs and was bursting with the health of a New England girl who lived much of her childhood outdoors. Her parents were one of the only interracial couples in the town where she had grown up in New Hampshire, and Charlotte bore traces of her redheaded mother in the burnt auburn of her hair, pale complexion and the smattering of freckles across her nose.

Though feminine and beautiful now, Charlotte had the kind of face that would gradually morph into 'handsome' as she aged, like Katherine Hepburn, Lauren Bacall or some other Old Hollywood beauty.

"It's fine. You can stay."

He had fallen asleep on her bed—the bed that used to be their marital bed—while watching the eleven o'clock replay of the evening news. Next to him on the nightstand was a glass of wine that he hadn't finished. After listening to Piper scream and cry herself to sleep he needed the drink to prevent himself from going into her room and smothering her with a pillow.

"Nah, I'll take the couch," Malcolm said, swinging his legs over the edge of the bed.

"Suit yourself. But you'll be more comfortable here."

Charlotte turned and went into the en suite, draping her jacket over a chair as she went, and unzipping the back of her skirt, letting it slide to the floor. She had a great body, which she pounded into submission with thrice weekly workouts with a trainer at a studio close to the firm.

On those mornings, she left the house at four a.m. That had been her routine for years, even while she and Malcolm were married. Back then he had respected her discipline, even while he regretted the loss of feminine softness it resulted in. Her hips were narrower, her stomach hard and flat, her arms as well-defined as those of an athlete.

"Piper flipped out on me tonight," he said sitting on the edge of the bed.

"Welcome to *my* world," Charlotte said. "It's become a thing with her lately. Just uncontrollable rages ..."

"She's a child. It's a *tantrum*, not a ... rage."

"Whatever."

"I think we need to be more firm with her."

"Like how? Beat her with a belt like your father did you?"

Malcolm rolled his eyes. "Can we not argue about this? Can we just try to get on the same page?"

"I turned off her phone. That should be good for a couple weeks. And then I'll have to turn it back on."

"Why?"

"Because she *needs* to have a phone, Malcolm. It's about more than her convenience. I use it to know where she is, and to keep her on track with appointments, and for Elisa to reach her. It's not just a luxury item." She made air-quotes with her fingers, alluding to his rants about all the material things they gave their children.

"Fine. Then ..." He ran a hand over his head. "I don't know what to do about things like her texting boys and getting into these questionable situations. I just don't ..."

"We do what we're doing now, Malcolm. We address each thing as it comes up, the best way we know how in the moment. We wing it."

"*Wing* it?" he asked, incredulously.

Charlotte shrugged. "I don't know what else to tell you. We had kids, and like most people we had no idea what we were getting into. Sooner or later, the piper has to be paid."

Laughing mirthlessly at her pun, she turned on the faucet at the sink and began washing her face.

FIVE

BLACK, NO SUGAR, NO CREAM

Malcolm was walking with Lorna through the streets of downtown Peekskill, occasionally pausing to look at vendors' stalls. The reggae festival began today—Friday—but the really good acts were slated for the next afternoon when the crowds would be largest. So, Malcolm and Lorna had wandered away from the main stage and were taking in the sights of the town itself. There wasn't much there, honestly. Located along the Hudson, and only a few miles away from Gilchrist College, it was once an industrial center, but in modern times had become more of a bedroom community for New York City.

"Really?" Malcolm said, looking at Lorna as she walked. "I guess I thought your daughter was older than that, though it makes sense since you're only ..." He let his voice trail off.

She was wearing jeans and sandals with a white cotton tunic blouse, and had pulled her wavy dark hair back into a ponytail. Instead of a leather purse, the bag she carried was a hobo, fashioned out of burlap. *Burlap.*

Malcolm almost smiled when he saw it, and tried to

imagine Charlotte with anything other than a sack of potatoes made of burlap. His ex-wife probably wouldn't carry a burlap hobo if she was an *actual* hobo living on the streets of New York. Lorna Terry carried hers with aplomb.

"People often think that about Riley when they hear about her." Lorna shrugged. "And when they meet her they're surprised to see she's practically a child."

Malcolm laughed. "It's because she's so accomplished."

"Not just accomplished," Lorna said. "Smart. She took a terrible situation and the attention that followed it, and made gallons of lemonade out of those lemons."

"That had to have been awful, going through that with her."

"It was ... manageable. Brought us closer. Helped me get to know my son-in-law better."

"So that's good then," Malcolm said.

"Yes. It is." Lorna stopped walking and looked up at him, forcing Malcolm to stop as well. "I have a feeling you want to ask me something. You didn't just idly bring Riley up."

"You know I have two daughters ..." He put a hand at her shoulder so they could keep going.

"You told me, yes."

"One of them—Piper—is thirteen. And I just, I can't shake the feeling that we're in for some tough times with her. She's so tightly-wound and at the drop of a hat she flies into these tantrums that ..."

"Malcolm." Lorna stopped him. "If you're looking for parenting advice, you've come to the wrong person. Riley practically raised herself. And the fact that I successfully got her to adulthood without serious incident has little or nothing to do with my aptitude as a mother, believe me."

"I don't need advice so much as I like picking your brain," he said. "You've got a big one, y'know?"

Lorna laughed. "Thank you?"

"No." Malcolm looked at her. "I mean it. I like talking to you, listening to you. It's ... refreshing to be with a woman who cares more about ideas than ..."

"Ooh. Stop. I hear an indictment of your ex-wife coming on. I'd really rather not, Malcolm. Become the foil for some other woman's perceived failures."

This time it was he who laughed. "See what I mean? Who *says* things like that? No one else I ever met, that's for sure."

"I'm glad you find me such a curiosity."

"Not a curiosity." He held her arm so she would stop walking and turned her toward him.

She smiled and he saw tiny crow's feet at the corners of her eyes. But her latte-complected skin was otherwise perfectly smooth. Her age was in the wisdom of her eyes rather than her features. They were knowing eyes, dark and almond-shaped, fringed by naturally long lashes that remained—in all the times he'd seen her—unenhanced.

"I don't find you curious at all," he said, pulling her closer. "I find you fascinating, intriguing ... sexy."

And then he kissed her. Right there out on the street. Something he hadn't done since he was in his twenties and prone to that kind of impulsive behavior. But Lorna didn't seem to mind; she kissed him back immediately, only pulling away when it appeared they were both about to get a little too exuberant about it. When he raised his head, she was smiling again.

He never knew what he was going to get with her—the prickliness, or the womanly softness like right now. Everything about Lorna Terry screamed 'Handful' and 'Trouble' but there was also something about her that was as bright and seductive as the sun. It was impossible not to look, even though you knew it may hurt your eyes.

"Should we find someplace for lunch?" she asked.

Malcolm nodded. "I could eat." When she turned to begin walking again, he took her hand and she didn't pull away.

They found a small Latin-fusion place that served only *tapas* and got several of the small plates with a bottle of red wine. Sitting across from Lorna in the almost empty restaurant, Malcolm regretted that their afternoon together would have to end before it became evening. He had to go back to the city to get his girls, and they would be with him for the entire weekend.

"Tell me about what's happening with Piper," Lorna said unexpectedly, as though she'd read on his face the direction his thoughts had taken.

"She was texting with an older boy from her school. So, her mother turned off her phone service as punishment and she flipped out on us both."

"But if she sees him at school, what difference does it make if you turn off her phone service?" Lorna asked reasonably.

Malcolm's shoulders sagged.

"I mean, at least with the phone, you monitor it and you can see where she is and who she's been talking to, right?" She bit into a small tortilla topped with fresh basil and goat cheese.

"You don't think that's objectionable? Spying on her."

"Spying on her? One can't 'spy' on one's own minor children."

Malcolm leaned back. "I'm surprised you would think that."

"Until they're adults it's our job to guide them, and the only way we can do that is with the best information. Information they don't always share willingly."

"Huh," Malcolm said.

"What does 'huh' mean?"

"I guess I just thought you would have a much more permissive view of things."

"Well, in some I probably do. For instance, have you talked to her about birth control? Had a doctor ..."

Malcolm shook his head. "Nah. Piper is light-years away from ..."

"*Older* boy. You said it not me." Lorna shrugged and ate another *tapa*. "But you know your child better than I do."

"You said something interesting. You said Riley practically raised herself."

"I was eighteen, just turning nineteen when I had her," Lorna said. She took a long sip of her wine. "I was in my freshman year at college. I was determined not to become what everyone said I would be—another girl who had ruined her chances. So occasionally, taking care of a baby came in second to other concerns."

"But you're close now."

"Very much so. And I'm grateful for that. It could easily have gone the other way. But I think Riley is ... temperamentally inclined to ... love." She shrugged.

Among the things he had heard about her was that Lorna Terry was professionally self-assured, almost cocky. But in the passing references to her personal life, she seemed remarkably humble, and not inclined to give herself credit for anything. So far, she'd implied that she had been a lousy mother, and that if her kid loved her, it was only because she was "temperamentally inclined" to do so. There was obviously a story there, but Malcolm sensed that if he simply asked what it was, all Lorna might offer was a sanitized version, or clam up altogether.

Deciding to let her off the hook, he changed the subject. "So. Did you ever think of a new title for your course?"

"Yes. *'Fifty Shades: An Examination of Post-Modern Female Sexual Permissiveness in Popular Culture'*."

Malcolm laughed. "Very good. Lots of opaque words that say very little strung together to sound intimidating."

"That's how they like it. Steven approved it right away."

"But it sounds like you're going to spend the entire semester talking about that book."

"That book?" Lorna echoed. "Do I hear sour grapes? *That* book outsold everything in print for a long, long time. How did yours stack up, Malcolm T. Mitchell?"

"It didn't, by comparison. Not even close. Horny house-wives trump everything. But anyway, I write literary fiction, not ..."

"Oh, I knew those jeans and folksy blazers harbored the heart of a snob," Lorna teased him. "No one has ever explained to my satisfaction the difference between popular and literary fiction. Seems to me it's a distinction meant only to belittle the people who outsell you."

"Ouch!"

"So, tell me then." Lorna leaned closer, and Malcolm had to repress the urge to kiss her again. "What's the difference?"

"Literary fiction examines the human condition through the characters, or offers criticism, or observation of society and its vagaries. Popular fiction just seeks to tell entertaining stories."

Lorna laughed. "I'm impressed. How long have you been working on *that* definition?"

"About seven months now. Ever since a reporter asked me the question back when my book first came out and I couldn't answer it," he admitted.

Lorna leaned back and smiled at him. They had been doing a lot of smiling all afternoon. But this one was different. It felt like yet another brick in the rock-solid wall surrounding her had been painstakingly removed.

DIGGING his fingers into the flesh of Lorna's ass, Malcolm thrust even deeper, feeling her nails rake across his back. They were both slippery and slick with perspiration because when they returned, it was to a warm house. Lorna said she hated central air, and instead kept her windows open, and ceiling fans on in the warmer months. It had been unseasonably warm that day, almost summery.

Just outside her bedroom window, a bird chirped, casually, lazily, oblivious to the intensity that was unfolding only feet away.

"*God* that's good ... like that, just like that ... just like that."

Lorna's warm breath on the shell of his ear, the smoky huskiness of her voice spurred him on. Malcolm flipped over, taking her with him so she was on top. Lorna leaned forward and licked his chest, taking a nipple briefly between her teeth so that inside her, his dick jumped and jerked.

"No, goddammit," he hissed, grabbing her face. "You're not going to cut this short."

"Why would I want to?" Lorna gasped.

Malcolm pulled her face down to his and devoured her, their tongues going at it like gladiators fighting to the death. Lorna pulled back and bit his lip, hard.

Tasting a hint of blood, Malcolm kept going but let his hands fall to her hips, stilling her so he could drive into her the way he wanted to, slowly arching upward, corkscrewing and pulling out almost completely. Lorna's head fell back and exposed the fair column of her throat. Releasing her hips from his hold, he pulled her down again, sucking her right at the spot where her neck curved, and loving how she moaned when he did.

Losing patience with the limited range of movement from

being beneath her, Malcolm flipped her over again, and grabbed one of her legs just behind the knee and slung it over his shoulder, plunging into her at an angle. He felt himself hit a spot that was softer, hotter and sweeter. She felt the sweetness too, because Lorna's cries grew louder and more high-pitched, her stomach and legs trembling and quivering. She was coming, but he still had a few more minutes in him.

Pulling out abruptly, he slid down her body and buried his face between her legs, covering her with his mouth, and sticking his tongue deep. Lorna bucked and he pressed her thighs flat with his forearms, forcing her to remain in place while he drank of her.

"Malcolm! Oh god … *Mal* …"

Raising his head just enough so he could see her face as she came apart, Malcolm tried not to smile.

That's what he wanted—to hear her say his name, so he would know that *she* knew just who it was that made her feel this way. She might have had more than a few before him, but he was going to be the one who mattered, even if it killed him. And hell, it just might. His heart was racing at a ferocious pace.

When she went slack, no longer able to fight the feeling, only occasionally jerking at the sensation of his tongue relentlessly stroking her, Malcolm covered her body with his again and shoved deep, grasping the sheets on either side of her head. Lorna's expression was one of incredulous pleasure. He kissed her, feeling her lips turn upward into a smile.

Sucking in a stream of air, he slid in and out of her in three last, long, deep stokes before feeling the tightness at the base of his stomach. Lorna felt it too and cupped his face in both her hands, kissing him hard. Malcolm groaned into her mouth and she took that in too, both of them disappearing into the feeling of perfect completion.

Malcolm was still dazed and waiting for his brain cells to

re-fire when Lorna shoved at his chest, reminding him that all his weight was resting on her relatively small frame. Rolling over, he watched through half-shut eyes as she got out of bed and pulled a kimono-style robe tightly around her, and briskly fastening the belt.

"It's just past four-thirty," she said. "You mentioned something about having to get to the city to get your girls?"

Malcolm raised himself onto his elbows and watched her.

She was at her dresser mirror and had begun scooping her hair up, trying to restore it to some semblance of order. The sheen of perspiration was visible on the backs of her calves, and at her nape when she lifted her hair. Outside, the birds still chirped as though the earth hadn't almost tilted off its axis moments before.

And apparently, Lorna Terry was determined to pretend she hadn't felt it either.

"Yeah. Thanks. I'll take a shower first if that's okay."

"Of course. You want tea?" She looked over her shoulder at him, but still didn't make eye-contact.

"Coffee's better if you have it."

"I have it." She turned away from the dresser as though to go make it.

"Lorna."

She stopped and looked at him again, her expression flat, giving away nothing of whatever emotions may have been beneath the surface.

"Bring your ass over here."

She hesitated.

"I'm not going to bite," he said.

Rolling her eyes, she came to him and he pulled her down onto his chest. Parting her robe, Malcolm looked at her breasts. Medium-sized, large nipples, and full in all the right places. He took one nipple between his teeth and nipped slightly.

"*Ow!*" Lorna smacked him on the side of the head, and he slid from beneath her.

"So, yeah, I lied. I do bite," he said before he left her there on the bed.

She had a strange look on her face—amusement, and something that was almost like gratitude.

For what, though? Lightening the mood?

In everything except for the interpersonal, she didn't seem to mind when things got heavy. If he suddenly wanted to argue politics or the existence of God right now, she would probably loosen right up. But one earth-shattering orgasmic experience—and he had no doubt her world had been shaken just like his had been—and she was ready to run for cover.

"Black, no sugar, no cream," he said before shutting himself in the bathroom.

PIPER STILL WASN'T SPEAKING to him by the time he got the girls packed and ready to go. And Malcolm couldn't say he cared, honestly. Hayley was immersed in a game on her iPad with earbuds in, and so the drive back was largely silent, giving him the space and time to think about his afternoon.

He could still taste her on his tongue, feel the sting where she had carved into his back and shoulders. And he had perfect recall of the look on her face—cool and expressionless—right after they'd rocked each other's worlds. He, at least, was willing to acknowledge that that was what happened. It had been no less explosive than the first time they'd been together, when she'd boldly walked right up to him at that faculty mixer, handily disposing of the other women who had been crowding him, and feigning interest in his work.

Malcolm had been tired that evening, having just come off

a pretty big fight with Charlotte and then driven upstate in bad traffic, moving himself into his small faculty house. He intended only to make a polite appearance, then skulk off to ponder the state of his life and get some sleep.

Then Lorna approached and made some smart-ass comment about his work. Wearing a black dress that skimmed what looked like a very nice figure, she twirled a glass of red wine between her fingers as she spoke, her gaze assessing, head leaning to one side.

He had heard of her because her name always came up when anyone mentioned Gilchrist College. She had been widely published in her field and had a reputation for being somewhat of a flamethrower. Her most prominent quote, and the one for which she had become somewhat famous, was when she called Newt Gingrich, who at the time was running for President, an "oversexed, markedly unattractive, aspiring-Alpha-male, who uses his positions of power like a prick—to fuck women, *and* fuck them over, at every opportunity."

Malcolm even remembered Charlotte reading the quote aloud to him and wondering aloud when it had become vogue for professors to use words like 'fuck' to make their point.

So he'd definitely heard of Lorna Terry, but when she introduced herself he was shocked at how attractive she was. And then he was embarrassed at being shocked, because wasn't that just a ridiculous stereotype, that feminists were women who couldn't even get a man if they tried? But beyond her physical attributes, Malcolm found himself turned on by their repartee. And soon, his fight with Charlotte, his exhaustion and every other woman in the room had drifted into the backdrop.

Take me home, Lorna said to him after they'd been talking for about an hour. *I'm way too drunk to drive.*

She wasn't that drunk, because when they got to her house, she invited him in and walked with a steady, confident gait up to her front door, never once looking back to see whether he was following. Malcolm wanted to strip her of that confidence; just strip her in general. And once inside, she made it clear that her intentions for how the evening would end were consistent with his own.

They didn't make it past the living room the first time, but eventually, they went to her bedroom. He woke up around one a.m. needing water and intending to leave after he drank it, but Lorna joined him in the kitchen, walking in completely naked and drinking from the same glass he held in his hand.

Parched, she explained.

But her eyes held the hint of a challenge; one he couldn't help but meet. He turned her around and took her from behind while she grasped the kitchen counter and let her head drop between her outstretched arms. Malcolm couldn't recall the last time he'd been with a woman who made him want to go more than twice in a night. And there was no denying that her being *The* Lorna Terry made him want to establish his *bona fides*, and put his best foot forward, so to speak.

It was only the next morning that he learned her age, and by then it didn't matter. *What was eight measly years anyway?* Nothing at all to him. But later, when his calls went unreturned, he figured they might mean something to her. Either that, or their interlude just hadn't been that significant.

And in all fairness, when he crossed the threshold into her house, Malcolm hadn't intended for it to be significant to him, either. But the idea of being so forgettable didn't sit well. Particularly since they'd breakfasted together, talked and laughed together. So, not knowing quite how it happened, he began to pursue her. And now, even after this afternoon, he still felt like he was in pursuit.

The irony was, he didn't feel equipped to be involved with anyone, let alone someone as obviously difficult as Lorna Terry.

And yet, each of her dismissals only had him slobbering for more. He'd always been a sucker for those women who were hard-to-get, sometimes finding it a little tough to distinguish them from those who were actually worth having. Something told him Lorna Terry was a whole lot of both.

"How much longer, Daddy?" Hayley had taken out her earbuds.

"Not much. About twenty minutes."

Piper groaned.

"We'll stop at Chick-Fil-A before we get to the house," Malcolm promised. "I know you both must be hungry."

"They're discriminatory," Piper said, her voice dripping with disdain. "I'm not eating from there."

Malcolm rolled his eyes. "Fine. We'll find a Burger King or get Chinese or something."

"I don't care what we eat," Hayley said helpfully.

"Yeah, you really don't," Piper said, her tone still snide. "And that's why you're going to be fat and disgusting before you're even ten years old."

"*Daddy!*" Hayley whined.

"Piper, if you don't have anything positive to say, feel free to fall back on silence as your alternate plan."

"Gladly," she said, sounding frighteningly like her mother.

This was the way Charlotte fought at the end of their marriage. Hot-and-cold, hot-and-cold until Malcolm thought he would be driven mad by all the back and forth. One day she might be meek, repentant and clingy, begging his forgiveness for going outside of their marriage, and the next, she was ranting at him for having changed.

You're not the same, Mal! she would scream. *I married an attorney. A man who wanted what I want. And overnight you tell me that was all just a pretense. You want to be a ... a... writer instead? I feel lied to!*

By then, he wasn't buying her bullshit. She didn't fuck another man because he spent evenings and weekends writing his novel. She did it because she wanted to, and because the man she'd been with was probably more consistent with her life-plan in the first place. And within weeks, Charlotte had confirmed that instinct by asking for a divorce. Of all the things that surprised Malcolm about the demise of his marriage, what surprised him most had to be the ease with which he agreed to end it.

"So what're we doing this weekend, Daddy?" Hayley asked.

"I thought we might do some hiking near the river. Maybe check out a street festival that's happening a couple towns over."

Piper groaned audibly, and Malcolm squelched the urge to pull over and shove her out of the car to walk the rest of the way.

He had many fears for how Piper might emerge on the other side of this phase she was going through, but one of his greatest was that he would wake up and realize he didn't like his own kid. That he would love her until the end of days wasn't in question, but *liking* her wasn't as certain.

They wound up getting Chinese, which they ate at his small kitchen table, Hayley talking a mile a minute and Piper saying nothing at all. Sitting in the center of the table, among all the cartons, soy sauce packets and plastic tableware was Malcolm's phone, face up. He itched to reach for it, to call Lorna just to check in, but she definitely wasn't a "check in" kind of woman, which felt ominous since it seemed as though most other women were.

Just after the separation from Charlotte, Malcolm had been on a few dates, just to cut his teeth again, and to break the oppressive silence of singlehood. The speed with which some women asserted ownership, and developed expectations had knocked him back. With one woman, a recently-divorced mother-of-three, it had only taken one coffee-date and a meeting for drinks before she began sending him text messages throughout the day—two or three on average—just to "see what's up." Before he could decide whether he wanted to see her again, she was there, crowding out his every thought with her unrelenting "check ins."

And she wasn't alone. There were others, most of them less obvious about it, but all of them pushing just a little too far, and a little too fast. In the end, Malcolm decided that the dating scene had probably changed during his fifteen years off the market, and that he wasn't quite ready for it yet.

And then he met Lorna Terry. He definitely wasn't ready for her. But still, he wanted to call, just to hear that warm, smoky voice; and to listen to her decode the world in her own unique way, firing up intellectual curiosity he'd believed long dormant.

Deciding to ignore the impulse to 'check in', Malcolm settled in to watch a silly preteen movie with his girls, and later, made sure they were comfortably situated in the spare bedroom. Once alone in his own room, he turned to his work, which at the moment consisted of re-reading his *New York Times* bestselling novel, 'Cadence'.

Though it—and he—had been hailed as overnight successes, the truth was Malcolm had been working on the novel for years, revising and fine-tuning it, changing characters, settings and even the underlying message several times before he was satisfied. Still old-fashioned enough to need external validation, he had submitted it to a publisher and was floored when they accepted it right away.

After many more edits and revisions, it hit the shelves to almost universal acclaim, as a "scathing commentary on race, identity-politics and the American Achilles heel of institutional racism". The reviews were so positive, Malcolm almost wanted to call bullshit on a few of them, but he didn't, because the book's success had yielded him a significant advance on his second book, and this gig at Gilchrist College. Now all that remained was proving that he wasn't a one-hit wonder, and cranking out something worthwhile his second go-'round. Easier said than done. So he was reading 'Cadence', hoping to rekindle some of that mojo for his current work-in-progress.

Too bad writing didn't work like that.

Sometimes, it was as though a magical being alighted on your shoulder, whispering the words in your ear, the rhythm and music of those words perfect for telling the story one wanted to tell. And at other times, that being—your muse—left you, or sat there on your shoulder stubbornly silent. Malcolm was suffering through that stubborn silence now. But he wasn't worried, yet. His first book had come too easily, it was practically a karmic requirement that the next one would be more difficult. Difficult he didn't mind; he just wanted to make sure it was good.

He read until it was late and he had to get up to check on the girls and secure the house. And just before turning in, he thought about Lorna again. And again, he resisted the urge to call, telling himself that if he knew anything about her by now, it was that she might not react well to being crowded.

So that was that. No phone call. Malcolm turned out the light and went to sleep.

SIX

GHOSTS OF MISTAKES PAST

"He's REALLY GOOD," Riley said. "Makes me wish I could write fiction. If I did, I like to think it would be something like this."

Lorna held the receiver away from her ear and looked at it in disbelief. High praise indeed, coming from her daughter.

"Why haven't *you* read it?"

"I'll get around to it," Lorna said vaguely.

"A little professional competitiveness, perhaps," Riley teased. "Can't stomach the idea of having to tell him how incredible it is?"

"*Is* it?"

"Is it what?"

"Incredible. That's quite a superlative."

"I like it enough to want to meet him. How's that?"

"Shawn wouldn't stand for you fawning over some writer," Lorna teased her back.

"Yeah, yeah. So you didn't answer my question. Why haven't you read it? And his name, by the way? How perfect is that for a book jacket? *Malcolm T. Mitchell.* It has such ... gravitas."

"You're beginning to sound like a groupie," Lorna quipped.

"Oh, I'm betting he has plenty of those as it is."

"Yeah," Lorna said dryly. "I bet he does."

"Well you should make yourself 'get around to' reading it. I think you'll like it. So you've met him, I take it."

"Yes," Lorna said. "We've met."

She didn't know why she was hiding from Riley the fact that she and Malcolm had been sleeping together for almost a month now. She didn't generally edit herself with Riley but this was the second time in as many months that it had occurred. With the grad student, it was because he was, well, a grad student. And with Malcolm, it was because ... Lorna had no idea why, actually.

But while she couldn't seem to cough up the most salient piece of information, she couldn't seem to make herself stop talking about him either. So she had recommended his book the last time she and Riley spoke, and now was getting the review. Apparently it was good enough that her daughter had read it cover to cover—all five-hundred-something pages of it—in a day and a half.

"So you are coming down for the big event, right?" Riley asked. "You were such a great coach last time that I'd kind of like you to be here."

"Is she expected to make an appearance on her actual due date?" Lorna hedged.

"If not sooner. I'm already dilated quite a bit."

Dilated. The language of childbirth. Why did it all have to sound so clinical and unpleasant?

"There's a thing that night. So I'll take Metro North and come down immediately after."

There was only silence on the other end.

Lorna shut her eyes and waited for what she knew was coming.

"I was hoping you wouldn't wait until the actual date, Mom. I want you to come down before. Like a couple days before."

She was only ever 'Mom' at times like this. Most of the time she was 'Lorna'.

"Riley, the college is only a forty-five minute train ride away from Manhattan. I can go to my faculty dinner and then come down right after."

"You hate those dinners," Riley said. "I can't believe you would prioritize an event you're bound to hate over the birth of your second grandchild."

"It's not as though you'll be alone. Shawn ..."

"Will be absolutely useless. As you well know."

Riley's voice had risen to an angry pitch. The pitch it only ever reached when they were fighting, so Lorna supposed that was what this was.

Sometimes she wondered whether her daughter made these demands just so she could orchestrate yet another demonstration of Here's-How-You're-A-Shitty-Mother. But she did have one thing right—Shawn was going to be useless. He had darn near lost his shit when Riley went into labor with the last kid, but that was entirely her fault for not taking the perfectly safe drugs, tested and tried a million times over with other more reasonable women who had given birth before her.

I don't want my baby coming out all doped-up, she'd insisted. *I don't need an epidural.*

And the result was predictable. Weeping, wailing, gnashing of teeth. And one very shaky husband, who throughout active labor looked like he was close to tears himself.

"How about I come down a couple days before, but come

back up just for the dinner and then return to the city right afterwards?"

Riley sighed. "Okay. Yes. That should work. Just so long as you don't dilly-dally after the dinner."

"I don't ... dilly-dally."

At least she didn't used to. But lately, her position of influence in the department was beginning to feel a little less assured. She was starting to think it had been the wrong move to turn her nose up at being the chair when it was offered to her three years ago. Now, she had a sneaking suspicion there were rumors that she had actually been *passed over* for the position. Because what idiot didn't accept that honorific when offered? *Stupid Lorna Terry, that was who.*

So some dilly-dallying *might* be in order at the dinner, just to get a sense of her standing among her colleagues.

"So we can expect you when?"

"I'll be there Wednesday."

"Good. And don't sound so oppressed at the thought, Mom. *God.*"

"Riley, I don't feel oppressed. But I have a lot of balls in the air right now. I need to make sure I don't lose sight of important ..."

"Important?" Riley cut her off. "Unlike me going into labor you mean? I'm sure that's a trifle compared to ..."

"That's not what I mean. And I'd appreciate it if you don't unleash your hormonal angst in this direction. That's what Shawn is for."

"That's a really *fucked up* thing to say," Riley's voice rose again. "Not to mention sexist. Something one would think you of all people would be sensitive to."

"I hate it when you brandish my political views against me like a weapon, Riley. It's become tedious."

"Y'know what's become tedious? This conversation. So I'm

going to hang up now. And I'll see you on Wednesday. That's if coming to support me through this birth rises to the level of being important enough."

Lorna took a deep breath, and the phone went silent. She'd been hung up on.

Sitting for a moment, quietly at her desk, she replayed those last few minutes of the conversation with her daughter and decided that she wasn't at all at fault for how it ended. Riley, whether she wanted to admit it or not, wasn't herself during the last few weeks of her pregnancy. No woman was. How could you be? You were literally *occupied* by another human being, after all.

Lorna decided she would call Shawn later and tell him to be extra sweet to Riley over the next few days until she arrived. And she had no doubt he would rise to the occasion. As he always did.

"HE SAYS YOU KNOW HIM," Inez said.

Lorna looked down at the message slip in her hand, written in Inez's neat script, letting her know that Todd Williamson had called, and wanted her to know that he had arrived on campus. She didn't know a Todd Williamson and had no clue why he thought his arrival would be of interest to her.

"Well, I don't," Lorna said with certainty.

Inez shrugged.

Truth be told, Inez was a lousy department secretary, and frequently got things mixed up. But she was somewhere in her sixties and almost an institution onto herself at Gilchrist, having shuttled among departments for decades. She knew everyone at—and just about everything about—the college and no one could muster the will to fire her. Especially since it was only by working at the school that Inez had been able to send her children there.

It was Gilchrist's liberal guilt—all employees and their families got free tuition, mostly because the employees came from the working class town in which Gilchrist was located; and because most could never in this lifetime afford to pay the full tuition, even if their kid was lucky enough to get in.

"If he calls again, could you ask him a few questions? Make sure I'm really the person he thinks I am?"

"Sure thing."

Inez was already looking back down at her magazine. When she did, Lorna saw that she had a significantly thinning patch at the crown of her head, which she had attempted to comb over.

The signs of old age were especially visible to her lately. Especially visible, and especially troubling. Lorna averted her eyes from Inez's balding pate and headed back to her office.

When she got there, the back of another head greeted her. She smiled and crossed the threshold, shutting the door and leaning against it. Malcolm turned at the sound and stood, coming toward her.

"Hi," he said.

"Hello."

They squared off in silence for a moment, like animals in heat, deciding on the best approach to the inevitable act of intercourse.

"You don't belong on this side of campus," Lorna said.

"I know. And yet I couldn't help coming."

"I'm not in the mood for you," Lorna said. "I had a terrible fight with my kid, went for a walk to clear my head and now have way too much work to ..."

"Shut up," Malcolm said.

He advanced on her and leaned over to lock her office door,

just before kissing her, in precisely the way she liked to be kissed. He teased the waistband of her skirt as he did, running the tips of his fingers just beneath it and stroking her skin where it had creased and puckered from the pressure of the fabric pressing into her flesh. She waited for him to undo the button, lower the skirt and suggest something naughty but he didn't.

"Actually, I'm on this side of campus because I have a meeting," he said when he raised his head. "I just wanted to stop by and say 'hi', and you see what you got me into?"

"What *I* got you into?" Lorna laughed. "But I shouldn't be surprised. You youngsters are insatiable."

"I really hate it when you do that," Malcolm said, lifting his eyes to look at her.

"Do what? Point out the obvious?"

"What's obvious? That I'm younger than you, or that I'm insatiable?"

"Both. But let's not start an argument. I've already had one of those today and I'd rather not have another."

"You did say that. What were you and Riley arguing about?"

"My lack of a maternal instinct, I think. It's the only argument we ever have. The details vary, but that's the crux of almost every disagreement we have."

Malcolm looked at her and seemed not to know what to say.

"I'm sorry, baby," is what he settled on.

Lorna generally hated it when men called women 'baby'. But when Malcolm said it, it felt different. Maybe because he said it infrequently enough that it wasn't a cliché.

"Anyway," she said, shaking herself loose of the feeling. "You have a meeting so I should let you go."

"I didn't realize you were holding me hostage," he said

lightly. But he reached for her door and unlocked it. "What time are you home tonight?"

"I don't know. Seven-ish."

"I'm coming to get you. Be ready at seven-thirty."

"Malcolm ..."

"I love how you say my name," he said before ducking out and shutting the door behind him, before she had a chance to refuse.

He was there and gone in less than fifteen minutes. Lorna could almost believe it hadn't happened but for the vague, throbbing ache between her legs that he had inspired but not relieved. She really should stop seeing him. Or at the very least, she should stop letting him dictate the terms of their seeing each other. But he just kept doing this, barging in and taking over, shoving himself into her life in a manner that was so over-whelmingly ... male.

Going to sit behind her desk, Lorna opened the drawer to the right where she kept her emergency antiperspirant, aspirin and assorted plastic utensils. In the rear, its flyleaf a little tattered, was Malcolm's book, 'Cadence'. Lorna opened it and read the dedication: *For my girls*.

Very artful of him not to name them. He said he had been writing it during the disintegration of his marriage. If the marriage had survived he could claim his wife was included in that group of 'girls' and if not, the dedication could be seen as applying only to his daughters. She wondered which was true.

The first chapter began with the lines: *When the news of Vernon's passing came, he knew he should cry; but instead he was awash with guilty relief. Good. The bastard was dead.*

"Malcolm T. Mitchell," Lorna murmured, leaning back in her seat and getting comfortable. "How very ... *dark*."

"WHITE WINE, WHITE PIZZA," Malcolm said, indicating the spread on his living room floor.

He had laid out a picnic blanket, and a bottle of wine was chilling in a chrome bucket with two glasses nearby. And at the center of the display, a large box from the most popular pizzeria in town. All the lights in the house had been dimmed, so that when he led her in, Malcolm had taken her by the elbow to guide her through to their destination.

"Is this what you had me get all dressed up for?" Lorna asked.

"You're wearing jeans."

"Oh. Right." She smiled up at him and he back at her.

"Let's eat," he said. "I'm starving and there's nothing more disgusting than cold white pizza."

They sat on the floor, opposite each other, on either side of the pizza box. While Malcolm poured them generous glasses of wine, Lorna inspected the pizza. It was still hot, and smelled delicious and garlicky.

"I started your book today."

"Yeah?" Malcolm handed her a glass.

"Aren't you going to ask me what I think so far?"

"Naturally, you love it,"

"I was prepared to hate it," she said matter-of-factly. "I was afraid I would. And then I would have to lie to you. But as it turns out, I don't hate it at all."

Malcolm laughed. He was handsome when he laughed. He was always handsome actually. But in an unexpected way, and at unexpected times. Just when she'd made up her mind that he was only generically nice-looking, his eyes would crinkle at the corners, like now as he laughed, and he was suddenly, startlingly, sexy.

"Why were you determined to hate it?"

"I wasn't *determined* to hate it. I just worried that I might."

"And?"

"And I'm not done yet, but ..."

"But," Malcolm prompted, taking a bite of his pizza.

"But I almost didn't answer the door when you came to get me because all I wanted to do was stay in bed and keep reading."

Malcolm froze, pizza still in hand, midair. The corners of his eyes crinkled as he smiled. "You can finish reading in bed later. In my bed, though."

Lorna took a sip of her wine. It was pleasantly cold on her lips and tongue, but warmed her throat and chest as it went down. Reaching out, Malcolm offered her a bite of his slice and when she leaned in with lips slightly parted, he held the pizza aloft, and kissed her instead. Lorna smiled against his lips and kissed him back, taking his glasses from his face so she could do it properly.

"Thank you," he said quietly, against her lips.

"What for?"

"For what you said about my book. Your opinion means a lot."

Lorna leaned back and raised the wineglass to her lips again.

"How about you?" Malcolm asked, taking another bite.

"How about me what?"

"Have you ever thought of writing a book?"

Lorna shrugged. "Not really. Although over the years I've had a few offers. Maybe one day I'll do some essays in a compilation or something."

"How many journal articles have you had published?"

"Dozens."

"Two-hundred and seventy-eight," Malcolm said.

Lorna's eyes met his. "How do you know? Did you look me up or something?"

He nodded. "I had this stupid idea that I would start reading them. So I could ... figure you out or something?"

"There's no need to decode me, Malcolm. If there's something that you want to know about me, ask."

"Really?"

"Yes, really."

"So why do you sound so agitated?"

"I'm not ... agitated. I'm just a little sick of people thinking that there's some past trauma that explains my politics. Or that ..."

"I don't recall having used the word 'trauma', or even the word 'politics'. I said I wanted to figure *you* out. Lorna Terry. The woman. Not the 'feminist', or 'the professor'. You."

"What's the difference?"

Malcolm was looking at her seriously now, fixedly.

"You don't think there's a difference?"

The question didn't sound like a challenge, but it felt like one. Lorna reached for a slice and took a large bite. It was warm, delicious and as laden with garlic as its aroma suggested. She closed her eyes as she chewed, concentrating on the taste.

"The difference ..."

Oh god. She'd been hoping he'd drop the matter entirely.

"... is that when I see you on campus you're stern, sometimes even what people would call formidable. And then I get you here, or I come see you in your space and you're witty, mischievous ... sexy, and very feminine. And it's all I can do to stop myself from kissing you all the time."

"You don't have to stop yourself," she said.

Malcolm smiled. "Yeah, I do," he said.

"Why?"

"Because I may not have you all figured out yet, but there's one thing I know for sure."

"And what's that?"

"While some women use physical intimacy as a way of pulling men in, you use it as a way to keep them out."

Lorna's heart thundered in her chest and she narrowed her eyes slightly, straining not to show just how unsettling she found this insight.

"This is great pizza," she said.

"That's the best you can do?" Malcolm asked.

"What do you mean?"

"To change the subject. Commenting on the pizza was the best you could come up with to change the subject? You don't like talking about yourself, do you?"

"That's ridiculous. Academics love talking about themselves. I'm no exception."

"No, you love talking about 'Professor Lorna Terry'. The image. The persona you've created. You don't like talking about yourself. The woman you are. Where you come from. Your family, your life, your background. D'you realize I don't know anything about you?"

"My bio is on the college website. You should read it."

"I did. It told me where you went to college, blah, blah, blah ... But nothing real."

"Honestly, Malcolm." Lorna shifted, unfolding her legs and folding them again on the opposite side. "If I'd known you invited me over to interrogate me ..."

"Why're you so jittery? Is it so weird that I'd want to talk to you about your background?"

"I'm not interviewing for a job at the State Department, so yes, it's a little strange that you would want to know about my ... background as you call it."

Malcolm took a bite of his pizza and looked undeterred. She was usually able to intimidate people when she took the tone she was taking now. But it wasn't working this time.

"I grew up dirt-poor in Louisiana," Malcolm said. "When

my publisher was writing my bio for the dust-jacket of my book, they decided to say I was from New Orleans, because people recognize it. But the truth is, I'm from a place no one's ever heard of in St. Mary Parish."

Lorna sat a little more upright, putting down her wine and giving him her full attention, surprised at the unexpected revelation, and at how interested she was in hearing more.

"You don't sound like you're from ..."

"It got 'educated' out of me," Malcolm said wryly. He looked down into his wineglass. "I got sent to a private boarding school in New Orleans when I was thirteen, run by a bunch of priests. Then I went to LSU for a year, then to Cambridge on an extended exchange program, and decided to finish my degree there. That's where I met Charlotte. She was doing her junior year abroad." He shrugged.

"You said you 'got sent' to boarding school. Who sent you?" Lorna couldn't help but ask, though she knew it meant that she would, sooner or later, have to reciprocate with information about her own life.

"My mother. I had a father who was mostly not around, and when he was, wasn't exactly a good provider, or a good influence. Or a good person. But my mother ..." He shrugged again. "She loved him. So she could never turn him away. One of my guidance counselors told her about a scholarship program for the school in New Orleans and so she applied for me, and I got it. I think as much as she loved my father, her worst fear was that I might grow up to become like him. So she sent me away."

Moving a little closer so they were only feet apart now, Lorna put down her wineglass. "That must have been quite a sacrifice for her. And difficult for you."

Malcolm gave a brief laugh. "Not at all. I was relieved to get away. And stay away. I only ever went back to see my mother, until she died six years ago."

In the silence, Malcolm drank more of his wine and ate more of the pizza.

Lorna felt frozen in place, knowing that she should reach out and touch his hand, or shoulder. Or share something about herself in return.

After a few moments, Malcolm stood and extended a hand to her. She took it, and he pulled her up. She followed him into the bedroom.

THEY MADE LOVE EASILY NOW.

He knew her body, and she knew his, and in short order, they could give each other pleasure. Making love was the thing they most often did together. And Malcolm wasn't sure any longer that it would be enough.

He gave in and led her to the bedroom because he knew she would be comfortable with the physical in a way she clearly was not with the emotional. But it wasn't even emotional. He wasn't asking her to make any declarations, but to simply give him *information*; to tell him something about herself that wasn't publicly available from an internet search, and she was unable to do even that.

Nothing about Lorna Terry was conventional. He knew that, and had known it from the moment they met. But he was unprepared for how completely guarded and shut off she was. He wasn't looking for her to bare her soul, because he wasn't ready for any soul-baring either. But what she offered was a void. Sex, and clever repartee during which she used words and took a tone that made it clear he was no closer to getting to know her than a star pupil sitting in the front row of one of her lectures.

A grand romance at this stage of his life may have been too

much, but what Lorna offered was beginning to feel like far too little.

"SO I GOT that information you asked for," Inez called out, just as Lorna was walking by.

She was running a little late for her train and on her way out the door when the department secretary stopped her.

Missing her train was out of the question since Riley was already at Peak Gestational Irrationality. The baby was due in three days, and she was going a little stir-crazy, sitting in her apartment all by herself, unable to leave and risk Shawn's displeasure.

In the morning, she had a doctor's appointment which, Lorna suspected would result in her being checked into the hospital to deliver. The timing couldn't have been worse since tonight was the faculty cocktail party. Going to the city now, in the afternoon, and returning in the evening was madness, but she had already broken one promise, to go down a few days ago, and didn't want to antagonize her daughter further.

"What information?" she asked Inez, shoving her bag higher on her shoulder.

"The guy who was calling. Todd whatshisname. I found out how he knows you."

"Who?"

"The guy who called a couple weeks back and wanted you to know he's on campus. He called back, and I did what you said and asked him a few questions. I know how you know him now."

"And?" Lorna asked, shrugging impatiently.

"He said he's from Ohio, and was in a graduate program there. And that you met at the NYU conference. In late May."

"In late ..." Lorna felt her throat clench. "He said he's *on campus?*"

Inez nodded and then turned her attention back to her computer monitor as though she had more serious business to attend to, but Lorna knew better. During the hours she wasn't looking at magazines or muddling up professors' schedules and phone messages, Inez was generally playing some silly game with a simulated restaurant where she "cooked" simulated food and served it to simulated "patrons."

"Yep. Left a number, which I got from him again if you want it."

Glancing desperately at the time, Lorna shook her head. "Just leave it in my mailbox or on my desk," she said. "I'll get it when I come back early next week."

Inez grunted and didn't bother looking up again.

Outside of Fenman Hall, Lorna's car was waiting—apparently a student who was doing Uber on the side to make extra cash. She kept her head down so he wouldn't try to make conversation, as they invariably did when they realized they were picking up a member of faculty.

Jesus. Todd whatshisname was Mr. Almost-Thirty-Years-Old. The graduate student she spent the night with? But what the hell was he doing here?

But of course, she'd met *lots* of people at the NYU conference. It didn't have to be him. And if he was planning to come to Gilchrist for any reason, surely he would have mentioned it, and she would have remembered. If he said he was coming to Gilchrist, if there was any *possible* scenario that involved her seeing him again, she never would have slept with him, that much was certain. She hadn't been *that* drunk.

Lorna made it onto her train with only three minutes to spare and collapsed in the only remaining seat in her car that didn't have someone else next to it. Of course, it was located right next to the bathroom, from which the strong and unmistakable odor of stale urine emanated. Add to that, the headache she was developing, from rushing around all morning trying to squeeze a full day's work into four hours, clean her house, and pack to go to Riley's.

The idea of getting there, spending a few hours reassuring her daughter that she would attend her delivery and then getting back on the train for the mixer felt like way too much. It *was* too much. She shouldn't have given in to Riley's prenatal hysteria in the first place. And if the way she was feeling now was any indication, she wasn't going to make it to the mixer at all, which was disappointing, because she wanted to go. Very much. And why not admit it? It wasn't just because she needed to do reconnaissance on her career. There was another mystery to solve. The Mystery of Missing-in-Action-Malcolm.

After their dinner at his house, during which he had poured out his heart—or at least attempted to—about his childhood, in a transparent shot at getting her to do the same, she hadn't heard from him. The evening ended the way all their evenings ended—in bed. And in the morning, he made them coffee and they talked the way they always did—about the news, about their work, about his developing frustration that his second book wasn't coming along as he'd hoped, about his volatile teenager ...

Everything seemed as it always was. Except now he hadn't called. And it was only once his calls stopped that Lorna realized something—she had never called him. Not ever.

And yet, she had come to look forward to hearing from him. And to expect it. And now he was missing. Or maybe not missing, but just ... done.

Leaning back into her seat, Lorna took a deep breath. Maybe that was it, then. He was done. *They* were done. Too bad, because she'd liked him. Still, she wanted to see him. At least to confirm her suspicion, that was all, and for no other reason.

Shoving aside the sudden rush of a feeling disturbingly like melancholy, Lorna reached into her overnight bag and pulled out his book. She was almost finished now. She had been savoring it, going slowly and looking forward to discussing it with him. But now, may as well get through the rest of it and turn her attention back where it belonged—to her family, and to her work.

SEVEN

FAMILY TIES

BOXED WINE AND BAD JOKES. THAT WAS HOW LORNA described what she expected of this mixer. But even so, Malcolm expected her to be in attendance. The president of the college, Julia Bond, was hosting at her home, so just about every faculty member on campus for the summer was present, milling around in the expansive living room in the House on the Hill, as the President's Residence at Gilchrist was called. A stately white colonial, it sat on the far, east end of campus, alone on a small sloping hill that provided the best vantage point from which to survey the entire property.

In the president's living room, there were few personal touches, but what looked like very old pieces of art, and furnishings that had probably been part of the property for many decades. None of the faculty, nor the president herself, looked completely at ease in the room, and Malcolm had begun to regret coming. Though he had—in his mind at least—ended things with the prickly Professor Terry, he now had to admit that part of his reason for coming tonight was that he wanted to see her.

And now, she wasn't even here. That was so completely like her, to keep him guessing and wondering, even though he doubted she'd spared him a second thought when she decided on her evening plans.

"Malcolm you're lost in thought over here! Writing your next book in your head, I'm guessing."

Malcolm turned toward the voice and smiled. Professor Rogers was wearing a white dress that stopped just above her knees, and had her long hair arranged in a high and intricate bun. She was definitely not one to shy away from dramatic effects. Or to shy away in general.

With as much gallantry as he could muster, he had been rebuffing her subtle come-ons ever since he arrived. Lately though, she'd been more overt, so he had taken to avoiding her. Especially since he was otherwise involved. But it didn't seem to matter. Wherever he was, she found him, like a homing missile. The only mercy was that she hadn't actually asked him out or anything. Probably because she was clearly the kind of woman who never *had* to ask a man out.

"How'd you guess? Thinking about a tricky scene in the third chapter," he lied.

"I'm sure you'll work it out and it'll be brilliant," she said with a graceful wave of a hand. "But if you ever need a reader, I'd be honored to help out. Are you happy with your editor?"

"Yeah. Pretty much. She always has good notes. But I tend to want to wait until completion before I show her anything."

"Well, we all have our process."

"You write?" Malcolm asked, trying to stop his eyes from scanning the room, periodically checking the doorway through which new guests entered every so often.

"Don't all English professors? I never had the guts to try to get anything published though. One day." She had an unnerving, fixed stare; unblinking eye contact that made him want to squint, or look away.

"How about journals? A short piece, maybe for *The New Yorker*, or something like that."

Professor Rogers shrugged. "One day," she said again, and then she continued to assess him with that disturbing gaze.

Before he had to think of something else to keep the conversation going, Malcolm felt his cellphone vibrating in his breast-pocket and reached for it. His phone had become an appendage lately, as he waited for Charlotte to call him about another episode of Piper's Acting Out. But this time, it wasn't Charlotte.

"Sorry," he said, giving Rogers an apologetic look. "I have to take this."

He stepped around her and headed for the foyer where it was quieter, pausing to unload himself of his wineglass.

"Hello?"

"Hi," the voice on the other end said. "So ... in recent news, I'm a grandmother again."

Malcolm smiled, looking around for a private place as a trio of faculty members walked by, conversing a little too loudly.

"Congratulations."

"Thank you. She was a little early. Just a couple of days, but completely ruined my plans for the evening, I can tell you that."

Shoving against the front door, Malcolm exited the house altogether. The evening was warm and muggy, so he shed his sport coat and took a seat on the front steps. The view was incredible, looking down across toward the main campus, the intermittent lights from the residence halls and academic buildings twinkling like stars.

"I wondered where you were," he admitted.

"Did you?"

"I did."

The silence between them stretched out for a long while, until he realized that what he was witnessing was Lorna Terry at a loss for what to say. And then he realized something else—this was the first time she had ever called him. He had been pursuing her so hard, he had somehow missed that little detail.

And when he stopped pursuing, and pressing and pushing her to reveal things, this was what happened. She called. And not to tell him she was a grandmother again, but to say: *if you stand back a moment and let me catch my breath, I will come to you. I will let you in.*

"I didn't know your daughter was pregnant. What did she have?"

"A little girl. They named her Cassidy. Cassidy Lorna, poor thing."

"That's a perfectly good name," Malcolm said quietly. "Gives her a lot to live up to, though."

"And a lot to live down."

That was precisely the kind of loaded comment that would normally have him pressing for more. But that was before. Now, with this one phone call, he was beginning to understand a little more about this inscrutable, perplexing woman. She could not be cajoled into greater intimacy. In fact, anything that smelled of 'intimacy' would probably have her scampering out of reach. Getting to truly know her would require the kind of stamina few men likely had.

Running a hand over his head, Malcolm issued a quiet sigh and wondered whether he had it. And if he did, whether he could afford it. He had a book to write, and a difficult kid to raise. He should walk away. Because Lorna Terry wasn't the kind of relationship one had casually, no matter what she liked to think. She was the kind of woman who required focus if you wanted to do it right.

"Does she look like you?" he ventured.

On the other end of the line, Lorna laughed. "Oh god, *not at all*. She looks like her father."

"So, Cullen and Cassidy, huh?"

"Cullen and Cassidy," she repeated. She was happy. He could hear it in her voice, though she may never admit as much.

"When are you coming back?" he asked, dropping his voice much lower.

"In a few days. When Riley realizes she doesn't need me nearly as much as she thinks she does right now."

"I'm sure she does need you, Lorna."

She said nothing.

"Will I see you?" he asked, his voice hoarse. "When you get back?"

"Yes," she said after a few beats. "You'll see me."

"You were right about the party, by the way," he said, reaching for safer ground. "Boxed wine and ..."

"Bad jokes," she finished.

"Yep."

More silence. But it was comfortable.

"I'd probably better get back to it. And let you get back to your family."

"Yes," she said.

"Okay, so ... goodnight then."

"Malcolm?"

"Yeah?"

"It's amazing, isn't it? How those ties form right away? From the moment they take their first breath—or even before—you just ... feel it, even though you just met them?"

"Yeah," he said. "It's pretty amazing."

SHAWN INSISTED that the baby sleep in the room with them, so she was there in a bassinet next to Riley's bed, swaddled tightly and sleeping as peacefully as though she was still in the womb. Wealth had some uses, and this was one. Lorna's son-in-law had been able to reserve a private suite for his wife—where she could give birth and be cared for in the days following—that looked like a room in the Four Seasons.

The bed was larger than the standard-issue hospital bed, large enough for Shawn to now be sleeping on it with Riley, her head resting on his shoulder, his arm wrapped about her. Cullen was with a nanny since Lorna's services as a back-up coach were needed at the hospital in case Shawn should prove not to be up to the task. But he'd performed well this second time around, and even cut the umbilical cord.

Now, he was sleeping like a man returned from battle, his mouth slightly open, snoring quietly. Lorna hated the term "son-in-law." Perhaps it applied to other people, but Shawn felt as much a son to her as Riley did a daughter.

Watching from the sofa-bed, Lorna knew that he would probably only sleep for another hour or so. Soon he would awaken and want to go home to check in on his son. She could practically write the script—he would be torn between leaving to see Cullen and staying with his wife and newborn, but eventually, Riley would persuade him it was fine to go, her tone a gentle lull that she reserved for her husband alone.

Where had her daughter learned to love like that? Not from her, certainly.

Turning onto her side, Lorna took a deep breath and shut her eyes. Before he left, Shawn would look to her as well, his eyes asking her to take care of his family in his absence, no matter how brief. It was. *His family*. Hers, as well. But more his, and more Riley's. She was at the same time an insider, and someone looking in from the outside. She would stay only as long as she needed to, and then she would go home, back to Gilchrist.

It was that knowledge which made her reach for her phone and call Malcolm, though just that afternoon she told herself she was reconciled to the end of their affair. Hearing his voice had made her day complete somehow.

After hearing her granddaughter take her first piercing cry, Lorna's heart seized in her chest. And seeing Shawn hold her, still covered in mucus and blood, and bring her to Riley had been overwhelming. She thought she was prepared, after having seen Cullen born, for the rush of emotion, but she was wrong. This time was just like the first time. A part of her flew out of her chest and attached itself to this tiny new human that she hadn't even yet begun to know. And Lorna wanted to share that insight with someone—someone who would understand.

Shawn and Riley were too immersed in their own little world, big enough only for the two of them, and Lorna again—as she had many times over the years—faced her one-ness, her soleness, her ... loneliness.

It wasn't often that she acknowledged its existence, and it wasn't an overwhelming and earth-shattering loneliness of the kind that made a person want to weep or curl up into a fetal position. And in any event, she wasn't the weeping or fetal position type. But it was a distant and dull ache, a hollowness and craving for just one other soul who might truly understand her soul. Lorna had never had that, and had been successful during many intervals in her life, almost convincing herself she didn't want it. But sometimes the hollowness reared its head again.

And tonight, here it was.

Talking to Malcolm both helped the hollowness and highlighted it. She sensed that he might be like her in many ways—the kind of person who feels so deeply that the safest course of action, was often to pretend not to feel at all. Getting more involved with him would only result in one or the other of them getting burned. And because of their natures, if that happened, maybe it wouldn't just be a burn; someone would be utterly consumed and go up in flames.

"Hey."

Shawn's gravelly voice caused her to lift her head. He was sitting up now on the edge of the bed, pulling on his boots, reaching for a shirt he'd shed.

"I think I'm gonna head back to the house," he said. "Just to see ..."

"Yes." Lorna smiled. "You go check on him. But he should be fine, Shawn. Probably sleeping by now."

"I know, but ..." He shrugged.

He didn't like nannies. He and Riley argued about it sometimes, the need to have strangers intermittently looking after their son while she worked. He wanted her to stay home, and would probably re-launch that campaign once the new baby was home.

The irony, Lorna always believed, was that the very things that caused friction in their relationship were the things Shawn loved about Riley. Her independence, and the firm yet gentle way she always asserted her individuality, and refused to let him change her. If Riley became a housewife, he would probably become bewildered and wonder where his real wife had gone.

"I know," Lorna said. "I'll be here. Go ahead."

GETTING Riley and the baby back to their condo later the next afternoon was akin to a top-secret operation, involving decoy SUVs and all kinds of foolishness like that. Shawn's superstar status made it as necessary as it was ridiculous, but both Lorna's daughter and son-in-law seemed to take the whole thing in stride. It was just one of the facts of their life together—he was a rap star, and the kind that seemed to provoke the most interest—the private and almost reclusive kind, with deep and cryptic lyrics and a stare of impenetrable intensity that made his public and groupies craven for details about what might lie beneath the surface.

Shawn never smiled for cameras, or glad-handed the press, which was one of the things Lorna most appreciated about him. He was, in a word, *unapologetic*.

At their Central Park West condo, the nanny was sent away, and a baby nurse showed up before Riley sent her away as well and instead called her best friend, Tracy to come over. Tracy showed up with Brendan, who also happened to be Shawn's best friend. He was a favorite of Lorna's—he was tall, and handsome but it was neither of those things that made her love him. Brendan was one of those people who had been born blessed with a never-ending wellspring of pure joy. When he smiled, it was a sight to behold. If she believed in them, Lorna was sure his aura would be bright, blinding and a hundred feet all around him, pulling everyone nearby into it.

With their friends there, Riley and Shawn were more animated, and everyone moved comfortably around the house, the nucleus being the living room, toasting to Cassidy, talking and laughing with lower voices so as not to wake her. Riley didn't look like a woman who had just given birth and certainly didn't move like one.

"Mom, have one of these mimosas. They're really good."

Riley was holding a glass in her direction.

"Did you *drink* one?" Shawn asked.

He had walked into the kitchen where Riley, Lorna and Tracy were working on shrimp fajitas, and keeping the steady flow of drinks for the men.

"I tasted one. Yes. But just a sip," Riley admitted, her expression daring him to complain.

Shawn shook his head but said nothing, just took the plate of fire-roasted shrimp and headed back out to the living room.

"Next time, he should be the one to carry the baby," Riley quipped.

"I can't believe you're already talking about next time," Tracy said. "You were like that with Cullen as well. What're you having? Painless childbirths or something?"

"Oh, believe me, it's far from painless," Riley said. "Right Lorna?"

Lorna shrugged. "I honestly can't remember."

Tracy and Riley both turned to look at her at once.

"What d'you mean you can't remember?" Tracy wrinkled her brow. "You don't remember the pain, or you don't remember ... childbirth?"

From the look on Riley's face, Lorna realized she probably shouldn't have spoken without thinking. Riley's births had been wondrous, miraculous, longed-for experiences. Nothing could be more different from Lorna's own path.

"Oh honestly, I don't know why we'd want to dwell on that," she said, hoping to divert their attention. "Let's just celebrate Cassidy. No matter how painful the process of getting her here." She raised her glass in a toast and Tracy smiled and nodded.

"To Cassidy," she said.

Riley, on the other hand, said nothing.

Later, when their guests had left, and they were cleaning up, the topic arose once again, as Lorna feared it might. Riley had never shown much curiosity about the circumstances of her birth, but now that she was a mother herself, she sometimes asked questions or wandered onto ground where Lorna would rather not tread. Most of the time, her references were oblique, her questions indirect, and Lorna was able to evade them without too much fuss. This time was different.

"I wonder about my father sometimes."

Riley was loading the dishwasher, bending carefully as she did. As the day wore on, she'd gotten visibly more exhausted and was moving more slowly. Her halting motion made her seem vulnerable, and her words hit Lorna in the center of her chest.

"What do you wonder?"

"Well ... for starters, whether he's even alive."

Taking a deep breath, Lorna reached for the dish that Riley was attempting to wedge between two others, and kneeling in front of the dishwasher found room for it. She stayed down there, rearranging things and taking out others.

"I don't know," she said honestly. "But I have no reason to believe he isn't."

"It occurred to me one day." Riley was still speaking very slowly. "It occurred to me as I was watching Shawn with Cullen, that he doesn't know his father either. He never did. He's met him, but doesn't know him. And his mother is long gone. He had his grandmother, and a cousin who helped raise him, but no real ... no parents, y'know?"

Looking up at Riley from her position crouched on the floor, Lorna nodded. This was the kind of conversation that merited eye contact.

"He never had either parent and I only had you. Never had a father. And here we are, he and I, trying to be the best parents we can for our kids. But sometimes ..." Riley paused and took a breath, then continued. "Sometimes it feels like we're faking it. Making it up as we go along."

"Riley." Lorna stood and closed the distance between her and her daughter. "That's all anyone does. No one knows exactly how to do this. *No one.*"

"Is that how you felt?"

Lorna gave a brief bark of laughter. "God yes."

"And you did it alone."

She shrugged.

"I have a million questions, but I don't want to ... hurt you by asking them."

"You're not going to hurt me."

Lorna reached out and pushed a strand of her daughter's hair from her face. She had let it grow long again. She had done the same when she was pregnant with Cullen. And just as she had done then, she would probably cut it all off when it became too much to maintain along with caring for an infant.

The hair—dark, smooth, tightly-coiled curls—may not have come from Lorna's side of the family. Lorna's own hair was flatter, straighter, and rumored to be the result of Seminole blood. But she didn't know for sure, because there was no longer anyone she could ask.

Riley looked very much like her father, at least as Lorna remembered him.

"There's a lot I want to know, of course. But maybe we could start with ..."

"Baby, she's up."

Shawn stuck his head in the kitchen, unwittingly interrupting what might have been arguably one of the most important conversations Lorna and Riley would ever have. And to her shame, Lorna was relieved. It had been emotional enough being present for her second grandchild's birth. The thought of resurrecting the circumstances that led to her daughter's entry into the world on top of all that wasn't nearly as welcome.

Riley looked at her, obviously torn. "I have to feed the baby, but ..."

"Go," Lorna said. "This conversation is probably long overdue, but maybe ..."

"Now isn't the best time," Riley finished for her.

Shawn was looking back and forth between them, his expression mildly curious, but mostly impatient. In the background, Lorna could hear the baby's mewling, that vaguely disturbing sound that was probably biologically programmed to produce anxiety in mothers.

"It freaks Cullen out when she cries," Shawn said as he and Riley headed toward the nursery.

Shutting the door to the dishwasher, Lorna chose a washing cycle and leaned back against it, closing her eyes.

EIGHT

WAR AND PEACE

"So where the hell is she, Charlotte?"

"That's what I'm telling you. I don't *know*."

"This is just not happening." Malcolm stood and began pacing his office, talking half to himself, half to his ex-wife. "So look, I can leave as soon as we hang up. But you have to give me some idea of where I need to go to. And whatever happened to using her phone to know where she is?"

"She probably turned the damned thing off. And there's no point in you coming down here. She's probably just with a bunch of her friends. We just need to figure out which one of them it was she left with, that's all."

Charlotte had called, just as he was winding down after a day of some pretty productive writing, with the news that Piper had given Elisa the slip. After picking her and Hayley up from school as she did every day, Elisa was persuaded by Piper to take them both to Serendipity 3 for Strawberry Supremes before heading back to Brooklyn. And according to Elisa, since Piper was being uncharacteristically sweet and cooperative, she hadn't wanted to refuse. So they cabbed it over and sat down for no more than ten minutes when Piper said she needed to go to the restroom.

And never returned.

Poor Elisa sat there for almost twenty minutes before she went to investigate and finding that Piper wasn't in fact in the restroom asked the staff in a panic if they had seen a girl in a St. Stephen's uniform. One of them had. Piper, it seemed, had gone skulking out the front with another girl in uniform, with blonde hair with blue highlights. And so Elisa called Charlotte in tears. Charlotte in turn called Malcolm, sounding remarkably sanguine about the whole thing.

"Do you know who that might be? A blonde girl with blue streaks?"

"No, Mal. I have no idea. That probably describes ten percent of the girls at that school."

"But who're her best friends, Charlotte? Kids she talks about ..."

"Piper barely speaks to me, or haven't you been paying attention?" his ex-wife quipped. "And Elisa said she was being 'sweet'?" Charlotte gave a bitter laugh. "You'd think it was her first rodeo with this kid. Piper is never 'sweet'."

"That's all very enlightening. But let's try to stay on task; where the hell do you think she could be? Should we call the police, or ...?"

"No. No police. I'll call Helen Crane. Her daughter is constantly pulling crap like this, so she's had to become like the KGB and knows all the little tricks of the trade with these kids, where they hang out ..."

"Okay, call whoever you need to. But if we don't know something within a half hour, I'm coming down there, and I'm calling the police."

"You with the police." Charlotte sighed. "She's a teenager, and this is the last week of school before summer vacation. This kind of thing was bound to happen sooner or later. Granted, it's a little early for the really big transgressions like ..."

"I wish you would stop talking about Piper's behavior like it's some rite of passage," Malcolm snapped, taking off his glasses and running a hand over his face. "This isn't the kind of shit we should be putting up with. And if she gets even a hint from you that you think this is some normal developmental milestone, she's never going to get her fucking act together."

"Don't curse at me, Malcolm. And if you want to save the lecture for later, I'll just go ahead and call Helen."

"You do that. And make sure you call me right back!"

The difference in their reactions probably came down to the difference in their upbringings. Malcolm had the kind of mother who could silence him with a look, and who meted out discipline for infractions as slight as *looking* at her with insolence. Charlotte on the other hand grew up in a home where the occasional bout of underage drinking or cursing at one's parents was considered a completely predictable "testing of boundaries."

Even once they were adult and engaged, Malcolm was shocked to hear Charlotte's sister use the word "fucking" at the dinner table in front of her parents. With no reaction on their parts whatsoever. It was the kind of thing that he should have known would be a problem in their marriage, especially once kids became part of the equation. But Malcolm made the mistake legions of people before him who had tripped into holy matrimony had made—he believed they would "figure it out."

Well, they never did, and still hadn't "figured it out" and he was losing hope that they ever would. From the time Piper was little, Charlotte's approach vacillated between structure and indifference.

She loved her kids, but at the end of the day wasn't that interested in them, nor would she be, Malcolm believed.

Maybe not until they were nineteen or so, and able to converse with her and conduct themselves with at least some semblance of what she considered rationality. Her insistence on order in their home only extended to logistics though—homework, piano practice, haircuts and doctors' appointments. In everything else, like Piper's increasingly erratic moods—she simply didn't have the patience to even try to comprehend when a crisis was brewing with their kid, and certainly didn't have much will to deal with them once they materialized.

Like today. She would call Helen Crane, sure, but was assigning the role of "worrier" to him.

Twenty-five minutes later, after Malcolm had almost paced a hole into his office rug, the phone rang. He answered without checking and was shocked to hear Piper's voice on the other end.

"Daddy," she said.

Malcolm's heart almost seized in his chest because clearly she had been crying.

"Baby," he said. "Where are you? What happened?"

"I'm in a cab. I'm on my way home," Piper said.

"Piper, Elisa said ..."

"I'm sorry, Daddy. I know I shouldn't have done that. But I really wanted to go to the party. And I knew Mom would say no, so I ..."

"*Party?* What party? Piper it's just four-thirty in the afternoon. How could ..."

"A bunch of kids were getting together at her apartment. Because it's the end of school. Emily invited me, and I thought ..." Piper was sobbing and gulping now, and barely comprehensible. "I thought they liked me. Emily's a junior, and I thought ... but it was just ... and all of them were ... laughing when I didn't want to drink and ... now everyone thinks I'm a *loser!*"

Closing his eyes in exasperation and relief, Malcolm massaged the bridge of his nose.

"So you were drinking alcohol, Piper?"

At thirteen! Visions of a drunken ten-year-old Drew Barrymore flashed through his mind. That was what privilege did to kids.

"I ... I tried it ..."

"And?"

"I didn't ... I didn't like it," she admitted between gulps. "And that's why Emily ... that's why ..."

"I don't give a shit about Emily," Malcolm said.

And his cursing made Piper's sobs stop dead in their tracks. That, and the steely coldness of his voice probably.

"I'm going to call Elisa and tell her to expect you, and to pay the cab when you get there," he said. "And then once you're home, I expect you to call your mother and apologize. And then you go sit your ass somewhere until I get there myself and deal with you."

There was nothing but silence on the other end of the line.

"Piper? Did you hear me?"

"Yes, Daddy." She sounded like she was five-years old again.

"Good."

Once he ended the call, Malcolm dialed Charlotte at work and filled her in.

"Thank God," she said. "Because Helen was no damned help. Her kid is probably at the same party. When I get home ..."

"What time will that be?" Malcolm interrupted her.

"I don't know. Usual. Around seven-thirty, I guess. A little later."

"You don't think this merits knocking off early?"

"No, Malcolm, I don't. So a bunch of kids tried some wine

coolers to make themselves feel grown up. So what? It's not the end of the world. It's not like we're talking hard drugs."

"No. That'll show up when she's sixteen. *If* we mess this up now."

"Don't be so fucking dramatic."

"Charlotte, I swear to God. I am driving down there tonight and when I get there ..."

"You are *not*. Because if you do in this frame of mind, you're bound to do or say the wrong thing. In fact ..." Malcolm could hear her moving around. "I'm calling my sister right now, and telling her to go to the house and get the kids. I'm not having you charge in and make a federal case out of ..."

"You know what could have happened to her? You didn't even have a clue where she was!"

"And neither did you, so ..."

"I'm not the custodial parent. If I were ..."

"You'd be as lost as I am, Malcolm. Stop kidding yourself."

At that, he said nothing. Because it was at least partly true. He might be lost, but he wouldn't be clueless like Charlotte appeared to be. Their kid was in trouble and Charlotte seemed hell-bent on doing nothing about it.

"Look," he said, willing himself to calm down. "If I don't come tonight ..."

"Don't."

"Okay, I won't. But you, Piper and I have to sit down together and we're going to get to the bottom of what's going on with her."

"Fine. Soon."

"Tomorrow or Sunday."

"No, not this weekend. I have plans with the girls."

He didn't want to ask what plans. Because if it was one of Charlotte's periodic spa days that she took Piper and Hayley on, he would lose his shit. But it would be just like her to think that an incident like today was no reason to reschedule her facial.

"Okay, not this weekend, but Monday."

"Monday," Charlotte confirmed.

———

LORNA SLEPT ON HER SIDE, her back turned to him, one arm extended, her head resting on it. She cuddled only immediately after sex, but beyond that was a self-sufficient sleeper, even with him in the bed, unless he pulled her close in the middle of the night. He did that often, liking the smell and feel of her.

Malcolm had been watching her for a few minutes now—long enough that he was starting to freak himself out a little bit. Because he didn't want to leave. If he did, Lorna would neither notice nor care; they would reconnect sometime in the afternoon, or the next day and she wouldn't even remark on his departure as most women might.

But it was he who didn't want to go.

"Hey."

He nudged her gently on her back and she moaned, turning over and facing him, her eyes half opening.

"G'morning," he said.

Lorna smiled, a sleepy, lazy smile.

"C'mon, get up," he said, playfully nudging her again.

"Why?" she croaked. Glancing past him she checked the time, and then her eyes fluttered shut again. "It's not even eight a.m. On a Sunday."

"I know. Let's go to church."

At this Lorna's eyes opened fully. "To church?" she said as though she might have misheard him.

"Yeah. There's a Lutheran church over on Main that I go to sometimes."

"And you want me to come with you."

"Yes."

"Why?"

"Why not? Are you a nonbeliever?"

Lorna smiled at the word. "You mean an *atheist*? No. Atheism is just egocentricity in disguise, in my opinion."

It was Malcolm's turn to smile. "Does everything have to be an academic lecture with you? Just get your ass up and be ready in an hour. I need to go home to shower and change into something suitable."

"Malcolm," Lorna groaned.

"An hour," he said, kissing her fleetingly on the lips and getting out of bed before she could complete her objection.

He was putting on his shoes, sitting on the edge of the bed, aware of her eyes boring into his back, waiting for her to refuse outright. But when she spoke again, it was to ask a question.

"Okay, so if I'm to get ready while you're gone," she said. "What passes as 'suitable' at this church of yours?"

Malcolm didn't turn to look at her, not wanting her to see him smile.

———

LORNA TERRY HAD NEVER LOOKED AS DEMURE as she did when Malcolm returned to pick her up. She wore a white cotton dress, simple with buttons running its entire length, and eyelet trim on the cap sleeves and at the hem. On her feet were nude flats, because Malcolm had come to learn that she disliked heels of any kind unless modest in height. But most impressive of all was the fact that she had pulled her hair smoothly back into a twisty thing that Malcolm had once heard his ex-wife call a chignon. A little lipstick and even what looked like eyeliner completed the look.

"The pastor had better not be boring," she warned as she slipped into the passenger seat next to him.

"You can judge for yourself," he said.

What Malcolm hadn't told her, though he forgot himself until they walked in, was that almost the entire Gilchrist faculty who attended church at all, attended the Lutheran Church of Hope. The small and unassuming red brick building was on the corner of Main and Spruce, and the Sunday morning congestion as people looked for places to park was considerable.

Usually, a good percentage of the congregation wound up parking on the street instead of in the small lot, and then walking down the block toward the church. That walk was like a parade of the Gilchrist community, from the college president on down to the most junior members of the faculty, and their teaching assistants.

So when Malcolm and Lorna got out of his car and made their way toward the church, they had quite the audience and were greeted by colleagues just about every three steps they took. A block away from their destination, he reached over and slid an arm through Lorna's and she glanced up at him, momentarily surprised, but not displeased.

"Would you look at you two?"

Professor Rogers was getting out of her VW bug just as Malcolm and Lorna approached the church door, dressed as usual in a manner that was markedly incongruent from everyone else, yet still just barely appropriate to the occasion. This time in a spring dress that clung, and sandals, she looked like someone who was attending a beachside wedding. Slinging a shawl about her shoulders, she fell into step with them, on Lorna's side.

"Lorna, I can't recall having seen you at Church of Hope before. Have I?"

"No. Probably not. Unless for a funeral or something. Did anyone on faculty die last semester?"

Malcolm tried not to smile and contented himself with shaking his head in amusement.

Professor Rogers didn't look amused, and didn't respond but simply broke away from them to enter the church on her own.

"I can see why some people find you hard to take sometimes," Malcolm said under his breath.

"Rogers finds me hard to take *all* the time. She's never liked me."

"And so you try to win her over."

Lorna looked up at him, her expression one of disappointment. "Is *that* what I should do? Soften my tone with her? Bake brownies and bring them to her office?"

"Or just don't talk down to her like she's someone's dullard child."

Lorna rolled her eyes. "It wouldn't make a difference. All I'm doing is living up to her expectations."

"Or down to them," Malcolm said, putting a hand on the small of her back and ushering her into a pew.

During the service, he expected her to fidget, or show some other signs of impatience, but Lorna was attentive and present, and even joined in with all the hymns. He on the other hand could hardly pay attention because now that they were here, it seemed almost like a watershed moment.

He had gone to church regularly with Charlotte and the girls when he lived at home. Not because either he or Charlotte were particularly focused on their spiritual life, but because it was such a New England, WASP-y thing to do. And Charlotte, though biracial was very much New England and at least one half WASP-y.

For Malcolm's side of things, he always believed there was some essential component kids missed if they had no bedrock of faith or religious doctrine in their lives. He'd seen it in some of the kids in Piper and Hayley's school—that look of arrogant self-certainty that if they wanted something, they should have it; and that if it felt good they should do it. Without the moral compass provided by some foundation of faith, he always wondered what kinds of human beings they could become.

Actually, he knew what kind. He worked with them every day when he was practicing law—people who broke rules with impunity all their lives because of wealth or privilege, and who when they finally encountered a situation where exceptions would not be made, or their "unique" circumstances not accommodated, they reacted poorly, and sometimes criminally.

Those were the people who made up about seventy-five percent of Malcolm's client list by the time he left the practice —people who had lived lives without accountability or consequences for far too long until they happened across a rule that even they could not break without being called to the carpet. The senator's daughter who reacted in tearful disbelief when told she might be charged with her best friend's overdose because she supplied enough drugs to down a horse (*"Does this mean I need to defer my enrollment at Stanford?"*); the Wall Street trader whose illegal trades emptied a pension fund (*"It's not like most of these people ever sail the Caribbean after retirement anyway. They say they will, but they never do."*); and the most common one, the multimillionaire deadbeat husbands and fathers (*"Hey, she lived a damn good life when we were together. What? She thought the gravy-train would never stop?"*)

By the time he started planning his exit from law, Malcolm had come to loathe most of his clients, and to fear that they might see that loathing in his eyes. But on some level he should probably thank them. It was they who helped birth Vernon, the main character in his novel, who gamed the system by exploiting the prejudices of a country that believed the only "way out" for someone like him was through the standby escape route for unprivileged Black boys—professional sports. Malcolm had written Vernon as though writing himself—as a young man who suppressed a lifetime of anger and through hard work and focus, transformed it into something else entirely—ambition.

Charlotte, after reading his first draft, hadn't understood Vernon at all.

I just don't see what axe he has to grind, she said. *He's both athletically talented and academically gifted. He should be the least angry Black man in America if you ask me.*

That disconnect, which secretly pissed Malcolm off, had been a recurring one in their marriage. There were some things that Charlotte just didn't *get* about the Black experience. She'd grown up in a town where people politely pretended not to notice that one of her parents was Black, which could mean one of two things: that they genuinely didn't care (Charlotte's interpretation) or had no clue that on some level the avoidance was nullifying of Charlotte's father's Blackness (Malcolm's interpretation).

But knowing Charlotte's father as he now did, Malcolm suspected that he had been content to assimilate, and if at times it was an isolating experience to be "the only one" at social gatherings, he contented himself with the knowledge that at least he was providing his girls—Charlotte and her sister—a good, clean Leave-it-to-Beaver life.

When he met Charlotte at Cambridge, Malcolm hadn't even considered her a romantic prospect. She was at first just a friend, while he pursued a Nigerian student named Abidemi, who had a seductively musical accent and the brain of a nuclear physicist. The very obviously American Charlotte Hayes had been no competition.

"Shall we go?"

Malcolm was brought back to the present by Lorna's voice at his side, and it was only then that he realized the service was over and he was creating a traffic jam by not filing out of their pew.

On the little front lawn of the church, clusters of church-goers had stopped to chat, but Lorna showed no interest in joining in, so Malcolm ambled behind her, enjoying the sway of her backside and wondering whether it was inappropriate for him to be thinking about what he might do with it later. Just as they reached the gate that opened out onto the sidewalk, a young man stepped forward and into Lorna's path. He smiled and Lorna looked up at him, apparently slightly taken aback.

An awkward hug was exchanged just before Malcolm joined them.

"Professor Mitchell!" The young man stepped forward, hand outstretched. "A double treat!"

"Malcolm, please," he corrected him, taking his hand.

"Malcolm. Sure. I'm Todd Williamson. I was just telling Lorna that it was crazy to run into her here. I've been on campus for a couple weeks and been having the hardest time reaching her."

Malcolm smiled. "Yeah. Tell me about it."

The young man's smile persisted, but he looked from Malcolm to Lorna and back again, until a slow realization dawned in his eyes, and then the smile slipped just the tiniest bit.

"Todd and I met earlier this spring," Lorna explained coolly. "At a conference in New York where I got into a tussle with a couple of baby feminists."

"Wasn't much of a tussle. You decimated them pretty handily, I think."

"Oh, it wasn't ..."

"It was." Todd looked directly at Lorna and his eyes had that little something like hero-worship. She probably met groupies like this all the time, Malcolm thought with amusement. He sensed the moment she grew impatient with the conversation.

"It's great to see you again, Todd," she said, angling her torso as though preparing to walk away. "You'll have to stop in and tell me what you're doing on campus."

"I will. I did. I mean, we talked about it in New York, but I guess that was a hectic time, so ..."

"So, we'll talk again sometime soon." She offered Todd one last smile and then looked expectantly in Malcolm's direction, silently urging him to get moving.

"One of your fans, huh?" he said as they climbed back into his truck.

"Oh, quiet, you."

"THAT WAS *SO* GOOD. And I should know because I'm a pro making omelets," Lorna said, setting her plate on the side table.

Malcolm liked how she looked sitting on his sofa, legs curled beneath her and the top few buttons of her straitlaced white church dress now open to her cleavage.

"You're welcome. My stomach was growling all through that service. Next time, we'll go to the eleven o'clock instead."

"Next time?" Lorna smiled slyly at him.

"Would you come with me again?"

She nodded. "I would, actually. It was like going to a spiritual spa."

Stretching her legs out in front of her, she turned so that she was facing him, feet on the oak coffee table between them.

"And what're your plans for the rest of the day? Going to see your daughter and her family or anything?"

"Nope. They're good. Nesting."

"So stay here with me."

Since she'd returned from the city about five days earlier, he didn't push as much, and she didn't resist as much. Their almost-break (Malcolm hesitated to call it a "breakup") seemed to have sobered them both and made them focus on something neither was ready to admit—they liked this, whatever-it-was that they had, and weren't ready for it to be over.

"And do what?" Lorna asked, her voice quiet.

Sometimes she was like a calm, gentle breeze; other times she was like a hurricane. Today, the breeze. She seemed comfortable and almost sleepy, her eyes heavy-lidded, her aura one of contentment.

"Nothing." He shrugged. "I plan to do some writing, then at sundown I'll cook for us and we'll ... I don't know ... whatever."

Lorna smiled. They did a lot of ... whatever. They did more 'whatever' than Malcolm could recall having done in a long, long time. In that, they were in perfect sync.

"Okay," she said.

"Okay?"

"Uh huh."

And then she pulled her legs beneath her again, let her head fall back against the sofa cushion and shut her eyes.

The rest of the afternoon passed in almost complete silence. Malcolm worked on his book, making occasional trips from his home office to the kitchen to refill his coffee, grab a snack and sometimes just to reassure himself that Lorna was still there.

She slept silently, with only the barely perceptible rise and fall of her chest, and periodic changes in position. Three hours in, Malcolm covered her with a blanket, and went back to work. He wrote fluidly, his fingers dancing across the keyboard, his excitement rising. He had no idea whether what he wrote was any good, but to write so easily once again was exhilarating.

When it grew dark enough for him to turn on lights, he went to check on Lorna again, and it was then that she issued a deep groan, turned over onto her side and opened her eyes. They were puffy and a little unfocused, and her hair had come loose from its style.

"Hi," she said.

"Hi," he said back. "You hungry?"

She nodded. "You?"

"Starving," he said. "Again."

"Have you been writing?"

"Yeah. For hours. All afternoon."

Lorna smiled, and pushed herself to a sitting position. "Well then you go back to it. I'll cook us dinner."

"I took out some steaks," he began. "And there's ..."

"Malcolm." She stopped him. "Go write. I'm sure I'll sort it out."

"You sure?"

"Positive. When your muse visits, you have to indulge her, or she may never come again."

"Why are you not a writer, spitting out lines like that?"

Lorna stood and walked by him, pausing briefly to rake her fingers across his scalp and to lightly caress his nape. "Malcolm. Go *write*."

An hour later, she came to get him in his office and led him to his own table where she had cleared it of books and unopened mail and set two places. There was an open bottle of red wine, an arugula salad with cherry tomatoes, and pepper-corn-encrusted steak with sautéed brussel sprouts.

Malcolm resisted making a crack about not knowing that she could be so domestic, and simply sat to receive her offering. They talked about his book while they ate—'Cadence', not the one he was working on, because he was a little superstitious about talking about work that wasn't complete—and Lorna asked a lot of questions about his characters, without even a hint of facetiousness in her tone.

When dinner was done, they washed up side by side at his small kitchen sink, their arms and hips bumping into each other as they worked. Afterward, when she sensed that he had a few more words in him before feeling like his writing day was over, she went to his bedroom to read a book she'd chosen from his bookshelf. But Malcolm was unable to concentrate knowing that she was there, in his bedroom, likely in his bed, and waiting for him.

Shutting down the computer, he shrugged his shirt over his head as he made his way to the bedroom. At the doorway, he paused because Lorna was already undressed and wearing one of his t-shirts, her legs under the sheets. She looked up as he entered and when he removed his pants, she set her book aside.

Saying nothing as he pulled the sheets back, she let her knees fall apart. Crawling between her legs, Malcolm spread them further, and pulling aside her underwear, lowered his head.

She tasted sweet.

NINE

ANCIENT HISTORY

"Fallon," Lorna said looking at the undergrad sitting across the table from her. "While I admire your enthusiasm, it seems a little premature for you to have completed your senior thesis already, the summer *before* your senior year."

"I know." The young woman said. "But I want to get a head-start, get your impressions before you have a million other students and issues when we start back up in the fall."

"And you're enrolled in my senior lecture?"

"Yes. I am, but ..."

"That's only eight students, Fallon. You'll get plenty of individualized attention, I assure you."

"But you have other thesis advisees."

"One other. Yes."

"Well ..."

There was always at least one student like this every semester—an eager young thing who wanted to set the world afire with their "original" ideas on feminist theory. But it was the first time Lorna could recall having one show up in June with a completed thesis that was due almost a full year later.

"You see, what I'm hoping for is to get something published," Fallon said. "Not just have something that gives me a passing grade and lets me graduate."

Lorna leaned back and looked the young woman over more closely. She was uncommonly pretty, but wore enormous owlish glasses that Lorna would swear were an attempt to emulate Gloria Steinem. Behind the glasses her eyes were large frank, and inquisitive.

"You're interested in a career in academia?"

"Yes," Fallon said nodding. "I would love to have ..." She broke off and laughed, "... *your* career basically."

"Well then prepare yourself for a lot of long sleepless nights when you're certain that in your last paper you had no idea what you were talking about. And there'll be gin. Lots of gin."

It took Fallon a moment to realize she was joking and then she smiled.

"Okay, Fallon. Let's see this premature thesis of yours." Lorna extended a hand into which the young woman placed what looked like a ream of paper.

"It's long, I know," Fallon said. "At least twenty pages too long. But I was hoping that that's part of what you could help me with. Figuring out which ideas should stay on the cutting room floor."

"This is going to be time-consuming," Lorna said flipping through the first few pages. "So I'll make you a deal."

Fallon sat forward.

"In the summer, I do my own writing and research. And in recent years, I've not used a research assistant. How about you become my assistant for the summer, for which I would of course pay you. And with the time your doing research for me frees up, I'll read this magnum opus of yours, and ..."

"I would be your research assistant?"

"I believe that's what I said."

"Professor Terry, I would love that." She sounded breathless. "I'll quit my other job at ..."

Lorna held up a hand. "I would have to check your grades first. I have fairly high standards, and would be depending on you to do digests and annotated bibliographies ... the usual. But all of that requires accuracy, and analytical skill."

Fallon nodded. "I understand."

"Okay. Well, I'll check into your transcript, and be in touch."

"Thank you so much, Professor Terry. I just ..."

"Yes, yes. I have another appointment. Thank you for stopping in, Fallon."

She stood, looking as though she might have something else to say. Lorna hoped not. She was way behind on some of the tedious paperwork she always postponed too long, and Riley was due for lunch. Thankfully, after a few moments and one final nervous smile, the young woman nodded and left.

"IT'S SO weird visiting you here," Riley said walking around the office. "I don't recall ever coming to your office when I was actually enrolled at the college."

"You didn't. But I wasn't in this office. When you were here, I had the much smaller one in Rayburn Hall."

Riley had left Shawn with the kids for the day and driven up. For lunch was what they said, though they both knew the real reason was to finish the conversation that had been started in Riley's kitchen a few days after she brought Cassidy home from the hospital.

Already, her daughter had resumed the size she was before her pregnancy—breastfeeding and her father's genes, probably. Lorna remembered carrying around an extra twenty pounds for months after Riley's birth. And of course, she hadn't breastfed hardly at all.

"Which classes are having their reunions this year?" Riley asked, lifting and inspecting a book on Lorna's desk.

"Not sure. I usually leave town for all that brouhaha."

"Which I'm sure makes the deans mad at you. I bet lots of people come just to meet you."

"Don't kid yourself. They come to get drunk and sleep with their old college boyfriend or girlfriend, to see whether all those sweet romantic memories are accurate."

Riley laughed. "Ever the cynic. I had lots of college flings. I can't imagine being even slightly interested in any of them now."

"Remember how you never wanted me to meet them?" Lorna asked gathering her bag and keys. "Now that you're older I can ask: *what the hell was up with that?*"

"I don't know." Riley shrugged. "I was probably afraid of them falling in love with you or something."

"Riley!"

"No, seriously. You always seemed to attract younger men in droves ..."

Lorna thought of the grad student, whose name she now knew well—Todd Williamson. And she thought of Malcolm, who lately had begun to seem less and less young.

"That's not true. *Is* it?"

"Yes, Mom. Seriously? You don't remember?"

"No, I don't. Like ... who are you talking about?"

"Like I could remember their names." Riley scoffed.

Though Lorna knew she didn't mean it to be cruel or judgmental, the comment stung. There had been men, for sure, but when Riley entered Gilchrist, Lorna hadn't yet turned forty. She was in her prime, so of course there were men.

"Did I ..." She paused while locking her office door. "Did I *introduce* you to them all?"

"If you could call it that. I ran into some in our kitchen when I stopped by the house, or in the bathroom, or ..."

"How is it we never talked about this?"

"What was there to talk about? You had lovers. You never hid that, and you always taught me it was nothing to be ashamed of. So I didn't ..." Riley shrugged again. "It was mostly no big deal. I can't believe you're saying you now don't remember any of this."

"No," Lorna said. "I'm not saying I don't remember any of it. I guess I just remember it differently, that's all. There were men who were around for longer. There was Earl, there was ..."

Riley seemed to detect her consternation and touched her on the forearm. "Lorna, like I said, it was no big deal."

"You said it was *mostly* no big deal, actually. That's not the same thing."

"Well I meant 'no big deal'. So anyway, let's go find someplace to eat. I feel like Italian. How 'bout you?"

They ate at *Andiamo!* which was a favorite of the Gilchrist community because of its enormous antipasti selection and could-stuff-a-horse entrée portion sizes. Riley ordered like someone who was still eating for two, but Lorna didn't bother remarking on it since her daughter never seemed to gain an ounce anyway, and wouldn't have cared if she did. Lorna herself had only recently begun to care about things like pant sizes and the number on the scale.

"So I want to talk more about me being a bad mother," Lorna said once they'd placed their orders.

Riley looked at her, freezing just as she was about to dip a piece of bread into the plate of olive oil and cracked pepper between them.

"Who said anything about ..? See this is why we never have

these kinds of conversations. When it's about you, you get incredibly sensitive. And yet you insist on doling out brutal truths to everyone else when it's about *them*."

"What you described earlier, men coming and going, is a pretty shitty mother, that's all."

"That's *your* judgment of yourself. I never said anything like that."

"I don't know how else to ..."

"Look, I came here because I wanted to ask you some questions about my father. And suddenly it's about you. It's *always* about you, Lorna."

"Ah. And now we get the truth."

"I always tell you the truth. And the truth is this: I never said you were a bad mother. Did I sometimes wish you made it to more PTA meetings? *Sure.* Did I wish my house didn't reek of pot when my friends came over when I was in middle school? *Of course.* Did I occasionally want you to bake some fucking brownies? *Yes!* But I never said you were a shitty mother!"

Riley raising her voice was so unusual that Lorna was or a few minutes, literally without words.

"I don't know what narrative you have in your head about yourself that you're hoping I'll confirm for you," Riley continued in a calmer tone. "But I had a pretty good childhood. Some of it not so good, but on balance, good. I don't know what else you want me to say."

"I'm ... sorry."

Riley looked up. She seemed surprised. Lorna knew it was because those two words were ones she didn't often say in sequence. The second one she didn't often say, period.

"You're right. This isn't about me. But I think some of what you said may have triggered me. Made me think of my own mother."

"What about her?" Riley asked slowly. "We never ... You've never told me much about your family. I don't even know if there's anyone left."

"I don't know either," Lorna said ruefully.

"Mom. Look. If today you don't feel up to ..."

"No. You came up here, so let's talk." She nodded. "Let me tell you about your father."

Riley bit into the crusty bit of bread in her hand, brushing away the crumbs that fell onto her shirt. "Okay, so ..."

"It's hard to talk about him," Lorna acknowledged.

"Why? Was he like, I don't know, an asshole to you or something?"

Lorna laughed. "No. Quite the opposite, actually."

She leaned back and took a deep breath before beginning to speak.

TEA USUALLY WORKED to help calm her when her mind was racing, or if she could not sleep. Something like chamomile or peppermint, neither of which she really enjoyed under usual circumstances. But the chamomile didn't work tonight, and neither did the one very small glass of chardonnay that she had immediately afterwards. Finally, Lorna tried just lying in bed, but when she closed her eyes, she saw Riley's face—the surprise, and the disappointment, the hurt and the withdrawal.

Sitting up cross-legged after an hour of fruitless tries to get to sleep, she finally gave in to the impulse she'd had since early evening. The jeans she had been wearing that afternoon were on the floor nearby. She put them on. Then she slid her feet into her clogs, pulled a random sweatshirt over her head and left the house without even bothering to check in a mirror to see just how crazy she might look.

Malcolm answered his door surprisingly quickly, and looked tired but not as though he had been asleep. He said nothing when he saw her, but simply looked surprised.

"Are you alone?" Lorna asked.

It had only occurred to her on the drive over that he might not be.

He nodded. "Everything okay?"

"No," she said. "Not really."

And then she took a few steps forward which made him step back. He shut the door behind her and locked it.

"Lorna," he said when they were facing each other again. "What ..."

"I was home, and couldn't sleep."

Malcolm waited for more, but then she saw him decide not to press her further about why she was there.

Lorna advanced slowly, and he watched her, waiting to see what she would do next. She didn't usually have to initiate anything, because he wasn't one to wait. This time he did.

Putting her arms up and around his neck, Lorna exerted gentle pressure to pull him down. She closed her eyes just before their lips met, and relaxed her body against his. His lips softened, but he didn't do what he always did. He was still holding back, to see what she might do. What she did was kiss him more deeply, press her tongue into his mouth, pull back and capture his lower lip between hers coaxing him, frustrated when he didn't immediately take charge.

Letting her arms drop, she took a step back and shook her head. "Maybe I made a mistake. I thought ..."

"What?"

"Nothing. I just wanted ..."

She turned away from him, but Malcolm grabbed her arm, pulling her back so she collided with his chest.

"You wanted what?" he demanded.

"I don't know. I just ..."

"*This?*" he said. His lips pressed into hers, bruisingly hard; and he kissed her the way she liked him to—no waiting, no hesitating, just taking. One large hand came up to almost span her neck. He tilted her head to the side, kissing her there as well, his rough stubble scoring her skin. "*This what you want?*"

"Yes." Lorna exhaled. "This ..."

Malcolm reached down and opened her jeans, sliding his hand down into it. He parted her with his fingers, stroking her while Lorna moved against his hand. His lips came to hers again, and he swallowed her moans, even as the rhythm of his fingers produced more of them. He moved her again, exposing the other side of her neck, licking and biting her there.

Now, he was out of control, but in charge at the same time.

"You came here to get fucked? Is that it?"

"Yes," she said again.

Abruptly, Malcolm lifted his head but his hand still worked on her. He looked angry. "I'm more than that, Lo," he said.

Lo. He had never called her that before. Endearment, even in anger.

"*We're* more than that," he added.

Lorna looked at him, or tried to. It was difficult to keep her eyes open or even to listen when he was touching her this way. She got on her toes, kissed him again and he made a sound of frustration. Then they were tussling with each other's clothing, moving, lifting, peeling away.

Malcolm had her naked in less than a minute and she had only succeeded in removing his shirt. Lifting her so her legs were wrapped around his torso, he carried her into his bedroom, which was dark. He had been writing, because the light and computer in his office were on. Lorna felt only the tiniest stab of remorse at having taken him away from his work.

And even that disappeared when he lay her across the bed and immediately spread her legs wide.

Without further preliminaries, he stripped off what remained of his clothes and sank between her knees, shoving hard inside her with one long thrust.

Gasping, Lorna clutched the sheets as Malcolm moved, each time with long, deep strokes. After her body's initial slight resistance, she loosened and softened around him, warming and becoming more liquid.

Bowing his head as much as he could, Malcolm captured a nipple between his lips, tugging and sucking on it. The feeling was electric. Lorna's hands came up atop his head, holding him there, and he nipped her, causing her hips to buck upward. When they did, he held her in place and pulled back, both of his hands pressing her immobile into the bed.

Shifting tacks, he pulled out of her completely and sat back on his haunches. Hands still on her hips, he dragged her forward so that her butt was on his thighs. Now grabbing her at the knees, Malcolm used her legs as levers while he pumped in and out of her, forward and backward, his eyes trained downward, watching himself.

Lorna's back was arched, only her shoulders and head making contact with the bed. She opened her eyes and saw only Malcolm's face in a scowl of pleasure and concentration, his focus on their bodies joining. He didn't look at her face, which was for a moment mildly troubling until the pleasure overtook all thought, and her head thrashed back and forth.

"This what you want?" Malcolm panted between breaths. "Like this?"

"Yeah," Lorna panted. "Like that. Keep it ... right there ... like that ..."

"Y'know what, Lo?" he said. He sounded angry. "*Fuck you.*"

Then he shoved her back further, so her butt was once again on the bed and he was no longer inside her. Lorna's body clenched, protesting his sudden absence and she opened her eyes, just in time to see Malcolm come for her again, this time slinging both her legs over his shoulders and stabbing at her like he wanted to drive her through the mattress. His face was buried in the space between her neck and shoulder, again, not looking at her. She shouldn't have cared, but she did.

Grabbing his face between her hands, Lorna forced eye contact.

"Malcolm ..." she forced out. "It's *you* I needed. *You*."

Something in his eyes shifted and he slowed.

"Please. Don't doubt that," she said.

He blinked slowly and lowered his head, kissing her.

———

LORNA'S HEAD was on his damp chest. Her hand stole downward under the sheet and she cupped him, feeling him stir. They hadn't spoken since the second round, and though both of them were now thoroughly spent, the desire didn't go away. The mind was willing, but the body might protest. She was still aching a little at her inner thighs, and felt raw between them.

"Talk to me," Malcolm said.

"I don't ... have many confidantes," Lorna said. Then she laughed. "None, actually. Riley is the only person who comes close. And Shawn in a way."

"The rap star?"

"I wish people would stop focusing on that," Lorna said into the dark. "It's the least consequential thing about who he is."

"Since you know the other parts, I can see how that would be frustrating. So you can relate to how I feel."

"What do you mean?"

"When you try to show me Lorna Terry, feminist theorist, college professor, man-eater all the time. When you try to pretend that's all there is when that's the ... how did you put it? The *least consequential* part of who you are. And then you show up here at one in the morning wanting to get screwed and pretending that's all it is, that something isn't bothering you."

"Is there a *problem* with me showing up at one in the morning wanting to get screwed?" she asked teasingly, hoping to lighten the mood.

"Only when you withdraw while you're doing it. You're the only woman I've ever known who pulls away after sex. And sometimes even during."

"You mean like men often do?"

"C'mon, Lorna." Malcolm made a sound of frustration and sat up so she was forced to do the same.

He flipped on the bedside lamp so they could see each other, and Lorna squinted against the sudden light.

"Stop with that bullshit. You see what I mean? I try to get to the real with you and you throw up some line from one of your lectures. That crap might've worked on that grad student, but it isn't going to work on me."

Stunned, Lorna didn't even have time to control her expression to pretend otherwise.

"Yeah," Malcolm said. "I know you fucked him. I could see it by the way you dismissed him outside the church. I recognized your posture, your ... distancing techniques. Because you sometimes use them on me."

"I'm not going to apologize for ..."

"And no one's asking you to."

"Nor am I going to explain whom I might have slept with and why."

"No one's asking you to do that either!"

"Then what are you asking?"

"For you to just ... talk to me. You came over here upset. I saw it in your eyes. And I was waiting for you to tell me. Man, I was ..." He paused and ran a hand over his head. "I was ... *excited* that you might want to tell me something about ... anything. And then you ... turn it into a booty call."

"I've never been in a position of having to negotiate for dick before," Lorna said ruefully.

Malcolm gave a brief laugh. "You know you can get that from me whenever you want it."

"And maybe tonight that's all I needed."

"I don't believe that. Something happened. Something that ..."

"I told my daughter the true story about her father this afternoon," Lorna said in a rush. Raking her fingers through her hair, she took a deep breath. "And it seemed to go okay, my telling her. But only because she hasn't processed it yet. And when she does, she ..." Lorna shrugged. "I don't know what'll happen then."

Malcolm said nothing. He leaned back against the head-board and watched her, waiting for her to go on. Without his glasses, which he wore only occasionally, he was more sexy-lumberjack than college professor. More so now because of the stubble on his cheeks and chin. It would be so easy to derail the conversation by dipping her head beneath the sheets and taking him in her mouth and for a while they would both disappear. But he would be angry as well, and then maybe they would be over. She didn't want that.

"When a father is absent, everyone knows not to ask why. Even the kid whose father is absent knows not to ask why," she said, pulling the sheet up to cover her chest and leaning against the headboard next to him. "And then certain assumptions grow around that when he doesn't show up. People assume, and the kid assumes ... that he didn't *want* to show up."

"But sometimes he does ... want to," Malcolm said.

"Yes. Sometimes he does. But the mother, blinded by her own heartbreak, or selfishness, doesn't allow it."

Neither of them spoke for a while, until Malcolm finally did.

"And so, did he? Want to show up?"

"Yes. When I got pregnant we were freshmen in college. Neither of us was ready to be parents of course. But when I got pregnant, I felt hopeful for the first time in a long time. That I might have ... a ... I don't know, a place to belong to.

"His parents were solid upper middle-class people, with a summer home and an extended family and holidays around a Christmas tree and Thanksgiving around a large table. I saw some of that when I was with him and I think I wanted it. I know I did."

"And so the pregnancy ..."

"Wasn't planned. But once it happened, I felt hopeful. I pictured that life for me and my baby, and Ryan ... that was his name ... was part of that picture but not a major part. I wasn't in love with him so much as I was in love with his all-American ordinariness, and the normalcy of his family and the ... niceness."

"And what happened?"

"Well, once he found out I was pregnant, he told his parents, and they invited me out for a weekend and there was a nice little chat. They said we were too young to get married, and that Ryan and I had to build our futures, that whether separate or together, time would tell. They were actually very civil about the whole thing. They told me that though the timing wasn't ideal, they would love their grandchild, and while I went through the pregnancy—if that was what I decided to do —they would help support me, and pay my medical bills."

Malcolm had slid his hand over and was resting it on her bare thigh. It was warm there, and comforting.

"And they were true to their word. But while I was pregnant, Ryan pulled further and further away. He was in college, he wanted to party, to go out, to be a college student. And so that's what he did. He was there for Riley's birth and his parents were there as well. And he was supportive and ... friendly. He intended to be there for her, but whatever we had was definitely over.

"I transferred after my junior year. From City College of New York to NYU. Ryan transferred as well, but to Boston University. And then went on junior year abroad. While he was gone, his parents still helped financially, and I'd dress Riley up in these little outfits and take her to see them. By then I was getting more and more into feminist theory, and I had all these new ideas swirling around in my head. And suddenly it felt so demeaning, like something out of a Colleen McCullough novel, me bringing my little bastard child to the big house and begging for alms or something."

Lorna laughed a little at the memory. Riley was such a pretty child, and Ryan's parents doted on her. But Lorna was impatient during those visits. She had schoolwork to complete, friends she wanted to see; and by then, always a lover as well.

"I started sending back their checks. Missing visits on purpose. I made myself scarce, so they didn't see her as much. And when Ryan came back from abroad, he came to see me and asked what was up. His parents had told him that I didn't take the money anymore and that they were having a harder time seeing Riley. I told him that we didn't need his family's money, and that we didn't need his family."

"And that was it?" Malcolm asked. "They left you alone?"

"No." Lorna shook her head. "It would make me sound so much better if I could answer yes to that. Riley asked me the same thing. It took years for them to leave me alone. Ryan visited, sometimes with his parents, sometimes not. Because he knew that I might never bring Riley to them, or might make excuses but so long as he just showed up, I would probably be cooperative. And I was, for the most part—cooperative but never friendly.

"So they came, they saw her and I sat there with a nasty scowl, waiting for them to be done and get out of my apartment. And then there was this one day when I was busy with school and they dropped in. Riley was fussy and getting over a fever, and she was crying, and I was exhausted ... and I screamed at Ryan and his mother and told them to leave us alone, that we didn't need them. Then his mother started crying as well ... it was a mess. She never came back after that. She sent word with Ryan that if I could just send pictures she would appreciate it. And that I should keep in touch.

"I did my Masters at Radcliffe, and I sent pictures for a while, sometimes not. Ryan stopped in for a while. And sometimes not. But finally, after years and years of me moving around for my studies and different academic programs, and him having to track me down because I conveniently never left a forwarding address, he finally had enough. He wrote a letter to Riley for when she was old enough to read it. It said that he loved her, that she was wanted and let her know how she would always be his daughter. He put in his full name, his birthdate, his parents' names and birthdates. He gave her everything short of his social security number. I was supposed to give it to her when she was eighteen."

Lorna could tell that Malcolm both dreaded and wanted to know the answer to the question he asked next.

"And on her eighteenth birthday, you ..."

"When Riley turned eighteen, she got into Gilchrist, where I was already teaching, and she got into Vassar, Dartmouth and Princeton as well. She was ...." Lorna felt her throat tighten. "She was brilliant. She was *amazing*. And confident and so fucking talented. And I was proud, and felt like she was *my* accomplishment alone. So I .... I chose ... I chose not to share her."

"What did you do with the letter?" Malcolm had removed his hand from her thigh.

"I ripped it up," she admitted. "I ripped it up and threw it away."

Malcolm exhaled, grimacing and squeezing his eyes shut.

"Lo ..."

"I know, Malcolm. *I know.*"

"And you told her all this, this afternoon?"

"Yes."

"How did she react?"

"I'm not sure she'll ever see me the same way again."

"Jesus Christ."

"And from the sound of your voice right now, I'm not sure you will either."

"No. That was you then. That isn't ..."

"I don't know that. *You* don't know that. I've lived a self-centered life, Malcolm. I've done what I wanted to do, when I wanted to do it and never allowed anything to slow me down. Not even my kid. I'm not sure too much has changed."

When he didn't say anything, Lorna braved a look at him. He was staring sightlessly off into the middle distance, his expression not unlike Riley's when she had shared the same story with her.

"Well," she said. "You were the one who wanted me to talk. So this ... this is what you get."

TEN

BEST LAID PLANS

"So what're your thoughts, Mal?"

"My thoughts? That maybe we should just have her committed to a mental institution because no way is this just 'normal' adolescent behavior. I'm almost expecting her head to spin around next."

"Very funny." Charlotte twirled her wineglass in her hand by the stem, flipping her auburn hair out of her eyes.

It wasn't politically-correct to think let alone say something like this, but Malcolm always thought her mannerisms were very much those of a White girl from New England than a Black woman from ... anywhere. Much of them seemed centered around her hair—twirling it, twisting it, flipping it—no matter her mood. He never used to notice it as much as he did now. Charlotte's body was always on the move. Even when she was sitting down, she was never still. Now, she was running her free hand along the length of her thigh as though testing it for muscle tone.

"Hayley will be at camp for most of the summer, but Piper I'd planned just to have stay home and maybe get a little summer job, go stay with my sister for a week, with my folks for another; and another with you when Hayley gets back. Now, I don't know."

The "camp" that Charlotte was referring to was actually an astronomically expensive summer program generally for wealthy Upper East Side kids whose families didn't even sneeze at the ten thousand dollar price tag. For that princely sum, a group of twelve kids was chaperoned with four parents and a "camp director" to Europe for five weeks.

Each year, apparently the itinerary differed, but this year it was Florence, Siena and the Chianti Region, with obligatory time in Rome. Places Malcolm wasn't sure he had even heard of when he was Hayley's age. This was the kind of thing that Charlotte thought of as necessary for their kids' futures, and because she had the kind of father who willingly helped bankroll it, Malcolm reluctantly went along with the program.

On the one hand, who wanted to deny their child the opportunity to see the world? And on the other, how on earth could you ever teach them how to earn anything in life if so much was so soon and so freely given to them?

"She definitely can't just stay home," Malcolm agreed.

"Not the entire time, for sure. I can shuttle her among family for these first few weeks but what about having her with you when you go to North Carolina?"

"With me?" Malcolm sat up straighter.

"Yes, with *you*, Malcolm."

He had a few weeks on the North Carolina coast planned for late June into July, when he hoped he would knock out the rest of his book. He would wander around the house in shorts and no shirt, only shave or shower when absolutely necessary and write thousands and thousands of words—that was the plan. Piper was not in the plan.

The thought felt uncomfortable. And selfish. For a brief

second, Lorna flashed through his mind, and her confession of self-centeredness at her daughter's expense.

"She'd be so bored though," Malcolm said. "Just me and her in a big old house."

"She needs to be bored. Have her bring some books and a swimsuit and figure out what people do when they have no friends to text with, or illegal drinking parties to run off to."

"Yeah, that'll teach her. A week at a beach-house. *Ooh.* Aren't we being too tough on her?"

"Don't mock me, Malcolm. If you have a better idea, I'm all ears."

"Well, what'll you be doing?"

"What do you mean? Working, of course."

And banging her boyfriend, probably. The man Charlotte had stepped out with was a partner at the firm. A married partner. A tall, blonde, corn-fed all-American boy who liked to clap you on the shoulder when he greeted you, all blue eyes and white-white teeth. His name was Spence of all things. Malcolm had disliked him long before he found out Spence had fucked his wife.

"She'll need to spend some time with you as well, Charlotte. Not just your sister, your parents and me. You know that, right? You can't avoid her forever."

"Avoid her?" Charlotte snorted and glanced toward the stairs up to the second level where the girls were presumably sleeping by now. "I wish. She walks around the house in a constant snit, slamming doors, clattering dishes and being a general pain-in-the-ass. *Every* day. You have no idea."

Glancing at the time, Malcolm prepared to stand. It was past nine and he wanted to get back upstate. He had only come down so that he and Charlotte could lay down the law to Piper for the millionth time. And so they could have this parent-to-parent huddle in person; and he could be a more visible presence for Piper lest she think she was free to pull another little caper like her last one.

Now that school was out, she had lots more rope and Elisa, spooked by Piper disappearing on her that time, had begun to hint that she would soon be moving on. Before she quit—which now seemed inevitable—Malcolm and Charlotte wanted to make a game plan for the summer.

"So? Can she?" Charlotte asked, standing with him. "Come with you to North Carolina?"

"Sure," he said. Because how could he say otherwise?

"Good. I'm going to work on a calendar, so we have her entire summer mapped out."

Charlotte walked him to the door where they both paused, standing and facing each other awkwardly. Out of long-established habit, they leaned in before recalling that they were no longer in that place. Now they were cordially raising children together, and nothing more.

"You know," Charlotte said, the hint of a smile dancing about her lips, "you could stay if you wanted."

Her brown eyes lifted to his, and she gave him a look that was clearly one of invitation.

If he stayed, it wouldn't be the first time. Mostly, it was strictly platonic, but since they had split, there had been a few occasions when they both gave in to the habit and comfort of each other's bodies.

Charlotte was an energetic lover, and liked to ride him, grinding her pelvis against his, then lying flat against his chest, legs together, squeezing him between her thighs while he slid in and out of her. It was good sex, sometimes even phenomenal. But since her infidelity, it always left him feeling empty and mildly disgusted with himself afterward.

"Nah," he said. "Not tonight."

"You're seeing someone, aren't you?" Charlotte smiled and sipped her wine.

"Yeah," he acknowledged.

"Someone who makes you turn down sex with me," Charlotte mused. She had always thought a lot of herself. "Should I be jealous?"

"Believe me. No one could be as unlike you as this woman."

"Ha. So maybe I shouldn't be jealous, but just insulted."

"You should be neither. Goodnight, Charlotte." He kissed her on the forehead and turned to head down the steps of the brownstone and into the street.

He drove straight to Lorna's without stopping in at home first, and rang her bell. It was almost eleven p.m.. She opened the door dressed only in a thin tank and her underwear, her hair disheveled. She had been sleeping.

"Thought you might want some company," he said.

They hadn't seen each other since she told him about her daughter's father. One solid week, during which neither of them had called the other. Seeing her now, Malcolm wondered how it was that he had managed to make it that long.

Without a word, Lorna stood aside, and let him in.

"I THINK I HAVE AN IDEA."

Lorna strode into Malcolm's office, and pulling his rolling office chair away from the desk, positioned herself astride him.

He had been typing away at his laptop and she was clearly interrupting his flow, but it didn't bother her at all because she had come to learn that it didn't bother him. In fact, he liked it.

"Ooh, I think I *like* this idea," he grinned, running his hands along her bare legs when she pressed closer against him.

"No. Listen." She placed her palms atop his. "Something's

been bothering me. Ever since I went to that conference in New York."

"The one where you delivered the smackdown to the young 'uns?"

"See? That's what's been bothering me. *That* was the head-line for anyone who went to that session. That one of the old guard lost her shit and delivered a 'smackdown' to the new, more dynamic, more *relevant* contingent of young feminists."

Malcolm shrugged. "Well if that's what happened ..."

"But that wasn't what I intended to happen. So it's been bothering me. And now I have an idea."

"Okay. Listening."

"I'm going to write a book, Malcolm."

He smiled even wider. "That would be pretty cool."

"Yes. It would be my first. But I think this might be the time."

Fallon, her new research assistant had been helping her pull out and catalog all her papers, including dozens of unpub-lished articles, musings and essays. For about a day, Lorna considered whether they might make a nice compilation that someone would want to publish, but then she had taken them home and began reading them.

And the fact of the matter was, many of them were, well, *dated*. She still didn't buy into the "*boss-bitch-ism*" stuff, but there was something there; something that women of her gener-ation would do well not to dismiss. It was worth analyzing at the very least.

"I have no idea how to actually structure it and I have only vague ideas about the thesis, but, yeah. I think I want to write a book."

"Forget about structure," Malcolm said. He had moved his hands up her thighs and they were now at her waist. He teased the edges of her underwear. "Just ... write."

"Maybe I should outline though?"

Lorna tried to ignore how good the light touch of his fingers felt. After he showed up at her place, they'd gone to his the following night, and now they had been together for five straight nights, broken only by the few hours a day they went to their respective offices on campus. And even those hours had shortened—from six, to four, to now just two hours apart today.

"Some do. I don't. I just let the magic flow from my fingertips."

"Those *are* magic fingertips," Lorna acknowledged letting her eyes close as he moved beneath the hem at the crotch.

"But I could help you name some chapters or something," Malcolm kissed her neck, his lips so feather-light, goosebumps rose on her skin. "Like maybe ... *'Beyoncé, Boss-Bitches and Bustiers: Reforming the Paradigm for Gender Equality'* ..."

"Hmm. I like that," Lorna sighed.

"What? The title, or ... this?" Malcolm brushed his thumb over her clitoris and Lorna smiled, leaning into him.

"Both." He kept his thumb where it was, making slow circles, while two other fingers entered her. "But ..."

"But what?" His lips were moving along her jaw now.

"You have to ... I have to go get my laptop. I've been disgustingly lazy while I've been here."

"Okay. But right now we're taking a break." Malcolm hoisted his butt off the chair just enough to slide his sweats part of the way down. Already erect, he became more so when Lorna reached down to touch him.

"There is nothing as beautiful as a hard dick," she said.

Malcolm grinned. "Oh if I could get you on tape saying *that*. What a scandal it would cause in the man-hating circles you travel in."

"We don't hate men. We love them. And that's why I need

to write this book. I think you—and most of society—have got us all wrong, Malcolm."

"Just shut up and sit on me," he said, maneuvering himself close, his mouth on her neck once again.

"No," Lorna said, sliding off him. "You're going to take too long that way. I need you to come quick, and hard, and drive me home to get my laptop."

Then, falling to her knees in front of him, she took him in her mouth.

———

WHEN LORNA OPENED HER EYES, she was on Malcolm's sofa, having fallen asleep writing with her computer on his coffee table. The smell of cooking had awakened her.

Getting up, she stretched and yawned, ambling over into the kitchen where Malcolm was shirtless at the stove. Walking up behind him, she wrapped her arms around his waist.

"Hi," he said. "Got some good rest?"

"Mm hmm."

"Got some good writing done?"

"Mostly notes. Ideas. Thoughts. Nothing coherent yet." She pressed her cheek against his back, moving it back and forth. "What're you making?"

"Writing food. Chicken-fried steak and mashed potatoes. And string beans in case we feel like being virtuous."

"Smells amazing. And you do too."

"Don't you start with that," Malcolm said. "We're both getting a lot of work done, so ..."

"Oh easy for *you* to say now that you got sucked off," Lorna laughed.

Malcolm turned to face her and Lorna let her head fall

back so they could make eye contact. His were amused, and curious.

"Y'know what?" he said quietly. "I like this. I like ... you."

"Good," Lorna said, her eyes dancing away from his. "Because all of the screwing gets awkward when people don't at least like each other."

"It isn't just that ... the screwing," Malcolm said. "And you know it."

"*Anyway*," she said breezily, letting the word drag on for a moment. "Tell me what you're working on. Or is it a jinx to talk about the new book too much?"

"It isn't a jinx. I just don't tend to do it." He turned to face the stove again and when Lorna tried to move away, he reached back and grabbed her wrist. "Nope. Stay right where you were."

Smiling, she put her arms around his waist and leaned into him again.

"I never did tell you what I thought of 'Cadence' once I was done, did I?" She spoke against his back.

"Nope."

"Are you curious?"

"Yeah. And a little scared."

"Don't be. I loved it. And I loved Vernon as a character. I wanted to follow him right into the book." She couldn't see it but could feel that that made Malcolm smile. "Though I *am* curious about one choice you made."

"I bet I know which one," he said.

"Tell me which you think."

"You want to know why I made Vernon fall in love with the White girl."

"Yes!" Lorna exploded. "*Why*, Malcolm? I was so ... crushed by that. I felt ..."

"Rejected?" He reached above the stove and took two plates from the cupboards above.

"Yes. Exactly. Also, you did this amazing manifesto about race and had this tall, handsome, intelligent, dark-skinned tree of a man who stands for everything that's good about Black men, and then he falls for a blonde chick? I just ..."

"I get it." He started plating their food. "Want to see what wine I've got? I think there's a sauvignon blanc in the fridge."

Lorna finally released him and went in search of the wine, finding it and then two glasses.

"It was part of the challenge. I wanted to test our views of race on all levels. Up until he met and fell in love with Emma ..."

"And *Emma*? You could not have found a whiter name."

Malcolm laughed. "I know. But that was the point. Until he met and fell for Emma, he was the best of what Black men offer. Almost cartoonishly so, right? A great athlete, good-looking, smart, dignified, self-possessed. And if Emma's responses are any guide, a good lay, too."

Lorna groaned. "I was literally envious of her when I read those scenes."

"Yeah, but of all the things Vernon was, did he become any less so, just because he chose a woman who's not Black?"

"No, of course not. And I tend not to give a shit about interracial relationships. I honestly feel that love and life happens wherever and however it happens. But I felt so ... set up by this romance with Emma. Vernon was ..."

"Like the Great Black Hope?" Malcolm took the glass of wine Lorna handed him and took a sip.

"I guess so, yes." Lorna shrugged.

"That was the goal. To have readers look at and confront their own racialism. Not racism, you understand. But *racialism*. It's a very different thing."

"Oh my god, Riley would *love* you," Lorna said.

"Grab your plate and let's go eat."

As they got situated at his dining table, Lorna noticed that Malcolm briefly bowed his head and said a silent prayer over his food. She had never noticed that before.

"Have you spoken to her?" he asked. "I mean, since ..."

"No."

"You have to, y'know?"

"Yeah. I know. But I want to give her some time."

"Time ..."

"To decide just how much she hates me."

"Lo. She doesn't hate you."

"*I* would hate me."

"Yeah, well ... that was a pretty far-reaching and ill-advised parenting decision for sure."

Lorna laughed and raised her glass to him. "Far-reaching and ill-advised. You are *definitely* a writer. All those words when you could have just said 'shitty'."

"It was a shitty decision," he said looking directly at her, his face unsmiling.

"And there's nothing I can do to change it."

"Exactly. So you just have to figure out a way to move forward."

"Once I told her. And told you? I heard it. I heard how awful it sounded. And how awful it was. She can never get those years back with her father and his family. And I don't even know. Maybe some of them are dead and gone by now."

"Do you think she'll look them up?"

"Probably. Riley is nothing if not a problem-solver. And depending on what she finds, she'll probably get angrier and angrier. What if she has siblings she's never met? Or what if her father died? I mean ..."

"There are a million 'what ifs'. But the good news is you

don't have to stay in the dark. You can help her find out. Or find out yourself."

"I could. It shouldn't be too difficult these days."

"But before any of that, you're going to have to call her."

"I know," Lorna said.

She had been thinking about it for days, wondering whether her silence was helping, or making things worse; second-guessing every detail she had shared, and those she excluded. And in her worst moments, she wished she could take it all back and resume the silence she had maintained all these years.

"Hey," Malcolm said.

She looked up at him and realized she'd been staring into space.

"C'mere," he said, lifting out of his seat and leaning in. Lorna did the same and he kissed her. "It's going to be okay."

And the way he said it made her believe it was true.

"I'M GOING to North Carolina at the end of June. Come with me."

He didn't plan to say it. As Lorna was gathering her things, preparing to get out of the SUV, the words just leapt out spontaneously.

"What?" she looked up from having just shoved her sunglasses into a case in her handbag. "You have a conference there, or something?"

"No. I rented a house on the beach. To write. I'll be there for at least two weeks, maybe for as long as five. And I want you with me."

Lorna's eyes softened. "Oh, Malcolm that's ..."

"Don't take that tone like you're about to pat me on the head, Lo. You know I hate that shit."

She looked at him for a moment then nodded. "You're right. But for *weeks* Malcolm, just you and me marooned in a beach house driving each other nuts? I'm sure we'll argue and get on each other's nerves, and ..."

"Cook, and write, drink wine and make love. Yeah, we'll do all that."

Lorna pressed her lips against his, then nuzzled him. "It does sound amazing."

"And anyway, there's one other detail. For at least one week, there'll be someone else to argue with and who'll get on our nerves."

"Who?" The question was asked cautiously.

"Piper."

Lorna pulled back. "Oh. No. I can't do that. No, I ..."

"She's a pain almost all the time lately, but beneath all that she's an amazing kid."

"I'm sure she is. It isn't that. If you're supposed to be spending time with her as a father-daughter thing, then I wouldn't want to intrude."

"Don't make this about Piper. Just say you'll come with me."

"I can't say that, Malcolm." Lorna opened the door to the truck and prepared to get out.

"Then say you'll think about it."

"Malcolm."

"I want you with me."

"I've *been* with you. All week."

"So what're you saying? I hit my quota?"

"Of course not, but ..."

He knew what she was thinking. It was her dumb thing about relationships. She didn't want to trip and fall into one by accident. She could think what she wanted to think, but Malcolm knew that the fall had already happened. They had both fallen headfirst and were now more than chest-deep in this thing, whatever the heck they called it.

"Then think about it, and let me know."

"When you say 'think about it' you don't give the impression you'll accept any answer other than 'yes'."

Malcolm shrugged and handed her her bag when she was out of the truck. "Yeah," he said. "Exactly."

ELEVEN

HOME REPAIRS

"So how is she?"

Shawn shrugged, his focus trained on the menu in front of him. "She says she's fine. But you know how she is."

"And how are you?"

At that, Shawn looked up at her and his eyes were hard, and almost completely closed off to her.

"You're angry with me too," she said, stating the obvious.

"That was some pretty foul shit you told my wife."

Whenever his protective instincts were aroused, he called Riley that—"my wife"—instead of using her name. It was proprietary and primal, and funnily enough, Lorna respected it under circumstances like this.

"It was."

"How could you even do something like that?" Shawn interrupted her. "I mean ..." He paused and shook his head, biting into his lower lip. "She thought he just didn't care. And I know how that feels, because I have a father who *really* didn't care. He was the *king* of not giving a shit."

They sat quietly for a few moments, Lorna looking aimlessly about the almost empty restaurant. After more than a week of silence between her and Riley, Malcolm had convinced her that she had to be the one to call.

You're the one in the wrong here, he said. *So you're the one who needs to extend the olive branch. Forget about that letting-her-process-it bullshit. Call.*

But even then, Lorna had been too afraid to call Riley directly and instead reached out to Shawn. He was truculent enough with her on the phone to make her offer to come into the city to see him in person.

And so now, here they were, in a café near his office at So Def Records. Lorna had asked Shawn to pick the place since he was more familiar than she with where he might sit for a conversation and not be interrupted by fans looking for selfies with him, or an autograph. And so far, no one had bothered them at all, which was a mixed blessing.

"I just realized I don't know much of anything about your family," Lorna said. "You've never talked about them to me."

"There were cousins. My grandmother. But actual parents were a little scarce where I grew up. So the waste of a perfectly good father?" He exhaled a puff of breath. "That offends me. On a personal level."

She didn't often feel humbled, but Lorna did now. As was often the case, in his frank and plainspoken way, Shawn had a way of putting things in perspective.

"I don't know. I guess you were young," he said, shaking his head.

Reaching across the table, Lorna briefly squeezed his hand. "That's kind of you. I *was* young. But the truth is a lot more complicated than that. And a lot less flattering."

"Anyway, I'm sure you two'll work it out. Riley can't be

mad at anyone for too long. And I'm not even sure she's mad. More hurt than anything else." Shawn looked up. "When I met my wife, you know what I remember?"

Lorna shook her head.

"That you were the first person I heard her talk about with ... admiration. I mean, Riley is just who she is, y'know? And she's comfortable in her skin, but you were the one person, the *one* person I think she ever wanted to be like."

"Shawn. You're not making this whole thing any easier."

"Why should it be easy?" he snapped.

"Okay. Point taken." Shawn prepared to stand and Lorna looked at him incredulously. "You're leaving? We barely just sat down."

He was hurt too; not just angry, but hurt. She saw it now for the first time in his eyes.

"Shawn. Stay. *Please.*"

He settled into his seat once again and Lorna touched his hand, pulling away when it stiffened.

"I usually have a way with words," she said laughing nervously. "And now I can't think of anything to say to ... fix the damage I caused. And that's why I haven't called her. But I see now that I may have damaged our relationship too. If that's the case, I ... I would hate that."

Shawn's eyes rose to meet hers. "If she's hurt, I'm hurt. You understand?"

"No." Lorna said firmly. She shook her head. "I'm not talking about the transfer of emotion between a husband and a wife, the sharing of grudges or that kind of thing. I'm talking about my independent connection to you, about *our* relationship. That's what I'm talking about. Riley and I *will* talk, but now I want to talk to you. *About* you. As a mother to her son. Because that's what you are to me. Not just Riley's husband."

Shawn stared at her for a long time and then a slow, reluctant smile lifted one corner of his mouth. "I don't think you have to worry about losing your way with words," he said finally.

"I'm so sorry, Shawn. To have hurt 'your wife' ..." She chuckled at her use of his phrase. "And to have hurt you. Riley and you and your children are my only loves. You know that."

"I know," he said, his voice hoarse.

"So should we have lunch? And then maybe ..." She wasn't sure how far to go. "Maybe you can tell me about this father of yours, the king of not giving a shit."

Shawn hesitated for a moment then nodded, picking up his menu and looking at it. "Sure," he said, his voice and face giving away nothing. "Why not?"

MALCOLM ALMOST MISSED the knocking on his door entirely because it was done so lightly, he believed it might be next-door. Only when he looked up did he see the face of a young woman looking in.

"Professor Mitchell?" She smiled shyly. "Your door was ajar, so ..."

"Sure. Come on in."

She shoved the door open and stepped across the threshold, beginning to pull it shut behind her.

"No. Leave it open, please," he said.

She smiled again. "Sure. Sorry."

"So, how can I help you?"

"I'm Fallon Wright," she said, pausing for a moment. "Professor Terry's research assistant?"

"Oh! Sure. So what's going on, Fallon?"

He noticed for the first time that she had two copies of 'Cadence' in her hand. Realizing that he'd spotted them, she stepped forward.

"Professor Terry is out of town today and she asked me to stop by and have you write an inscription in her copy of your book?"

She spoke with a lilting at the end of her sentences that so many young women had these days; every statement sounded like a question. Malcolm could only imagine how that drove Lorna nuts, since she was so declarative about everything, even her questions.

"She wanted *you* to get me to write an inscription in her copy of my book?" he repeated, grinning.

"Yes." The young woman looked confused by his obvious amusement.

He was amused because twenty-four hours ago, when he was with her, he spotted his book in her bag as he prepared to take her home and asked jokingly whether she wanted him to sign it.

What am I? she asked, almost haughtily. *One of your fangirls? Of course I don't want you to* sign *it.*

"And the second book?" he indicated the other one in Fallon's hand.

"This one is mine," she said blushing. "I hope I'm not being too presumptuous."

"Of course not. Give it here."

Fallon took two steps forward and handed him the books over his desk.

"This one is yours?" he asked, holding up the newer of the two.

Fallon nodded, and Malcolm pulled out a pen and wrote something generically appreciative, handing the book back to her. In Lorna's he wrote something decidedly more risqué and personal. When Fallon extended a hand to take it, he shook his head.

"This I'll return to her myself," he said. "Thanks for stopping by, Fallon."

But the young woman remained where she stood. She was tall, maybe five feet ten inches or so, and slender with wildly curly strawberry-blonde hair, streaked with a much paler, almost platinum-blonde. Her skin was a brownish honey-tone.

"Was there something else?"

"Yes. I hope you don't mind me saying, but your book ... it felt so personal to me. There was so much about it that I connected with."

"That's very nice of you to say. And no, I don't mind at all."

"See," Fallon continued. "My parents are an interracial couple. *Were* an interracial couple, I mean. They're divorced now. But anyway, I used to have a hard time seeing how they got together, y'know? Because my Dad, he's just all about being a strong Black man. And the Black part... I mean, that's really an important part of his identity so I always wondered how they ..." She stopped and laughed, probably realizing she was babbling. "Anyway, I just wanted to thank you. For giving me a little insight, I guess."

Malcolm nodded. "You're welcome."

He waited for her to leave, but she didn't. Instead, she shifted her weight from one leg to the other, the motion causing her hip to jut out a little, like a beauty pageant contestant posing at the end of a runway. She touched her neck and offered him one last coy smile.

"Thank you, Fallon," he said, pointedly looking in the direction of the door.

"Oh. Yeah, well ... thank you. For the ..." She held up her book one last time before turning to leave.

Leaning back in his chair, Malcolm sighed and shook his

head, recalling the conversation he had had with Shane Tiller, the only other Black man close to his age on faculty. Tiller taught biology, so there would be very few occasions where Malcolm ran into him but he made a point of seeking Malcolm out when he first arrived on campus, and asking him out for a beer.

Take it from me, man, he said. *There's some little hot-to-trot honeys at Gilchrist. Smart, pretty, fiending-for-a-brother type chicks. But whatever you do, look if you have to, but never, never touch. You feel me?*

Not surprisingly, Gilchrist had a strict policy against student-faculty relationships. Even if the student in question wasn't *your* student. Apparently there had been a scandal a few years back where a male professor and a senior got embroiled in a relationship that both managed to keep discreet and adult.

Until the breakup.

And then the student suddenly cried foul, saying she had been taken advantage of. After an investigation, the faculty disciplinary committee found no wrongdoing or coercion on the part of the professor, and that should have been the end of it. Except that the student later attempted suicide.

From what I heard, she was a little bit of a histrionic type to begin with, Tiller explained. *But it didn't matter. The professor had to resign and the policy was tightened up to prohibit all relationships between student and faculty. Don't get me wrong. It still happens, but my advice to you is don't check for none of these girls. It ain't worth it.*

The story was interesting and all, but Malcolm had no intention of giving it any relevance in his life. He was at Gilchrist to solidify his career in academia, and to finish his book, and that was all. And as far as anything else was concerned, with the likes of Lorna Terry on his hands, there was no way in a million versions of hell that he could ever be tempted to do something stupid with a college girl—no matter how pretty—like Fallon.

Getting up and going to shut his door, firmly and completely this time, Malcolm almost got slammed in the face when it swung open again almost immediately.

"Oh my gosh! Sorry, Malcolm! Did I get you?"

"Nope. I'm fine."

He stepped back and admitted Eve Rogers, holding back his exasperation. He got more work done at home—even with Lorna walking around in nothing but his t-shirts and both of them pawing each other every fifteen minutes—than he was getting done here today.

"I just saw one of your fans leaving and thought I may as well strike while the iron is hot," she said giving him a twist of her very full lips.

"How'd you decide she was a fan? And what iron were you hoping to strike?" he grinned.

"Well, she was practically fawning as she left, clutching your book to her chest," Eve said. "And as for the iron?"

She sat in one of his guest chairs and Malcolm perched on the edge of his desk, facing her.

Today she was in a long, wide floral skirt, high-heeled sandals made of a rough, ropelike material, and a white tank-blouse that hugged her curves. Her lipstick was the same crimson as some of the flowers in the print on her skirt.

"I'm here to ask you to dinner," she said.

Malcolm scratched the side of his neck. "Oh," he said. "I ..."

"Don't tell me you're surprised," Eve Rogers said.

"A little, yes."

"Well, if I'm out of line, please tell me," she said, looking up at him, eyes a little wide. "I know I've seen you with Professor

Terry out and about, but I guess I assumed it was just … casual. Given … well, given her …"

"Let me think about it," Malcolm said, talking over her, afraid she might finish her sentence with the word, 'reputation'.

If that was her intent, he didn't want to hear it. In fact, if that was her intention, he would be *pissed*, and he didn't want to start collecting grudges against his colleagues in the department before the fall semester even began.

"Of course. I know it can be awkward, being in the same department and all. But we're adults …" Eve Rogers stood and took a step toward him. She reached out and stroked the front of his shirt. "Aren't we?"

"Yeah. We are."

"Good. So, when you've had a chance to ruminate, let me know what you come up with." Eve Rogers shot him one last smile before turning and flouncing out through the open door, her bright skirt swirling around her.

"I'D LIKE TO MEET HER."

"Why?"

"She's your daughter. More than your daughter. Why wouldn't I want to meet her?" Malcolm asked.

"I don't recall banging down the door to meet your two," Lorna said, reaching over and spearing one of the carrots on his plate.

"I know. Which I find kind of insulting if you really want to know the truth, but we'll leave that discussion for another day. Tonight, I want to know why I can't meet Riley."

"Well she isn't talking to me right now, for one thing."

"That'll pass. You said things went well with your son-in-law, right?"

They were in the Portman Arms. It was a shabby, pretentious little restaurant the next town over from the college where
people went to meet when they were having adulterous affairs
and inappropriate relationships with their students. Lorna and
Malcolm's thing wasn't inappropriate on any level but by
suggesting this clandestine meeting place when Malcolm said
he wanted them to go out for a change, Lorna felt it kept everything very tongue-in-cheek, and not quite as serious.

But now he was pressing her to meet Riley.

"Why do you find it insulting that I haven't been asking to
meet your children?" Lorna asked leaning forward in her seat.
"I find families complicate things. Especially kids. Don't you?"

"I generally don't think of my children as complications,
no," Malcolm said, taking a bite of his glazed salmon.

Lorna smiled.

This was why she liked him so much. A different, lesser
man might have been peeved at a comment that implied that
his kids were anything other than the "joys of his life", or
"apples of his eye" or some other such triteness. Malcolm was
many things, but he was not trite. She liked that about him.

Lorna had been sleeping with him for almost eight weeks
now. That was how she liked to think of it, "sleeping with",
though they did many more things together now than just have
sex. Mostly they talked, debated, brainstormed. He was her
intellectual equal, possibly her superior, and the mixture of
competitiveness and awe she felt toward him was the most
potent aphrodisiac she had experienced in a long, long time.
And even the fact that he was nine years younger had become
less significant to her.

But lately Malcolm had been making overtures, expressing
curiosity about the rest of her life, especially about Riley and
Shawn. Just when she thought he might have forgotten this ill-
conceived quest to dig further and further, her daughter or son-

in-law would show up in the media somewhere, and Malcolm's curiosity would be piqued once again.

This time, his interest was revived because Riley had been quoted in *The New York Times* (which both irritated Lorna—she *had never been quoted in The Times!*—and made her ridiculously proud) making some remark that Malcolm found amusing. Asked about the influences for her new contribution to an anthology on race and gender, Riley had quipped that her influence on gender was undoubtedly her mother, Dr. Lorna Terry, who was a "staunch feminist, or as my husband Shawn would call her, a 'fucking-feminist'."

Lorna didn't mind the quip, nor the reference to Shawn calling her a 'fucking-feminist'. He'd called her as much to her face which Lorna didn't mind because she adored him and knew full well that he thought the same of her. Anyway, Malcolm found the comment intriguing, and it only re-lit the flame of his curiosity about Riley and her unlikely mate, the world-renowned rapper, *blah, blah, blah.* Such an old and tedious storyline, in Lorna's view. Riley and Shawn were a couple in love, whatever the hell that meant.

Malcolm particularly wanted to meet Riley because like him, she was obsessed with writing about race. Not that Lorna took any issue with an interest in racial politics, but as a twenty-first century topic of focus, she had begun to believe it was all so retrograde. At some point Black folks needed to stop crowing about their Blackness and just get on with it. Of course, Riley would argue—as had Malcolm—that she was just as anal retentive about discussing gender bias in *every single little thing*.

"Does she even know about me?"

"Does who know about you?" Lorna asked, taking in a mouthful of pasta primavera.

Malcolm held his fork still, aloft and midway to his mouth, and looked at her.

"Okay fine, yes, she knows about you," Lorna admitted. "But only in the most academic sense."

"What the hell does that mean? How can she know about me ... academically? Either she does or she doesn't."

"I think she knows that I'm seeing someone. And that it's one someone."

"As opposed to ...?"

"As opposed to *more* than one someone, Malcolm," Lorna said pointedly.

Malcolm paused once again. "Maybe we should talk about that as well."

Then he took a sip of his pinot.

Uh oh. Here it was. The Monogamy Lecture.

Women generally initiated this talk, but Lorna almost never had. Not since she was about twenty years old. Her theory of relationships was one of non-attachment, which was really a misnomer because of course she formed attachments, just loose ones. The kinds that were easy to let go of when the time came. Non-Attachment was far easier if one wasn't monogamous, and if every relationship was viewed as an opportunity for learning rather than a lifelong partnership.

"What would you like to talk about?" she asked, as if she didn't know.

"Eve Rogers asked me to dinner the other day."

Lorna almost spluttered her pasta across the table and onto Malcolm's very well-tailored, perfectly-fitting summer blazer.

Eve Rogers, the pushy English professor who hated women had asked him out, huh? Well. Lorna couldn't say she was surprised that Rogers would ask him out; she was however surprised and a little disappointed that Malcolm would consider it. Not because he shouldn't keep his options open, of course, but because Rogers was so obvious.

"And what did you say?" she asked, taking a delicate bite of penne.

"I was noncommittal," Malcolm said. He looked at her over the top of his glasses, the way she imagined he would look at his students during his lectures.

"That's not like you," she said lightly. "Why the hesitation?"

"Because I'm otherwise occupied," he said. "Except the extent of it ... this occupation isn't clear."

"The occupation being ...?"

"You." He put down his wineglass and for a moment gave her his full and complete attention.

So, she was correct. This *was* the Monogamy Lecture. But leave it to Malcolm T. Mitchell to be so stealthy about it. It was a question wrapped in a threat, swathed in a gently prodding inquiry: *"I want to meet your daughter but is it necessary if I'm seeing someone else? And by the way are you also seeing other people?"*

"Malcolm, what we are is what we are. I see no need to define it. If you'd like to go to dinner with Eve Rogers, you should feel perfectly free to do so."

Why was that so difficult to say? Why did it make her feel like each and every word was choking its way past her lips?

"Really?" he asked. Then he looked at her plate. It was almost clean as was his. "Dessert for you? I'm feeling like something sweet tonight."

Then you'd better get something sweet here, Lorna thought. *Because there'll be no sweetness for you later, that's for damn sure.*

"Just coffee," she said. "And yes, really."

Her voice had taken on an edge, though she was trying valiantly to control it.

"So you would have no issue with me taking Eve Rogers to dinner?"

"None," she enunciated.

May as well let him know now. She was not That Woman. The clingy, 'I-want-you-for-myself' woman. The 'your-dick-belongs-to-me', 'where-were-you-all-evening', 'I-need-to-know-where-I-stand' woman.

She was Lorna *Fucking* Terry. *Asshole.*

"Then we may have a problem," Malcolm said. He raised his hand, trying to get the attention of the waiter.

No shit, Sherlock.

The waiter responded to Malcolm's summons and took his order for tiramisu and Lorna's for a double espresso. And then they were alone once again. She wanted to, but could not resist asking: "What would be the problem?"

Malcolm looked at her, giving her the full Malcolm T. Mitchell He-Man stare. The one he gave her when they were in bed and he wanted her positioned differently than she was. The look he gave before he grabbed her by the ankles and yanked her toward him, with not a hint of gentleness. The look he gave her before he took her like no man ever had.

Malcolm had discerned about her what no other did, which was the paradox that as a feminist, she felt most powerful as a woman when she was with a man who *knew* how to be a man. There were no kid-gloves in this thing they had—Malcolm gave it to her straight, and always had.

"The problem would be," he said, "that in telling me I should go to dinner with Eve Rogers, you might be under the impression I would be equally understanding if you were to go to dinner, or anywhere else for that matter, with any man but me."

Lorna sagged in her seat. *Now he'd gone and done it.*

"Malcolm," she sighed, her voice kind as though addressing

a three-year old. "I wish you hadn't said that. You had to know that I'm not one to stand for ultimatums. Especially not those that would tell me what to do, and with whom. You *had* to."

"Yes," he said, downing the last of his wine and meeting her gaze evenly. "I do know that. And you had to know that I'm not one to sit blithely by while you squander a good thing on some half-baked notion that you're polyamorous or some such bullshit. You *had* to."

They went back to his house and had sex anyway. Angry sex, because they were both unfulfilled by their conversation at dinner. Neither had gotten what they wanted, and later there would be a reckoning.

Later, but not now.

Not now because the challenge Malcolm issued turned her on. Lorna was certain she was going to have to leave him, but that didn't mean she couldn't revisit, just one more time, the heady, achy, exhilarating feeling of being taken by a man who knew exactly how to take her.

As soon as they made it inside, they were shoving each other against walls, pulling aside clothing, nipping at necks, nipples, stomachs, thighs. Wide-open mouthed kisses, thrusting pelvises, grasping and grappling hands, noisy climaxes.

Afterwards, Lorna let him talk her into going back with him into his bedroom. The wine at dinner had done her in. She wanted to close her eyes for only a few minutes before shaking Malcolm awake and having him drive her home to sleep in her own bed. The idea, of course, was that once she was there she would simply disappear from his life.

Avoiding him would not be too difficult. He was all the way across campus most of the time and their schedules did not coincide. They were able to have time together only because they made time. She would stop. That was the plan. No more time, no more Malcolm.

But when Lorna opened her eyes again, it was morning, and bright sunlight was bathing the stark white sheets in Malcolm T. Mitchell's bed. And he was lying partly atop her, his limbs intertwined with hers, and her arm was wrapped about him, his face buried in her neck, and she didn't want to move, and didn't want to disappear from his life, nor have him disappear from hers.

Shit.

TWELVE

ACQUIESCENCE

GROUPIES. HE DIDN'T KNOW WHAT ELSE TO CALL THEM.

Lorna was virtually surrounded by people—no fewer than eight—and they were all edging closer to her as she spoke, trying to position themselves in the center of her field of vision. And Lorna was enjoying it, though Malcolm was pretty sure she would deny it later.

Earlier that evening when they spoke on the phone, she said she wasn't even sure she was coming. But when one of the department heads invited you to their home, it was poor form not to at least put in a brief appearance so she eventually relented, and they planned to meet there and leave together. But ever since she'd walked into the room, Lorna had barely spared a glance in his direction.

The host of the party was chair of the English Department, Dr. Diane Ramsey. Dr. Ramsey was somewhere in her mid-seventies, sharp-witted and sharp-tongued, and took no mess. It was she who had recruited Malcolm for the position, very baldly stating in their first conversation that *"Of course you're a brilliant writer, but the fact of the matter is, Gilchrist needs*

Black men. We don't have enough Black men!" He'd liked that about her, her frankness about the fact that his race and gender were at least *among* his key qualifications.

Her home was as eccentric as she—with what looked like artifacts from trips to every conceivable continent. There were masks from Africa, figurines that looked like they might be from China, paintings in the style of the Old Masters. And everything was crammed into her little bungalow, which was surrounded on three sides by bushes that were badly in need of a pruning.

Dr. Ramsey, or her helpers, had cleared much of the furniture in her front room to the walls and in the center placed a large buffet of finger foods, and a cluster of various alcoholic and non-alcoholic beverages. People wandered in and out of her kitchen in search of ice, and groups of what appeared to be grad students alternated between helping to replenish food and drinks and participating in the little satellites of conversations around the room.

Lorna was at the center of one of those satellites. She was obviously very popular with the students, but Malcolm noticed, not as much with her fellow faculty. They all greeted her cordially enough, but rarely lingered to talk for more than ten minutes, which was interesting since he had never heard anyone say so much as a negative word about her. After a while observing, Malcolm thought he knew what it was—Lorna was The Rockstar—every college had one. She was the instructor who had the magnetic power that all college professors secretly wanted—students looking at them with something like worship in their eyes, hanging onto their every word. Whatever commanded that kind of reaction, Lorna had it in spades, and used it to her fullest advantage.

Malcolm tossed back the remainder of his now lukewarm

beer and turned toward the refreshments table, eying the mini-quiches.

"When I was a grad student, I used to crash these things just to get dinner," a voice off to his left said.

He smiled at Eve. "The good ol' days, huh? Where'd you go to school?"

"Here," she said raising her wineglass as if in a toast. "I'm a lifer at Gilchrist. Been here since undergrad in fact."

"That's pretty incredible. No urge to wander?"

"I did wander. Every once in a while. A semester here, a summer there. But it always felt like home, so I always came back."

"I'm hoping to find that someday."

"Someday could be now," Eve ventured. "Gilchrist could be the place."

Malcolm gave her his full attention for the first time since she approached. She had beautiful eyes. They were her best feature, and should have been the one thing she left alone, but instead, she wore mascara, liner and shadow to draw attention to them.

Charlotte did the same—tended to play up her best features, to overplay them at times. In her case, it was her legs. She had lots of short skirts and snug pants in her wardrobe.

"How much of the town have you seen?"

"Not much, honestly," Malcolm admitted.

Eve Rogers tilted her head to one side and lowered her voice.

"I'd love to show you around. There are some real gems in the area. Secret little streams here and there, even a waterfall. Beautiful places perfect for a quiet picnic and some conversation, or ... whatever."

There was no reason not to say 'yes'. The only one he had, seemed more and more to be a reason of his imagination—that he and Lorna were developing into something more than a series of one-night stands. Whenever it seemed like he might be making some headway, she did something like she was doing tonight—holding up a hand like a traffic cop, and shoving him back several paces beyond arms' length.

"Maybe we ..."

"Eve. I didn't see you come in."

Dr. Ramsey had approached, so they both turned to make idle conversation with their hostess for a while and Malcolm thanked his lucky stars she had inadvertently short-circuited his impulse to do something he would probably regret and wasn't even that committed to doing in the first place.

"Lorna is in rare form this evening," Dr. Ramsey said.

The sound of her name drew Malcolm's focus back to the conversation. He followed Dr. Ramsey's gaze over to where Lorna was now sitting on a window seat, and next to her was the grad student from the church garden, the one she admitted she'd slept with.

Two other students stood in front of her, and all of them were laughing at something, as though it was the funniest thing they had ever heard. For a flash, Lorna lifted her eyes, and then her glass, toasting to Dr. Ramsey from across the room.

"She has such a spirit, that one," Dr. Ramsey said. "A real natural for reaching young people. It's a skill some can culti-vate, but few are naturals at it like she is."

"It's all a matter of style," Eve said, her voice a little brittle. "Some of us prefer not to get quite so ... intimate with our students. Maintaining some aloofness has always served me well."

"Oh, me as well," Dr. Ramsey said right away, clearly missing the snarky undertone. "But then again, we can't all be Lorna Terry."

Malcolm sensed, rather than saw the tension rise to Eve Rogers' shoulders.

Dr. Ramsey waved at someone else on the other side of the room, then excused herself, heading off in that direction and leaving Malcolm with a now decidedly more ill-tempered Eve Rogers. She twirled her wineglass restlessly round and round between her fingers and sighed, then cleared her throat.

"I should probably make the rounds myself," she said without looking at him. "I hadn't planned on staying this long. So ..."

"Goodnight, Eve," Malcolm said.

She looked at him for a few beats, and then cleared her throat again, gave him a curt nod and walked away. And just as she did, his eyes met Lorna's across the room.

Without a word to the students who moments before had been hanging on her every word, she stood and crossed the distance until she was standing directly in front of him.

"So," she said. "When's the big event?"

"What big event?"

They were the first words they had exchanged in person that evening.

"Your date with Eve Rogers."

"I'm not going on a 'date' with Eve Rogers."

"Is that why she looked so crestfallen when she walked away just now?"

"You'd actually like it if I went out with her, wouldn't you?" he said looking down at her.

She had her hair out tonight, which was a rarity. It reminded him of how he liked to grab it, and pull her head back, exposing her neck. He wanted to grab her now, because she just made him so damned ... crazed.

"Why would I care?" she returned.

"Oh, you'd care," he said with certainty. "But you'd also feel validated."

"Why would I feel validated by you going out with Eve Rogers?" Lorna feigned a laugh.

Malcolm leaned in so he could be sure only she heard him. "Because then it would fuel this little fiction you're crafting in your head that what's going on here is only physical."

Lorna lifted her eyes to his, her expression flat. "Are we about to have another 'relationship conversation', Malcolm? Because I'm getting really bored with those."

"So let's stop having them!" he said sharply. "And just have the damn relationship instead."

Lorna's eyes widened slightly and she seemed poised to speak then stopped herself. Finally, she gave a barely perceptible nod.

Malcolm leaned in. "*What* was that? I didn't quite ..."

"Fine."

"Fine, *what*?"

"I don't know what you think this proves, but, if it's what you want ..."

"What *we* want. This isn't me twisting your arm. *We* want it. So let's stop behaving like we're fucking fifteen-year olds."

Lorna pulled back in surprise, her mouth falling open.

"Yeah, I said it. It's immature bullshit that neither of us have time for. I've got a book to write, and you have whatever the hell it is you do when you're not driving me out of my mind."

"Could you lower your voice?" Lorna hissed. "I'm not having this discussion with you in a room full of students and colleagues."

"Then meet me outside at my car in five minutes. It's time we left anyway."

Without waiting for her inevitable protest at *how* he'd

asked her, or maybe even her outright refusal to comply, Malcolm brushed by her and headed for the door.

Eight minutes later, he was sitting behind the wheel when Lorna opened the door and climbed into the SUV. They both sat there, staring ahead.

"So when is this trip you've been talking about? To North Carolina."

When he heard her take a breath, he knew she was about to speak, but he could not have anticipated that that was what she might say.

"In a week and a half. Just after Reunion Weekend."

"And we would stay how long?"

"We have no summer courses, so as long as we wanted. Piper would be with us for a week, or maybe two if she and we can stand it."

"Okay," she breathed.

"Okay what?"

"*Jesus*, Malcolm! Are you going to want some blood too? I said I'd come, and that we're 'doing the relationship' thing, whatever the hell that means. I think that's plenty enough concessions from me for one night, don't you?"

"No," he said. "There's one more thing. You're staying at my place tonight."

Lorna expelled a long, deep sigh, but didn't fight him. Malcolm started the engine and pulled away from the curb.

———

COFFEE WAS MADE when he woke up; the aroma was what helped bring him to wakefulness, but the house was silent. Malcolm showered and threw on sweats and a t-shirt before going out to the living room to confirm what he already knew—Lorna was gone.

Sighing, he went into the kitchen to get his first cup when he saw it. An index card propped against the coffee carafe.

'Meeting with Steven this morning so I had to run. See you later, maybe. L.'

He picked up the card and smiled. She'd left—which wasn't unusual—but she'd also left him a note, which was. But being Lorna, she couldn't just say 'see you later'. She had to retain that last tiny bit of control and add: 'maybe'.

Whatever made her feel better.

Malcolm put down the note and poured his first cup of the day.

"SO MAYBE I'LL fly down and drop Piper off, or something."

"Why would you have to do that? She'll just drive down with us."

"Do you really want to be in a car for thirteen hours with Piper? And besides, I want to meet this person."

"*This person* has a name. A name I've told you, now about three times."

"Yes, I've been Googling her since we've been on the phone. I mean honestly, Malcolm, how old is she anyway?"

"Charlotte, was there something else?"

"I think I'm completely within my rights to want to see and meet the person who's going to be spending so much time with my child. And I hope you know Piper is bound to hate her."

Malcolm stretched while holding the phone between his head and shoulder. "No one's arguing with your rights, just your wisdom. And Piper hates everyone. But believe me, if anyone can hold her own, it's Lorna Terry."

"Is that admiration I hear in your voice?" Charlotte asked, sounding more than a little bitter. "If so, then I'm happy for you. *I* certainly wasn't able to provoke that response in all the years we were married."

"There's not a whole lot that's admirable about adultery."

"You always like to do that—reduce what we had to our worst moments. Pretend that it wasn't good for a long, long time."

If he had to guess, Malcolm would say that something was going on with his ex-wife. She only liked to revisit her fairytale version of their marriage when her current situation wasn't what she wanted it to be. Maybe Spence wasn't looking like he intended to hold up his end.

When all was said and done with the dissolution of their marriage, and Malcolm and Charlotte had finally been able to have a conversation without screaming and yelling at each other, she made a confession. She and Spence made a bargain, once their affair turned serious, that they would both leave their marriages for each other.

Charlotte had done so first, but Spence had younger children, and Charlotte agreed that it might—and probably should—take him a little more time. But there had been hiccups and fits and starts that Charlotte had confided in Malcolm about, usually when she had a couple too many glasses of wine; and once when they wound up in bed together. Spence waffled a little bit sometimes. He had spells of renewed devotion to his wife and two small sons, or he was wracked with guilt about the kind of role model he would be for his boys.

Malcolm kept his mouth shut, but his money was on the divorce never happening.

"We had plenty of good times, Char," he said dutifully. "But in the end, I guess they didn't outweigh the bad."

"You didn't answer me. How old is she?" Charlotte pressed.

"Didn't Google tell you?"

"It says she's forty-six. But that's on Wikipedia, so I

wondered whether it's accurate. She's attractive enough, I guess."

"Charlotte, I was writing when you called, so ..."

"And far be it for me to take you away from that. Her Wiki page is very extensive. And ... does she even like children? Will Piper ..."

"Wait, what?"

"I asked whether she even likes children. She has some pretty harsh things to say about pregnancy and motherhood. Comparing pregnancy to *slavery*? Like, who thinks something like that?"

"Where are you *reading* this?"

"It's a quote from one of her articles, where she talks about how she felt when she was pregnant. And I quote: '*At times, I recall feeling a sense of enslavement; my will was subsumed to the will of the tiny being who occupied me, dictating where I might go, what I might do and even which substances I might consume or imbibe.*' I'm not sure I would like her very much. I'm not sure why you do."

Malcolm sighed. "She's just a ... deep thinker, that's all."

"Huh. Sounds like a cold fish to me. I can't imagine what her kid thought when he or she read that little nugget. And I can't imagine what it would be like to sleep with someone like that either."

He let the comment hang there, knowing full well it was really a question.

"Anyway, I'm very excited to meet her now," Charlotte said, not bothering to lighten up on the sarcasm. "I guess I'll let you get back to your work."

Then she hung up without another word.

And because he let his curiosity get the better of him, Malcolm immediately Googled Lorna and checked her Wiki page, searching for the quote Charlotte read to him.

It was part of an article she wrote almost fifteen years earlier, called '*Demystifying Motherhood: Social Constructs and the So-Called Maternal Instinct*'. One part of the title was particularly jarring: the "*so-called maternal instinct.*" He had to agree with Charlotte—that couldn't have been fun for Riley to read. It only made him more curious about her daughter than he had been before. He wondered at the extraordinary resilience of the young woman who would have survived, and by all accounts thrived, with a woman as challenging as Lorna as her only parent.

But more than curiosity, Malcolm felt a little sympathy as well. Lorna was not an easy partner, not an easy *person*. And what she had shared about the way she extricated Riley from her father's life ... that was tough stuff to stomach. It made his ongoing fascination, and the other feelings he was beginning to have about her much more confusing.

What the hell was he getting himself into?

THIRTEEN
WIDE OPEN

"Fallon, I'll need you to index all of these according to subject and date," Lorna said, handing her research assistant a pile of pages, pulled from magazines, and some of them printouts of pages on the internet.

Fallon took the pages and nodded, smiling as she noticed the image of the pop star on the page at the top of the pile.

Lorna noted the smile but didn't comment. In a moment of jest, Malcolm had given her a great idea, and she was going to run with it. In her book proposal, she was going to use the overly-sexualized images of today's pop icons—some of them self-identified feminists—to make the case that modern feminism over-identified with the sexual liberation element of feminist theory but often missed the point. And the point, she would argue, was that liberation could very easily become self-exploitation.

Somewhere in the back of her mind, she was playing with the idea of comparing it to women who prostituted themselves for their own gain, versus those who were pimped by someone else. Was the degradation different? But it was an imperfect analogy, so she would have to think it through.

Maybe, in North Carolina, she would find the clarity of thought she was seeking. Because lately, it had been difficult to find on campus. Steven had called her in for another meeting and said there was a rumor; a rumor about her having been involved with a student. Of course, she denied it categorically. Of all the missteps and poor judgment calls she had made in her career, sleeping with a student had never been one of them.

Steven accepted her denial at face value, but had cautioned her about the 'unfettered access' she gave to the young people she taught. It sounded like he was chiding her for something that he claimed to believe she hadn't even done. Though she wondered at the source of the rumor, she didn't have time to dwell on it.

"Should I put them in this box you're taking with you on your trip?" Fallon asked. "Once they're indexed, I mean."

"Yes. Thank you. That would be great." Lorna looked up absently and nodded.

"Y'know, Professor Terry, I could just scan them all, put them on a flash drive and give that to you. And I could still index them." Fallon shrugged. "But it would be electronically."

Lorna laughed. "Of course. Why didn't I think of that? I guess I'm still being dragged kicking and screaming into the digital age. And of course, flash drives get erased, so ..."

"Well, we can back it up on a cloud for you as well."

Lorna opened both hands, palms up, indicating she was out of her depth.

"Do whatever you think will work, and let me know. But the books, I do need, so please be sure to pack those."

She turned her attention back to her monitor and expelled a rough breath when her phone immediately rang.

One week. She had one week to get things organized for

what could turn out to be a month-long absence, and she felt nowhere near prepared. And whether she wanted to admit it or not, some of it was just plain ol' nerves. Weeks holed up with Malcolm, and sharing some of that time with his high-strung problem-child was cause enough for anxiety without being under the gun to pack her work into two neat little boxes and schlep it all down south.

"Hello!" she almost barked the greeting, causing Fallon to lift her head in surprise.

She had set up her laptop at the small circular meeting desk in the corner of Lorna's office and customarily worked there.

"Mom."

Lorna instinctively sat up straighter at the sound of Riley's voice. It had been two weeks since they spoke, and she had missed her. It seemed like much longer.

"Riley."

"Yes. Hi." She sounded as though she had made the call under duress. And maybe she had. Shawn had been remarkably forgiving, and probably had been lobbying on her behalf. But of course, he forgave her; it wasn't his father who had been denied him.

"I'm glad you called."

Lorna vaguely registered Fallon getting up and leaving the office with a sheaf of papers in her hand.

"Yeah, well, I think it's probably time for us to talk. Again. I mean, talk again."

Now she sounded nervous. And it broke Lorna's heart. She and her kid had the rarest of rare relationships. They were mother and daughter, but friends, too. She always thought they were the exception to that rule—that one shouldn't and couldn't be 'friends' with one's children. But even if that were so, she had definitely betrayed that friendship, by keeping something so important from Riley, and for years at that.

"Of course. Whenever you want to. Wherever you want."

"Reunion Weekend?"

"That's this weekend. And then after that I'll be gone for a while."

"Gone? Where are you going?" Riley's voice rose.

"Just to North Carolina. With ... I'll tell you all about it when we see each other."

So much seemed to have happened in such a short time. She was 'seeing' Malcolm officially now, and they were going away together. And she was working on a book. In the blink of an eye, she and Riley had lost a little bit of their touch with each other's lives.

"How's Cass?" she asked. "And Cullen?"

"Good. They're both good. Cass is changing so much already. I'll bring pictures."

"Pictures? Why don't you bring *her*?"

"Because I want us to have uninterrupted time to talk. Really talk. You can see her another time."

"But after Reunion Weekend, I'll be leaving that Monday, and ..."

"Mom, we're not going anywhere, and I assume you'll be back at some point. So, seeing Cass can wait."

Seeing Cass can wait?

For one panicky moment, Lorna wondered whether Riley planned to give her a taste of her own medicine, by denying her access to her grandchildren. The thought of it made her surprisingly fearful, but only for a millisecond. Because Riley didn't have that kind of nature. She was as unselfish a person as there was. Unlike her mother.

"Okay. So, you'll come alone then?"

"Yes. For the Friday night thing they have. I'll spend the night and take the train back late Saturday morning."

"You want to spend the night?"

"Why? Do you have plans?"

"No. Just surprised is all. It's been a long time since you spent more than a few hours here. And you don't mind going to the dinner? We can skip it if ..."

"No, I'll go. It's only a few hours. And the rest of the time, we'll, you know, talk."

"Okay. So Friday then."

"Yeah. Friday. 'Bye Mom."

She hung up and Lorna held the receiver for a long while. Riley hardly ever called her 'Mom' and only when she was a little vulnerable, or wistful. Sometimes, if she was really annoyed she might call her 'Mother.' But 'Lorna' was what was most familiar, most comfortable for them. But this time, this conversation, Riley had not once called her by her name.

"SO IT LOOKS like you'll get to meet my kid after all."

Malcolm looked up at her, but Lorna said nothing further, keeping focused on her food.

"So, she's coming up here?"

"Yes. Friday. For the reunion dinner, and then to ... talk." Lorna made air quotes.

"That's good."

"Yeah, I guess it is." She picked through her plate, eating nothing.

On her way back from campus, the idea of going to an empty house didn't appeal to her, so she stopped at Parthenon, a Greek restaurant on the edge of town, and then called Malcolm to see whether he wanted a platter as well. He sounded surprised to hear from her, but said he would be waiting, and now they were sitting in his living room across from each other, eating directly from the aluminum containers with the plastic utensils, the take-out bag and condiments on the coffee table between them.

"But you're worried about it."

"Yes." Lorna looked up at him.

"Understandable," Malcolm said.

He had a five o' clock shadow dusting his strong, masculine jaw, which made him look even manlier. And he wasn't wearing his glasses.

Lorna had learned that her instinct was correct—they were only a mild necessity, for comfort and ease rather than a true requirement. When he didn't wear them, he looked younger, and much better looking than he probably should if he wanted to be taken seriously as an academic. Hunky professors were in actuality, very few and far between.

Lorna smiled at the thought. Those female undergrads were going to eat him alive come fall. She could only imagine the swarms of them lined up outside his office with contrived questions, just hoping to catch his notice.

"You're smiling," Malcolm observed.

"My mind wandered for a moment," she explained.

"This lamb is good," he said, taking another bite of food. "Thanks for picking it up. I hadn't even begun to think about dinner."

"So Malcolm," she said, having a thought. "You haven't said much about Piper lately. What's going on with her?"

"Yeah, I should probably brief you before you find yourself, what did you call it? *Marooned* with her for a couple weeks."

"That's not why I asked," Lorna said. "I just realized I've been a little self-absorbed lately, what with my own little family drama."

"Since when have you ever been concerned about being self-absorbed?" he asked with a small smirk.

Lorna felt a ping in her chest. "Malcolm, please ... I don't feel like ... debating tonight. I just ..."

He looked at her, and their eyes met. She saw compassion in his and looked down again hastily, trying to concentrate on her meal.

"So," she said again. "How's Piper?"

"She's like a walking minefield is how she is. You never know what's going to set her off. Been acting out a lot. And I can't shake the feeling that something's going on with her. Like something's bothering her. But Charlotte comes from the school of thought that all prepubescent girls turn into monsters at some point and so I'm worrying for nothing."

"But you *are* worried."

"Yeah. There's no book, right? That can tell you how your kid should be acting. But you just have to know *your* kid. And my gut tells me that Piper isn't okay. But you want to know what the most uncomfortable thing is?"

Malcolm looked up at her and Lorna nodded, prompting him to continue.

"The most uncomfortable thing is, I'm starting to realize that Charlotte *doesn't* know our kid. It isn't just a difference in parenting philosophy. She's not worried because she doesn't even *know* Piper well enough to know that something isn't right."

"And how do you say that to her, right?"

"Exactly. There's no way to say that and have it come across as anything other than an accusation."

Lorna nodded.

"Anyway," Malcolm said. "That's what's happening in my world."

Giving him a wan smile, Lorna moved from her place on the armchair opposite where he was on the sofa and went to sit next to him instead, leaving her food behind. She didn't have much of an appetite anyway.

Once next to him, she leaned against his shoulder, and Malcolm lifted his arm, putting it around her. Lorna slid down, lay on her side and rested her head in his lap.

SHE WOKE up in his bed, with no recollection of how she'd gotten there. Next to her, Malcolm was on his side, his arm draped across her middle.

Lorna sat up, thinking that she should probably go home, but instead she shed her clothes, down to her bra and underwear and lay down again.

Malcolm stirred just as she put her head on the pillow.

He opened his eyes, and they took a moment to focus.

"Hey," he said, hoarsely.

Lorna offered him a small smile but said nothing in return. She reached out and traced his nose, down the bridge, over the lips, pausing at the seam and running her fingertips horizontally along it. Watching as Malcolm's eyes darkened, she smiled again.

Reaching forward and behind her, he found the clasp on her bra and unfastened it, sliding the straps down her shoulders while she lifted slightly to help him. When her breasts were free, he bowed his head, took a nipple in his mouth and teased it with the tip of his tongue.

As he moved from one to the other, Lorna let her hand rest lightly on his head and closed her eyes, exhaling softly between her parted lips. Moving closer, Malcolm let his hands roam down her side and back, sliding her underwear low on her hips.

Lorna maneuvered them completely off and shifted so she was astride him. Lifting his body, with her still straddling him across the hips, Malcolm removed his boxers. They were kissing now, panting heavily, taking and giving each other breath.

With hands grasping her buttocks, he lifted her, and pulled Lorna back down onto him. She cried out against his lips and he held her there, for the moment both of them completely still.

"Open your eyes," Malcolm breathed.

His tone was so urgent, she did as he asked, immediately.

What she saw in those eyes made her blink back tears. What she saw frightened her. She didn't care to think of what he might be seeing in her eyes.

"*Lo ...*" he said.

She began moving, slowly at first and with increasing frenzy, grinding against him, rather than rising and falling. Malcolm's hands remained on her hips, his eyes held hers. Lorna felt the wetness against her face, and realized that the threatened tears had spilled and were overflowing, though she couldn't for the life of her imagine why.

Lifting a hand to wipe them away, she was surprised when Malcolm grabbed her wrist.

"*No,*" he said, shaking his head. His voice was deeper, hoarser. "It's okay. You get to cry, too, Lo. *You get to cry too.*"

———

THE REST of the week went by very quickly, with Lorna spending most of her days writing in her office, Fallon buzzing around providing information and cataloging research Lorna planned to take with her to use in North Carolina. Fallon had turned out to be quick, quiet and accurate and efficient—all the things Lorna needed in an assistant.

She made a mental note to take the girl's premature senior thesis with her so she could read it on the long ride down south.

If it was any good, she would do what she could to help Fallon's ambition of being published come true, because she had been invaluable over the past few weeks.

Almost every evening, Lorna spent with Malcolm, though they generally didn't talk much. They ate dinner together, exchanged basic information about their days and then he went in to write. He apologized for his long silences, and for being scarce after dinner, explaining that he was in that place Zadie Smith called "the middle of the novel" which didn't mean he was halfway done, just that he was fully and completely immersed and the physical world had become distant while the one he was creating took over.

And Lorna, in return, explained that she didn't mind. She liked the combination of silence and the knowledge of his presence. They didn't need to speak. Instead, she read, and to her horror, had begun watching more and more television, though with the volume low so as not to disturb Malcolm working in the next room. While they didn't exchange many words, they always made love when he later joined her in his bed, sometimes in the very wee hours of the morning.

Whether she was awake or asleep, he reached for her, pulled her to him and spread her legs, tasting her, then taking her. Lorna thought it had something to do with the excitement of writing, but there was no gently inquiring hand on her thigh or breast, Malcolm simply took her as though she was his to have at will. And she found that she liked it.

But now it was Friday, and Riley was due, so her time in the office was short, and Lorna had forewarned Malcolm not to expect to see her until she and Riley made it to the dinner that evening.

Glancing at her office clock, Lorna hurriedly shut down her computer and shoved it into her bag before Fallon stopped her.

"I haven't loaded the new stuff onto it yet," she said.

"Remember you said you wanted it both on your hard drive and the cloud?"

"Yes, but I'm late to pick up my daughter at the train station, so ..."

"I could always drop the laptop at your house tomorrow or Sunday?" Fallon suggested.

Lorna considered for a moment. She probably wouldn't be doing much work with Riley there, and with the dinner and everything.

"Sure. Yes. That sounds good. And the books?" She indicated the box she had been gradually filling, as she identified books she needed from the library that she might need as references while she wrote.

"I'll bring those too," Fallon said with a reassuring calm that Lorna appreciated.

"Wonderful. Thank you, Fallon. You've been a lifesaver. I ..."

"You can go, Professor Terry," Fallon said. "I'm happy to take care of it. See you this weekend."

Pausing one last time, Lorna nodded. "Okay. Yes. Thank you again."

She got to the train station just in time to see Riley exiting, a leather duffle over her shoulder, wearing jeans and a tank with ballet flats, a light summer scarf around her neck.

Lorna smiled because, as she'd predicted, Riley had once again cut her hair, though this time not as much. It was still long enough for her to have it in a short, curly ponytail. Standing and looking around for a moment, she finally spotted Lorna's car and gave a brief wave, starting in her direction.

When she got into the car, she smelled like citrus and looked beautiful. Lorna smiled at her, feeling the pride she always felt just looking at her only child.

"Hi," she said, leaning over and hugging her, holding her a little longer than she might normally have done.

When she released her, Riley looked at her searchingly. "You okay?"

"Great, now that you're here."

Riley offered her a smile. And how grateful she was for that smile.

"I'm glad I'm here, too, Lorna."

"Are you hungry? Or do you want to go to the house and get straight to the hard stuff?"

"Hard stuff as in ...?"

"Our conversation," Lorna said laughing. "I didn't mean hard liquor. Though depending on what you want to say to me, I might need that as well."

"Let's maybe go have something light to eat?" Riley suggested. "Since we have that dinner tonight, no sense over-doing it."

"Yes, that's right. And tonight you get to meet Malcolm T. Mitchell. I've told him you're a fan." Lorna pulled away from the curb, keeping her eye on the road.

"That'll be cool. Did you tell him I was geeking about his insights on race?"

"I told him you were geeking about him in general. Kind of like you're doing right now. He enjoyed hearing that. Very much."

"Wait, is there something ...? Lorna are you, like, *involved* with him?" Riley smacked her on her thigh.

Lorna laughed. "How could you tell something like that from ..?"

"It was the look on your face. In your eyes. You're sleeping with him, aren't you?"

Lorna was surprised at how jarring that sounded to her now. Sure, she and Malcolm were sleeping together—if one wanted to use that silly euphemism—but now, it sounded wrong for so many more reasons.

"We're involved," Lorna acknowledged. "And he's the person I'm going to North Carolina with."

"Are you serious?"

"Yes. On Monday, we're leaving at the crack of dawn."

"No, Mom. I mean are you and he ... serious? Relationship-wise."

Before making the turn onto Main Street, Lorna glanced at her daughter who was turned almost completely around in her seat.

"What would make you think that?"

"How many times do I have to say it? I *know* you. You're different when you talk about him. There's a ... tenderness in your voice."

"Shut up, Riley."

"No, I mean it. Usually when you talk about men you're seeing, it's with cynicism. Like they're specimens or something."

At that, Lorna gasped. "Are you seri... *specimens*?"

Out of the corner of her eye, Lorna saw Riley shrug. "Just calling it like I see it."

Even though she didn't much enjoy what was being said, Lorna had to admit that she liked that they seemed to have fallen back into their usual frank and comfortable banter again. Later, things were likely to get tense when they broached the reason for Riley's visit, but for now it was as though they hadn't missed a beat in their normally close relationship.

"And you're not talking about this guy that way. You're talking about him like a person. A person you like, and ... respect, even."

"I do respect him."

"And you like him," Riley prompted.

"Yes," Lorna forced out. "Very much so."

Next to her, Riley leaned back into the seat, looking ahead for the first time. She did everything short of rubbing her hands together in satisfaction.

"Well, this visit just got *a lot* more interesting," she laughed.

FOURTEEN

GRACE

"So what's in North Carolina?"

"What I'm *hoping* is in North Carolina is the second half of my book," Malcolm said.

Riley Gardner laughed and nodded. "Oh, I bet."

Physically, she looked only vaguely like Lorna, but there were similarities in the way they made unflinchingly direct eye-contact when speaking or being spoken to. Three hours earlier when she entered Stratford Hall where the Reunion Dinner was being held, walking next to Lorna, Malcolm had been immediately struck by her quiet grace. Her energy was the very antithesis of her mother's.

While Lorna's presence was attention-grabbing and raw, Riley had a quietude of demeanor that was, in its own way, just as striking. It immediately called to mind something Lorna had once told him about her daughter and son-in-law's relationship. Malcolm had asked how it was they met, and how it was they fell in love—the rapper and the intellectual seemed such an unlikely match.

She interviewed him, Malcolm recalled Lorna saying. *But*

when you get to know them, you'll get it right away. He's very temperamental, very brooding and temperamental. And she's his calm.

And him? Malcolm had asked. *What is he, for her I mean?*

Riley, if left to her own devices would live almost completely by the dictates of her head, Lorna explained. *Shawn is the reason she lives life with her heart as well.*

And now that he'd spent this much time sitting and talking to her, Malcolm saw how much of Riley Gardner was about her intellect. Apart from her mother, she was the first person in a long while who held Malcolm's interest completely, alternately probing him with questions about 'Cadence' and telling him about her work.

By dessert, she had convinced him to write a piece for her journal in the fall, and maybe even to be interviewed once his new book came out. She and her mother had that much in common—they were the kinds of women men couldn't help wanting to please.

The obligatory speeches and awards passed by almost unnoticed while his and Riley's conversation continued, and now there was dancing as the event began to wind down. Lorna had been pulled away and come back several times; and finding them still deep in conversation shook her head and went away again to find other people to entertain her.

"How long did it take you to finish 'Cadence'?"

"First draft was a matter of weeks. And then refining it took a couple years. I had no real sense of wanting to 'complete' it. Just of wanting to get it right."

"And this one?"

"*Lots* of pressure to complete it," Malcolm admitted. "Everyone wants to see whether you can beat the sophomore curse and all that."

"Well then I hope you're able to do that in North Carolina."

"Here's hopin'" Malcolm lifted his wineglass.

Riley lifted her glass in answer to his toast, and took a sip of her wine, making a humming sound as she swallowed. Then she laughed.

"I haven't been drinking at all," she explained. "Pregnancy, and now breastfeeding. So tonight is my first taste of wine in about a year."

"That's right. Congratulations on the baby. Lorna called me the night she was born."

Riley looked surprised. "She did?"

"Yeah. She sounded thrilled."

"Huh." Riley shrugged and then gazed past Malcolm's shoulder as though searching the crowd for a glimpse of her mother. "She's not the most conventional grandmother in the world, but she does love my kids."

"And your husband," Malcolm added.

At that, Riley gave a genuine smile. "Yes. She definitely loves Shawn. Very much. They have a very ... easy and comfortable relationship."

Something in her voice told Malcolm that she was saying more—that *her* relationship with Lorna on the other hand might not be quite as easy, nor as comfortable.

"I tease her sometimes that my husband and son are the only men she's ever loved."

For a moment, her eyes grew distant and then Riley focused again, giving Malcolm a brief but determined smile.

"Would you excuse me for a few minutes? I just realized I haven't spoken to them tonight, so I think I'll go make a quick call to check in."

"Sure. Of course."

Malcolm stood as she got up, and left the table, and when

she was gone, did some looking around himself. He spotted Lorna nearby, deep in conversation with two other women.

Tonight she was in a semi-formal black chiffon dress with a Grecian-style neckline and high-heeled black sandals, the heels a rarity for her. Around her neck was a long gold necklace that she fidgeted with as she talked, and small gold drop-earrings adorned her ears. The soft waves of her hair had been pulled up and away from her face, in a loose knot. And for only the second time since he'd known her, there was even makeup in evidence.

Malcolm took advantage of being alone and undetected to watch her—the way she knitted her brow and pursed her lips, which he now knew meant she disagreed with something that was being said, but was restraining herself from saying so; and how she raised her right hand to the back of her neck, where there was usually a curl loose that she habitually twisted around her forefinger when deep in thought.

He stared at her for so long, she must have felt it, because soon Lorna looked up and directly at him. Her eyes changed, then; her eyes, and something subtle at the corners of her mouth.

Crazy as it sounded, he'd missed her today even though not twenty-four hours ago—and for several nights before that—she had been with him, and in his bed. When Lorna let her guard down and just let herself be, there was nothing like it, and no one like her. Since that evening when she'd cried in front of him, there was one less wall between them. All but gone were the mini-lectures and professorial pronouncements.

Finally, it felt like they were just a woman and a man, stripped bare of all their stuff and getting to know each other.

Now that Lorna had caught him staring, Malcolm didn't bother looking away or pretending he hadn't been doing it. He kept his eyes on her, and she did the same. There was no denying it anymore. Between them, something electric was happening.

AFTER THE DINNER, Malcolm drove home and let himself into his house, tossing his keys on the kitchen counter and grabbing a beer from the fridge. He hadn't done much drinking at the dinner since it was all about meeting alums, impressing them and having them empty their pockets into Gilchrist's coffers for another year. Not that he'd held up that end of the bargain too well tonight.

Most of his time had been spent in the company of Lorna Terry and her interesting daughter, and Malcolm only vaguely recalled one or two brief conversations with alumni who wanted to share how much they loved his book. A few others had actually brought along copies for him to sign, which he did obligingly, and then returned his attention to the women in his company.

The way Lorna talked about her parenting history, one would have to believe that Riley became the woman she was in spite of her mother, and not because of her. But after meeting Riley, Malcolm didn't believe that for a second. Lorna had to have done something right.

Emptying the beer bottle, he slid off his formal jacket and walked through the house, checking doors and windows. As he did his walkthrough, he noticed the odd books everywhere, lying open on their faces, stray t-shirts and coffee mugs on different surfaces, including the windowsill in his office. Lorna Terry was a little bit of a slob. But he liked finding traces of her in just about every room in his house.

ust as he sat on the edge of his bed to shed the rest of his clothes and hit the shower, his cell rang.

Reaching for it, he answered without looking at the console.

"Mal?"

"Charlotte. Hey." And then a thought struck him and he stiffened. "Is Piper ...?"

"No, she's fine. Sleeping the sleep of the high-strung and not-so-innocent. Elisa is with them."

"Elisa is with ... and where are you? Still at work?" He glanced at the clock. It was past eleven, but it would not have been the first time that Charlotte burned the midnight oil, especially if the case was an important one.

"I'm outside your house."

"Wait. Outside *my* house?"

"Yes. Open the door, would you?"

Without hanging up, Malcolm headed back out to his living room and then to the foyer, peeking out through the blinds. And sure enough, idling at his curb was a white M-Class Mercedes. Charlotte flashed the high beams before turning off the headlights altogether, and then she was getting out and walking up his front path.

Breaking the connection on the cell, Malcolm went to open the door, waiting until Charlotte made it inside. She was wearing a plain black t-shirt, flip-flops and jeans, and had pulled her hair back into a loose ponytail.

Holding back all the questions that sprang to mind, Malcolm locked the door behind her and followed as Charlotte headed for his living room.

"Didn't even know you knew my address," he said.

"It's on your checks," Charlotte said. "I just got the most recent one today. Thank you, by the way."

Malcolm said nothing.

He and Charlotte had a very detailed, and by some measures complicated, divorce settlement. He paid child support according to a percentage of his net income, a formula they both devised and agreed to, filing it with the court as part of their divorce. Both of them being members of the bar had saved them a mint on hiring lawyers, and besides, they had enough experience to know that lawyering up sometimes protracted conflict rather than resolving it.

"What's going on, Char?"

Charlotte collapsed onto his sofa and looked around, not acknowledging his question.

"This looks like the home of a college professor," she said idly. "Did it come with all this furniture?"

"Most of it." Malcolm sat opposite her and tried to make eye contact, but Charlotte was avoiding it.

"Hayley loves coming here. Piper said it's like sleeping in a musty old library."

"Well you know Piper. Always looking on the bright side of things."

Charlotte offered up a brief laugh and finally looked directly at him. "I think I might have messed up," she said.

"Why? What happened?" Malcolm leaned forward. "Something happen at work?"

"No, Malcolm. Not at work."

"Then what?" Malcolm felt his exhaustion overtaking his patience.

Charlotte sighed. "I just ... I was in bed replaying some things, and I wonder now whether I might have ... whether I was too hasty when ..." She looked at him and there were tears brimming in her eyes. "Do you ever wonder whether we were wrong ... to get a divorce?"

Actually, he never wondered that. Maybe in the very beginning when he confronted the horrors of being single again, and of dating. But now, never. He was sure they had done the right thing.

"I know you think it's because things aren't exactly going according to plan with Spence ..."

"How *are* things going with the ass-hat?"

"You are *so* fucking sanctimonious when you want to be, y'know that?"

Running a hand over his head, Malcolm took a deep breath. "Charlotte are you telling me you drove all the way up here because you're having some drama ... some completely *predictable* drama, by the way, with your married boyfriend?"

Charlotte gave a wry smile. "I guess it is predictable, isn't it? I don't know why I thought ..."

"That you and Spence were different? That you could take the fantasy and make it a reality?"

Staring at him with flat eyes, Charlotte heaved a deep sigh. "Do you have coffee, or ..."

"Tea," Malcolm said standing. "It's too late for coffee. You may as well stay and leave first thing in the morning."

He tried not to notice the vaguely hopeful look in her eyes. Knowing her as well as he did, she was probably thinking that staying over gave her more time to exercise her persuasive talents, and that they would end up in bed together. But as he pulled out things for brewing tea, Malcolm was as certain as he had ever been of anything that there was no way he would wind up screwing his ex-wife. Not tonight, and probably never again.

Charlotte didn't really have doubts about Spence; at least no more doubts than she'd had weeks, months or even a year ago. Now, though, she sniffed competition and she didn't like it. That was her nature, and that was how they'd gotten together at Cambridge.

Malcolm had been green and inexperienced, a boy from small-town Louisiana who had never been out of the conti-nental United States, and Charlotte was the already well-traveled and somewhat privileged girl from New England who was always happy to teach him the ropes of being an American expat living in a strange new world.

Malcolm had been seeing Abidemi at the time, a beautiful Nigerian, herself from an impressive family who placed an extraordinary amount of emphasis on achievement and education. Abi was the first actual African he had ever met, and she shone for him like a beacon, belying all the negative things poor Black kids in America are taught about the so-called Dark Continent and its people.

Abi was beautiful, witty, and intelligent; and had the broadest worldview of anyone Malcolm had ever met. He was proud that she had chosen him.

While he was focused on the arts, Abidemi was an economist. She called him "William Shakespeare" with a mixture of admiration and amusement, and in an accent that was part British, part Nigerian. He believed himself in love with her, and occasionally fantasized that he might stay, and that somehow Abidemi's disapproving father would see that the Black American of indeterminate heritage was good enough for his daughter after all.

But none of that happened. Instead, during a rare argument with Abi, Charlotte had taken him to a pub where they drank and talked late into the night. Malcolm remembered being relieved to be with someone who understood the same cultural references, and who wasn't quite so intimidating, nor so ... foreign. And Charlotte's sexually aggressive approach was—for that night at least—a welcome change from the quiet reluctance with which Abi sometimes approached sex. But after he slept with Charlotte, Malcolm regretted it immediately.

Later, somehow Abi got wind of the one-night stand (Malcolm sometimes thought from Charlotte herself) and just as suddenly as she had turned her favor in his direction, she took it away. After that, Malcolm defaulted into Charlotte, the American girl who was both safe, and in the States, probably a little out of his league.

Once, after they had been coupled up for about a month, they spotted Abi near Saltmarsh Dining Room, and Charlotte, clinging a little tighter to his arm as though he might sprint away in that direction made a derisive sound in the back of her throat.

I can't believe you would have picked her *over me,* she said.

It was such an insignificant moment. But all these years later, Malcolm still recalled and occasionally returned to it. Because he believed, and probably had always known, that it was a tiny window into Charlotte's true character.

"What kind would you like?" he called out toward the living room. "Black, or green?"

There was no answer, but shortly afterward, Charlotte was standing at the kitchen door. "I looked around," she said. "Cute place."

"Black, or green tea?" Malcolm repeated.

"Green, I guess. Does she come here? *Dr.* Lorna Terry?"

"You're not an invited guest, Charlotte. You don't get to show up at my house and start quizzing me about my private life."

"I'm not 'quizzing' you, Malcolm. I was just curious. Lord knows I've over-confided in you about my personal life."

"Yeah. Over-confided is right."

"Did it make you jealous?" she asked, moving closer.

Malcolm felt her hovering over his shoulder as he turned off the burner under the teakettle.

"It used to make me angry," he acknowledged. "In the beginning."

"And now?"

"Now ..." He turned to face her. "I think you need to sleep in the bed you made."

"Nice to see that your lapsed Catholic sense of retribution is still intact," Charlotte said sarcastically.

"You'll find everything you need in the fridge and cupboards. I'm tired and going to bed," Malcolm said walking around her.

"Malcolm, I ..."

He was just at the door when her voice stopped him.

"What?" he paused without turning to look at her again.

"I'm sorry," she said.

"Yeah. Get some sleep, Charlotte. You're leaving first thing in the morning."

After he showered and turned off the lights, it was hard to get to sleep himself. He heard Charlotte moving around elsewhere in the house and remained alert for a long time, hoping he wouldn't have to deal with some embarrassing scene of her coming into his bedroom.

But she didn't come, and Malcolm was relieved.

"ARE YOU COOKING?"

Charlotte came ambling into the kitchen the next morning, looking well-rested. Malcolm had coffee on, and was preparing to make eggs.

Leaning against the kitchen counter, he watched as she helped herself to some of the coffee, casually going into his refrigerator for creamer. He waited until she added sweetener and had taken her first sip.

"What happened last night," he said. "That can't happen again."

"Because you might not have been alone? I realize that

now. So ...”

“It can’t happen again because you weren’t invited Charlotte and there’s nothing here that’s yours, or that has anything to do with you.”

Only once he said the words did Malcolm realize that Charlotte’s coming over had brought the past sailing in with her through the front door. Just as he was beginning to build a comfortable present, and future.

“You stop by my house uninvited all the time,” she pointed out.

“Because there *is* something there that’s mine. My children. But ...” He shrugged. “You’re right. The boundaries haven’t been clear. I’ll make sure to call first from now on.”

Charlotte’s eyes met his over the brim of the coffee mug. “I don’t actually care about that. And the girls like it that you sometimes just stop in.”

“But still ...”

“You’re really serious about this then, huh? And about this person.” She looked off into the middle distance. “I guess it was bound to happen sooner or later. You’ve moved on.”

“That happened when I signed the divorce papers.”

“Did it?” She looked at him again. “I’m not sure. And I’m not sure I moved on then either. Maybe I thought that we might go through some changes, and then, I don’t know, find each other again.”

“So, Elisa is with the girls you said last night? You’d better ...”

“Yes. I’d better hit the road.” Charlotte took one last, long gulp and put the mug in the sink.

“Do Piper and Hayley know where you ...”

“No. They have no clue I came up here. It was just a bad decision, fueled by wine and ... nostalgia.” She gave a wry laugh.

He walked her out to the living room and when she grabbed her keys and purse, tried to think of something positive or reassuring to say. But honestly, he just wanted her gone.

Last night, he'd been on a high after the evening with Lorna, and getting to know Riley. He was pleasantly tired and looking forward to his thoughts and a shower, followed by restful sleep. And then Charlotte showed up, crowding it all out.

It was too much like the last years of their marriage when she resented his writing, because it closed him off in a way she couldn't understand. And because it had nothing to do with her. She used to barge in then as well, making up household chores, family outings or other tasks, just to tear him away from his laptop and make him focus once again on her, even if she had no intention of focusing on him.

"Well," Charlotte said as they stood at the front door.

Malcolm opened it. Lorna was standing there.

Her eyes flitted from Malcolm to Charlotte and back again, and slowly, she smiled. To anyone who didn't know her, the smile might have seemed polite, and even pleasant. But Malcolm recognized the cynical resignation beneath it.

"Lorna," he said.

"Malcolm."

"Lorna, this is Charlotte; Charlotte, Lorna."

Charlotte seemed frozen in place for a moment but finally recovered and extended a hand, which Lorna took. Both women exchanged 'nice-to-meet-you's' and then Charlotte shrugged.

"This is great timing in a way," she said. She sounded a little rattled. "Since you'll be with Piper for part of the summer, it's good that we would meet."

"Yes, it is." Lorna said, not a trace of strain in her voice. "I've heard a lot about how spirited Piper is."

Charlotte laughed a brittle laugh. "That's nice of you to say. Spirited. Yes. Anyway ..." She glanced at Malcolm. "I have to get back, so ... we'll talk later, Mal?"

"Sure," he said. His voice sounded tight, even to him. "Talk to you later."

He and Lorna watched Charlotte make her way down the path and get into her car before they went inside together.

"Is that coffee I smell?" Lorna turned away from the front door, heading for the kitchen.

"Yeah. But I should probably make a fresh pot."

He followed, trying to read something, anything from the posture of her shoulders. There was certainly nothing in her voice to give her emotions away.

"So, just so you know," he began, "that ..."

"I just dropped Riley off at the train," Lorna interrupted him. "I was thinking that I wanted to download a little of what we talked about. And so I came here to do that with you."

"I'm glad you did," Malcolm said.

Taking a sniff of the coffee in the carafe, Lorna emptied it in the sink and rinsed the container.

"You're right," she said. "It smelled a little stale."

"Lorna, listen ..."

"If you're about to give me an explanation I haven't asked for, there's no need."

The studious calm in her voice when Charlotte was there was gone, and now there was just the tiniest of tremors. She still hadn't turned to face him, and was busying herself with the coffee filter now.

"I don't believe you," he said quietly.

Lorna made a sound of exasperation, but still didn't turn to look at him.

"I know you. You're going to pretend this doesn't matter,

but later, when I least expect it, you're going to come up with some *really* creative way to make me feel your displeasure."

"Malcolm, I don't know what you *think* you know about me. But you screwing your ex-wife isn't that surprising. And it definitely isn't my business."

Grabbing her by the shoulders, Malcolm spun her around.

"Listen to me," he said firmly. "It is your business. And there was no *screwing* of anyone. She stopped by without calling, just as I was about to go to bed. I gave her a cup of tea and told her to leave in the morning since it was already late. And then I went to sleep. Alone."

Lorna's nostrils were slightly flared, and her eyes were hard, emotionless.

"Charlotte sometimes gets a little ... conflicted about her new reality. But I'm not," he continued in a softer tone. "I'm not conflicted about mine. *At all.* Okay?"

Lorna looked down at the coffee filter in her hand and then up at him once again. Under his hands, Malcolm could feel some of the tension release from her arms and shoulders. She wasn't angry *at him*, exactly, he realized. She was angry because she cared—Charlotte's being there had mattered to her, and she didn't like that.

Taking a deep breath, Malcolm leaned in, nuzzling the side of her neck.

"You smell amazing," he said into her skin, feeling her relax against him even further. "Like coconut and ... fresh air."

After a moment, her hands were on his back, moving higher. Turning his head, he kissed her jaw, and then her mouth, pulling back just a little, just so he could give her a brief smile.

"Good morning," he said.

Lorna smiled back and brushed her lips against his. "Good morning."

FIFTEEN
THE DISTANCE

Lorna let herself into her house and headed straight for the kitchen, pouring herself a glass of water and leaning against the counter as she drank it, one slow sip after another. She wasn't thirsty. And she definitely wasn't hungry after the enormous breakfast Malcolm had made them—bacon, eggs and even hash browns with onions. What she was, was restless. Restless, and unsettled.

Even after they sat together at his dining table and ate, drinking large mugs of coffee and talking about the latest political scandal in Washington (involving yet another intern and an affair with a randy congressman) she couldn't get the image of the ex-wife out of her head.

She had never been the kind of woman who looked at other women with envy. It was one of her favorite attributes about herself, her ability to observe the assets of other women and feel nothing but admiration. It was one of the things that she believed made her a womanist—women were her allies, her compatriots, her sisters-in-arms. And though she didn't have many that she considered friends, the cause of her life was making sure the female of the species was never overlooked, taken advantage of, or abused.

So to look at Malcolm's ex-wife, a woman she had never met and knew little of, and feel an immediate spark of competitiveness and even something close to animosity? It was nothing short of horrifying.

Running a hand over her face, she tried to shake it off.

Charlotte ... was her last name Mitchell still? Charlotte whatever-her-surname-was was a striking woman. Fair skin, a few freckles, and interesting coloring that probably had people doing a double-take. She looked athletic as well, like one of those women who treated their body like a machine, always improving and refining it, paying meticulous attention to every wrinkle and sag as it appeared.

Lorna was decidedly not that kind of woman, nor did she care to be. But who would have thought that Malcolm, the *cerebral* Malcolm would go in for that type? And who would have thought that Lorna Terry would be standing in her kitchen obsessing about what "type" a man might like?

It was bad enough that she had showed up at his place unannounced—only the second time she had ever done that, by the way—but it was now much worse because she was actually ... jealous to find another woman there. And what was even worse yet, Malcolm knew she was. He knew she was, and had reassured her.

"Ugh," Lorna said aloud to the empty room.

Putting the empty glass in her sink, she opened her refrigerator and assessed what would have to be thrown out, and what she might simply stash in the freezer while she was in North Carolina. Suddenly, the trip that had her a little apprehensive was filling her with something like actual fear. There would be no distance between her and Malcolm while there; no distance and no escape.

Once, when they were in bed together and she'd gotten up to dress, minutes after he made her climax so hard her vision blurred, he'd reached out and stroked her naked back.

Hey, he said. *You're leaving me?*

She'd answered that she had to, because there was something she had to do, somewhere she had to go. She couldn't recall now what excuse she'd used.

You're like a jack-in-the-box, he said. *I make you come and you jump right up afterward and run out of here.*

No, I don't, she insisted.

You do, he said.

And when Lorna turned to look at him, he nodded.

I won't do that anymore, she'd promised. *I guess my work will go undone, my responsibilities all neglected ...*

And Malcolm had simply smiled and tugged her back down to him.

That time they'd stayed in bed almost the entire day.

It had been little things like that, things like that had been tiny, incremental steps to the place she was right now—a place she didn't like and probably had no business being. Not at this time in her life. And definitely not with a man almost nine years her junior with a pretty ex-wife. And now with this trip to North Carolina? It would only make things worse. She was going to have to get out of it. And she had less than forty-eight hours figure out how.

"SO I'VE ORGANIZED them according to author, date and then cross-referenced by topic. I think I picked most of the keywords you might use, so ..."

Lorna listened as Fallon described the system she had devised for organizing the hundreds of documents and articles she had scanned, uploaded to Lorna's cloud drive, and also saved on the flash drive. The girl had obviously put a lot of work into it, so there was no point telling her that the trip that made the process necessary might actually not be happening after all.

The filing system, complete with file paths and annotated descriptions were all typed up in a neat five-page document that Fallon had printed for Lorna's easy reference, and she was reviewing it now to make sure it would be easy to follow. Mentally, Lorna added one more thing to her checklist—to remember to read Fallon's thesis. She had gotten more than her money's worth with her as a research assistant, so she would make time to help refine the thesis and maybe even pull a couple of strings to get the thing published in a journal somewhere.

"So, I think that's it," Fallon said, looking up. She was sitting at Lorna's desk in her home office because in addition to reviewing the reference document, she had just gotten through showing Lorna on her laptop how to access the cloud drive.

"Wonderful. Thank you, Fallon. And the books?"

"Oh! In my car. I boxed them up for you. I'll just go get them."

Just as the girl sprang from her seat in front of the computer, Lorna's cellphone, sitting next to the laptop buzzed. They both glanced at it.

Malcolm. Again. He had been calling on and off since Lorna left him that morning, and she hadn't answered any of his calls.

Fallon, noticing the name on the console, looked quickly away and offered Lorna a brief smile.

"I'll just ..."

She left the room and Lorna looked down at her phone when it offered one last chime. Malcolm had left her a message.

Instead of listening to it, Lorna picked it up to turn it off altogether when there was more ringing, though this time from her house phone.

Grabbing it from the cradle, she answered without considering that maybe Malcolm was trying her landline instead. It wasn't Malcolm.

"Hey. I'm shocked to get you."

"Hello ..." Lorna's brow furrowed as she tried to place the voice.

"It's Todd," the caller said. "Todd Williamson?"

Still, she couldn't quite ...

"Oh, Todd! Hello." Mr. Almost-Thirty. *How in the heck had he gotten her home number?* "How are you?"

"I'm great. It's been a killer trying to get in touch with you. I guess your summers are as busy as the semester can be."

"Yes, sometimes," Lorna said vaguely. "So ..."

"I wondered whether we could meet. I wanted to talk to you about something and I thought it might be best to do it in person."

Wrinkling her brow again, Lorna tried to think of what he could possibly need to talk to her about. They met at a conference, and she had ill-advisedly slept with him thinking he was someone she would never see again. And that was about the extent of it as far as she was concerned. But now he was at Gilchrist. The last thing in the world she needed was for him to think was that she had any intention of being anything to him other than a cordial acquaintance.

"Well, the thing of it, Todd, is that I'm busy preparing to go out of town ..." She would think later about how to avoid Todd now that she wasn't *actually* going out of town.

"So maybe I could stop by there," he said quickly. "Just for a few minutes. I promise I won't take too much of your time."

"Well ..."

"Just for a few minutes. I promise."

Taking a deep breath and silently releasing it, Lorna tried to take a measured tone. "Sure. If you're certain it won't take too long ..."

"It won't. How about around seven this evening or so?"

"Seven. Yes. That should be fine."

She had just hung up and was vaguely wondering how Todd even knew where she lived when Fallon returned bearing a banker's box, filled with books. She placed them near the door to Lorna's office and stood upright again, looking expectant as though awaiting further instructions about what to do.

"Thank you, Fallon," Lorna said for the hundredth time that morning. "I think that's it. You go ahead and enjoy the rest of your Saturday. There's the Alumni Parade and other Reunion Weekend activities that I'm sure you'll want to take part in."

"Not really." Fallon shrugged. "I've been to a few Reunion Weekends."

"Oh. Really? You're a legacy student then."

"Yeah, my mother went here. I've been wearing Gilchrist t-shirts since I was a baby, pretty much." Fallon leaned back against the doorframe and Lorna swung around in her office chair to face her fully. "She drilled it into me that when I went to college, this was where I would be."

"So being at Gilchrist isn't exactly your choice?"

Fallon shrugged again. "It isn't as though I had any better ideas and it is a great school, so ..."

"And how about your course of study? Is that your choice? Or ..."

"Oh, for sure!" At that, Fallon's eyes brightened. "That worked out at least. This is a great place for Women's Studies. Thanks to you, of course ..." She paused and blushed.

"And many others who came before me," Lorna said

nodding. "So you're serious about this? A career in this field, and in academia?"

"Yes, very serious."

"I haven't yet read your thesis ..."

"Oh."

"But I intend to," Lorna said hastily. "In the next week as a matter of fact. So then we can get down to it, you and I. Figuring out how to get you published, perhaps."

"Professor Terry ..." Fallon seemed at a loss for words. "That would be ... I couldn't even begin to thank you, if that were to happen."

"So let's work toward it."

Fallon nodded. "I will. For sure. And ..." she started to say something then stopped.

Lorna smiled. "What is it?"

"I wondered, if it's not too presumptuous ... The research you're having me do? It's kind of ... interesting. And ..."

"Unconventional?" Lorna supplied.

"Yeah, exactly. There are lots of articles about female pop stars, and they're the ones no one would think of as feminist necessarily."

"Yes, that's correct. I'm working on a book proposal," Lorna explained. "More or less, it's about how traditional feminism might have created a somewhat constricting view of what is normative for feminists—rejection of overt femininity being the one most people think of; but beyond that, how use of sexuality as a core source of power is frowned upon by so-called *real* feminists. But now I'm interested in challenging that, using as case examples some of our current pop icons who embrace the label 'feminist' but refuse to adopt its norms."

The girl's eyes lit up with excitement, and something that Lorna had grown accustomed to seeing from her students—

awe. It never ceased to amaze her how excited some of them got at ideas. Just *ideas*.

In the undergrad world, students like that were few and far between. Most were interested in one thing—getting enough credits to graduate, and if they had plans for another degree, they wanted the grades that would get them into their first choice among graduate programs. Those pursuits sometimes made it difficult for the simple appreciation of new and provocative information.

But then there were students like Fallon Wright, who grew visibly animated when someone lit a spark of an idea that they had never had—nor heard—before. Those students were the ones Lorna enjoyed most, and there was no point pretending that she didn't also enjoy their admiration.

"Now it makes sense. All the stuff about ..."

"Yes. So I've had to look at some non-traditional sources, pop-culture magazines ... I've even started watching *Entertainment Tonight*."

Fallon laughed. "Oh my god, it's going to be amazing."

"It's just a book proposal at this point," Lorna demurred. "So we'll see how amazing it is, or isn't. Or if it ever is anything at all other than a bright bulb that came to me in the middle of the night."

"Maybe you could ..." Fallon cut herself off once again.

"Fallon, please. If there's one thing I'd hope you would learn from me it would be to be bold about expressing your ideas. Even the ones you believe might be stupid sound considerably less so if delivered with confidence."

Fallon smiled. "Okay, well ... So I was thinking that if you want to do something on contemporary pop stars, isn't it just as important to find out why contemporary women might accept them as feminists? So ... I mean, it's one thing to figure out why a certain popstar thinks of herself as a feminist, but even more importantly don't you want to know why modern women *accept* her as such?"

Lorna thought for a moment and then smiled. "You're absolutely right. After all, who knows why she adopted that label? A publicity stunt maybe? It is interesting though that most people seem not to have challenged it too much, despite ..."

"No, but some *do* challenge it," Fallon said, sounding considerably more confident now. "But those voices aren't nearly as persuasive as the ones who accept and defend her, so ..."

"They're just fans, maybe," Lorna suggested. "Who would accept whatever she says."

"Or, they're explicitly rejecting what you call 'the constricting normative view' of feminism. That's a genius phrase by the way."

Lorna laughed. "Thank you. And ... again, thank you for this." She patted the pages on her desk. "But I really should get some work done. And let you enjoy the rest of your Saturday."

"Of course." Fallon pushed away from the doorframe. "Have a great rest of your weekend. And a great trip."

"Yes. And I have your cell, and you have mine, if anything should come up. I've given Inez instructions to give you access to my office while I'm gone."

Why was she still pretending to people she was going anywhere? At this rate she would have to hide out in her house for two weeks to maintain the charade.

"Okay. Safe travels."

Once Fallon was gone, Lorna turned to her desk and picked up her cellphone, considering whether to listen to Malcolm's message. It wasn't likely he had anything momentous to say, and she didn't need to hear his voice right now. All it would do was weaken her further, and remind her of how weak for him she had already become.

LORNA HAD COMPLETELY FORGOTTEN about Todd Williamson.

Until he was standing at the threshold to her front door, it had slipped her mind entirely that she told him seven o'clock would be a good time for him to stop by. The afternoon had rushed by in a flurry of cleaning—which she did when she wanted to play around with ideas in her head—and writing. There was nothing coherent that could be considered a book chapter yet, but she had what she believed to be a solid over-view and outline, and a few bits and pieces that could probably later be cobbled together for the introduction.

All day, her phone had chimed on and off, her house phone ringing at least twice, and though she formed the intention to stop working and check messages, she hadn't. And now, it was dusk, the light softening and the shadows lengthening. She planned to work herself into exhaustion. And then the doorbell rang.

Answering the door, Lorna found herself facing Todd Williamson who, just as had happened with his voice, seemed like a total stranger for a few moments. But finally her brain churned into gear and she placed his pleasant, crooked smile, curly, sandy brown hair and semi-tousled style of dressing.

In her academic career she had met a total of one Black man with any interest in Women's Studies and feminism. The men were all mostly like Todd—mild-mannered and somewhat self-effacing younger, White men who were raised with mothers who admired Gloria Steinem and raised their sons to reject gender norms.

"Todd!" she said, stepping aside. "Come in."

"You look like I caught you in the middle of something," he said, entering the house.

"Yes. I was writing," she said, hoping that the confession would cause him to state his business and be shortly on his way.

Todd had a slow, ambling kind of walk, like someone taking a Sunday morning stroll. It made him look like a slacker.

Lorna remembered thinking he was cute when they first met. Not handsome, not sexy, just cute. Like something one might pat on the head. How she had gotten drunk enough and foolish enough to actually sleep with him she could not for the life of her understand. Now, he looked so completely ... unremarkable.

"Can I offer you anything?" she asked. "I'm guessing you were over at the college for some of the parade and all the rest of it?"

"Yes. Stopped by. There was someone from the Class of 1939. It was weird. She was the only one, and had to be pushed in a wheelchair, waving her class flag."

"Wow. That would make her well into her nineties, wouldn't it?" Lorna asked, trying to sound interested and amazed.

"Something like that, yes. And yes, if you have some cool water that would be great."

"I'll get it for you. Make yourself comfortable."

She left Todd in her living room looking at the African masks on her wall, and scanning the books on her shelves. Already, she regretted telling him he could come over. He hadn't yet said why he was there and it was beginning to feel like she had invited a ... fan into her home, rather than a student or colleague. And the truth was, but for them having had a one-night stand, Todd was a complete stranger, and more like a random admirer than either a student or colleague.

Lorna poured him a glass of water from her Brita pitcher and brought it back into the living room, handing it to him, and standing nearby rather than sitting. Sitting would make him think they had time for a longer conversation, and to shoot the breeze. She definitely didn't want to do either.

"So, Todd," she began. "What's on your mind?"

He took two sips of water and then turned to look directly at her. He cleared his throat before speaking. "I think I get it now," he said.

"Get what?"

"When we met in New York," he continued. "That night? I mentioned that I was thinking of Gilchrist for a place to continue my Masters coursework. I told you I'm studying Beowulf?"

Lorna nodded though she didn't recall any of that. *He was studying an Old English poem for his Masters?* Now she was even more confused about how they had wound up in bed together. What an effete course of study.

"And you said it was a great place, that you enjoyed it here. And that ... you would be happy to introduce me to people, that sort of thing."

"Oh." *Time to come clean.* "Todd, of course I'm happy to do all those things. I just, I honestly didn't remember. I'd had a little too much to drink the night we met, was a little rattled by that session I was in, and ... anyway, I'm sorry if I created some expectation that ..."

"No, no. That's not what I'm saying," he said quickly. "It wasn't that you created the expectation. I actually know a few people here through my family. It was that I just ..." He shrugged. "I *hoped* we would reconnect."

Lorna let that hang there. She could address neither his expectations nor his hopes. But she had a sinking feeling she knew what was coming next.

"So I just wanted to be upfront about that. So you wouldn't think I was, I don't know, stalking you with all those messages and everything."

She had been ignoring his messages as a matter of course for so long now, she had no idea how many there might be, or whether the sum qualified as "all those messages". Now she was beginning to wonder. And maybe even worry a little bit.

"You said you were going away for a while, but I just wanted to stop by and state my intentions. I'd like to take you to lunch, or coffee, or ..."

Lorna's shoulders sagged, and she sighed. "Todd." She reached out and briefly touched his arm, shaking her head. "I don't think that would be a good idea. Now that you're a student here. And also ..."

"Professor Mitchell?" Todd asked.

Lorna nodded. Putting aside for the moment that she had no idea what she was going to do with or about Malcolm T. Mitchell, he definitely had his uses right now.

"But we can certainly be friends, Todd." *Distant friends.* Wave at each other from across the Quad friends. "I hope that'll be enough."

"I guess it has to be enough," he said with a brief laugh. "And let's face it. This was a shot in the dark, wasn't it?"

"Todd. You're so much ..."

"Younger than you?" he asked, intuiting what she had been about to say. "Yeah. But I was hoping you didn't care about that. Since, you know ..."

At that, Lorna let her hand drop. "Yes. I know. New York. That was bad judgment on my part."

Todd's face fell.

"I enjoyed our time together," she amended quickly. "But it wasn't the best idea given what you've just said. The age ..."

It was a poor excuse, and what's more, it wasn't even completely true. But before she could complete her sentence, her doorbell rang once again.

Turning toward the door right away, Lorna felt only relief

at being rescued. She didn't even stop to think about who it might be, or why they were there. She only barreled toward the door like it was the lifeline rescuing her from a sinking ship.

Swinging it open, she was still relieved, but that relief only evaporated when she saw that on the other side of the door was Malcolm T. Mitchell.

SIXTEEN
UNDERSTANDING

"I've been calling you all day. Thought you might be hungry."

Malcolm held up the bags from the Greek restaurant that Lorna had turned him on to a couple weeks earlier, and only registered that she wasn't alone when she glanced over her shoulder and toward the living room.

Standing there, a glass in hand, looking inquisitively toward the front door was the grad student. The one whose name Malcolm had forgotten, but who—and *this* part he remembered quite well—Lorna had admitted having slept with once. Or, *was* it just once?

"I've been working." Lorna stepped aside to admit him. She reached up to play with the curl at the nape her neck. "Todd just stopped by for a ... Anyway, he was just leaving, so ..."

"Oh." Todd grinned a little sheepishly. "Yes. I just ... well ..."

He stepped forward and handed Lorna the glass, then taking another two steps, extended a hand.

Malcolm hesitated a moment before taking it.

"Good to see you again, Professor Mitchell."

Malcolm nodded but did not speak, still trying to read the mood in the room, and figure out what he might have walked in on. His gut told him it was probably nothing. But the side of him that had laid his claim to Lorna Terry still didn't like it that Todd was there at all, no matter how innocent the reason.

"I'll go put this in the kitchen," he said. "Good to see you again as well, Todd."

When he left the room, he heard bits and pieces of Lorna sending Todd off, thanking him for stopping by, telling him that he "shouldn't worry about the other thing" and that she was "glad to have it all cleared up." And Todd, sounding a little embarrassed as he said his goodbyes. Then there was only silence from the next room and moments later, Lorna joined him in the kitchen.

"God. Today must be the day for awkward encounters or something, huh?" she said. "What'd you get? I'm starving."

Hand resting on his back, she peered around him at the containers he was removing from the plastic sacks on the counter. He wanted *not* to want to ask her what the grad student had been doing there. Especially since they'd done this very same dance just hours earlier with the Charlotte episode. But then, he told her she was entitled to ask the question, so it only stood to reason that he could as well.

"What the fuck was he doing here?"

He didn't mean for it to come out *quite* like that.

The hand on his back fell. He turned to look at her, arms folded.

"*Malcolm.*" Lorna both sounded and looked surprised at his tone.

He shrugged. "I asked you a question."

"It's not that you asked the question," she said slowly. Then she seemed to reconsider. "It's not *just* that you asked the question. It's also how you asked it."

"Who gives a shit how I asked it?"

"I give a shit. Especially since you're not even asking, you're *demanding*. And you know I don't do demands."

"At least I have the emotional honesty to let you know that when I show up at my woman's house and see another man there, I want to know why. Particularly when you've been unreachable all damn day, and ..."

"I told you this morning that I had a lot to do."

"Not so much that you can't entertain guests though."

"Unplanned, random guests."

"No, not random, Lorna. Someone you were involved with."

"Involved with." She made a scoffing sound. "He was just a ... a ... *thing*. Hardly even worth mentioning. And in fact, I didn't mention it. It was something you ferreted out, from reading my body language or whatever the hell it was you said you did outside the church that day."

She tried to turn away but Malcolm grabbed her arm.

"So why was he here?"

Lorna shook her head, her expression incredulous. "I'm having a hard time believing we're even having this conversation. Are you seriously threatened by ... *Todd?*"

No. He wasn't. Not really. But this woman, this maddening, confounding woman ... who the hell knew what was going through her head at any given time? She had been upset about Charlotte being there this morning, he was sure of that. And then they have a perfectly pleasant breakfast together and she leaves, only to ignore his calls all day.

"Are you thinking that Todd could be, what? Like a *revenge-fuck* because of your ex-wife being over this morning?

Some childish tit-for-tat ..." Closing her eyes, she shook her head slowly from side to side. "If you think something like that, then you don't know me at all."

Running a hand over his face, Malcolm took a deep breath. "I don't think that," he said finally.

"Then ..."

"It's just ..." He searched for the right words. "You always feel like any moment you're going to just ... slip away."

Looking directly into her dark, brooding eyes, Malcolm saw something there he couldn't identify. She touched him and took two steps closer. Then she did something so tender, so unlike her, Malcolm literally held his breath. She pressed her cheek against the center of his chest, wrapping her arms around his waist. Malcolm felt her shoulders heave.

"I'm not slipping away," she said, quietly.

THEY TOOK the food out to the living room and ate there, and Lorna talked about her book proposal and the ideas that had been coming to her all day; coming so fast, she said, that she almost couldn't type them all. She sounded excited, and energized, and Malcolm was glad she was having this conversation with him and not with someone else. Although to hear her tell it, there weren't too many 'someone-elses' that she would talk to like this.

"You never mentioned how things went with Riley," he said, reminded of her as he was thinking of Lorna's few confidantes. "Now that she's had time to process what you told her about her father."

Lorna paused with a piece of a pita midair. "I never did, did I? That's why I stopped by this morning."

"Yeah, but after Charlotte left, you still didn't tell me."

She shrugged and took a bite of the bread.

"So what happened?"

"We talked almost until dawn," Lorna said, speaking as she chewed. "About you at first. She was very impressed by you, asked if we were ... serious. Whatever that means."

"What did you tell her?" Malcolm grinned.

"That you're ... not inconsequential."

At that he laughed aloud. "I bet you *did* say that, didn't you?" He shook his head. "But I'm guessing she's probably used to your little avoidance techniques by now."

"Anyway, she liked you very much."

"And?"

"And what else? She liked you. That's all."

"I meant what about the conversation about her father?"

Lorna put down the bread and brushed her palms clean.

"That conversation wasn't as easy," she said wryly. "She's all the things you'd imagine she would be—angry, hurt, confused ... conflicted."

"Is she going to try to find him?"

Lorna looked up. "She already has. Turns out he's been under our noses all along."

Leaning in, Malcolm put down his fork. "Have they ...?"

"No, she hasn't reached out. But she knows where he is. Apparently in Connecticut. Not too far away. And he's married, but she doesn't know yet if he has kids. That he might ... that's why she hasn't done anything with the information yet. She's worried about his other kids. If he has them. She ..." Lorna's voice faltered a little. "She doesn't want to do anything to hurt them."

Sitting back, Malcolm waited for her to continue.

"I could tell she's angrier at me than she even knows how to express," Lorna said. "She's not used to being that angry. I'm not even sure if she knows the extent of her own ... rage about this."

"What makes you so sure she has it? Maybe you're projecting."

"No." Lorna shook her head. "She was different with me. Not the entire time, but here and there ... just a little more standoffish, a little more guarded."

"But that's probably to be expected."

"Yeah." She stared off into space, her eyes unfocused.

"Hey," Malcolm said.

She looked at him, her eyes, still slightly dreamy in expression.

"I'm sorry that this morning when you came by to talk I wasn't ... available right away. I'm sorry that Charlotte was there."

Lorna shrugged. "She's the mother of your children. She'll always be there in one way or another, won't she?"

Malcolm shook his head. "Not like that, no. And never again when you need me."

Lorna looked up, a little smile on her face. "Who said I *needed* you?"

"You did. Just by showing up."

She smiled again, but didn't deny it. Instead she stood and extended a hand.

"Come," she said.

———

"*THERE ... RIGHT THERE ... THERE.*"

It seemed to go on forever, but Lorna didn't want him to stop the slow grind as he pressed into her, leaving not even a fraction of an inch between them. She heard Malcolm's slow, rhythmic breaths in her ear, felt them stirring the damp hair at her nape. His arms were beneath her, cradling her torso, his hands gripping her shoulders from the rear. His body seemed to have melted into hers, one indistinguishable from the other. She felt him inside her, around her, on her. She smelled and tasted him, heard and felt him. There was nothing else.

Sex, fucking, lovemaking ... for her it had always been the same—pleasurable, but mindless. If a man aroused her body, she disappeared from the thinking realm and was only a bundle of nerve endings and pleasure centers. He could be anyone.

But not with Malcolm.

Malcolm was thought and feeling all at once. She heard *his* voice, tasted *his* tongue, smelled *his* scent and felt the indescribably delicious sensation of *his* dick, deep within, stroking, thrusting, slipping, sliding, and pulsing. He wasn't just any man. It was Malcolm who made her feel these things.

Lorna tried to shut off all thought when he was inside her, but it was impossible. All of it was mixed up, together and inseparable—his patience, his humor, his intellect, his hands on her ass, his mouth on her breasts, his hand between her legs; his talent, his graciousness, his tongue on her clit, his lips pressed against her ear. She couldn't parse any of it. She wanted it all. And she wanted it all the time.

HE WAS GONE when Lorna opened her eyes again. The sun outside was bright and high in the sky, and she was alone.

Turning over in bed, she tried to get back to sleep but could not, so instead she got up and took a shower. Her entire body ached in places she didn't know could ache, and she groaned at the wonderful feeling of the hot water pelting her back, chest and legs.

Afterwards she made herself coffee and sat in her kitchen, watching the numbers change on the clock above the stove. For almost an hour she sat, her mind flooded with memories.

Of Earl. Malcolm reminded her of him. Not because the two men were anything alike, but because Earl had been the only other man who had moved her. Not even Riley's father had managed to move her in the way Earl had. She wasn't yet thirty when she first met him, and he was with her until she was thirty-four. They met at some random party at the house of people whose names Lorna had long forgotten.

He was the proverbial tall, dark-as-night and handsome man, and had eyes as black as coal. He told her he worked for the Metro North transit system, so Lorna assumed from his physique that he meant he worked on the tracks; something physical in any event. But Earl was a civil engineer and though he spent a good amount of time on sites, he mostly worked in an office and with paper and documents, just like her.

When, after their first night together he'd cleared up that misunderstanding, he laughed at her and her preconception—that a man who looked like him had to be a construction worker, or laborer of some sort. That was how Earl was—he laughed at her and at himself constantly. He taught her, the newly radicalized feminist, not to take herself so seriously. Lorna had loved him. Deeply, and for a long time. Even after he left her.

Getting up from the kitchen table, Lorna finally made her way into her home office where she worked without pause until well into the afternoon. The only interruptions were her thirst and her bladder, and then around four p.m., her hunger. She made a sandwich and threw out the remaining bread because it would be stale when she returned from her trip.

Somewhere in the middle of the lovemaking, she had decided that she would go after all. Eating alone at her desk while drinking coffee, she realized that she was lonely. Not just for any companionship, but for Malcolm.

He hadn't called and she had a feeling he would not.

At seven-thirty, when it was time to walk through the house and turn on lights, and to think about locking doors, she got up and did so. And then she called Riley. She could hear Cassidy in the background, making little mewling noises.

"That sounds like a happy baby," Lorna observed.

"She is. For the moment. I'm nursing." And then a pause. "You breastfed me, didn't you?"

Lorna held her breath. There had been many questions like this since Cassidy, more so than when she had Cullen. With Cullen, Riley had been too immersed in the wonder and newness of the experience of motherhood to subject it to examination. She and Shawn had walked around for months just bewildered with joy.

But with Cassidy, she had begun to want to know the answers to questions that all boiled down to three things: *did you love me like I love my children? Were you happy when I was born? Did you nurture me, or was I just an annoyance?*

"I did. For a little while. Not as long as you breastfed Cullen." But that was an outright untruth. Lorna tried breastfeeding for all of one week before giving up in frustration.

Riley had breastfed for a year, stopping only once her OB told her she had plateaued as far as the benefits to the baby, and because she suspected Shawn had begun to grow a tiny bit envious of the singular attention that breastfeeding conferred on Cullen.

"So ... all packed and ready to go to North Carolina?" Riley asked in an abrupt change of subject.

"No. Not yet."

"You're leaving in the morning, aren't you?"

"Yes," she said quietly.

She thought about Malcolm's silence all day. His frustration with her the evening before. As far as she knew she was leaving in the morning. It was probably only fair that she get a taste of the uncertainty he complained about. She wasn't sure now that he would show, and it was uncomfortable thinking that he might not.

"*Aren't you?*"

"Yes, Riley. I'm leaving in the morning."

"Oh. For some reason I thought you might make up a reason not to go."

This child. She knew her too well. "Why would you think ...?"

"Because I realize what it is now. Remember when we were talking about the men you were involved with? How they're often younger?"

"How could I forget?" Lorna asked dryly.

"Well I figured out why. It's because you didn't want men who would challenge you. They were all self-fulfilling prophesies—men who couldn't measure up. And if they were younger, less experienced, less accomplished than you, it was easier to ensure that. Made it easier to drop them, too, probably. Not as ..."

"I don't feel like being psychoanalyzed tonight, Riley. Honestly."

"Okay, fine. But the point I'm making is that though he's younger, Malcolm Mitchell is definitely not like those men. He's an adult. I think he could be good for you."

"Why?" Lorna asked. "Because he's written a critically-acclaimed book? That's hardly ..."

"No. Because I don't see him taking any of your *shit*, that's why."

"Stop cursing in front of my grandchild," Lorna said for want of something better to say.

On the other end of the line, Riley was laughing and after a moment Lorna joined in.

"He's taken a lot of my shit already, I think. Maybe too much," she confessed when they had both calmed down.

Riley said nothing for a few long moments, then took a breath. "You need to let yourself be happy."

"What makes you think I'm not happy? Have I ever ..."

"*With* someone. You need to let yourself be happy *with someone*, Lorna. Not just in your work, or in your obviously superior intellect. All of that ... at the end of the day, it's hollow. So what if you're the smartest person in the room always? Does that comfort you?"

It did. For many years, it really did. Lately, she wasn't as sure.

"Go put that baby to bed. Kiss Cullen and Shawn for me."

"Mom ..."

"I'm fine, Riley. I just want to get some more work done before I throw some clothes in a bag and go to sleep. Malcolm plans to get here at five a.m. or some ungodly hour like that. I'll call you from the road."

"Do that. Promise?"

"I promise. Go take care of your family."

"Lorna?"

"Yes."

"I love you, y'know."

"I know. I love you, too."

She spent the rest of the evening packing with the television on as background noise, hoping to distract herself from the fear that Malcolm might not come after all. Wanting him, and wanting to be with him used to come with an undercurrent of resentment, because she didn't *want* to want him. Now, there was no resentment, just wanting.

Lorna must have fallen asleep around midnight, but woke again around two and tidied her bedroom, showered again and dressed for the drive to North Carolina. Then she lay across her just-made bed. Her packed bags, the box of books Fallon had brought her, and her keys were all set out at her front door so she could make a quick exit.

Around four-forty a.m. her eyes opened for no reason that she could identify. And then she heard it, a few quick honks of a car horn. Heart racing, she got up and went to the front room, looking out the window. At the curb, idling in the grey, early morning light, was Malcolm's Range Rover. Lorna felt her shoulders heave in relief.

She brushed her teeth quickly, splashed water on her face and checked once again to make sure all her doors and windows were secure. Grabbing everything she could carry in one trip, she opened the door and headed down the path. She was overburdened and could barely hold it all, and after a moment, the door opened on the driver's side and Malcolm got out. He came around the truck, and met her halfway.

"Here," he said, reaching out to lessen her load. "I've got it."

Inside the truck, he watched as she got settled and snapped her seatbelt into place, but said nothing, even when they pulled away from the curb. They drove for almost fifteen minutes without speaking, passing Gilchrist where there were still traces of the weekend's revelry—odd signs and exuberant banners—'Class of 1984!'—discarded on the side of the road, along with red plastic cups and assorted bits of litter. Lorna's eyelids grew heavier by the second.

"Malcolm?" she said.

Now that he was here, she felt herself being pulled under by exhaustion once again. Waking up and falling asleep on and off had taken a toll, as had the worry that he might not come. And now she felt like she could sleep for hours. But she had one question she wanted to ask.

"Yeah."

"Why did you leave this morning?" she asked. "I woke up and you were gone."

SEVENTEEN

JOURNEY

SHE NEVER NOTICED BEFORE WHEN HE LEFT.

This time though, she sounded almost vulnerable. Not a word, or emotion that he was used to associating with her. For Malcolm it was like being in a deep, dark hole and finally, when he had almost given up hope, spotting a sliver of light.

Turning to look at her, he was planning to be careful not to betray how Lorna's words affected him. But it didn't matter because within moments after speaking the question, she had fallen asleep.

He almost felt like waking her up and demanding she explain herself because *what the fuck was that?* Since when had she ever cared that he left while she was asleep? Just when he started to adjust his behavior thinking he was playing by her rules, she was starting to come around to his?

Running a hand over his face Malcolm made a sound of impatience. Next to him, Lorna didn't even stir.

He left because he decided to give her some space; *that* was why he left. He left because after they made love and she drifted off to sleep, he was awake. Wide awake and lying in her bed, he replayed over and over in his mind her reaction to his outburst when he asked her about the grad student being there. And then he felt like an insecure asshole. And what about when he bitched-out and spouted that crap about her slipping away? Lorna Terry, if he let her, would have his balls in a vise.

Between Charlotte being at his house when Lorna dropped in, and then her inexplicable silence while he tried to get her on the phone, Malcolm had panicked, plain and simple. So he'd gone to grab them some dinner and simply stopped by. Finding that she had company—male company—had thrown him, and then it was off to the races after that.

This woman had him acting like he was seventeen again and his girlfriend had paid too much attention to some other guy during prom; doing the kind of dumb shit he had stopped doing around the time he was in his twenties. Dumb shit like changing his behavior based on some anticipated response from a woman he didn't understand, but wanted nevertheless.

He'd woken up and dressed, leaving Lorna in bed because he thought he was crowding her. After the concessions she made about labeling what they had a "relationship", coming to North Carolina and accepting his explanation about Charlotte, he felt like he owed her something she seemed to want—space. So to find out she *didn't* want it, and in fact wanted him there when she woke up was beyond frustrating. She was making him as crazy as she was.

Malcolm laughed out loud.

Again, Lorna did not react, too deeply asleep now to register anything at all, her head lolling back against the head-rest. By her own admission, she didn't have relationships like the one they were beginning to build. So why the hell would he even consider following *her* lead?

Lorna turned in her seat and made a slight moaning noise. Her wavy hair was loose, and fell to one side, partly obscuring her face. Her lips, bracketed by laugh lines, were full and a natural dusty rose color. They parted, as though she was about to bestow a kiss. Malcolm's chest filled with a rush of possessiveness, and he stared at her for a few seconds before reminding himself to turn away and pay attention to the road.

"Enough of this bullshit," he mumbled to himself.

From now on, they were doing things his way.

"LOT LIZARDS."

Until he heard her voice, Malcolm didn't even know Lorna was awake. He had just pulled into one of the larger rest areas on the New Jersey Turnpike, thinking it was good a time as any to grab breakfast and awaken Lorna to use the restroom so they could push on through to Pennsylvania before stopping again. But it appeared the cessation of motion had woken her up before he had a chance to.

"What?" he asked, thinking he had misheard her, or that she was speaking aloud the remnants of a dream she'd had.

"Lot lizards." She pointed across the massive parking lot to where the big rigs were parked, and truckers on cross-country trips had pulled in to sleep or fuel up. "There."

Malcolm followed the direction she was pointing in and shrugged.

"Those women. See them?"

Among the trucks, a few women milled and wandered, some of them looking like they were waiting for rides.

"That's what they call them. They're being prostituted."

'Being prostituted'. She didn't say they were prostituting *themselves*, nor that they were 'prostitutes', but chose words that recognized the women's victimization.

Looking once again, Malcolm noticed that many of them

were wearing shorts and mini-skirts, tank tops and close-fitting dresses. The weather was warm enough, so at first glance, there was nothing unusual about their attire. A few were also in clunky high heels and wedges, but by no means did they look even marginally sexually-enticing. If anything, they looked like hitchhikers, or migrants.

"All the way out here?" he asked.

There was nothing but highway for miles around.

Lorna nodded. She had turned in her seat a little but her cheek was still resting on the headrest, her eyes still a little bleary from sleep.

"The first published article I ever did was about these women. Or at least some of them are women. I've been in places where some are as young as fourteen. Girls who're trafficked, runaways who get exploited. And it happens right here in plain view."

Malcolm looked yet again, his eyes following one woman who was swaying back and forth, standing in place, occasionally becoming more alert when a man walked by. She said something to one of them. He ignored her and kept walking. She lit a cigarette and ran a hand through her hair.

"The pimp is somewhere around," Lorna said. "Sitting in one of these cars. Watching them, waiting until they get a customer. And afterwards, they'll walk over to the car and give him the money. They could be out here up to twelve hours at a time."

"That's terrible. I never heard of ..."

"Probably because these women and girls are lower on the rung than even street prostitutes in the city. They're practically sub-human as far as society and even the police are concerned. Hence the name ... lizards, creatures that crawl on their bellies."

Her voice was subdued as she spoke, and Malcolm could tell she was reminiscing about something. Or someone.

"What made you decide to write about them?" he asked on a hunch.

At that, Lorna turned and focused on him, a vaguely haunted look still in her eyes.

"When I was seventeen, I took a bus ride from South Florida to New York City. And, early in the morning, the bus driver stopped at a rest stop so everyone could freshen up, have a meal or whatever. I sat in the diner alone and this girl my age came and sat in the booth with me. Asked if I could buy her breakfast, or a sandwich or something. And she was looking around, kind of fidgety ...

"And I said I could spare a couple dollars but she didn't want the money, she wanted food. Mine was already on the table and she asked if she could just have that. It was half-eaten ..." Lorna paused and took a breath, running a hand over her face. "I couldn't understand why she would want that ... food some stranger had already picked over. But I let her have it. She ate it like she hadn't had a meal in ages. And then she calmed down a little once it was done. I asked where she was headed and she seemed confused, and said she wasn't headed anywhere. She was waiting on her daddy."

It was a few moments before Lorna was able to continue. And when she did, her voice was even quieter. Malcolm had to lean in closer to hear her properly.

"I thought she meant her 'father'," Lorna said laughing mirthlessly. "Then a car pulled up outside and she just got frantic, I mean, she was *scared*. She gets up, runs outside and a man gets out of the car. He drags her by the arm and I think he's going to put her in the car. But he doesn't. He drags her halfway across the parking lot over to where the trucks are parked and shoves her. And she was just sort of ... standing there, waiting or something. And I realized, she didn't want to wait for food to come out because she knew her "daddy" was coming soon and that if he did, he wouldn't let her eat it.

"When I got back on the bus and it was pulling off, I saw her get into one of the rigs with some other guy. And that's when I figured out what was going on." Lorna shrugged. "I wasn't a sheltered kid by any means, but I just ... the sight of her out there, being dragged and shoved by one man, and then being ... bought by another. That girl, she could have been me, Malcolm. Could so easily have been me."

When she finished, Lorna looked at him and gave a little shrug.

There were a million questions he wanted to ask: for starters, why she would be taking a bus on her own from South Florida all the way to New York before she was even eighteen. But the revelation came only because she was talking about something else, someone else other than herself. And if he pushed, she might clam up on him. But no matter. He had time. They had time—and thanks to this trip, they would also have the space—to really get to know each other.

So Malcolm let it go and instead reached out and touched her cheek.

"What d'you say we go get something to eat?"

Lorna nodded.

Inside, there was a food court, teeming with activity. Without discussing it, they both seemed to have decided to get back on the road as quickly as possible, so after they went to the restrooms, and picked up breakfast sandwiches and coffee, they headed directly back to the car. All that talk of prostitutes and the selective blindness of everyone around them had put a damper on Lorna's mood, but Malcolm was glad that at least she was awake and he would have her company for the next few hours of the ride.

"So when is Piper coming?" Lorna's voice broke the silence.

"Not sure. I figure we'll want to have a little while just the two of us. So maybe the second week."

"How long are you staying?"

"I hope four weeks."

Then there was silence again.

"Was that you making conversation?" he asked, amused. It was one of the first times within memory that Lorna seemed not to know what to say to him.

"Yes. And you're making it excruciating, just so you know."

Malcolm laughed. "I don't mean to. I'm just still trying to get used to the idea that you actually came with me."

"Pinch yourself," she suggested, her trademark sarcasm finally making a reappearance. "The dream is real."

He looked at her and they both smiled. Then, to his surprise, Lorna's hand crept across the distance between them and rested on his thigh.

"Want to stop in Philly?" he asked.

"Is it out of the way?"

"Little bit. But we're not on anyone's timetable, so we could hit a couple galleries, spend the night, have a nice dinner, maybe?"

Lorna made a noncommittal sound. "Whatever you want is fine. I like Philly."

"Whatever I want?" He glanced at her. "Since when have you been so easygoing about letting me decide for both of us?"

"I pick my battles," Lorna said, a smile in her voice.

THROUGH THE WONDER of modern technology, they managed to find a last-minute hotel room in Center City, checked in and considered what to do with the rest of the morning. Finally deciding on the Philadelphia Museum of Art, they walked instead of taking a cab, ambling along and pausing to look in store windows or at whatever caught their eye. Somewhere around Chestnut Street, Malcolm pulled Lorna out of the path of a runner, with his arm over her shoulder, and it remained there for a few minutes, until he let it fall, instead taking hold of her hand. She returned his firm grip with her own, and so they walked that way, hand in hand until they were at their destination.

Wordlessly, they moved through the Thomas Eakins Collection, perusing pieces of art that they had both probably seen many times before. But Malcolm found himself watching Lorna out of the corner of his eye, gauging her reaction to each one, but reluctant to break the comfortable silence.

In the hotel room, before venturing out, she had hastily changed into a pair of white sneakers, put on a cardigan over her plain white t-shirt, and pulled her hair up into a ponytail. Dressed that way, she looked fifteen years younger than her age. Malcolm liked that there was nowhere for her to go, nothing for her to do other than be with him.

After about an hour of walking around looking at paintings, he detected a pattern. When she liked something, she at first grew very still and stared, barely even blinking; and then her hand would go up to her neck while she played with that errant curl that was almost always hanging free.

Once, she caught him looking at her while she studied a large oil portrait, of a young woman with dusky skin, and dark, silky hair.

"Italian, you think?" she asked. They were the first words she had spoken in a long while. "Or a little African blood in there muddying up the bloodline?" she added with a hint of teasing. Stepping closer to read the plaque, she turned to look at him, and shrugged. "An actress, Suzanne Santje."

"Sometimes I like it better not reading the plaques," he said. "Preserves a little mystery."

"*You* like mysteries?"

"Why so surprised?"

"Because we had barely met before you were trying to pry loose a million intimate details about my life."

"Where you grew up and how you grew up doesn't really qualify as 'intimate' in my book."

"That's because you have no idea how horrific childhood can be."

He looked at her, for a moment at a loss for what to say until she touched his arm.

"Not mine, silly. There were some rough patches in mine for sure, but I wasn't referring to *my* childhood as horrific. Just saying that in general, maybe you should consider that some people's stories are a little grittier than others'. And maybe not something they'd easily share."

"Fair enough," he acknowledged. "But it wasn't as though we were strangers. And I wasn't asking about those hypothetical 'other people', I was asking about you."

"Okay, so ask ..." Lorna said.

"Why were you on a bus from South Florida at seventeen?"

Lorna blinked. Maybe she'd forgotten that she shared that, because she had been talking about something else entirely at the time.

"I was going to New York for college."

"At seventeen?"

She shrugged. "I'd skipped a grade."

Walking over to a nearby bench, Malcolm sat and waited. Lorna still stood, a few feet away. Finally, she sighed and came to sit next to him. "Any chance I'd get away with leaving it at that?" she asked.

Malcolm shrugged. "I'm through trying to force you to do anything."

At that, Lorna touched his thigh. Whenever she touched him, he felt it almost profoundly. Everything about her had weight and consequence.

"I don't know why I'm making it all such a big deal, honestly," she said quietly. "I just haven't been used to spilling my guts to anyone. And it's been a long time since anyone's asked the kinds of things you ask."

"I find that hard to believe."

Lorna shrugged. "It's true. And of course, few people are as relentless as you, Malcolm."

"I don't know any other way to be."

She smiled. "I like it," she said. "The way you are."

Squeezing his thigh, Lorna leaned in and so quickly he could almost tell himself he'd imagined it, she kissed him on the lips.

"I'm tired of Eakins," she said briskly, getting up from the bench and beginning to walk away. "Let's go. I have an urge to look at something modern."

LATER, though Lorna wanted to eat dinner in the room, Malcolm managed to drag her out to a Korean restaurant that was one of his local favorites by pointing out that they had plenty of time when they got to North Carolina to eat in bed, drink wine and have lazy, half-drunken sex.

Oh, I know, she said flirtatiously over her shoulder as she headed in to take a shower. *But can one really have too much lazy, half-drunken sex?*

So he did the only thing he could do as a red-blooded man in the prime of his life—he followed her into the shower.

They made it to the restaurant around nine, a full hour later than their reservation, but still managed to get a table, which they shared with an elderly couple, the hibachi grill in the center between them.

Lorna had never had authentic Korean before, so Malcolm enjoyed explaining all the side dishes, and then watching her mull over each one. While he explained, he noticed that the couple sitting across from them was listening keenly as well, so after a while, he was making suggestions for their meal and describing items from the menu.

"It's our fortieth anniversary," the woman explained. "Benjamin had the idea that we should do something different."

She was dressed in a powder blue dress and her hair beautifully-coiffed, her husband in a grey suit with a tie matching her dress.

"Wow. Congratulations," Malcolm said, reaching across the table to shake Benjamin's hand. "Happy anniversary to you both."

"It's been an eventful forty years," the woman said smiling at her husband. "I'm Patrice, by the way."

"I'm Malcolm. And this is Lorna."

"Good to meet you both," Lorna said, reaching across to shake hands. "Should we all take the plunge together?" she asked indicating the menu.

Benjamin and Patrice looked at each other for confirmation and then nodded.

"I was in Korea when I was in the Service," Benjamin said. "Thought I remembered all of this, but ..."

"It was a long time ago." Patrice patted his hand. "So why not let these young people help us out of this pickle you've gotten us into?"

"Speaking of pickles," Malcolm said. "You're going to love the kimchi."

They ordered four dishes for the table, and wine to accompany the meal, and the conversation flowed naturally, the older couple enjoying telling stories about their marriage, their children and the different places they had lived. Lorna was a spirited part of the conversation, easily making jokes and exchanging amused glances with Patrice when Malcolm and Benjamin got into good-natured debates about sports, politics and even childrearing. Occasionally, Malcolm felt Lorna's hand on his thigh, resting there lightly, gently squeezing, or moving idly back and forth.

"And how long has it been for you two?" Patrice asked as she helped herself to a third sampling of the dried squid pickle.

Lorna looked at Malcolm and smiled. "Oh, only about five minutes." Her eyes were warm.

"So a new relationship." Patrice's eyebrows lifted. "But you seem so ..."

"Well-suited," Benjamin finished for her.

Malcolm's eyes held Lorna's. "I think we are. *She* still needs some convincing."

Patrice smiled and nodded as though she knew something they didn't. "I'm sure she'll come around."

They made it back to the hotel after midnight, having been among the last to leave the restaurant, and parting with the other couple at the curb with handshakes and hugs.

In the suite, Lorna was quiet and thoughtful, or maybe like him, she was just tired. They changed, washed faces, and brushed teeth in silence, and it was only once they were in bed and the room was dark that Malcolm spoke. He could feel that next to him, Lorna was lying awake as well.

"I just realized, I don't know if you were ever married." he said.

"No. Never was."

"Did you ever want to be?"

"I've been asked. Once."

"And said no."

"Right."

For a while they said nothing. And just as Malcolm made up his mind to let it go, Lorna spoke again.

"His name was Earl. He wanted to be my husband and a father to Riley. And for us to have other babies and live happily ever after. But I messed that up."

"How?"

"I cheated on him. And made sure he found out."

Turning onto his side to face her in the dark, Malcolm moved closer, resting a hand across her stomach.

"Why?"

"I was scared to want it, I guess. I was just coming into my own as a feminist and as a woman. And I was ... scared. That I could so easily want to sell it all out to make babies and be married to a big, strong man who wanted to take care of me."

"You thought of that as selling out?"

Lorna laughed softly. "You know how it is when you're young. I was a black-and-white thinker. So that was it for Earl."

"You sound like you regret it."

"I regret hurting him. And hurting Riley. She loved Earl. And I took him away from her. Just like I did with her biological father. I guess it took me a long time to stop repeating the same mistakes."

"She loved him," Malcolm said carefully. "But did you?"

It took Lorna almost a minute to answer. "Yes."

"How about now?"

"Now? Do I love Earl *now*?"

"No, I mean, would you get married now? Or do you feel the same way about it?"

"I don't know what purpose it would serve now. I'm at a different place in my life."

"What *purpose?*" he asked. "How about you want to commit to spending your life with someone?"

"I can do that without getting the government to certify my intention to do that, Malcolm."

He released a puff of breath and rolled over onto his back once again. "That's such an old hackneyed argument ..."

"It's not an argument, it's a fact. If I made that commitment, I would make it. It wouldn't need a certificate ... And coming off a divorce, I would think you of all people ..."

"I intended to be married for life. Charlotte was the one who had other ideas."

"And do you regret that?" Lorna asked, echoing the question he'd asked her about Earl.

He wanted to say 'yes'. But he couldn't.

After his marriage was over, Malcolm had had to face some hard truths about it. He had loved his wife. But once they split, he had barely even missed her. What he missed was the rhythm of being part of a couple. The rolling over in the middle of the night and knowing there was someone there. The coming home and seeing evidence of another life being lived intertwined with his. But he had missed Charlotte almost not at all.

"Maybe I was married to the wrong woman," he said finally.

"Or maybe you were with the right person for that time in your life. But once it was over, it was over. And maybe being 'married' only made it more difficult for you both to acknowledge it once it was."

"Yeah ... well, we're just going to have to agree to disagree on this one," he said folding his arms behind his head.

"Or we can agree *not* to disagree anymore tonight," Lorna said.

Malcolm closed his eyes, and opened them once again when he felt that Lorna had moved astride his hips. She shrugged her shirt over her head and then reached down, cupping and feeling him.

"Let's not fight," she said, her voice a whisper. She leaned in to kiss him, her lips gentle against his, the tips of her breasts brushing his chest. "Okay? Let's just ... not fight."

Rather than respond in words, Malcolm kissed her back, holding her by the hips and letting her guide him inside her. He wasn't fighting.

Where Lorna Terry was concerned he had surrendered a long, long time ago.

EIGHTEEN

QUIET STORM

LORNA STRETCHED AND TURNED IN THE RUMPLED BED, opening her eyes slowly and smiling at the view, of breakers crashing against the shore, and at the long stretch of unbroken sand and blue water. Malcolm, when he had woken—probably hours ago now—must have opened the French doors that led out to the small balcony overlooking the beach. The beige cotton curtains whipped in the warm, salty breeze making Lorna want only to turn over and sleep for another few hours.

But she couldn't, because elsewhere in the house she could smell coffee being made, and a breakfast that included bacon. And who could stay in bed when there was bacon to be had?

Sitting up, she groaned at the pleasant ache in her muscles.

"*Coffee?*" Malcolm's voice reached her from the kitchen.

"Thank you," she called back.

Moments later he joined her with two mugs in hand, barefoot and shirtless, golden-brown from many hours in the sun.

For the first two days on Bald Head Island, they had done nothing but swim and sleep, eat, drink and make love. Neither of them read, nor did they write.

They just talked—every day for hours, and sometimes at night as well, long after all the lights were off. But the time after sundown was mostly reserved for walks on the beach and long stretches wrapped around each other on the large bed, tangled in the sheets. There was a television set, but they didn't turn it on, though they sometimes listened to music, streamed from their phones into the Bose wireless speaker Malcolm had the foresight to bring along.

Smiling as he handed her the mug, Malcolm's eyes dropped to scan her nakedness. Lorna wasn't at all self-conscious being bare-assed in bright sunlight around him anymore. He had seen it all by now—the slight lip of extra flesh at her waist, the tiny ripples in her thighs, the faint tributaries of stretch marks around her nipples. None of it seemed to dull how much he wanted her.

Cupping her hands around the mug she took her first sip and moaned.

"Perfect," she said. "Thank you. How did you know I was awake?"

"I could feel it," he said sitting next to her.

Funnily enough, she knew what he meant. After a few days of being in each other's company alone, Lorna thought she could detect subtle changes in energy when he was near. Even if he was downstairs, having just come in from a solo walk, she felt him. If he was in the living room on the sofa and woke from a nap, coming to sit with her on the balcony, she knew he was coming long before he arrived.

"We're out of eggs," he said. "And a bunch of other stuff. We should probably go get groceries before Piper gets here tomorrow."

"What time are we going to get her?"

"You're coming with me?"

"Sure. Why not?"

Getting it out of the way was probably for the best, especially since from all Malcolm had told her, Piper was bound to hate her anyway. But Lorna had no fear of difficult tweens; she could use the time to start reading Fallon's thesis, and to begin writing again. These last few days she had been intoxicated, sluggish from sun and sex and large glasses of the mid-priced wine she and Malcolm drank with dinner.

"We'll pick her up at the airport around three o'clock. She's flying alone."

"Okay, so I guess I'll have to wake up long before noon. *That'll* be hard."

"Come join me for breakfast," Malcolm said getting up and heading back toward the kitchen. He briefly tugged on a lock of her hair before he left. "It'll be ready in a few minutes."

Lorna watched him go, taking in the muscles of his back, his firm ass and calves. She had always believed him a handsome man, but now he was more than that.

Now, she thought of him as beautiful.

Now she thought of him as hers.

Finishing up her coffee, she showered, putting on a light-yellow cotton shift, and her swimsuit underneath in case they went swimming later. Most of their afternoons they spent on the beach, or tooling about the island in the little golf cart they had rented. There were no cars on Bald Head Island other than official vehicles, just bikes and golf carts. It was small, quaint and unapologetically White; populated mostly with well-off old Southern families who had scooped up prime real estate along the fourteen miles of beachfront, or further back in the marshes. It was a beautiful, unspoiled and quiet place and Lorna had loved it right away, despite the scarcity of people who looked like her.

The house Malcolm had rented was perfect. A three-bedroom craftsman style cottage painted white and dove-gray, it had an open floor plan that allowed the ocean breeze to pass through the rooms unobstructed, and sat on the sand with stilts to protect it against high-tide. All the bedrooms faced the sea and watching the sun set was a transcendent experience. All the furniture was white or denim, in sturdy fabrics perfect to withstand salty air and the occasional soaking wet swimsuit.

Walking out into the living area, Lorna decided that one day she would consider buying a place like this. Somewhere else though, where the base asking price for a beachfront home wasn't $1.5 million.

Malcolm had set their breakfast out on the large oak kitchen table, poured glasses of juice and portioned out scrambled eggs with the bacon. Just as Lorna sat down, he put toast on her plate.

"You're spoiling me," she said. "I don't know what I'm going to do when I have to go back to my old barren existence of cooking for myself every day."

"Who said you have to go back?"

Lorna took a gulp of orange juice to avoid answering. Malcolm took a long sip from his coffee mug and looked at her expectantly, one eyebrow raised.

"I'm going to have to start working soon," she said. "I feel lazy. And you have a book to finish."

"I've finished it."

Lorna laughed. "When? In between all the walks and drinking, eating ..."

Malcolm grinned at her and tapped his temple with two fingers. "It's all done, up here. Now I just have to write it down."

Joining her at the table, he reached for his fork and dug into his eggs. Both their appetites had been voracious since they got there. Something about the sound and smell of the ocean seemed to make them hungry all the time.

"Is that how it works for you?" Lorna asked. "You work it all out in your head before you write?"

"Sometimes. And other times I sit at the keyboard and begin typing and it all seems to come from nowhere."

"Where do you *think* it comes from?"

Malcolm shrugged. "I have no clue. All I know is … I experience life in words."

Narrowing her eyes, Lorna paused with a piece of bacon halfway to her mouth. "What does that mean?"

"Like …" Malcolm chewed and swallowed then spoke again. "Let's say I'm watching you walk into a room. Most people experience that in images. And that's how their brain processes it. I see you walk into a room and I think, *'the gentle sway of her hips, the swish of her skirt about her knees, and her delicate tread were almost hypnotic in their rhythm.'*"

In spite of herself, Lorna felt a slow grin spread across her face. "Oh, so that's what you think, is it? When I walk into a room?"

Nodding, Malcolm shoveled another forkful of eggs into his mouth. "Stuff like that … and other stuff too dirty to say at the breakfast table."

"Professor Mitchell, you are going to be fighting off those eager undergraduate Lolitas," Lorna said shaking her head.

"I'm sure I won't even notice them," he said meeting her gaze.

"Don't be so sure."

Adoration was a heady thing. Even for the most principled of instructors.

"What about you?" Malcolm asked. "I know you have your fan club. Have you ever been tempted?"

"Not attracted to women, no."

Letting his head fall to one side, Malcolm gave her a look. "You know what I mean. Some of these guys, like Todd what-shisname? I bet plenty of them get hot for the sexy feminist professor."

"I love that you think I'm sexy," Lorna teased.

"No, seriously. Do they ever give it a shot?"

And Lorna could see that he *was* serious. Malcolm was naturally possessive, she had come to learn. Though he had probably matured out of much of it, it was obviously his basic inclination—to have and to keep his woman close.

Lorna noticed the way *he* noticed when other men spoke to her, and she watched him hold himself still, and hold himself back. He was what her son-in-law might mellow into, in another twenty years.

Or maybe not. Shawn would never be "mellow" about other men's interest in or attention to Riley.

"You're not answering," Malcolm said. "So, I take it that's a yes."

"No, my mind wandered for a minute, that's all," Lorna laughed. "But the answer *is* yes. Some of them try, in their clumsy collegiate way."

"And have you ever been tempted?"

"Tempted? By *what*? Some long-haired emo-boy in Birken-stocks who thinks calling himself a feminist will make him get laid more often? Who'll go down on you for a half hour because he can't make you come with his dick alone? Honestly, Malcolm."

"*Whoa!* For someone who says she's never tried these emo-boys as you call them, you sure seem to know a lot about how they ..."

"I never said I never tried them. I did. When I was an undergraduate myself," she added quickly.

"Oh." Malcolm took another gulp of coffee and stood,

beginning to clear his dishes. "And for the record," he said as he walked away, "*I* like going down on you for a half hour. And it has *nothing* to do with not being able to make you come with my dick alone."

Lorna smiled and rolled her eyes.

"SO, HOW'S IT BEEN?"

"It's been fine."

"Fine? That's not very descriptive. You aren't already looking for an exit strategy, are you?"

"Riley. I've only been here four days."

"Which for you may as well be an eternity. Especially with no one else around to break up the monotony."

Lorna held the phone away from her ear, for a moment resenting just how cynical her daughter was about her ability to maintain anything resembling a relationship with a man.

"There's nothing ... monotonous about Malcolm."

A long silence was the response from the other end of the line. So long that Lorna checked to see whether her cellphone had dropped the signal.

"Mom ..." Riley said slowly. "Are you *falling* for him?"

Lorna's face grew hot and she shifted in her seat, edging forward. "I don't even know what that means, *falling* for him."

"Yes you do. That's why you're blushing. I can hear it in your voice."

"Riley ..."

"If you're not comfortable talking about it, that's okay. Just ... enjoy it. It's the first time since ..."

Lorna knew she wouldn't say his name. Riley and she rarely spoke about Earl and when they did, it was very briefly. And the last thing Lorna wanted to do was entertain a long conversation about yet another father-figure she had driven out of her daughter's life.

"Anyway, just enjoy it," Riley said again.

"I *am* enjoying him," Lorna admitted. "Very much."

More than she intended to. More than was wise, when she knew that at some point, inevitably, it would have to end.

"I'm tempted to come down there and witness it for myself."

"It would be a very full house if you did. His daughter is coming tomorrow."

"Oh yeah. The difficult one?"

"The very same."

"Well that ought to be interesting." Riley laughed.

"I plan to make myself scarce and get some work done while they bond or whatever," Lorna said.

"I'm guessing that won't go over too well."

"Why wouldn't it?"

"Lorna, for someone who's so smart, you can be so clueless. Malcolm didn't invite you on a vacation with his daughter so he could have you two *separate*. He obviously wants you to get to know each other. Which means even if you're not serious about the relationship, he's definitely serious about you."

Lorna thought for a moment.

But Malcolm hadn't mentioned anything that led her to believe he actually thought she would be spending time with Piper. Of course they would probably take meals together and do an occasional outing, but his daughter would be there to spend time with him, not with *her* surely.

"I think you're wrong," Lorna said simply, choosing not to engage on the whole "serious about the relationship" business.

"Okay. I'll talk to you in a few days and we'll see who's wrong. Where is he anyway, while we sit here discussing him and his kid?"

"Went to get groceries. But enough about Malcolm. I was curious about whether you've ... moved ahead with what you were thinking about doing. Reaching out to ..."

"No. I kind of think ... I think I need you to do it with me."

Sitting upright, her legs falling from the table and onto the wooden deck, Lorna gripped the phone tighter. "Do what with you?"

"Come see my father."

"Riley ..."

"I don't want to do it alone. And if for some reason things went south, Shawn is just going to ... I don't know, flip out on him or something. So he can't come. I need you."

Running a hand over her face, Lorna took a silent breath. It wasn't often her kid said she needed her for things anymore. But this ...

"I realize facing your mistakes head-on is something you dislike doing, but ..."

"Wait a minute! I didn't say 'no' and what I *really* dislike is this snide attitude you've adopted with me lately, Riley!"

"Forgive me for being snide," she said ... snidely. "But I only recently found out that my father didn't abandon me but had been chased off. Some people, maybe even most people, would never speak to a parent again over something like that."

"So, congratulate yourself for being a bigger person than that, and let's move on."

"Move on? Are you fucking *kidding* me?"

Riley rarely cursed, so Lorna knew she had gone too far.

"You really need to take a good, long look in the mirror, Lorna. Because all these things that you've gotten used to chalking up to as *your* life lessons? They affected *other* people's lives as well! *Mine.* My father's ... and god knows how many other men who made the mistake of thinking that the ease with which you opened your legs would equate the ease with which you'd open your heart!"

With those last words, they were both stunned into silence. Lorna felt pinpricks at the back of her eyes, and her lower lip trembled. The silence stretched out a few moments, then finally Riley sighed.

"Mom. I'm sorry. That was ... I'm ..."

"Let's just talk later. Okay?" Lorna managed. "Let's just ..."

She ended the call and ignored it when it immediately rang. Just as she was about to turn it off altogether, a text message came through.

I'm sorry, it read. *That's the worst thing I've ever said to you. To anyone. I love you, and I'm sorry.*

The devolution of 'conversation' into 'argument' was too common an occurrence between them lately. *Of course* when she said 'move on' she hadn't meant to imply that Riley should abandon her plan to reconnect with her father. She only meant she needed to get past the resentment. But maybe that had been too much to expect as well.

Of course, Riley resented what had been done to her. But Lorna had been spoiled all these years—Riley was an even-tempered baby who turned into a sunny child, remarkably steady teenager and then a well-balanced, serene adult. She had made things easy for Lorna, all her life.

Whatever she may have wanted, she never demanded; the things she needed ... well, Lorna acknowledged now, maybe there were times Riley had to seek those out on her own as well. Like Shawn. They both, after unconventional childhoods, had found each other and built the most conventional of families—Mom and Dad, desperately in love with each other, and in love with their children.

What Riley said *was* the worst thing she had ever said to her. But Lorna was fairly certain she deserved it. It wasn't the kind of thing one said to their mother, but it was the kind of thing that could probably get said when, from the time she could speak, you encouraged your kid to call you by your first name.

———

"HEY."

Lorna opened her eyes and looked up at Malcolm, standing over her, amused.

"You went back to bed?" he said, stating the obvious. "You're right. You *are* getting lazy."

"Yeah ..."

She had gone to lie down, just for a minute, after that awful exchange with Riley and somehow drifted off entirely.

Blinking lazily, she turned onto her back as her vision came into focus. Malcolm was wearing a light-grey t-shirt with the picture of a Coors beer can on the front. The shirt was well-worn and a little frayed at the sleeves and hem, like he'd been wearing it every summer since he was in college. It stretched across his chest and at the arms, showing off his very solid and lean physique. Between that and the sun-kissed, reddish-brown hue of his skin, and the scruff on his face, he was beyond sexy.

Reaching out, Lorna grabbed ahold of one of the strings hanging from his cargo shorts and pulled him toward her.

"Join me," she said.

Malcolm laughed. "No. Let's go take a walk. It's beautiful outside."

"I don't want to," Lorna moaned, tugging harder.

Malcolm took two steps forward, grinning down at her, and relenting when she began pulling at the waistband of his shorts.

"Let's just stay in bed and screw until we're sore," she said. "After tomorrow we won't be able to do it as often, and ..."

"Who said we won't be able to do it as often?" Malcolm had begun shrugging his shirt over his head.

"Piper will be here," she reminded him.

"I can be quiet. *You* on the other hand ..."

"It's not just a question of being quiet, Malcolm. I'll be off writing someplace to give you guys your space, and ..."

He froze, his hand halting hers where it had begun pulling down his zipper. "Who said we need *space?*"

"So you and Piper can do the Daddy-Daughter thing."

She looked up at him and he was biting his lower lip.

"Sure, we'll do some of that, but we're all going to be here together, so ..."

Lorna let her hand drop. "But not all the time, Malcolm, that's all I mean."

"No, but ... I'd like her to know you, to ... *what?*"

"Nothing."

"You made a face."

"I didn't mean to." She sat up and Malcolm sat next to her.

"I hope I didn't overshare on how difficult she can sometimes be. I'd like for you and her to get along."

"Sure. But I hope you know I'm not up for any substitute mothering, or ..."

Malcolm's head snapped back. "Substitute *mothering?*"

"Because I'm not up for that," Lorna continued. "You and I both know I'm not the type. So if your thought was that ..."

"Slow down. What the ...?"

"I talked to Riley and she said something that made me wonder whether what you expect is for me to ..."

"You talked to Riley?" Malcolm interrupted. "When?"

"While you were gone." Lorna shrugged.

"And what else did you talk about?"

Sighing, Lorna let herself fall back into the sheets again. "What difference does it make? She asked about Piper coming and made a comment that made me wonder whether your expectations are that I'll be some Summer Charlotte-Substitute for your troubled ..."

"She isn't *troubled*, Lorna. She's a kid who's a little turned-around right now. Because of her parents' divorce, puberty or both. And as for my expectations of you, believe me, they're very low right now."

"Good! Because where mothering is concerned, I couldn't possibly meet them!" She kicked the sheets aside and shoved herself up and off the bed. "Come to think of it ... why am I even here? You should be with some limber thirty-year old who doesn't take afternoon naps and ... and ... does yoga on the beach. Someone who would give you your own little Malcolm in a year or two ..."

She intended to make her way to the balcony to get some bracing salty air and clear her head, but he grabbed her by the arm, none too gently either, and pulled her back down to the bed. Lorna struggled for a moment until he pushed her back and covered her body with his.

"What the fuck is going on with you?" he demanded.

"Nothing! It just all became clear to me. This ... *joke* we're conducting. You have a young family. You're young enough to make *another* one. I don't have time to get entangled in some surrogacy situation with your ... *complicated* pre-teen, when all I want is some solitude to begin to write my book!"

Something in Malcolm's eyes shifted and he braced himself on his forearms on either side of her head. His chest was moving as he breathed. Lorna felt his heartbeat against her, and it made her want to hold him closer, even though everything she said was intended to push him away.

"What else did you and Riley talk about?" he asked quietly.

"You could, y'know?" Lorna said, ignoring his question.

"Start another family. Have a boy this time. Men are always interested in having boys, aren't they?"

"I have all the children I'm interested in having, Lorna."

"You never know. You could change your mind."

"I could," he said slowly. "I could meet a woman who's so interesting, so ... smart, sexy, fascinating ... so fucking ... *complex* that I might wonder what it would be like to make a baby with her. But ..." Malcolm rested his weight on one elbow and with the other hand touched her face. "But maybe she's past wanting that. And if she were, I would be cool with it."

Lorna braved a look into his eyes once again, and what she saw there was tenderness. And understanding. Something in her chest tightened.

"We're at such different places, you and me," she said, as his thumb caressed her jaw. "You're just beginning to realize some of the tests of parenting. I've already ... failed at all of mine."

"Lo, you haven't failed at anything. What ... Tell me what you and Riley talked about. Is that why ..."

"We talked about normal things for a while, and then it was back to her father and she said ..." Lorna's throat tightened and she swallowed hard. "I don't even want to repeat what she said."

"She's angry," Malcolm said simply. "She has a right to that. But you didn't fail at being her mother."

"I did, though. Maybe the only real thing a mother has to do is always put their kid's interest before their own, at least when they're little. And ..."

"Wow. Really? Doesn't sound like good feminist theory to me," Malcolm teased.

Lorna managed a smile. "Fuck feminism."

At that Malcolm laughed, letting his head drop so his face

was buried in her neck. *"Fuck feminism?"* he repeated, lips pressed into her skin. "She must have really let you have it."

Lorna relaxed beneath him and put her arms up and around his waist, basking in the slightly tingly feeling his kisses produced, and shutting her eyes.

"She did. It was terrible."

Malcolm lifted his head and raised the weight of his torso once again, so he was on his forearms. "Look at me," he said.

Lorna looked.

"It's probably going to be terrible for at least a while," he said. "Don't you think?"

She nodded.

"But it doesn't mean you get to fight your way out of it ... especially if the person you keep trying to fight with is me. And you don't get to fuck your way out of it either."

Lorna attempted a smirk but knew that what surfaced instead was a sheepish smile. "You think you know me so well, don't you?"

"I do." Malcolm reached down between them and with one hand began working on removing her underwear. "I know every nook ..." he kissed her neck. "And every cranny ... and all your special spots ..." His fingers brushed over her clitoris and Lorna turned her head so their lips could meet.

"I thought you said we weren't going to fuck our way out of it," she said.

"Today only," Malcolm said as she smiled against his lips. "And only because you're such a slow learner." He maneuvered his shorts down and over his hips. Lorna felt him kicking them off.

"Slow learner? Not interesting, fascinating ... *smart?*" Pushing up against him and raising her hips, Lorna spread her legs to make way for him.

"Who said I was talking about you?"

Malcolm heaved and exhaled deeply, as he pushed inside her.

Lorna's body resisted a little, because she was slightly swollen and a little sore. Fortysomething year-old bodies weren't made for sex at the frequency she had been having it lately. But it didn't matter. When Malcolm was inside her, it felt like it was precisely where he was meant to be.

NINETEEN

THE BIG SHIFT

"You look at your phone even more than I do. Does my dad give you a hard time about it, too?"

Piper was in a good mood. She seemed buoyant, even. When Lorna and he had picked her up at the airport, she had been escorted by a flight attendant from the secure area and was talking so animatedly to the woman, she didn't even notice Malcolm until he was right in front of her.

Wearing a pink t-shirt and denim shorts with white high-top sneakers, she had her dark auburn hair pulled into a side-swept ponytail that swung around her head as she walked. Her legs were long and brown. She looked like ... a teenager.

Oh hi, Daddy! she said when she finally noticed him. As though she'd run into him by accident while out lunching with friends.

Hey. How was the flight?

He hugged her and pressed a kiss to her forehead, then turned to the flight attendant to thank her for her help.

It was no problem, the woman said. *Piper was a delight as unaccompanied minors go. No trouble at all.*

And Malcolm had to resist the urge to make a crack about maybe having the wrong kid. Piper turned and beamed at him, her smile the open, beautiful, irrepressible one he thought he would never see again once she turned thirteen.

So where's the girlfriend? she asked.

Oh that's right, Malcolm thought then. *She's saving the really bratty behavior for when she has a new audience.*

But no. Piper had been perfectly gracious and polite when they got into the rented car where Lorna was sitting, idling at the curb, prepared to circle the terminal if asked by traffic control to move along. And now, here she was, making conversation while Lorna scrolled through messages on her cell phone.

"I actually haven't checked it in more than a day," Lorna said, still looking down. "Not generally a big fan of things that help people locate you whenever they want to. But seems like I missed a million messages."

"Anything important?" Malcolm asked, glancing over at her in the passenger's seat.

"A couple from the college. I'm guessing Steven. So, I should probably call him back at some point." Her brow was furrowed.

"What do you teach?"

Piper was positively garrulous today. Malcolm wondered whether someone had slipped her some alcohol by mistake.

"Women's Studies." Lorna smiled and glanced toward the backseat to make eye-contact when she answered.

"What's that about? Studying women?"

There was the smart-mouth he knew so well.

"Some. But also studying woman*hood*."

"Hmm," Piper said. "There were a couple of really interesting women on the plane sitting next to me."

"Oh really?" Malcolm asked. "How so?"

If Piper was in a chatty mood, he wasn't about to stop her, because if she was quiet and sullen, he didn't have the time or patience to draw her out, and Lorna was unlikely to notice or care.

"One of them was a little on the heavier side. She sat in the window-seat. She came on board with a pizza, a tub of gummy bears and a chocolate bar and ate the whole time. And then when the air hostess walked around with snacks for sale, she bought even more! Like, with the pizza *open* on her tray table, she asked for the snack pack, Pringles *and* a Diet Coke. It was disgusting."

"Piper," Malcolm chided.

"It was, Dad! I mean, the flight is only like an hour and a half! And she ate like it was the end of the world or something."

"Yeah, but we don't call people disgusting."

"Yeah, but what if they *are*?" Piper leaned forward in her seat for emphasis.

Lorna laughed. "We call them what you called her before," she suggested. "Interesting. What about the other woman?"

"Oh yeah. She sat in the aisle seat. The minute she sat down she takes out hand sanitizer and she goes, '*I'm not a germophobe*' like anyone even *asked* her, or said anything. And then she puts on her seatbelt, and takes out some spray thingie and like sprays it right up her nose ... *ugh*."

"That *does* sound interesting," Lorna offered. She winked at Malcolm and he smiled back at her. "Pretty eventful for an hour-long flight."

"It was. Between the fat lady and the one with the chemicals, there was a lot of stuff you could talk about in your class, I bet."

Piper leaned back again and Malcolm heard her fidgeting in her backpack for something. Finally she pulled out her iPhone. The offending iPhone on which she communicated with older boys and arranged to go to parties she had no business being at.

"This rental doesn't look like it has Bluetooth so I'm going to listen to music. Daddy? Is that okay?"

"I'm sure Lorna would love to hear about ..."

"No, it's fine," Lorna chimed in. "Piper and I have plenty of time to get acquainted over the next week. And we're stopping to eat before we get back to the island, right?"

"Yeah," Malcolm said, shooting her an amused look. "Go ahead and listen to your music, Piper. But it goes back in the bag when we stop."

"Okay."

Once he was sure she had her earbuds in, Malcolm reached over and touched Lorna's thigh, this time keeping it closer to her knee and PG-13, rather than higher up where he normally liked to touch her.

"Thank you," he said.

"What for?" Lorna looked surprised.

"Being so ... yourself with her."

"Oh, that." She shrugged. "I just don't have the energy to try to be anyone else, that's all."

"LO."

Groaning, Lorna turned over and away from the hand on her shoulder. Vaguely, and in the distance, she heard the sound of the surf, making it more difficult for her to wrestle free of the sleep clouding her mind.

"*Lo*."

"Malcolm, be quiet and go to sleep," she mumbled. "It's still dark out."

"I know. It's almost five-fifteen. C'mon, I want to show you something."

"Well I don't want to see it."

"*C'mon ...*"

Lorna felt his arms steal about her waist and she was dragged back against him. His morning erection pressed between her butt-cheeks; and instinctively she arched her back, pressing into it.

"See, I know you're not that tired. Let's go. Get up."

Turning to face him, Lorna opened her eyes and tried to focus in the hazy, gray morning light. The previous evening, they had slept with the French doors leading out to the balcony open. There was no crime to speak of on Bald Head Island. Like many places populated with the well-off and filthy rich, it was well protected, patrolled by a small force of fewer than a dozen sworn officers that guarded the less than three hundred full-time residents. The wind from the ocean and sound of the waves made it easy to get to sleep, but very difficult to wake up.

"Where's Piper?"

"Sleeping, I'm guessing."

"Like we should be," Lorna tried to turn her back to him again, but Malcolm leaned forward, kissing her on her bare shoulder, moving down the outside of her arm. Goosebumps rose on the surface of her skin.

"When she wakes up I'm taking her to brunch and we're going to be gone all day. Maybe see some of the sights on the island."

"Good," Lorna groaned. "I'll get some work done, finally."

"You don't mind?"

"Of course, I don't mind. I'm relieved." This time she did turn over and show him her back.

"Well maybe I mind," Malcolm said against the nape of her neck. "Maybe I'm going to miss you after being together all day every day for almost a week. So I want to do something before I go, just for us."

Lorna smiled sleepily. "You're such a romantic sap," she teased.

"Guilty. So c'mon, let's go. We're going to miss it."

"Miss what?"

The sunrise. That was what.

And once Malcolm managed to get her up and out on the sand, Lorna was glad he had. The sand was cool beneath her feet, and a little damp when they sat, side by side, watching the awesome display of golds and yellows, of silvery blue and magnificent purple. They watched, but did not speak, as the colors spilled around them, banishing the dark and bringing everything back into vivid focus. And with the light, the world around them seemed to come alive; even the sound of the waves seemed suddenly louder.

Leaning into Malcolm, her chin on his shoulder, Lorna spoke softly.

"How were you ever able to arrange that?"

"I know people," he said, turning his head.

Moving in closer, she kissed him, putting into it all the things she wasn't sure she would ever be able to say.

FALLON'S PROSE was a little clunky, and the ideas she expressed were not particularly inspired. Twice, Lorna had put her research assistant's thesis aside to go wake herself up with a short walk, or a glass of juice. Around noon, she stopped altogether to make herself something to eat, and while doing so, decided to call Steven back to see whether he was the one behind all her missed calls from the college.

"I've been trying to get ahold of you," he said, when she

reached him in his office. He sounded rushed, and a little irritable.

"I'm sorry. I'm out of town and not always near my phone. What's going on? More requests for course title changes?"

"What?" He exhaled. "No, Lorna ... nothing like that. This is something else entirely. Do you know a student named Todd Williamson?"

What the ...?

"Yes. He's an acquaintance. Why?"

"How *much* of an acquaintance, Lorna?"

"Before I answer that, I'm going to have to ask you why you need to know."

"Todd Williamson is the son of one of our trustees. He's apparently a pretty mixed-up kid; a ne'er-do-well from a family that generally does *very* well, full of academics and writers and the like. He's been flitting around for years from college to college trying to finish a degree that never quite gets finished and finally his father pulled some strings to get him a place here."

"And what does that have to do with me, exactly?" Lorna asked though she had a sinking feeling she knew.

"He told his father you and he were having ... a relationship."

"That is absolutely *un*true," Lorna said. "And why would he tell his father a thing like ..."

"I told you, he's a mixed-up, fucked up kid. The father thinks he was trying to impress him. The Williamsons are an old family that doesn't like ... messes. And no matter how impressive Todd might have thought it was to tell his father he bagged the illustrious Dr. Lorna Terry, his father is apoplectic that a member of faculty could have taken advantage ..."

"*Taken advantage?!* He's hardly a child, Steven. He's ..."

Almost thirty. Lorna broke off and closed her eyes, emitting a mental groan. There was always that thing about Todd. A vaguely Peter Pan affect. Like a child in a man's body.

"So I take it something is ... or did happen with him."

"Not since he's been a student. And not on campus."

"Lorna," Steven said, sounding weary. "When the hell are you going to stop with the ...?"

"I'm not going to sit here and listen to you lecture me about my sex life, Steven," she snapped. "I met Todd Williamson before he came to Gilchrist and had no clue he was *about* to come to Gilchrist. Nor did I have any idea who his father was. I *still* have no idea. All the trustees look like one big amorphous blob of ... White *maleness* to me."

"That's the kind of smart-assed comment that's just going to make this thing worse," Steven said, his voice sounding tight. "So wherever the hell you are, and whatever you're doing, I suggest you take some time to think of a ... cleaner way to spin this while I try to smooth things over here."

Swallowing hard, Lorna ran a hand over her face and looked down at the sandwich fixings on the kitchen counter, waiting for her to assemble them.

"And you should know it isn't just his father he's told. Apparently, you're one of his favorite talking points at campus parties. Even Eve Rogers came to me with this story of you banging the grad student."

"Rogers!" Lorna scoffed. "Since when was *she* appointed the grand marshal of the Moral Majority Parade?"

"You can try to kill the messengers all you want," Steven said. "But the message still looks pretty damn bad for you. Where did you meet Todd Williamson anyway? *If* I'm permitted to ask."

"It depends on the capacity in which you're asking, Steven. As my friend, or as a representative of the college."

"As a friend, Lorna. This is still an informal, confidential inquiry at the moment."

"I met him at a conference," she said. "In the city."

"So you were there with your Gilchrist College credentials."

"What the hell does *that* mean? Even if I go to Target for dishwashing liquid, I go 'with my Gilchrist College credentials'."

"You know perfectly well what I mean. You were there in your role as a representative of the college!"

Lorna exhaled. "I suppose one could say that."

"And while there, you slept with a student who you knew was about to matriculate at ..."

"No, I told you I *didn't* know."

"Okay. Look ... I may need to reach you again. Just make sure you answer your phone," Steven said before he hung up.

Lorna put her cell phone on the kitchen counter and leaned back against it, trying to convince herself that a mountain was being made out of a molehill. If Todd had been nineteen instead of twenty-nine she could understand the fuss. She had done no more than any of her colleagues had done over the years, and continued to do.

How many times had she walked into one of the male professors' offices only to see him standing just a smidge too close to his undergraduate research assistant? Or looked the other way when a comely, young graduate student came slinking out of an esteemed member of faculty's hotel room late at night during a work-related trip? She never cared about that kind of thing because it was none of her business. As a rule, she felt that people's sexual proclivities—as long as they didn't involve minors, the mentally-impaired or animals—were their own business.

But none of her rationalizations could drive away the tiny

pinprick of dread she felt once Steven had uttered that one sentence, possibly innocuous, but more than likely not: *This is still an informal, confidential inquiry at the moment.*

It was the last three words that bothered her most: *at the moment.*

"IS this where you've been all day?"

Piper came bounding in, finding Lorna sitting on the sofa, the sheaf of papers that were Fallon's thesis fanned across the coffee table in front of her. After her talk with Steven, she had thrown herself back into the task with renewed focus, trying to find something—*anything*—to occupy her mind other than the potential brewing scandal back at the college.

"Pretty much," Lorna looked up at the girl and smiled. "What about you?"

"Saw the entire island, I think," Piper said sitting in one of the chairs nearby and sliding off her white Keds.

She was a long-limbed girl, who when she was older would probably be described as 'statuesque.' Like her mother, she had tiny freckles across her nose, reddish-auburn coloring, and light-colored eyes. But Lorna saw traces of Malcolm as well—in the seriousness about Piper's mouth, the full sensuality of her lips. Maybe, one day, she would even be considered beautiful.

"Where's your Dad?"

"He dropped me off and then realized you'd probably be hungry so he went to get something to eat so you don't have to cook."

Piper made that announcement as though it had some significance. Like she wanted Lorna to react in some way. So she did.

"That's very considerate of him. I wouldn't have minded cooking. I bet you're both tired."

"Yeah ..." Piper folded her legs beneath her. "It's a nice place, this island. Everyone's rich. And blonde."

Lorna gave a dry laugh. "When I first got here, I noticed the same thing," she said.

"It's kind of like where my Grampy and Nana live. In New England. Rich and blonde. Grampy is like the only Black guy for miles, I think."

Not knowing how to give a neutral response, Lorna instead set about gathering Fallon's thesis into a neat stack.

"What is that?" Piper asked.

"Someone's senior thesis. I'm her advisor next year."

"What's it about?"

"About a writer named Susan Sontag."

"Is it any good?" Piper asked. She fished a piece of gum out of the pocket of her khaki skirt and unwrapped it, popping it in her mouth.

"I'm afraid not," Lorna said.

"Are you going to give her an 'F' then?"

"No. It's good enough to give her a 'Pass'. For your senior thesis, you don't get a letter grade, just a 'Pass' or 'Fail'. So, I guess she could hand this in and be fine."

"I failed a class once. My Dad went ballistic on me."

Smiling, Lorna tried to think of Malcolm going 'ballistic'. She couldn't quite picture it.

"Did he?"

"He said it was because I didn't even try. And he was right. I just don't like math. And whenever I have to look at a page of solid numbers, I just feel my brain shut down or something."

"So maybe you're meant to be a writer, like him. I assume words don't make your mind shut down."

"No, but I think a lawyer is probably what I'd want to be."

"Again, just like him."

Piper shrugged. "I don't know. I think I want to do something different. Like maybe human rights law, or something like that. On career day at school, my friend Jess' mom came and talked about what she does. She works for the U.N. and does this really cool stuff with refugees and people who get thrown out of their countries because of war ...." Piper let her voice trail off. "But I don't know. I guess I'll decide later."

"Yeah, well there's plenty of time," Lorna said. "And the good news is you get to try out different things in college before you decide. That'll be the fun part."

Piper rolled her eyes. "I'm not sure about going to college. It just seems stupid. Like when I turn eighteen and can do whatever I want, why would I go to school where I have more people telling me what to do?"

"Well, for one, because you couldn't be a human rights lawyer otherwise."

"That was just *one* idea of what I want to do," Piper said, sounding, suddenly, very much her age again. "I could also do something where school isn't a part of it."

Lorna shrugged. "Yes. Like become a cleaning lady, or a supermarket cashier."

"That is like, so classist. What's wrong with being a cleaning lady or a cashier?"

"Nothing. And yes, it is classist. But you see, Piper, someone who went to school to become a human rights lawyer *could* one day just up and become a cleaning lady or cashier if they choose to. But it would be a lot more difficult if someone who chose a life as a cashier or cleaning lady wanted to up and become a human rights lawyer."

Rolling her eyes, Piper shoved herself up from her chair.

"Call me when my Dad gets here with the food?"

She ambled off toward the bedrooms while Lorna watched her, recalling what kind of pre-teen Riley had been.

Quiet. Artsy and contemplative. Hardly any work or trouble at all. And when she made trouble, it was generally for herself only, and very ... quietly. Riley was the nerdy girl who didn't realize she was also very pretty. And when she discovered she was, she didn't quite know what to do with that discovery, so there were a couple of high school relationships where she was taken for granted, and treated with less value than she was worth. Lorna had very promptly set her straight so that later, if she made missteps in her relationships, it was never *that* mistake.

Piper already knew she was pretty, was Lorna's guess. And she was going to take her parents on a merry chase around the mulberry bush a few times before it was all over. Poor Malcolm. He had no idea what was in store.

Returning her attention to Fallon's paper, Lorna neatened the stack she'd made and put the television remote on top to anchor it. She would call the girl in the morning to give her detailed comments and notes over the phone. The call with Steven had altered her mood and she wasn't sure she would have the patience to be gentle in her delivery of what was fairly unpleasant news: the thesis was competent enough to pass, but not nearly original enough to merit being published anywhere.

Depending on Fallon's response to that, Lorna was prepared to either work with the girl to improve it, or help her with choosing another topic. She sincerely hoped that Fallon opted for the latter, because she would be occupied with researching for a new paper for the rest of the summer and into the next school year, freeing Lorna from the task of helping her make a silk purse out of this sow's ear.

Sighing, she went to brew herself some tea—she had

already had way too much coffee for the day. But it was busy-work. She didn't really want tea either.

Where the hell was Malcolm?

Moments after she hung up from speaking to Steven, Lorna had found herself longing for Malcolm's calming influence. He would put things immediately into perspective and help calm her down. He had that effect on her, and she was coming to depend on it, and yearn for it. Not that she considered herself particularly high-strung or anything, but she definitely tended to disappear inside her own head, and it was a welcome change to have someone to whom she could pour out those thoughts in spoken words. Someone who didn't care about tiptoeing around her feelings and would "call her on her shit" as Riley would put it.

She'd thought about him way too often during the day, her mind drifting toward silly things, like the way he ran the wash-cloth gently down her back when they showered together, or how he sometimes playfully grabbed a handful of hair and used it to yank her head back so he could attack her neck with deep, soulful kisses. Lately her worries about his age were making a reappearance. He hadn't even hit the Big Four-Oh, yet, and was only three years past the age that Lorna thought of as the marker for genuine adulthood.

Lorna had been with a man once, who insisted he didn't want children. She was forty and he was only a year younger. Jared Townes was his name. He lasted a year before he started dropping hints about it maybe "not being such a bad idea to at least think about having a kid". Marriage he actually, really didn't care about, which made them seem well-matched at first; at least for a long-term thing, where he lived in the city and came over on some weekends, and where Lorna never troubled him about what he might be doing otherwise and with whom.

And because men tended to be shortsighted where relationships are concerned, Lorna knew that Jared would go on like that indefinitely, even counting himself lucky that he had a woman who gave him his "space". Until the inevitable day came that he realized he was in a relationship that was essentially uncommitted to a woman who would never, ever, want to bear his seed. And then he would resent her, because he was fifty, she was fifty-one, and children—even with another woman—had become a remote possibility.

So Lorna ended it, the way she almost always did. With minimal conversation, and by simply disappearing from Jared's life. To his credit, he didn't take too long to catch on, and soon the phone calls, emails, and text messages ceased. Only once had he tried to come by.

And to her complete *un*-surprise, Jared was married and procreating within eighteen months. Last she heard, he had twin boys, and she was happy for him.

Lorna could imagine Malcolm with boys. Even though he had children now, she could imagine him with boys, especially. They would be lively and bright, handsome like their father. And he would rear them to be strong, powerful, intelligent Black men. Something in Lorna's stomach tightened, clenching at the prospect of that happening with Malcolm and some other woman.

Trying to banish the thought, she concentrated on her tea, chiding herself not to compound her worries. As if she didn't have enough to think about with Todd Williamson running around the Gilchrist campus pretending they had some great love affair. What if he was truly deluded, and mentally unstable? He had seemed to be many things, but not crazy. Surely, he could be reasoned with. She could explain to him that what he was telling people—most especially his father—was damaging to her reputation and wouldn't do him any favors in his academic career either.

For a moment, she considered calling and confronting him, then remembered that she didn't have his number. Although, hadn't he called her that time just before she left New York? Reaching for her cell phone, Lorna scrolled through her incoming calls but couldn't find anything that looked right. Or had he called her home phone?

Making a sound of frustration, she put the phone down again. If it wasn't for the fact that they weren't exactly on the best of terms right now, she might call Riley. Except ... didn't this latest little tawdry affair basically confirm the truth of what Riley said? So no, she wouldn't call Riley. She would sit tight, sleep on all this and decide tomorrow whether there was cause for panic.

But dammit, where the hell was Malcolm?

TWENTY

COME BACK TO ME

Malcolm glanced out onto the darkness of the beach, unbroken except for the occasional flash of white, of the waves breaking on the shore. She had been gone for almost an hour, and he was beginning to wonder if he should go out looking for her.

After a dinner of crab cakes, scallops, and steak fries, when Piper turned on the television, Lorna said she needed some fresh air and would be back soon. But it wasn't soon, it was—he glanced at the clock—forty-seven minutes, and she had still not returned.

Next to him on the sofa, Piper was dividing her attention between a sitcom on the television that had for the first time been turned on since he got there, and someone she was text-messaging. Normally, he would tell her to put away the phone and be 'present' with him, but he wasn't exactly present either.

While they ate, Lorna's mind had clearly been elsewhere and Malcolm was planning to talk to her when they were alone. But instead she chose to be *alone*-alone. He wondered whether it had anything to do with the hour he'd left her with

Piper, and itched to ask his daughter what they'd talked about, if anything.

But Piper was being so incredibly unlike herself that he didn't want to say anything to risk upsetting that apple cart. She would be sure to interpret his question as an accusation and it would be off to the races after that. Even the day they'd spent together had been remarkably drama- and tantrum-free; so much so that he even called Charlotte while he was waiting for the take-out, just to let her know they didn't have to schedule that exorcism for their kid after all.

How is she getting along with the professor? Charlotte asked, not commenting at all on his mention of Piper's good behavior.

Because of the sarcasm, Malcolm could only assume that things in her own love-life hadn't improved any.

Pretty good so far.

Mm, Charlotte said. *Let's hope for your sake* that *lasts.*

But her tone of voice suggested she hoped the opposite. Then she had put Hayley on the phone so he could wish his younger daughter a great trip for her summer "camp" abroad, and tell her to Skype and call as much as she wanted to.

"I wish you got dessert while you were out," Piper said, tossing her phone aside. "You think there's a place where we could just go get some ice cream or something, Daddy?"

"Maybe. I don't know. Probably."

"So could we? Just go get some?"

Malcolm glanced out toward the beach once again.

"She's an adult. I'm sure she can find her way home. Just leave the door open or something."

"That's not safe," he said.

"I don't think crooks can afford this place," Piper said, laughing at her own joke.

Malcolm said nothing. He didn't want to leave while Lorna

was still gone, just in case ... in case what? Piper was right. She was an adult, and there were few places in the continental United States as safe as this island. He could simply leave the door open, and Lorna would be back when she felt like it.

"Okay," he said, standing. "Let's go find some ice cream."

Piper leapt up like a lottery winner. "Cool! Lemme get my flip flops."

They rode in the golf cart to three places before they found one that sold ice cream that met Piper's specifications, and then they made their way back to the house. Once there, Piper went bounding up the steps to the entrance, tapping her feet in faux-impatience as she waited for her father to open the door.

Under normal circumstances, Malcolm would have enjoyed her playfulness and been grateful for it even, but he was only partway paying attention, wondering instead whether Lorna had returned from her nighttime trek on the beach.

Inside, the house was precisely as they had left it, and Piper resumed her place in front of the television, beginning to dig into her carton of ice cream.

"Don't eat that whole thing, Piper," Malcolm said absently as he headed for the master bedroom.

When he got there, he found Lorna, sitting fully-clothed in the center of the bed, her legs stretched out in front of her. She looked up at him impassively. In her hands was a copy of his book.

"Hi," she said. "Where'd you two get off to?"

He resisted the urge to throw the question back at her and instead sat on the edge of the bed.

"Ice cream," he responded. "Piper wanted some. If she hasn't already scarfed the whole thing down, I could bring you a little."

"No thanks. I'll probably get up and have some tea in a few minutes."

"Doing a re-read already, huh?" he said, indicating the book. "I'm flattered."

"I thought I might like your voice in my head," she said. "To replace my own for a little while."

Then she set the book aside and unexpectedly, lay on her side, resting her head on his lap.

Momentarily surprised, Malcolm didn't know what to do but finally, when Lorna shut her eyes, he stroked her hair a little, and she made a soft sound, almost like a purr of pleasure. Something was wrong. He knew her well enough now to realize that much. And he also knew he would have little luck finding out what it was by asking directly.

"I have to go back," she said quietly.

Malcolm sighed silently. "Why?"

"There's something I need to take care of. Something that ... well, it's important and won't take care of itself."

"Is it Riley?"

Lorna made a soft snorting noise. "Well, there's that too. But no, it's something else."

"Something I can help with."

"No." Lorna moved closer. "Not really. But just in case, I'll be taking you with me." She patted his book, lying next to her on the covers. "At least, taking your voice. So I can have that in my head. Instead of my own ... stuff."

"Are you coming back?"

"I hope so," she said. And sounded like she meant it.

She snuggled closer still, and Malcolm continued the gentle motion of his fingers in her hair.

"When I was seventeen, I took the bus from Miami to go to college," she said, "because I'd graduated early, and ... because my mother had died."

Malcolm's hands in her hair halted for a moment, then he

resumed stroking, not wanting her to catch on how surprised he was.

"She'd actually been dead almost a year when I left. I spent the last semester of high school living with an uncle. His name was Claude and he was a fixture in my life for my whole life. Kind of in the background, sometimes present, sometimes not. And so when my mother died, I went to live with Uncle Claude. Most of the time he left me to do my own thing, just gave me money and things I needed for school, occasionally hassled me about keeping my room clean, things like that. Nothing out of the ordinary."

Lorna took a deep breath, but she didn't open her eyes.

"There was a school play one night that I wanted to go to. I forgot to tell Uncle Claude about it, and when I got home it was late. Much later than I'd ever been home before, because I'd spent a little time after the play talking to this boy I liked. And it felt good, y'know? It was the first time since my mother died that I was feeling like I could maybe be happy again one day. The boy was cute, he paid me a lot of attention, flattered me ..."

She stopped talking for a few moments and then took another breath and resumed.

"I got home and Uncle Claude was waiting for me in the living room. He'd taken the seat almost directly opposite the front door and when I walked in, he asked me where I'd been. He asked if I was with a boy, and I said something like, '*yes, but just talking.*' And then ..." Lorna opened her eyes for this part. "I saw something in his eyes. It wasn't the anger of a parent or guardian. It was jealousy. And possessiveness. Like a man has for a woman. And he said, '*you know, I'm not your real uncle, right? Not your blood-uncle, anyhow.*'"

Malcolm held his breath.

"And there it was," she concluded.

"There what was?" He couldn't help but ask.

Lorna sat up and looked at him. She looked him directly in the eyes. "I knew right then that I wasn't safe. He was just waiting. Biding his time until ... who knows what? Until I turned eighteen maybe? I left Florida the very next week. And never looked back."

"But he didn't ...?"

Lorna shook her head. "He never touched me. That night I came in late? That was the first time I felt unsafe under his roof. Unsafe and ... dependent. He could have done with me whatever he wanted. The thought of it made me angry. Angry at him, at my mother for dying so unprepared to have someone look after me ... angry at myself for being afraid and for letting myself feel safe."

"*Letting yourself* feel safe?" Malcolm echoed. "You have a right to feel safe."

Lorna shrugged. "I don't know how to explain it. That's just how I felt. Like I was foolish to have gotten complacent, and I promised myself that from that moment on, I would be on my guard. I wouldn't feel dependent, and I wouldn't put myself in a position where I counted on someone else to ... keep me safe."

"So, your mother had no other family? No real family that ...?"

"None that I ever met." Lorna stood. "It was always just me and her."

"Where are you going?" Malcolm asked, frustrated that she was walking away from him just as they'd finally started to communicate.

"To take a shower. I got a little sweaty during that walk so I want to freshen up before bed, and before I have that cup of tea."

"Lo, *wait* ... but your ... so how did your mother die? You were only seventeen so she had to have been fairly young, right?" He spoke to her retreating back.

"She *was* pretty young," Lorna said, her voice oddly emotionless. She didn't look back as she walked into the en suite bathroom. "She killed herself. She was forty-six."

AFTER HER SHOWER, Lorna emerged from the bathroom with wet hair and walked right by Malcolm who had already undressed for bed, presumably going to make her tea. Minutes later, he heard her conversing with Piper, evidently deciding to drink the tea out there. *So that was it then.* That was all she intended to share for one evening, and this was his cue to keep his distance.

Forcing himself to remain where he was, Malcolm found an old copy of *The Economist*, probably left there by the previous renter, and tried to keep himself occupied.

But his mind was racing. He remembered once reading an article about the children of suicides. One man had distilled it in a way Malcolm thought both sad and chilling, saying that the cruelest legacy of a suicide by a parent was that *"what might have once been considered unthinkable, suddenly begins to seem like a viable option."* Though he didn't think for a moment that Lorna was suicidal, Malcolm wondered about her moodiness, and her silences, her frequent need for solitude, and whether she carried that awful legacy with her as well.

By the time she came back, Malcolm had dozed off to a commentary in the magazine about the failure of the euro to live up to its promise as a regional currency, and the rest of the house was dark and quiet.

Lorna padded into the bedroom quietly and reached over

to turn out the bedside lamps. He watched her undress, silhouetted against the dim light of the moon outside.

"You're awake," she said, half statement half question.

"I was waiting for you."

"I had a lively debate with your daughter about the value of a college education," she said, chuckling a little as she climbed onto the bed on her hands and knees. "Her arguments were no good, but she definitely has the staying power to exhaust her opponent."

"Tell me about it," Malcolm said wryly.

"She's a great kid, Malcolm," Lorna said, in a tone that sounded truly heartfelt. "She's going to take you through the wringer a million times over, I bet. But she's such a great kid."

"It means a lot hearing you say that."

"Why? Because I'm such a parenting guru you mean?" Lorna laughed.

"Lo, anyone who watches you with your daughter for ten minutes can tell you have an uncommonly close relationship. Stop minimizing that."

"I know we're close. But was I a mother? That's the thing I sometimes wonder."

"There's more than one way to mother your child. You of all people should ..."

"*Wow*. Has Malcolm T. Mitchell finally taken a sip of the feminist Kool-Aid?"

She was right next to him now, her lips directly at his left ear, her bare thigh touching his. Malcolm felt his manhood twitch.

"Maybe. And what about you? Are you beginning to doubt your own dogma?"

"Yes," she said, opening her mouth against his neck.

Malcolm's dick woke up in earnest.

"You want to know my deepest, darkest secret? Well that's

it. I am nothing if not *riddled* with self-doubt. And that, Malcolm, is why I work so hard at seeming *so* certain."

This was just like her—to spark his mind and his libido to equal fervor. But tonight, he decided, he would let his libido win.

"*C'mere*," he said, frustrated when she moved just out of his reach. That was the story of their relationship—Lorna, just out of his reach.

Sliding down, she tugged impatiently at his boxer-briefs until he lifted his hips and she was able to pull him free. Then her lips had covered him, and she was sucking, licking and pulling him in.

Issuing a low groan, he managed to lift his head just enough to confirm that the bedroom door was firmly shut, before Lorna drove every coherent thought out of his head.

With a rhythmic bobbing of her head, she stroked and caressed him with her tongue and lips, alternately slow and steady, then when he pushed upward, increasing in speed and pressure. He knew where she was trying to take him, but he wasn't ready to go there yet, so with all the will he could muster, Malcolm pulled back and away from the delicious warmth of her mouth.

Lorna laughed softly. "You are *so* tiresome," she said, and he laughed with her, dragging her up to him so they were face to face.

He kissed her hard, their tongues dueling, lips sucking and nipping each other. Even with their kisses, they both struggled for domination, but Malcolm knew that at the end of the day, in this arena Lorna preferred to lose. She wouldn't surrender easily, but surrender she did.

Reaching down between them, he spread her with his fingers, and stroked and rubbed her, making soft circles and then pushing two fingers into her with gentle thrusts until she was climaxing, soft like hot molten wax all over his hand.

"I want four," he said against her mouth. "At least four tonight."

He felt her smile, and she panted against him, her tongue touching his fleetingly before she switched tacks and instead sucked on his lower lip.

"I may not have four to give you."

"Oh, we'll find them," he promised.

Grabbing her behind her knee, Malcolm lifted one leg and plunged into her at an angle, stroking her hard and deep. Beneath him, Lorna whimpered and moved her hips in a corkscrew motion, straining to get more of him. Seeing what she wanted, Malcolm pulled back and almost out, reveling at the angry frustration that he could just about make out as it crossed her features.

"You're not in charge here," he said, pausing before pushing inside her once again.

Lorna gasped and clutched his ass, her nails digging into it.

"I know," Lorna breathed. "I know ... but harder, Malcolm ... *please* ..."

He obliged, but only for a few strokes before pulling out of her entirely. She all but screamed, trying to grab hold of him and pull him back down to her.

"*Shut up,*" he said. "You're the one who said she could be quiet, remember?" He kissed her deeply, but evaded all her attempts to impale herself on him once again.

"Oh, I see what's going on ..." Lorna said, still breathless from the paces he'd taken her through moments earlier. "You're upset with me." She sounded incredulous.

"Why the fuck are you leaving?" he demanded as he shoved her back against the sheets and moved down her body. Stopping at her stomach he lightly bit her there. "*Why?*"

"Malcolm ..."

"Why?" He spread her legs wide and pressed them open with his forearms. "*Tell* me."

"I have ..." Lorna gasped when he swiped her with his tongue. "I have ... business to take care ..." She seemed to have forgotten the rest of her sentence when he pushed his tongue deep into her, curling it as he tasted her. She tasted like the briny seawater they swam in every day since they'd been there, and like sunshine. She tasted perfect.

Malcolm didn't let up until she stiffened and then collapsed against the sheets. They were both covered with a thin sheen of perspiration, so there was almost no friction as he made his way back up, his chest sliding against hers and feeling the hard rubbery sensation of her nipples.

"*Two*," Malcolm said against her neck, sucking her there. "Tell me why you're leaving ... and what business you have to take care of."

"Why do you ...?"

He slid into her this time with no resistance whatsoever, she was so wet. Lorna gripped both his triceps, heaving at each thrust, pulling back a little as though he was going too deep.

"Malcolm, I can't ... I ... can't ..."

"Can't what?" he asked. "Tell me what your business is? *Why not, Lo?* You have me wide the fuck open, and yet everything with you is a secret ..."

"No, I mean, I can't take ... I don't know if I can take ... any ... more ..."

She gasped at a particularly hard thrust and he slowed, raising himself on his extended arms to make sure he wasn't really hurting her. Her chest heaved and she looked directly at him, their eyes locking for a few moments in a wordless exchange of a strong, yet-to-be-named emotion.

"You want me to stop?" he asked, finally.

Lorna shook her head.

"Say it."

"No," she said. *"Don't stop."*

With that, he ground himself into her, feeling the hard clash of their pelvic bones and the soft grasp of Lorna's womanhood encircling him. Remaining in that position, arms extended, Malcolm was able to watch her face, the wonder and pleasure in her eyes, the erotic 'o' she made with her moist and swollen lips, and the way she bit down on the lower one when he pressed farther and higher.

Beads of sweat rolled down his face, dripping from his chin and onto Lorna, pooling in the indentation at the base of her neck, joining her own perspiration.

"Why're you leaving me?"

"I'm not," Lorna groaned. "It's just for a few days. I ... Malcolm, you have to ..."

"Come for me, again," he demanded.

"Malc ..."

Reaching down, he forced a hand between them and stroked her, his fingers moving in time to each stroke inside her. Lorna was keening and crying now, and neither of them gave a damn anymore about being quiet. Malcolm sure didn't. She was so hot and slick, he couldn't help but remove his hand for a moment, putting his fingers to his lips.

Watching him, Lorna opened her mouth wide and with a loud moaning cry, she came again.

"Three ..." she said, her eyes half shut. "That's all I've got." And then she smiled, a lazy satisfied smile that made his heart quake.

Malcolm, in spite of himself—and how frustrated he was that Lorna was planning to slip away yet again—smiled back at her. And then he kissed her, with all the feeling he had for her, that he felt forced to keep bottled up inside for fear of scaring her off.

Rolling away, to relieve her of his weight, Malcolm pulled her back against him, his still hard member pressed between them.

"Lo," he said. "You can let yourself feel safe. With me."

It seemed like an eternity before she spoke.

Her voice was barely above a whisper. "I know."

The next time was unlike the others—gone was all the competitive ferocity, and the barely restrained anger.

Lorna climbed astride him, and with her head buried between his neck and shoulder, rode him in slow, churning waves, moving sensuously, and in almost perfect time to the accelerating beat of Malcolm's heart. His climax approached like the ascension to a place almost divine, timeless and mind-less. And then there were stars, explosions and nothingness. Vaguely, dimly and from far, far away, Lorna whispered in his ear.

"Four."

TWENTY-ONE
FACING THE MUSIC

Thankfully, she didn't look as crappy as she felt.

Lorna looked herself over in her dresser mirror and pulled back her hair, fastening it at her nape in a knot with two bobby pins. Her skin was still golden from all the hours in the sun over the past week, so she looked the picture of health and composure. Riley had always said that was her "superpower"—the ability to appear unperturbed, no matter the circumstances.

Nothing could be farther from the truth today. She had a morning appointment with Steven in his office, and in the afternoon, she was taking a train into the city for a sit-down with her daughter.

Better, she thought when she made her plans, *to get all the unpleasantness out of the way right off the bat.*

Although seeing Riley was never unpleasant, no matter how difficult things might be between them.

Last night, she had spent the most uncomfortable evening that she could recall ever having spent in her own bed. Lorna tried to chalk it up to the bumpy flight from North Carolina, and New York's rainy welcome at LaGuardia Airport. She had a connecting flight that would have taken her to the small regional airport near Gilchrist, but had chosen not to take it after seeing the gun-metal gray and ominous skies. It was depressing enough leaving the bright sun and blue water, the salty air and the aggressive cleanliness to return to smoggy, rainy New York.

The ride upstate in the car she hired seemed interminable and it was dark when she got home, peeled off her clothes and collapsed into bed, not bothering to call and let Malcolm know she had arrived safely as promised. Sometime in the middle of the night—she had no idea what time—she heard her cell phone chiming and ringing on and off, but was too sluggish to bother getting up to get it.

Outside she could hear the music of the rain dancing against the gutters, and it lulled her back to sleep almost immediately. And besides, Lorna didn't particularly want to hear his voice. It was bad enough she'd found it so difficult to leave without compounding things with an emotionally unsatisfying call that would only leave her missing him more.

No. While she was here, she needed to focus on what was at hand—neutralizing this little virus of a mini-scandal. When going to war, it was best to travel light.

Choosing a lightweight blouse and her favorite jeans, Lorna slid her feet into her sandals and grabbed the brown leather hobo that her son-in-law had given her the previous Christmas. It was enormous and could easily contain a stack of papers, her small laptop, wallet and even a change of clothes for an impromptu overnight without looking sloppy.

He's on a mission to upgrade you, Riley had whispered when Shawn wasn't looking. *He says your clothes drive him nuts.*

And Lorna had smiled and shook her head. Shawn did have a way of gifting her items that gradually 'upgraded' but never changed her. Except now her boho-wear was more likely to come from Neiman Marcus than some low-cost chain. God, she loved her kids. She hoped he was in the city when she got there, because she definitely missed him, not to mention the babies.

The campus was almost deserted. Steven had suggested they meet in his office over coffee at eight-thirty. *I'll bring the coffee*, he added. By summer standards, that was incredibly early. Most of the summer classes started after ten a.m. Lorna wondered whether his suggestion of a meeting time had been by design, so that fewer people, or no one at all, would know that he was meeting with her.

Headley Hall was quiet as she entered, and her sandals made slapping noises against the stone floor and she headed down the hall toward Steven's office. He had the large one, the coveted one—the one she might have had if she hadn't turned up her nose at a position as chair. In retrospect, it was a foolish and prideful decision, as though she was above all that and immune to the career-climbing aspirations of her fellow professors.

"Lorna."

Steven stood as she entered, and Lorna noted that not only did he have coffee, but he had a plate with mini-croissants and danish as well, and had set everything up in his small sitting area.

"The coffee cup on the right is yours," he said as she unloaded her bag and sat on the small sofa.

"Thank you." She picked up the cup and took an exploratory sip. "You remembered."

"One sugar, very little cream," Steven confirmed. His dark blue eyes were genuinely warm when he looked at her.

Their affair had been brief, and not filled with passion by

any means, but instead marked by friendship and companionship.

Steven was a by-the-book kind of man, from traditional Midwestern roots. He had been the first in his family to go to college and never stopped carrying that mantle of exceptionalism. He wanted his life to be an example to his nieces and nephews back in Small Town USA, who viewed him with as much awe as though he'd flown to the moon. So, he needed a wife and family life to round things out, and Lorna's casual approach to sex and relationships had never been comfortable for him. After a few months, he had been the one to back away, and Lorna understood. It had been completely expected.

"So what're we going to do, Lorna?"

"I don't know that there *is* anything to do, Steven. It is what it is."

He shook his head impatiently. "You don't seem to understand what's going on here."

"I understand perfectly. A bunch of old White men are practically salivating at the idea that I'll get taken out by the very same things I've been preaching all these years—sexual and personal liberation for women."

Rolling his eyes, Steven leaned back and took a long sip of his coffee. "It's just like you to make some kind of holy war out of this. It's a lot simpler than what you're saying."

"Then simplify it so *I* can understand."

"You screwed a trustee's son. A student ..."

"He was not a student."

"He was *about to* be. What do you think would happen if professors went around sleeping with prospective students at academic conferences as a habit?"

"I'm not sure professors *don't* go around screwing prospective students at academic conferences, Steven."

"Okay, for the sake of argument, let's say they do. You're

the one who got caught. And you're the one who was unlucky enough to come across the son of a trustee of Gilchrist College."

"The *adult* son of a trustee of Gilchrist College!" Lorna ran a hand over her head. "Honestly I can't even believe we're talking about this! It's insane. What does he say? Todd, I mean. Is he feeling like I *exploited* him? Took *advantage* in some way?"

"I don't know what he's saying. Apparently his father has gotten him to shut up finally."

"So ... fine. What am I supposed to do now? Is there anything I need to be ...?"

"I haven't been on the inside track on this thing, but I know it's still being discussed. So I think you need to be practicing looking and acting like you've eaten humble pie. And if they ask for a meeting, be prepared to be contrite, and ..." Steven took note of her grimace. "Yes, Lorna, I mean it. *Contrite.*"

Picking up one of the mini-danish, she took a bite. "But so far no talk of anything else that you know of?"

"Like what? You stepping down? No, nothing like that," Steven said with a wave of his hand. "But this particular man, Williamson, he's a hard-ass so I wouldn't expect him to go too easy on you, either. If he meets with you, you'll want to do more listening than talking."

Grunting, Lorna chewed on her pastry. Inside her bag, her cellphone began buzzing and she reached for it. Malcolm. Sending it to voicemail, she let it drop into the bag once again.

"I'm hoping it's been pretty much contained," Steven said. "It's summer, and they'll want all of this dead and buried before the new class gets here. So if you do get called to a meeting, just don't ... piss anyone off, okay?"

"I'll try. But it can't have escaped you that this is just the kind of thing I teach and lecture about, how the standards for women are so much more ..."

"Yeah, yeah, I've heard all your lectures," Steven said smiling.

The air in the room lightened considerably and Lorna smiled back at him, settling into his comfortable sofa and enjoying the coffee and pastries.

"So, what was it, really?" Steven asked after a moment. "With you and Todd Williamson."

"One night. One less than memorable night."

"And have you been seen together, or ... has he ..."

"He called me a lot when he first got to campus. I didn't even remember his name. And then we ran into each other a time or two, and oh! He stopped by my house Reunion Weekend, and wanted to ask me out." She rolled her eyes.

"He was at your house?" Steven looked slightly more troubled.

"Yes. But so what? This is Gilchrist. We're encouraged to have students over. And you know as well as I do that on any given day, some professor is using students to go get their car cleaned, or pick up their kid from school, to make them dinner, or ..."

"And all of those things are within the realm of what's socially-acceptable."

"Using students as slave labor?"

"You know what I mean." Steven shook his head. "Just don't ... mention that to anyone. The part about him being over at your house. Was anyone else there?"

"Well ... Malcolm showed up, but he wouldn't say anything."

Steven's eyebrows lifted. "Mitchell was there when Todd Williamson showed up?" He looked amused.

"The other way around, actually. Todd Williamson was there when Malcolm showed up."

Leaning back, Steven grinned and nodded. "How'd *that* go over?"

"Not very well," Lorna laughed.

"I wouldn't think so. Mitchell has a certain urbane, He-Man thing going on."

Lorna stifled a smile. "Yes. That he does."

"So what's going on there? Is it serious with you two?"

"It's not *un*-serious."

This time it was Steven who laughed. "I guess that's the most I can expect to get out of you," he said shaking his head.

"Yes," she confirmed with a sly smile. "It is."

"YOU LOOK WELL."

"I look *well?*" Lorna kissed Riley on the cheek before sitting. "That sounds like you're greeting the Queen of England. I sure hope things haven't broken down *that* badly between us."

"Well you do. Look well." Riley said, smiling. "And you're the one who hasn't been calling me back."

"It's been kind of an eventful week."

Lorna lifted the menu and looked it over, without interest. She wasn't hungry. They were in a diner near Penn Station, because Riley had been eager to get out of the condo for a couple of hours. Apparently, Cullen was beginning to act up a little bit because of the new baby, and she had hired a nanny to help her through this crazed new period for their family.

Shawn, who still didn't like the idea of a stranger looking after their kids—no matter how necessary he now recognized it to be—was working from home and so Riley had taken advantage of the chance to get out in the real world once again.

"Why eventful?"

"I'll tell you about all that later. Most of all I want to hear about you, and what your plans are with, you know."

"Getting in touch with my father? Well, I haven't done anything yet, if that's what you're asking. And I'm still hoping you'll help me."

"Of course I'll help you," Lorna said right away. She had learned her lesson since last time when she hesitated and Riley melted down on her.

"I was hoping you'd make the initial call."

Lorna took a breath. The idea of calling up Ryan after all these years, and confessing that he had never heard from his daughter because she had blocked it made her want to throw up, right there on the table. But if anyone should deal with that discomfort, of course it should be her.

"Okay," she said.

Riley looked surprised. She raked her fingers through her short, curly hair, and for a moment looked like she hadn't thought past that ask. Perhaps she'd expected a fight over it.

She pursed her lips and finally, smiled, nodding and reaching over to touch Lorna's hand briefly in gratitude.

She looked pretty with her hair short. Like a pixie. Pert, pretty and graceful. Whenever she saw her these days, Lorna had to resist the urge to reach over and smooth a hand on her daughter's cheek. She was growing sentimental in her middle-age.

"So, I have his numbers and everything," Riley said. "And I thought since you're probably leaving soon, we might do it today. Or tomorrow if you have time to ..."

"No, we may as well do it today," Lorna said, her voice suddenly hoarse.

Riley removed her hands from the surface of the table and instead ran them back and forth on her thighs.

"What do you think? Should we do it at my place? Shawn's there, and the kids ...but we could lock ourselves in the master bedroom and ..."

"Wherever you're comfortable. Though you might want Shawn nearby afterwards, so yes, maybe back at your place is best."

"Shawn." Riley made a puffing sound with her lips and shook her head. "He's been trying to talk me out of it a little. I think he's scared I'll get my heart broken or something. That my father will reject me, or something."

"He told me what happened to him," Lorna said.

Riley nodded. "Yeah. His father was pretty much uninterested when he found him. But it was before all the money and ..." Riley shrugged. "And then afterward, when all the fame and money came, and his Dad reached out, Shawn said he couldn't trust his motives, so..."

Lorna nodded. "That must have been difficult."

"But y'know what occurred to me?" Riley said, looking down. "I'm kind of well-known as well now. Because of Shawn, and because of you. So if he wanted to, my father could have ..."

"He wanted to," Lorna said. "I'm almost certain of it. If he didn't reach out, it was only because he believed that you didn't want it."

"Or maybe he just moved on. Had a family, was happy ..."

"I suppose it's possible, but I doubt it very much."

Ryan had never been that kind of man—even as a young man—who would leave his child and go on blithely with his life. There wasn't very much about him that Lorna recalled in detail, but that she knew for sure—family was important to him, and it had been to his parents as well. She could barely stand to think of the pain she must have caused them all; and just because she was young, foolish and self-centered.

"So before we go face the music, should we have some cheesecake and coffee?"

"Yes. Let's do that." Lorna nodded.

For the second time that day, her cellphone interrupted an important conversation, but this time when she glanced at it, the call was from Fallon. She had plans to meet her research assistant for dinner that evening so they could talk over her thesis, and the plan, the hope, was that she would have concluded all her business in New York for the time being and could return to the beach.

But now, less than twenty-four hours later, the beach felt more like a mythical, almost imaginary place—somewhere idyllic that she had dreamed up. If she remained in New York more than another day or so, it was likely she wouldn't return to the beach at all, she would fall back into her habitual groove. And Malcolm would be livid, or worse yet, hurt.

At the curb at the airport, he got out of the car when she did, and wrapped a solid arm about her waist, pulling her close. Then he'd kissed her just beneath her ear as Piper looked on from the car, rapt at the sight of her father kissing someone other than her mother.

Come back to me, he said.

And inside Lorna's stomach, a thousand tiny butterflies fluttered.

AFTER THE COFFEE AND CHEESECAKE—NEITHER of which Lorna even tasted because of her frayed nerves at the thought of the call—they went back to the condo. When Riley opened the door, it was quiet. Calling out to Shawn and the nanny and receiving no response, she shot off a quick text message, and got back a prompt response.

"He's out with Mrs. Park and the kids," she explained. "So we have the place to ourselves for about an hour or so."

Mrs. Park was the woman they had hired to be a baby nurse and temporary nanny for Cullen and Cassidy, and had come highly-recommended as someone accustomed to working for high-profile couples. A middle-aged Korean woman with a few grandchildren of her own, Riley told Lorna over coffee that the woman was perfect for the job because she didn't follow popular culture, and neither knew nor cared why most of her clients were famous.

Cullen has just the right blend of respect and affection for her, Riley had explained with a laugh. *So he does whatever she tells him to without much fuss.*

Huh, Lorna had commented. *That's great because he does nothing that I tell him to.*

"Should we just go do this then?" Riley asked, suddenly sounding nervous. She unloaded her handbag on a nearby sofa and idly picked up one of Cullen's toy trucks that was on the floor.

"Yes. But I'd like it if you'd wait in the bedroom. Until I come get you," Lorna said. "I'd like to talk to him in private first."

Pausing for a second, Riley finally nodded. "Just so long as you promise not to sugarcoat anything for me afterward."

"Have I ever sugarcoated anything for you, Riley?"

"Okay. Fair enough. Let me get you his numbers."

Moments later, Lorna was sitting alone in Shawn and Riley's stylish living room, her damp fingers toying with the piece of paper with the numbers that were a doorway to her past.

Now, today, it was difficult to understand how she could

have been so shortsighted as to not know that this day would come. Even as a very young child Riley had been curious about almost everything. How could Lorna have believed she would never turn that curiosity in the direction of her absent father?

Picking up her phone, Lorna dialed the first number with shaky fingers. She had no idea whether it was a business line, or a personal one, so the voice of a young woman answering the phone had no context or significance.

"Ryan ..." Lorna hesitated over his last name. She hadn't spoken it in so many years. "Ryan Nicholl, please."

"Shall I say who's calling?"

"Lorna Terry," she croaked. "You can tell him Lorna Terry is calling."

Lorna heard the phone being put down and then the young woman calling. "*Dad!* Someone's on the landline for you! A Lorna Terry?"

Gripping the arm of the sofa, Lorna shut her eyes. There was a daughter. *Another daughter.* Riley had a sister. She waited, and heard voices in the background, the sound of someone picking up the phone and then silence. Moments later, another sound, like that of a door being shut.

Finally, a deep breath and a voice from her long distant past. Deep, sonorous, different and yet familiar.

"Lorna," Ryan said. He sounded cautious. "Is this really you?"

"Yes," she said. And out of nowhere, and for no reason that she could discern, there were tears in her eyes. "Yes, Ryan, it's really me."

TWENTY-TWO

"IT'S WHAT I KNOW HOW TO DO."

"Look what the cat drug in!"

"*Dragged*," Malcolm said reflexively. "For the hundredth time, Piper, '*drug*' is not the past tense of 'drag'."

"Jeez." His daughter rolled her eyes and lay on her back once again on the lounger next to his. "I didn't know I was at *grammar* camp."

"And anyway, what're you talking about?"

Piper raised a hand and pointed back over her shoulder toward the house.

They had been on the beach all morning, Malcolm writing on his laptop and Piper getting way too much sun, so she was turning red across the bridge of her nose. Turning, he saw a figure making its way across the sand toward them. His heart thrummed in his chest, and he shielded his eyes to get a better view.

Wearing a white maxi-dress, the hem balled up in one hand to prevent it from sweeping in the sand, was Lorna. She had on shades, and her hair was pulled back. In the hand that held the dress, she also carried her brown sandals. The same sandals Malcolm had grown accustomed to seeing at the front doorstep of the summer rental over the course of the days they had spent alone together. The sandals he had looked for, hoped to see, for a week now whenever he and Piper spent the day out and returned.

"Took you long enough," Piper said when Lorna was standing right in front of them.

"Piper," Malcolm said.

"Well it did."

Malcolm looked at her, and said nothing. She did the same, at first, then finally sat at the edge of Malcolm's lounger. Only yesterday had he stopped calling, texting and waiting for her to come back. But seeing her now, he knew he hadn't stopped waiting. Not really. And that only made him angrier.

Lifting a hand, Lorna put it at his cheek. Their eyes met again.

"You have every right to be angry," she began.

Still he said nothing.

"I should have called or something ..."

His lips twitched, and Malcolm willed himself not to say something he would regret. Something that shouldn't be said with Piper nearby looking on.

"... but this past week, I've had my ass handed to me, and I just ..."

"Piper," Malcolm said, talking over Lorna's explanation. "Could you give us a minute?"

"Sure," Piper sang. "I kind of knew that was coming anyway."

She picked up her towel and stood. Lorna turned and smiled at her as she left. Malcolm set his laptop under his lounger and then faced her once again.

"Look," he said. "I get it now. You're not ..."

Before he could finish, Lorna had his face in both her hands and was kissing him. She forced her way past his initial defenses until he was the one holding her, pulling her closer and pressing his lips hard into hers, punishing her and relieving his own need.

When they came up for air, she looked chastened—an expression not often seen on Lorna Terry's face.

"I know you're angry," she said again. "And you have every right to be. But everything else was difficult enough without ..."

"Everything else?" he said, shaking his head, exasperated. "That's the problem, Lo. I don't even know what the 'everything else' is! You left without explanation and then you stayed away and wouldn't answer my fucking calls!"

"I wasn't sure what I might be walking into, so I had to ..."

"Back up. Walk into 'how'? What are you talking about?"

"Two days before I left, I talked to Steven and he told me that there was a potential problem. With a trustee. That there was an informal inquiry into my relationship with a student."

"Your ... what the ..."

"It isn't true," Lorna said. "At least not really."

"What the hell does that mean, 'not really'? Did you have a relationship with a student, or not?"

"It's Todd. Okay? The grad student we ran into at church. The one who was at my house. That's the relationship they're looking into."

Malcolm narrowed his eyes, trying to understand.

"But he's ..."

"He wasn't even a student when he and I ... Anyway, there was no relationship. Just one night. And then he'd been calling, and I had no idea that he was so ... It turns out his father is a Gilchrist trustee. So it's gotten messy and ..."

"Slow down a second. You knew all this before you left? And yet you didn't *tell* me?" He shoved himself up from his seat and away from her, taking a few paces and then spinning to face her again. "Why the hell ...?"

"I was hoping to go clear things up, Malcolm, that's why. It doesn't have anything to do with ..."

And seeing the look on his face, she seemed to decide that it was advisable not to continue with that sentence.

"I'm not used to this," she said instead. "Having someone to share things like this with, to check in with. And Piper was here, and it seemed like a bad time to ..."

"Don't use Piper as an excuse," he warned. "You wouldn't have told me anyway."

"I may have. I don't know. But the point is, I didn't tell you because it's my mess to clean up. And I didn't want to bring that here. I just wanted to go back, take care of it, and then come back to you."

"So did you? Is it cleaned up?"

She shook her head. "Not really. And then there was the thing with Riley and her father. She wanted me to call him, so ..."

"Lo," Malcolm ran a hand over his head. "You see, this is what I mean ... you have all this shit going on and never thought to tell me?"

Lorna stood and came to him, wrapping her arms around his waist. "I know. *I* get it now. I promise you, I do."

"Do you?" he demanded. "Because it feels like you don't. It feels like you prefer to be on your own, and I'm starting to think I should just let you do that."

Her arms dropped and she stepped back from him. "If that's how you feel, then maybe that's where we are, and I should ..." She turned to leave and he grabbed her by the arm pulling her against his chest.

He kissed her again, and Lorna relented, leaning into the kiss and putting her arms up around his neck.

"*I'm in love with you,*" he said against her lips. "I love you, but I can't ... keep *doing* this shit, Lo."

"I know," she said. "I'm sorry."

"And you can't keep being sorry, either. I need you to just ... let me know what the fuck is up sometimes. I'm not trying to control you and I'm not trying to box you in, if that's what you're afraid of."

"I know you're not. And that's what I lo ... I know you're not, Malcolm. But this is me. This has been me for a lifetime. And overnight, you're expecting things from me that no one's ever expected. I just need you to be a little patient."

Leaning in, his forehead touched hers and then he nuzzled her, their noses brushing against each other. She was asking for his patience, and his understanding. She was saying she was sorry. This woman, who apologized for nothing, asked for nothing and sometimes seemed to need nothing from him was asking for this. From him.

"I'm *trying* ..."

Her lips brushed his, and he kissed her again. They stood there for a long while, arms around each other, the unforgiving Carolina sun beating down on their heads and backs.

"TELL ME WHAT'S GOING ON."

They were in bed. Of course they were. It was their salve, and their solace for every difficult thing that might spring up between them. Malcolm knew it couldn't go on like that forever, and that if they were to go on, one day, they would need to find another path to intimacy. But right now, sex was the most potent weapon in his arsenal.

The sun was setting, slashes of crimson and orange, purple and blue crossing the sky. They had left Piper to her own devices for the balance of the afternoon, with stern instructions not to wander too far. She had rolled her eyes and mumbled, *'whatever'* but hadn't gone anywhere. The entire time he and Lorna were in the bedroom, Malcolm heard her watching television, moving around in the kitchen and talking on the phone with friends.

Propping himself on one elbow he looked down at Lorna, naked among the sheets, her hair loose and tousled.

"What's the deal with this Todd guy?"

"There is no deal," she said. "That's the thing. But apparently, he's been saying otherwise to everyone who will listen. Including his *father*. And now the father, along with the other trustees, are considering whether they should have an inquiry or something into my conduct."

"How old is he?"

"Todd? About thirty. That's the thing. It's just so irrational, Malcolm. And he wasn't even a student at the time. I never knew he intended to be. It was just ..."

"Yeah. A one-time thing. So you keep saying." He fell onto his back, looking at the ceiling.

For a few beats, there was silence.

"Are you ... you can't possibly be upset with me about this, too, can you? For something that ...?"

"That what?" he cut her off. "Happened before we met? Didn't *mean* anything?"

"Yes. Exactly."

"If you think either of those things make a damn bit of difference in how I feel about it, you don't know men as well as you think you do."

He felt Lorna's hand on his chest, making slow circles, then she kissed him there.

"Well, you'll excuse me if your stupid jealousy is the least of my worries right now," she said. "I'm a little more concerned about the damage to my career over what was a mediocre lay at best."

Malcolm bit down on his lower lip and shook his head. "*And* she's back."

Lorna laughed. "I'm sorry, but it's silly. You have me, Malcolm. I'm here. Todd was a mistake. As unsatisfying as a ... second slice of cheesecake when you knew you didn't even need the first."

Rolling his eyes, he sat up. "Let's go see about getting dinner. And later you can tell me about Riley and her father, and what happened there."

"Or you could tell me how the book's going," Lorna suggested. "And how things have been with Piper. Wouldn't you rather talk about that?"

"No. I wouldn't rather. Nice try though. Get your ass up and let's go eat."

———

SOME THINGS COULDN'T BE un-said, or un-heard once said. Things like, *I'm in love with you ...*

Lorna couldn't get it out of her head. Not while she showered after their impromptu bedroom romp, nor now, while she, Malcolm and Piper sat on the deck off the living room, eating the burgers and fries they had picked up for supper. Piper was babbling about a bunch of kids her age she'd met on the beach, asking whether it was alright for her to go hang out with them the next day, and Malcolm was asking all the necessary fatherly questions, while Lorna's mind wandered.

Her thoughts were a jumble, falling one over the other. She thought about Ryan, and about Riley; about the conversation the two had, when Lorna finally handed her daughter the phone. She thought about the look on Riley's face, of flushed pleasure when on the other end of the line Ryan must have said something that pleased her.

And she thought about how when Shawn got home with the kids, Riley had thrown herself at him, arms wrapped tightly about his neck, and cried with real, pure joy. And then Lorna thought about how the cold, dark fingers of guilt wrapped themselves around her heart, along with the relief that Riley had gotten what she was too afraid to say all these years she wanted.

And she thought about her last call to Steven before she left New York again, and how he said he'd been '*firewalled*' from what was going on with President Bond and the trustees, and her case. '*I think it's been elevated beyond my pay-grade at his point, Lorna,*' were his exact words. That, and the fact that she was now considered a "case" were not a good sign.

But finally, now, she was thinking about Malcolm, and those words: *I'm in love with you,* and what that meant for them, and for her.

"*Don't you think so, Lorna?*"

She looked up and saw that both Malcolm and Piper were gazing expectantly at her.

"Don't I think what?"

Piper sighed. "You weren't listening? My Dad thinks he has to meet the parents of the girl who asked me to come swimming at her house. Even though she lives like two feet from here. I think it's stupid. I'm just going to swim."

"Not two feet. More like four hundred yards. But why get bogged down in details?" Malcolm said.

"I think he's absolutely right to want to meet them," Lorna said.

Malcolm smiled at her gratefully, though she knew that *he* knew she had been a much more permissive parent than he was. At this age, Riley had been doing sleepovers with families she'd never met. Now, she was honest enough to admit that it had less to do with her parenting philosophy than it had to do with her own convenience at the time.

"You guys are so old school," Piper said. "I know a kid who once went to like, *France* with a family without his parents meeting them."

"And we'll probably read about that kid in the papers a few years from now, too," Malcolm said. "Driving drunk on the FDR, or ..."

"Shooting up a post office ..." Lorna chimed in.

"Or he'll be the obviously drunk kid at graduation ..." Malcolm said.

"Whose parents didn't even bother to show up," Lorna added.

Then they looked at each other and laughed, aware that they were being inappropriate but unable to help themselves because they were both still a little giddy from their reconciliation and the two hours they spent consummating it.

"That is *so* mean," Piper said looking at them both in horror.

She pushed back from the table and went stomping inside, leaving Malcolm and Lorna sitting alone on the deck, stifling their laughter. As their laughter and smiles faded, Lorna let her hand creep across the table and cover his.

"You were too angry to say as much earlier, but did you miss me when I was gone?"

Who was *this woman?* That asked questions such as this? Surely not her.

"I thought I *showed* you how I much I missed you earlier,"

Malcolm said, turning his hand upward, so they were touching, palm to palm.

"You did. But one of the things I most like about you are your words; your beautiful, beautiful words."

At that, Malcolm smiled, his eyes crinkling at the corners.

"Well, you inspired quite a few choice words this past week when you didn't answer my calls. And I'm not sure they were what you'd call beautiful. And as far as writing goes, I might even have killed off a character unnecessarily because of you."

Lorna smiled back.

"Is that why you keep leaving me?" he asked, the smile fading. "So I can prove, over and over again how much I hate it when you're gone?"

"No." She shook her head, and looked down at the table. "I keep leaving because ... it's what I know how to do."

"It breaks me," he said.

She looked at him once again. "What?"

It frightened her when he said things like that. And shamed her, because she would never, *could* never be as brave as he was to expose himself in that way.

"When you leave. Every single time. It damn near breaks me. Because I never know if you're coming back."

Lorna moved her hand, which until then was still resting on top of his. Or rather, she tried to move it, but Malcolm was too quick for her and grabbed it, interlacing their fingers.

"See?" he said. "See what happened there?" He shook his head. "Don't do that anymore. Don't run away from me."

Her heart hurt. It hurt as though Malcolm had grabbed it in his fist and twisted it like a wet rag, wringing it to bleed from her every ounce of feeling she tried to keep hidden away.

"There they are," she said, struggling to keep her tone light. "Those beautiful words of yours."

TO STAVE off a meltdown by Piper, Malcolm and Lorna later walked over to the house where she had been invited to go swimming. She trailed behind them, complaining the entire way, but Lorna could tell she was secretly a little bit pleased.

Malcolm and his ex probably hadn't figured it out just yet, but they would—Piper wasn't difficult so much as she was a prima donna. If given a daily dose of focused and undivided attention, she would be infinitely easier to handle. The fact that her father and Lorna were spending some of their evening planning for something so inconsequential as a swimming date for her was just the sustenance her little pre-teen ego needed.

The house was set high on the dunes, and had a wide imposing path leading from the street and up to the front door. Like many homes on the island, it was painted dove-grey and white, with an immense wraparound porch and balcony. Inside, the lights were on, and the French doors on the lower level had been flung open, so it was possible to see right through the house from living room to kitchen as they ascended the steps to the entrance. Piper had texted her new friend to make sure it was okay for them to stop by, so just as soon as they made it to the top of the steps, the front door opened and a startlingly blonde woman was standing there.

Wearing white linen shorts and a multi-colored top that Lorna recognized as from the same line of colorful Lily Pulitzer garments that Professor Rogers back at Gilchrist seemed to favor, the woman was also holding a frosted glass of something that looked like a mojito.

"Come in!" she said, stepping aside. "I'm Steffie. And you must be Malcolm ... and Lorna. Hello again, Piper!"

Every word was pronounced with such exuberance, Lorna

could practically see the exclamation marks popping up around the woman's head as she spoke.

"Don's out back laboring over the grill," she explained. "And Piper, you'll find Marley up in her room."

She indicated a wide white staircase, which Piper wasted no time bounding toward and up.

"Thanks for letting us stop by on such short notice," Malcolm said.

"Oh gosh, it's no problem. People drop in and out all the time. Especially during the summer. And when I heard who you are, I just had to meet you."

Lorna took in their surroundings as Steffie gushed. Almost everything in the house was white, which seemed to be a theme on the island—in more ways than one—along with the craftsman style architecture which was a perfect blend of elegance and rusticity.

"Oh, well that's nice of you to say. So, did Piper ..."

"She just told us your name and of course Don and I were excited as all get out. Come this way ..."

Steffie led them through the foyer and an expansive living area out to an equally expansive deck, upon which a tall, blonde man in khaki shorts and a white t-shirt was grilling what looked like whole halibut on a state-of-the-art outdoor grill.

Turning at the sound of their approach, he extended his hand right away. He was handsome, with a ruddy complexion, and tousled hair just as blonde as his wife's.

"Malcolm T. Mitchell," he said. "*God*damn."

The two men shook hands and Don pumped Malcolm's like he wanted to yank it off. Smothering a smile, Lorna waited for them to get through with that and finally, Malcolm put a hand at her back.

"Good to meet you, Don," he said, laughing a little, obviously embarrassed by all the fuss. "This is Lorna."

Don's hand was a little moist and sweaty, and Lorna had to resist the urge to wipe her palm against her skirt when he released it.

"Can I offer you both something to drink?" Steffie asked. "Just made a pitcher of mojitos. And if I do say so myself, they're as good as you'll get."

"Would love one," Lorna said.

"Me too. Thank you," Malcolm said shrugging.

Steffie turned to head back inside, presumably to the bar, then paused and glanced in Lorna's direction. It took her a moment before she realized she was meant to follow, and so Lorna obliged.

"We'll just let them have their man-talk," Steffie said in a stage-whisper as they walked away.

Lorna smiled politely, willing herself not to roll her eyes.

It was two hours before they were able to pry themselves away from Don and Steffie. And by then Lorna had heard the couple's entire life story—about how they met in college and continued dating afterward, and how Don was completely unsuitable to Steffie's old Charleston family but soon proved himself in business. So Steffie's father relented and approved of the marriage, even gifting them with their first house.

And the rest was history, according to Steffie—the girls, Marley and Dylan were born, named after Don's favorite singers. And then they just sort of ... settled in. Steffie actually said that—they "settled in."

Settling in involved Don making oodles of money as a builder, scooping up prime real estate on the island and having this summer home, and one other for the winter out West, custom-made. Steffie had never worked outside the home. She said she "just wasn't that curious about the whole independent woman thing." The entire evening was spent in two pairs—men and women separated, with Lorna yearning to participate in what she imagined was a much more interesting conversation between Don and Malcolm.

But as they walked back to their much more modest rental house, Malcolm assured her that wasn't the case.

"Jesus," he said. "I can't remember being so bored ever before in my life. I just kept drinking to amuse myself. And man, he sure could toss one back."

"Daddy, that's so impolite. You were their guest," Piper said.

"Says my daughter who *majors* in impolite," Malcolm mumbled as Piper skipped ahead of them. "So how was it with Steffie? And what kind of name is that anyway?"

Lorna laughed. "It's short for Stephanie, I'm guessing. Probably about the same as your night. But she did give me some ideas for my book."

"Really?" Malcolm sounded surprised.

"Yeah. Not ideas she had, but listening to her made me think about the burdens of feminism. We don't talk about that a lot, but ... I don't know, Steffie made me think about it."

"What do you mean by burden?"

"Okay, so I'm going to say something. And it's only because I'm a little drunk that I'm going to confess it. Tomorrow, I'll likely deny ever having said it."

Malcolm laughed. "Okay. Hit me."

"There's ... a certain freedom in being able to depend on a man."

Malcolm looked at her, and Lorna could barely make out his features in the dark. About a dozen yards ahead, Piper was still skipping, obviously pleased by how the evening had gone since it virtually assured that she would have swimming dates with Marley whenever she wanted for the remainder of her stay.

"Freedom."

"Yes," Lorna said. "In feminist theory, we talk about the limits of dependency, the chains, and what it prevents you from doing. But listening to Steffie I was just struck by how idyllic her world is. Her father took care of her and made all the tough decisions, and then later, Don did. And to hear her tell it, they both have done a really good job.

"So there's freedom in that—she doesn't worry about bills, about not doing well in her career, about supporting a household ... or anything else for that matter if its unrelated to keeping her children and husband healthy and happy. And herself too. I mean, did you see her figure? She looked like she was twenty-five! Probably does Pilates three times a week, yoga twice and cardio for the other two. Gets facials, pedicures ..."

"Would you want that life?" Malcolm asked.

"Oh god, of course not," Lorna laughed. "I think too much. I would be bored out of my skull. But the point is, not everyone is me. Not everyone wants what I want. The women like Steffie, the ones I write about as though they're oppressed? Maybe some of them feel very, very free. And if that's the case, who am I to judge?"

"This can't be the first time you've had this realization, right?"

"No, but I think it's the first time I've allowed it to penetrate. The truth is, old-style feminism has an element of tyranny in it, the whole, *'believe as we do, or you're anti-woman'* thing. I think in my book, it would be good to openly acknowledge that, and call it out, y'know?"

"Could be revolutionary. Lorna Terry publicly softening her stance on what it means to be a womanist."

"Softening? I don't know. Maybe just being honest, finally."

They were approaching the house now, and Malcolm slowed her with a hand on her arm.

"I want to say something to you," he said, lowering his voice.

"You *guys*!" Piper was at the front door, waiting. "I need to go!"

"Door's open, Piper," Malcolm called.

Once she disappeared inside, he turned once again to Lorna and held both her arms, just above the elbows, his hands running up and down, along the surface of her skin.

"Look," he said. "I know this has been an adjustment for you, this whole ... relationship thing. But when I'm with you, like now, like tonight ... something just feels right. Like we fit. The things we talk about, the way we talk ... it enriches me, it inspires me ... I don't know if after having this, I could ever go back to being without it."

"Malcolm ... you're scaring me. You're not about to ..." Lorna's voice faltered for a moment. "Propose or anything like that, are you?"

"I know that might sound crazy to you, but it doesn't sound crazy to me," he said.

"Malcolm ..." Lorna tried to step back, but he held her tighter, pulled her closer.

"Wait. I know that's probably not something you're even willing to think about just yet. And that's cool ... but whatever we call it, whatever you settle on, I just need to know that all bullshit aside, we're in it, and we're doing this thing."

"And 'this thing' would be what? Marriage? Living together? What exactly is it you want?"

"Everything you can give."

Lorna shook her head emphatically from side to side. "No. That doesn't answer the question. I can give what I can give. That doesn't tell me what *you* want."

Malcolm laughed. "The always-challenging, Lorna Terry. So what, you want a list?"

"Do you have one?"

"I can give you one on the fly. As long as you understand I may want to add stuff later. We *have* been drinking all night after all."

"Understood. So, go. Give me your list."

"*Monogamy*," Malcolm said right away.

Lorna laughed softly. "Of course."

"Yeah. That one's really important."

"I knew it would be. What else?"

"*Communication.* No more of those fucking secrets you've been keeping from me. *Co-habitation.* I want us to live together, sleep together every night. *Partnership.* I want us to agree to decide the big things together. I don't get to run off to Portugal to research a book without consulting with you first, and you don't get to disappear for a week without telling me why."

As he spoke, Malcolm had pulled her even closer. Lorna smelled the not unpleasant mint and alcohol on his breath from Steffie's mojitos.

"And friendship, and collaboration, and all the things that already make us, us." He lowered his head, speaking against the shell of her ear, making Lorna tingle. This man, *made her tingle.* "I want all of what we have now. And more shit that we'll make up as we go along."

"Well," she said. "Is *that* all?"

"Is that a 'yes'?"

"That's an '*I'll think about it.*'"

"I'll take that," he said. "For now."

"Good."

He released her, but kept his hold on her hand and they started walking again until Malcolm stopped her once more.

"I thought of one more thing," he said.

"What's that?"

"Honesty," Malcolm said. "And that's a dealbreaker. Right

up there with monogamy. After what I went through with Charlotte, I'm not doing that again. Between the ugly truth and beautiful lies, I'll take the truth every time."

"Sounds reasonable enough," Lorna said, trying to sound airy.

And it was reasonable—more than reasonable—to ask for honesty if they moved forward.

But what of the lies she'd already told?

TWENTY-THREE

IDYLL'S END

MALCOLM HOISTED PIPER'S BACKPACK OVER HIS SHOULDER and waited at the foot of the steps for her to drag the last of her luggage from the Audi. How someone could accumulate that much stuff after a two-week stay on an island, he would never understand.

Originally scheduled to return home within a day of Lorna's return, Piper had successfully negotiated with her mother to let her stay until the end of the month, with Malcolm's consent. She had made new friends, and formed an alliance of sorts with Lorna, so he saw no harm in it. For the last two weeks in North Carolina, all three of them had developed their own rhythm; one which allowed both Malcolm and Lorna ample time to write, and Piper long hours on the beach.

"You have your keys, right?" Malcolm asked for the umpteenth time. He hit the fob to lock the car when Piper finally extricated all her belongings.

"Yes, Dad, I have my keys."

Charlotte had promised to leave work early so that shortly after he and Piper arrived, she would be home. While Piper had been a model of good behavior in North Carolina, neither of them were optimistic enough to believe that meant she was a wholly transformed kid.

Just as Piper inserted her keys into the lock, the door swung open.

"Surprise!" It was Charlotte. Wearing jeans and a white tank top, she was barefoot and barefaced. "I decided not to go to work after all. Wanted to be here to greet my baby."

"Hi Mom." Piper accepted her mother's tight embrace but glanced over her shoulder at Malcolm as though she suspected the woman hugging her might be an impostor.

"Let me look at you." Charlotte held her at arms' length and smoothed a hand over Piper's hair. "You look all tanned! And maybe even a little taller. Is she taller, Mal?"

Malcolm shrugged. "Could be."

"I'm going to go upstairs and put up my stuff," Piper said. "Mom, what's to eat?"

"Good to see some things never change. I'll order Indian or something in a minute, okay?"

"Or Thai," Piper said. "I ate all kinds of fried crap when I was in North Carolina so I need something light."

Malcolm and Charlotte exchanged amused looks as Piper went traipsing inside and up the stairs to her room.

"She scarfed down all that 'fried crap' without a peep while we were there, though."

"I bet she did. So ... thank you for those extra weeks. Sounded like she was having an amazing time, so I hated to kill that. Not to mention, she would have come back with all kinds of attitude."

"Yeah," Malcolm said glancing at his watch. "I think that's a fair assumption. So ..."

"You're not going to run off right away, are you?" Charlotte said, letting her head fall to one side. "Come in and have a coffee or something. You have a few hours at least before you have to worry about rush hour."

Rather than reminding her that just about every hour was rush hour in New York, Malcolm accepted her invitation and went in, following Charlotte as she padded toward the kitchen. Heading for the Nespresso machine, she got it started and reached for two mugs from the cabinet overhead.

"So, how was it?" she asked, as she moved about the kitchen.

"It was fine," he said, his mind already drifting to what awaited him upstate.

Lorna had left for New York a day earlier than he and Piper, planning to meet with Steven Hunt to get updated on what might be happening with the trustees. For the last two weeks, there had been nothing at all and so they were both hoping that it had all blown over and been recognized for the big nothing it was. But until he talked to Lorna, he couldn't rest easy.

"Everything? She got along with ..."

"You've asked me that a thousand times, Charlotte. So for the one-thousand-and-first time, yes. Piper and Lorna got along great."

Charlotte shook her head and exhaled a quick breath. "Of course they did. Sometimes I wonder if she does it to spite me."

"Who? And does *what* to spite you?"

"*Piper!*" she hissed, shooting a look in the direction of the stairs. "If you weren't around to see some of it as well, I would almost believe she's trying to make me look crazy."

"I'm sorry. I'm not following." Malcolm wiped a hand over his face, already sorry he'd agreed to the coffee.

"She goes away this difficult, hard-to-control kid, at least according to me. And yet when she's with you, she's the very picture of an angel. So I wonder if it's me she has it in for."

"I'm sure that's not the case, Char."

"Are you? I mean, what if I'm just a bad mother?"

"You're not a bad mother, Charlotte. That I know for sure isn't the case."

Charlotte smiled and came over to the counter where Malcolm was sitting, resting her hand on top of his.

"Thank you for that."

Sliding his hand from beneath hers, Malcolm cleared his throat. "So what'd you do with all your child-free time?"

"The same. Worked. Went to dinner a few times." Then she looked at him, biting into her lower lip. "Broke things off with Spence for good."

"Oh yeah?" Malcolm asked, surprised by how little he cared.

She may as well have been talking about a relationship between strangers. With each passing day and week away from his marriage, the more of a stranger Charlotte felt; the more of a stranger the man he had been with her felt.

"Yeah. It's done. It feels ..." She laughed a quick, dry laugh. "Like waking up from a bad flu. Suddenly I'm feeling all clear-headed and ... foolish."

"Look. Charlotte ..."

"You've said my name maybe five times in the last fifteen minutes," she mused. "That only happens when you're losing patience with me." She came around the counter so she was standing directly in front of him. "*Are* you losing patience with me?"

"Charlotte ..."

She laughed lightly. "*Six* times now. I'll take that as a 'yes'." But still, she put a hand up to his cheek. "You were always very patient. A very patient husband. A patient father. It was one of the things I loved most about you."

Malcolm turned his head to break the contact, but Charlotte cupped his face instead.

"I always felt like I could screw up and you would wait. You'd give me a chance to realize it, and correct it. Even after the divorce, I felt like that. But now ... I don't know. It feels different."

"That's because it is."

"Yes, but 'till death do us part, Mal. That's what we said. And when I said it, believe it or not, I meant it. I ..."

"Did you mean it when you were fucking Spence?"

"Yes, actually. I think I got ... caught up in the excitement of it. And just like you said when I stopped by your house, I guess I tried to make the fantasy a reality. But it was never real. I see that now. What we had was real. Our *family* is real. And I want that back."

Charlotte got up on her toes and leaned in, and a second before her lips met his, there was a loud exclamation of an expletive. They both spun around to find Piper at the kitchen door.

"Are you *serious*?!" she demanded.

"Piper ..." Charlotte stepped away from Malcolm and he took a deep breath.

"You're *divorced!*" Piper shrieked. "And you ..."

She stabbed a finger in Malcolm's direction. "You are *cheating* on Lorna!"

"That's not what's happening, Piper," Malcolm began.

"I saw it with my own eyes! You two make me sick!"

She turned and ran out of the room, and moments later came the sound of a slamming door, slammed so hard, it may have loosened the hinges.

Malcolm sighed. "Well ... thanks for that, Charlotte."

"Look ... I'm ... let's go talk to her. I'll explain that ..."

"*Let's* go talk to her?" Malcolm repeated. "No." He shook

his head and reached for his car keys. "I'm going home. You go talk to her. That's your mess, so I suggest *you* clean it up."

"HEY! What're you doing here? Are you lost?"

Lorna had just rounded the corner in the approach to her front door and there was Malcolm, sitting on her stoop like a teenage Romeo, waiting for his Juliet to make it home from school.

"Nope." He shoved himself to his feet and waited until she'd opened the door. "Swung by here on my way home, got out of the car and then couldn't muster up the energy to get back in and leave again. It's so freaking hot."

Lorna laughed, shoving the door open so they could both enter. "What if I didn't come home for hours?"

"Then I would have gone in search of you."

Pushing her back against the door, Malcolm kissed her as though he hadn't seen her just two days ago.

"Are you just getting back to town?"

"Yeah, just." He kissed her neck, pulled her t-shirt aside at the neck, and moved to her shoulder.

"Then you must be tired," she suggested, feeling her breath hitch in her throat.

"Not really. Annoyed. Horny. But not tired."

"Let's start with annoyed." Lorna shoved gently against his chest so he would take a step back. "Horny is kind of self-explanatory."

"Just some dumb shit with Charlotte. As usual."

"What happened?"

Lorna listened as he described the scene in his ex-wife's kitchen, and Piper's reaction when she walked in on it. Smiling, she looked up at him, then shook her head, kicking off her slip-ons and shedding her pocketbook.

"That's funny to you?" he asked.

"No. Actually, it kind of makes me angry," Lorna admitted.

"Angry?" Malcolm gave a laugh. "And your reaction to anger is to ... smile?"

"No, I'm smiling because it's strange that I would be angry." She turned to face him. Malcolm's expression was quizzical. "It means I feel ... possessive of you."

At that, Malcolm gave a brief smile, his expression transforming to predatory as he advanced closer. "You do, huh?"

"I do. Which is really kind of silly if you think about it because ..."

"I *don't* think about it," Malcolm said talking over her. "In fact, my ambition for you is that one day you'll just feel your feelings, and not analyze them so much."

"Well," Lorna said letting the word drag out. "That's going to take a while."

"Why is it going to take a while?"

He had backed her up against her sofa so Lorna had a good idea what was going to happen next. She was already sopping wet anticipating what would happen next.

"Because a lot of what I feel for you is new. Some of it I've never felt before," she said, shrugging.

The admission caused her heart-rate to increase. It felt dangerous and reckless, like stepping out on a limb without the assurance of a safety net underneath. And the significance of it wasn't lost on Malcolm either, because for a split second he froze and then he was smiling again.

"Oh, wipe that silly grin off your face," she said.

"You're smiling too."

"Yes," she said, allowing him to push her back onto the sofa.

With his leg, he parted hers, standing between them and beginning to work on his belt. "But for different reasons."

"What are *your* reasons?"

"My reasons," she said. "Are that I have a sense that I'm about to feel your mouth on me ... feel you inside me. Very soon. And I've been wanting that, and thinking about it all day."

There. Now *that* was much easier to say. And better yet, it had the desired effect.

Malcolm's grin widened. "Nah." He shook his head. "See, you were wrong. We weren't smiling for different reasons. That's exactly why I'm smiling too."

Then he was on his knees, and yanking her pants from the waist, not bothering to loosen the buttons. With it he dragged off her underwear as well, so she was bare-assed on her sofa, and they were poised to pretty much ruin it.

"SO, ANY NEWS FROM THE COLLEGE?"

She watched as Malcolm got up and walked naked to her kitchen, returning with bottles of water for them both. Lorna took the one he handed her and turned, snuggling into the afghan. He looked amazing naked. Some men, no matter how impressive they looked in clothes, seemed a little absurd when naked. Malcolm was definitely not one of those men.

"I think so," she murmured.

"What do you mean you think so?"

"There was a letter in my mailbox. I didn't open it. It's in my bag."

"Why the hell didn't you open it?" Malcolm reached over and snatched up her pocketbook from where she'd discarded it on the floor about forty-five minutes earlier.

"Because the minute I got in the door you attacked me?" she said matter-of-factly, reaching for the bag.

Opening it, she looked inside and fished out the envelope that had been in her box when she got to her office that morning. Lorna had spent the entire day, aware of it, but reluctant to open it. Probably, she could admit now, because subconsciously, she'd been waiting for Malcolm and wanted him there when she did.

"Here it is." She handed it to him.

"You want me to do it?" he confirmed.

"Please."

Glancing first at the envelope, he looked at her again. "It's from President Bond's office. Not the trustees. That's good, right? Or at least not as bad?"

"I don't know. Let's open it and see."

Lorna closed her eyes, listening rather than watching as Malcolm broke the seal on the envelope. A few seconds passed and she opened her eyes. He was reading, his brows furrowed.

"For god's sake, Malcolm, what does it say?"

"It says ..."

Lorna only focused on a few phrases: '... *calling into question your position as a member of faculty in good standing ...*' and '... *resolve this matter in a manner that takes into account your best interests, those of the student involved, and of course Gilchrist College.*' And finally, the one she expected: '... *meet to discuss this matter in person with all interested parties.*'

But there was more.

"And it says," Malcolm was speaking very slowly. "That you're free to come with representation if you wish."

"So there you have it," Lorna said.

"There we have what?"

"They're going to try to get me to resign, take a sabbatical, or accept some form of censure."

Malcolm shook his head. "They're not going to ask you to *resign* over a one-nighter with a thirty-year old man."

"They're going to ask for something. Some pound of flesh. Because if that wasn't the case, they wouldn't tell me I could bring a lawyer. They're going to offer something that I probably won't want to take. That's why they think I need representation."

"Maybe, but ..."

"But nothing. That's exactly what's going to happen."

She felt strangely dispassionate about the whole thing. The long reprieve, when it seemed like the entire thing was going away, was probably just the time it had taken for Gilchrist to consult their own attorneys and figure out what they could offer, and what they could get away with.

"Baby ..." Lorna looked up at Malcolm's concerned face. He had touched her hip, but she barely felt it. "You okay?"

"Fine," she said, her voice hollow.

"Look, I know plenty of lawyers. We can find ..."

"No. I'm not walking in there like I have some reason to lawyer-up. Like I committed a *crime*."

"Then I'll come with you."

"No." She sat up. "Are you insane? You haven't even taught your first class at the college yet. Barely even signed your contract. You can't get mixed up in something like this."

"*Mixed up* in it?" he demanded. "Lo, look at me. *Look* at me!"

She looked.

"Whatever happened to partnership? Huh?"

"There's partnership and then there's career suicide. And besides, I never said yes to your little ... list of ultimatums."

Malcolm snorted and let his head fall back. He looked at the ceiling for a long while, as though the secrets to the universe might be etched there.

"So we're back here again? First sign of trouble and we're already back here?"

"This isn't the first sign," Lorna said holding her voice as steady as she could manage. "There have been *plenty* of signs, Malcolm, and you know it."

"You're just going to flip the switch to 'off' again? Just like that, huh?" He picked up the letter and shook it. "This doesn't say anything we didn't think it would say. Nothing's changed! So why are you suddenly so ..."

"Because I actually thought it would be over with," she said slowly. "It seemed so ... remote. So asinine that an almost twenty-year career could come down to this ..." She laughed harshly. "This little farce of a *non*-scandal."

Malcolm was watching her, not saying anything, looking like he didn't know what she might say or do next.

"If I'd known." Lorna sat up and shook her head, grabbing her t-shirt from the floor and pulling it over her head. "If I'd known how expensive a roll in hay it was going to be, at least I would have made sure he'd done it the way I like it."

"Lorna ..." Malcolm said warningly.

She knew he hated to hear her talk like that, to talk about other men she had been with, and how it had been with them.

"I would have had him go down on me a couple times more, you know what I mean?" She looked him directly in the eyes, seeing his anger, and the pain beneath. "I would have had him fuck me *harder*, like you do ... or longer, or ..."

"*Shut up, Lo*," Malcolm said. He pulled his pants on and was reaching for his shirt. His underwear was somewhere. Forgotten.

"I would have taken it *up the ass*, if I knew I was going to wind up bent over a barrel anyway."

"*Shut the fuck up!*"

Lorna jumped at the sound of his voice. Louder than she

had ever heard it before. Angrier than the angriest she had ever seen him. His chest was heaving, and his face had the appearance of a thunder-cloud.

"You should go."

"Lo ..."

"I *want* you to go," she amended.

"If I go this time," he said. "If you send me away now ..." Malcolm shook his head. "I won't be back."

Lorna gave half a shrug, and ignored the sudden painful pounding of her heart.

When going to war, it was best to travel light.

"Yes," she said quietly. "I know."

TWENTY-FOUR

NO RULES BROKEN

"GETTING ALL SETTLED BACK IN?"

Malcolm looked up and toward the doorway of his office. He'd left the damn thing ajar again. Eve Rogers was looking in, her long curtain of hair falling to one side.

"Hey, Eve," he said, mustering what he hoped looked like a collegial smile. "How've you been?"

"Good. Excellent." Evidently, she took that as an offer to enter, because she shoved the door open and crossed the threshold, immediately taking a seat on the arm of one of his guest chairs. "So when did you get back?"

"Late last week."

"And you were in ...?"

"Down south," he said vaguely. "You know. Getting some quiet, getting some work done."

"How'd it go?"

"Well. Very well. So ..." He smiled again, this time apologetically, getting ready to let her know that he had work to do, and not much time to chit-chat.

"Look, I know it must be awkward," she blurted out. "What with Professor Terry and you ... and everything. But I ..."

"*What* must be awkward?" he asked.

Lorna had never liked Rogers, but he had remained largely indifferent to her. Now, though, he thought he could detect just the tiniest bit of satisfaction on her face and in her tone. And more than a little falsity.

Lorna may have been scathing in her judgment sometimes, but she was generally spot-on when it came to figuring out people's motives. He had always believed—perhaps egotistically—that Lorna disliked Rogers primarily because of Rogers' interest in him. But maybe there was more to it than that, and always had been.

"You know," Eve Rogers blushed a little, playing with a strand of her hair and for the first time not meeting his gaze. Usually, she more than met his gaze, she almost aggressively sought it out. "The whole thing with the student, and ..." She let her voice trail off when it became clear he wasn't about to give her anything approaching a reaction.

"Yeah, well, I have a lot to do, so ..." Malcolm indicated a phantom pile of work on his desk.

"Of course. Having been gone so long and all. And just so you know, we're all rooting for her. This could have happened to any one of us, so ..." Apparently she had decided to try another tack, seeing that her thinly disguised gloating hadn't gotten her anywhere.

"You think so?" Malcolm asked on a hunch. "That it could have happened to any one of us?"

This time Eve Rogers played with the sleeve of her blouse.

"Any one of us who might have ... met someone who we found attractive who then turned out to be ..."

"Because I actually don't think it could have happened to any one of us. This whole thing has the feel of, I don't know, a *witch-hunt.* Don't you think?" This time he was the one looking her directly in the eye. "Almost like someone deliberately fanned the flames and ... ginned things up a little."

"I don't know what would make you think that. From what I hear the young man in question told his father, who happens to be a trustee. That seems to me to ..."

"So that's pretty open knowledge then, huh?"

Eve Rogers gave a thin smile, then stuck her chin out, defiant once again. "He told everyone who would listen that he was sleeping with her," she said.

"Including you?" Malcolm leaned back in his chair, arms folded.

Rogers said nothing.

"And who'd *you* tell, Eve?"

"You haven't known her very long, Malcolm. But Lorna Terry has never been one for ... discretion. I'm not sure anything I could have shared would have gone too far beyond what she herself would have."

"Did you tell Steven Hunt?" he asked, cutting to the chase.

"Look." Eve Rogers stood, smoothing out imaginary creases in her skirt. "I only stopped by to say 'hello' and see how you were holding up. Considering she's meeting with President Bond and the trustees today. I imagine it's a stressful time for ... for you both."

"I'll pass on your good wishes," Malcolm said dryly.

When Rogers was gone, he glanced at his watch. It was just after eleven a.m. Not that the time had any significance to him. He had no idea when precisely Lorna might be going to her meeting because they hadn't spoken. For five whole days, they had no contact of any kind. Nor would there be. Not if he was the one expected to initiate it.

He had pursued Lorna Terry longer and harder than any woman he had ever known, and still felt only slightly closer to catching up with her. Whenever he thought he was getting somewhere, she just ...

What did it matter? It was all done with.

Expelling a hard, frustrated breath, Malcolm shifted in his seat. *What if she was there now?* He knew her. She would be terrified, but pretending not to be. Her work meant everything to her, and she would be scared to death of losing it.

That day at her house, Malcolm knew exactly what she was doing. He knew what she was doing even while she did it— goading him, taunting him, trying to make him angry and jealous so he would leave—and still, it had worked. She could wind him up like no one else; that was for damn sure. And in the end he hadn't left because she made him angry, he left because in trying to make him mad, she was telling him that yet again, she preferred to go it alone.

And chances were, she always would.

As hard as it was going to be, he would just have to train himself not to let it get to him. And if for some reason, some day he happened across Lorna with the next sucker who got pulled in by those eyes, that smile and that sharp, smart tongue of hers ...

Malcolm groaned and shifted in his seat. Taking a deep breath, he tried to focus on his computer monitor. His browser was open on a page that he no longer recalled looking for, or why.

He could still hear her voice in his head.

I'm glad I'm here.

I'm glad you're here too.

Malcolm had traced a line from the nape of her neck down to the slope of her ass, feeling her stir beneath his touch, and feeling his manhood stir as well, again. With her everything felt new, as though he hadn't experienced it before. Lorna was for him the rush of first love, of his first kiss, of the first time burying himself deep inside a woman, all over again.

No, she said turning onto her side so she could look at him. *I mean, I'm not just glad I'm here. I'm glad I'm here with you. With* you.

And then she leaned in to kiss him.

That was their second night in North Carolina, the night when they'd made love three times and he came so hard, he thought he would pass out. Which would have been embarrassing and hard to live down. But that was what Lorna did to him.

Damn her.

"YOU HAVE TO UNDERSTAND, Lorn ... Professor Terry. It's the lack of judgment we're concerned about," President Bond said.

Lorna smiled. "I wondered when we might get to that word —judgment. That handy catch-all for when no rules have *actually* been broken."

Julia Bond sniffed and looked away.

She was a regal woman, about sixty-five or so. She looked like a Hollywood casting director's version of a college president, complete with fitted tweed riding jacket (in the summer, no less!), knee-length A-line skirt and heels of modest height. Her chestnut hair was only just beginning to show signs of gray, which contributed to her authoritative mien.

Lorna liked Julia, respected her even. But she was no heroine, and wasn't about to throw herself on her sword for this cause, or any cause for that matter. President of the College earned well over three hundred thousand a year, and enjoyed many perks, like the mansion, the prestige and invitations to loads of fashionable parties thrown by wealthy alums. To her credit though, coming up on what was the tail-end of an hour, Lorna could see that the meeting was wearing on the college president. She didn't like being here. She didn't like it one bit.

Even Julia, Lorna assumed, could see how terrible the optics of the situation were—Lorna, the lone person of color, and a woman, sitting in this Victorian parlor of an office opposite a roomful of White men (and one Asian man, but why get technical?) and defending her sexual choices.

They had done the round Robin of introductions when they all sat down, so Lorna now knew which of them Todd Williamson's father was. He was portly and stern-faced and looked like a villain from a Charles Dickens novel. He had barely nodded his acknowledgment when introduced. Lorna wondered if he really thought she had *taken advantage of* his adult son. If it wasn't for her career being on the line, she might have laughed at the whole damn thing.

"So you think good judgment has no place among the attributes of a Gilchrist College tenured professor?" one of the trustees challenged.

Lorna couldn't recall his name.

"I think good judgment wasn't even a factor in this circumstance," she said.

"I'm quite surprised to hear you say that. You were at an academic conference, paid for by the college, and representing the college. How you conducted yourself while you were there, you don't see as requiring good judgment?"

"I met Todd ... Mr. Williamson ..."

At the mention of his son's name, the elder Mr. Williamson's lips tightened into an ugly, white line. Part of her wanted to yell at him: *Lighten the hell up! Your son got the best lay of his almost-thirty year old life!*

"I met Mr. Williamson after-hours at a social event organized for the conference. I had no idea why he was there, who he was, nor did I know that he intended to enroll at the college."

"And are you in the habit of spending the evening with men you meet in this fashion at academic conferences, Professor Terry?"

Lorna opened her mouth to answer when someone else cut her off, which was just as well since she was seconds away from saying something that would almost certainly have gotten her fired on the spot.

"You see, that's the judgment we're talking about," the interrupter chimed in. "Whether your conduct at these gatherings could bring disrepute to Gilchrist, or ..."

Lorna laughed. "Have any of you been to one of these conferences? *Ever?* I promise you, the 'conduct' rivals what you might see at the most boisterous undergrad keggers. And if you're concerned that what I did was in some way of out of the norm ..." She broke off and laughed again. "Well, you can rest easy on that one."

"So, everyone else is doing it? Is *that* your defense?" the elder Williamson spat.

"Actually, no," Lorna said, straightening her shoulders. "I have no defense. Because what happened was no one's business but mine and Todd's. That he chose to share it with all and sundry ... well, I would call into question his judgment. Not mine."

"Lorna, please." Julia Bond raised a hand, obviously hoping to quiet the inevitable blow-up that was imminent. The elder Williamson had gone positively purple with rage. "Let's try to stick to the matter at hand. We want to know that you at least, after some reflection, regret what happened and that it happened with a student. And that you're prepared to offer an assurance that it won't happen again."

Julia Bond's eyes were imploring her to be cooperative. Begging her almost. This was her signal, from one woman to another: *give them what they want, whatever will satisfy their need for a show of contrition and walk out of here scot-free.*

Lorna took a breath. That might satisfy these men, but her? She wasn't so sure.

Of course, she could say she was sorry. Three simple words, and maybe, it would all go away. They would give her a slap on the wrist, maybe take away one of her freshman courses and bump her out of line for any higher office at the college. And then she could go back to her life, and write her articles and her book and pretend this whole thing had never happened.

But wouldn't that be flying in the face of everything she believed, everything she had been teaching young men and women for more than ten years now? That their sexuality was their own? That between consenting adults, no one else had the right to impose their notion of morality? That women, *most especially women*, should be *unapologetic* about their desire to be touched, held, fingered, fucked ... whatever made them feel good, as long as they felt good about *themselves* as well?

No. *Apologizing was out of the question.* If she did so now, when there was actually something that mattered to her at stake, then she would be nothing but a fraud.

Shooting Julia Bond an apologetic look, Lorna slowly shook her head.

"I can't offer you regret," she said. "And the only assurance I can give is that while a member of faculty, I never have, nor *will* I ever knowingly get involved with a student."

A few of the trustees nodded as though satisfied, but the elder Williamson looked far from it.

"Well," President Bond said. She smoothed her hands over her skirt, and Lorna wondered whether her palms were clammy too, whether she too, had damp patches under her arms. "Thank you for coming in to meet with us, Professor Terry. I'll be in touch if there's anything further, but I think it's fair to say you should hear from me either way, very soon."

What 'either way' meant, Lorna wasn't sure. But she was glad the meeting was over. She stood, nodded at the assembly of men—her jury—and turned to leave the room.

SMILING at President Bond's receptionist as she made her way out of the parlor, Lorna took a deep breath. The air felt lighter suddenly. Now, the chips would fall where they may. At least she had made it out of the meeting with her temper and her dignity intact.

The last several days, waiting for today had been like preparing for battle. And as she always did when she knew she had to face any difficult or challenging task, she had drawn into herself, living almost monastically—spending her time thinking, meditating, planning, and when she was hungry, eating; when she was tired, sleeping. But very little else.

She neither answered nor made any calls, she didn't write and she didn't read. She channeled all of her energy into being Lorna-*Fucking*-Terry, the woman who never backed down from a fight, especially those she knew she was expected not to win.

Come what may, she felt almost triumphant for having made it through that ridiculous, sexist inquisition, and wanted to unload and discuss it with someone. Anyone. Well, maybe not anyone. A very specific ...

Opening the door to the outer vestibule, it took her a moment to process what she was seeing. What she focused on first was the baby, an infant young enough that it could be almost *any* infant, except that Lorna recognized the shock of silky, dark hair and the eyes. It was her granddaughter.

Cassidy was being held in strong masculine arms, though not those of her father. He looked up, and then stood up.

Malcolm.

"Mom!"

Before Lorna could react to the unexpected and dissonant sight of her Malcolm holding the baby, Riley was there, hugging her.

"What were you *thinking* not telling me?" Riley hugged and held her for a long time.

Lorna wanted to respond, but she was still reeling from the sight over her daughter's shoulder, of Malcolm, holding the baby, cradling her head gently in his large hand. He gave her a half-smile, far less than the smiles she was accustomed to from him. And his eyes, which she usually could read with little effort, gave nothing away.

"How did you ...?"

"Malcolm told me," Riley said. "He called and said it was important I get here right away, and so I did. I didn't even have a chance to ..."

"Where's Cullen?"

"Shawn's got him," Riley said impatiently. "That's what you're asking me right now? Where Cullen is? I can't believe you didn't ..."

"In about five minutes, a gaggle of outraged men will be walking through here," Lorna said. "So maybe we should take this little family reunion outside?"

"Fine, but you have some explaining to do, Lorna. I can't believe y ..."

"Yes, yes, we covered that." With a hand at Riley's back, she ushered her daughter toward the building exit, with Malcolm following silently, still carrying Cassidy.

"My car's over here."

Riley indicated a black SUV, the standard mode of transportation she and Shawn used when they were being chauffeured anywhere. And if Lorna knew her son-in-law, the driver would be some mammoth of a man, large enough to engage and overcome just about anyone in hand-to-hand combat.

So Malcolm had called. But how did *he* know?

Lorna hadn't spoken to nor reached out to him in any way since that scene in her house the previous week, hoping to retrain herself to be without him. Almost convinced just that morning that the retraining was successful, she now knew she had been lying to herself. Seeing him confirmed it, and knowing that he had gone to the trouble of finding the one person—other than himself—she might want to see after this meeting, only *re*confirmed it. If only they were alone, and she could talk to him, and...

And say what, though? She had pretty firmly shut the door on whatever might have been, and ultimately, it was probably for the best. She had never been one for relationship postmortems. When it was done, it was just done, no matter how it might hurt, no matter what her regrets. But she did want to thank him, for giving her what she didn't acknowledge she needed.

"Give me the house-keys," Riley was saying now. "I'll meet you back at your place. So get your car, wherever it is, and come straight home, okay?"

Lorna nodded, unable to keep her eyes off Malcolm and Cassidy. He was no longer looking at her though, but instead bouncing a little on the balls of his feet to keep the baby quiet, clumsily, the way men do.

"Lorna. Are you listening? *Straight home* so we can talk about this."

"For god's sake, Riley. You know I hate it when you talk to me like I'm a child. Yes! Straight home. I heard you."

"Good."

Then she was turning away and going to retrieve her child from Malcolm whom she paused to kiss briefly on the cheek.

Watching the exchange, Lorna wondered for a moment how they had talked about her—probably the way parents would about a wayward and hard-to-control teenager. The way Malcolm probably talked to his ex-wife about Piper.

As Riley approached the SUV, a man every bit as burly as Lorna expected, got out from the driver's side and opened the door for her, helping her in with the baby and then shutting the door. When the SUV pulled away, Lorna and Malcolm were left standing there, facing each other, wordless.

He was first to break the silence.

"You okay?" he asked.

Lorna nodded, feeling a lump, like a pebble in the back of her throat.

"So ..." Malcolm shoved his hands deep in his pockets. "Any conclusions, or ...?"

"No. Not yet. They expressed their shock and outrage, I gave my explanation and ..." She shrugged.

"Yeah, well. I'm glad you're alright." He turned to walk away.

"Malcolm."

He stopped but didn't turn around.

"That you called Riley," Lorna said. "I can't begin to tha..."

"Then don't," he said. "Just take care of yourself, Lorna."

He continued walking and didn't look back. Not even when he was at his car. He just opened the door, got in and drove away.

"YOU DIDN'T THINK I might want to know?"

The baby was asleep in the next room in the middle of Lorna's bed and Riley was unleashing, letting Lorna have it, the way she knew she would. But her mind was elsewhere. Not in the room full of men wearing suits and disapproving stares, but in the parking lot outside afterward where she had watched Malcolm walk away.

"Mom! I asked you something."

"You were already dealing with something else that was pretty intense, Riley. I thought ..."

"You thought," Riley scoffed.

"Okay, so I should have told you. I admit that. Okay?"

Looking at her with narrowed eyes, suspicious by her uncharacteristic lack of pushback, Riley came closer.

"So are you going to tell me now?"

"Didn't Malcolm tell you when he called?"

"Very little. He assumed I knew. And then when he realized I had no idea what he was talking about, he just told me I had to come right away. That you needed me, and it was urgent that I come immediately. Scared me to death. Do you have any *idea*?"

Lorna felt herself deflate. She was so tired all of a sudden. Tired of fighting in general, but most especially tired of fighting with those she loved. Those she ... loved.

"I just said, I should have told you," she repeated.

"So tell me now. Everything, Lorna. And leave nothing out."

Woodenly, and without emotion, Lorna recounted for Riley the entire Todd Williamson saga, beginning with the moment she woke up in her hotel room, regretting the one-night stand that had been far from worth the trouble, and ending with the receipt of the letter summoning her to a meeting with President Bond and the trustees. By the time she was done talking, Riley was sitting on the sofa, hands clasped between her legs, an exhausted and exasperated expression on her face.

"And what did Malcolm say about all this?"

"What does Malcolm have to do with anything?" Lorna asked, turning away and heading for the kitchen. "I'm about to make some tea. Do you want some?"

"He's the person you're involved with. He has to have an opinion. And I could tell he was worried when he called so I'm just curious about what he ..." Riley's voice followed her as she walked away.

"It doesn't matter anymore. We ended it," Lorna said from the safety of the kitchen.

She looked for and found that weak jasmine tea she knew Riley liked, and the much stronger English Black for herself, putting on the kettle.

"Why?" Riley's voice, surprisingly close behind her caused her to jump.

"Why what, Riley?"

"Why'd you end it?"

"I didn't say I ended it. I said we ended it. And why does *any* relationship end?" she asked. "It just ..."

"*Ran its course,*" Riley finished for her. "Right?"

Lorna spun to look at her. "After the day I just had, the last thing I need is ..."

"Someone telling you the truth?" Riley asked. What was unsettling, wasn't what she said, it was the way she said it. Sadly. Sympathetically.

"*Riley.*" Lorna took a deep breath and leaned back against the kitchen counter.

"You are so amazing, Mom," her daughter continued. "*So* amazing. I just ... I wish you would let yourself be with someone who believes that just as much as you *pretend* to believe it. I mean, what do you even get out of those little ... trysts like the one you had with this guy who got you into this mess with the trustees? Do you get *anything* out of it anymore?"

"I'm not about to be lectured ..."

"I know, because you prefer to be the one doing the lecturing. Always the professor," Riley said wearily, turning away from her again. "I'm going send the driver home, and call Shawn to let him know that Cassidy and I'll be staying the night. Then I'm going to take a nap."

The only sound in the kitchen was that of the kettle coming to a boil. Within moments, it was whistling, the high-pitched noise growing louder and louder until soon it was a shriek, like that of a soul in distress.

TWENTY-FIVE
AUGUST

It was amazing how easily, in the face of something that felt like a catastrophe, the world continued to turn. At the very least, Lorna expected a few whispers behind hands, or for someone who normally would have given her an enthusiastic greeting to look away and pretend they hadn't seen her at all. But none of that happened when she walked into Steven and Lisa Hunt's living room.

The barbecue was one of Steven's traditions. In the late summer, he invited everyone from the department, and a few faculty members from other departments over for a family-friendly day of grilled food, card games and over-indulging in alcohol. Most people opted to leave the kids at home because of the overindulging part, but since Steven had had children of his own, now there was more PG-rated fun to be had—games of horseshoe, a bouncy house and even popcorn and cotton candy stations. The festivities started around one p.m. and the parents with small children usually departed around four, after which the adult fun would begin.

For the past couple of years, Lorna made it a habit to get

there at five, entering through the house to first greet Steven's wife and make polite inquiries after their children whose names Lorna could never remember, and to grab a glass of chilled chardonnay before venturing out to the smoky backyard.

This year, she followed that practice and was, as always, greeted by Lisa Hunt, Steven's country bride in her LL Bean activewear. And as always, her fellow faculty who were in the room nodded and smiled their greetings, and one or two inquired about how her summer was going.

It was August now, and in three weeks the students would begin arriving. Classes would begin, and life would go back to normal. Except Lorna still had no idea what her new normal might be, because though it was almost ten days since her meeting with the trustees and President Bond, she had heard nothing.

Life went on. Apart from occasional calls with Riley, she had spoken to no one, not even her research assistant who was making increasingly frantic phone calls to ask about whether she still had a job, whether Lorna could talk to her about her thesis which she had done lots more work on, and finally, just to "make sure you're okay." She didn't mention the dinner appointment they had, a while back, that Lorna had not kept.

The energy it might take to call the girl back and hand-hold seemed like much more than Lorna had in store, so she simply ignored the calls, promising herself that after "just one more day" she would rejoin the land of the living, including dealing with Fallon. Steven's barbecue was her coming-out party of sorts—the first time since everything that she had ventured out in a social setting.

Because it was so hot, she wore white linen shorts and a lightweight orange top in a breathable cotton with her brown sandals. When she was getting dressed, the shorts that had once fit her perfectly, felt a little loose at the waist. She had lost weight, but she couldn't imagine when and how, since the entire time in North Carolina, she and Malcolm had eaten every saucy, fried and rich food known to man.

Out of nowhere, Lorna recalled one afternoon when they were sitting by the water, eating out of styrofoam containers. Fried clams and French fries from a small Mom-n-Pop place on the island.

This is so good, Malcolm said with his mouth full. *I could eat this every day. And that's sayin' something because the only other thing I want to eat every day is you.*

Oh is that right? Lorna flirted. *Well you haven't had me today.*

Don't worry, he said giving her his bedroom eyes. *I'm definitely getting some of that later.*

Lorna thought then that they were the exception to that rule—that the people who talked about it all the time weren't getting it *nearly* as much as they pretended. They got "it" plenty. And they liked talking about it—before, during and after, like they were twentysomethings, or teenagers who were entirely new to the mating dance and so, delighted in naughty conversations.

Malcolm never minded that she sometimes talked dirty, nor that she often liked it rough and rugged. Some men she'd been with had. Often, they seemed vaguely uneasy with her raw and vocal appreciation of what it felt like to be fucked, and fucked *well*. Malcolm never had. Instead, he ...

Who cared? It was over now. And ...

... that was when Lorna stepped out into the backyard and spotted him immediately.

Standing near the grill with a cup in hand, Malcolm was engaged in a conversation with Joel Wolfe. Joel was one of the older and more esteemed members of the Sociology Depart-

ment who liked to tease Lorna about her politics in a good-
natured way. *Burn any bras today, Lorna?* he might ask as they
crossed paths in the halls. And he always got a kick out of it if
she responded in kind. *Nope. Too busy giving out birth control
pills to teenage girls!*

Lorna could see Joel finding Malcolm's work interesting,
and imagined they would have plenty to talk about. Under
normal circumstances, of all the clusters of conversations in
the yard, that would have been the one she might have
chosen to join. Not just to be close to Malcolm, but because
…

Blushing at the thought, Lorna shook her head and laughed
a little at herself. So what? Of course she liked being close to
Malcolm. Their chemistry was electric and intoxicating. There
was a charge between them, like the emotional equivalent to
that low, almost inaudible buzzing noise one hears when they
stand too close to an appliance.

"Well if it isn't the scarlet woman."

Lorna turned to smile at Diane Ramsey, the English
Department chair, and even leaned in to give the older woman
a brief peck on the cheek. She appreciated people who didn't
beat around the bush, and tackled difficult subjects with
humor.

"Yes. The one and only," Lorna said.

"I wouldn't be so sure about that," Diane Ramsey said with
a sly look.

Lorna laughed aloud and noticed out of the corner of her
eyes that her laughter had alerted Malcolm to her presence.

"So how are you holding up?" Dr. Ramsey asked, lowering
her voice a little.

Shrugging, Lorna took a sip of her wine. "Fine under the
circumstances, I guess."

"You mustn't let them see you sweat, Lorna. You've always

been good at that. Come out more. Make sure your colleagues see you being part of our community, just like always."

"I'm here." She raised her wineglass. "And it hasn't been that I was hiding myself away. I was out of town for a while."

"With the delicious Malcolm T. Mitchell, I heard."

"How did you hear that?" Lorna pulled back a little.

"Oh, my dear. Are there any secrets on college campuses? If there were, it wouldn't have spread so fast about your fling with that silly little boy."

"I guess you're right about that," she said.

"And as for that. One day over a very large glass of wine, you'll have to tell me exactly what it was you saw in him."

Lorna laughed again. "It'll take a lot more than a couple of glasses of wine for either of us to answer *that* question."

"Oh. Don't I understand that. Well, in the meantime, let me introduce you to my brother and nephew. He's going to be at West Point in a couple weeks, and the worst chauvinist you'll ever have the misfortune to meet. Just like his father. I think I'd like to hear you two talk about women in the military or something," Dr. Ramsey added mischievously.

Grateful for a diversion, Lorna followed her over to the far end of the yard where a young man whose bearing screamed 'Armed Forces' and a middle-aged man with a vague resemblance to Dr. Ramsey were tearing into pieces of barbecue chicken.

———

BY THE TIME she managed to extricate herself from the Ramsey family, Lorna had had enough socializing and was ready to go home. It was getting dark, and the tiki torches were being brought out to guard against mosquitoes. Her shorts offered her the perfect out, and she was definitely going to take it.

Looking around, she found her host, talking—as bad luck would have it—to Malcolm. She had successfully avoided him without looking like she was avoiding him since she spent the entire afternoon with Ramsey and Company, but now she would have to speak.

Striding over to them, she mustered up the most sincere smile she could.

"Steven," she said. "Malcolm."

"Hey!" Steven leaned in to offer a quick hug. "I saw you in that intense conversation with Dr. Ramsey's brother and didn't want to interrupt. How've you been? I've left you messages to ..."

"I was hibernating for a little. We'll talk soon." She could feel Malcolm's eyes on her. And that electrical charge. "But I think I'm going to head out. The bugs are going to eat me alive if I don't get out of here before dark."

"Oh, but Lisa's bringing out the ..."

"I should probably go anyway. I think the sun wore me out a little."

"Did you drive?" Malcolm asked.

The sound of his voice cut right through her, penetrating every single defense. She had missed him. And now, hearing his voice, the idea that she might stop missing him anytime soon seemed ludicrous.

"No. It's a short enough walk. So ..."

"I'll drive you home. I was about to head out myself."

Steven looked back and forth between them, sensing some subtext. He smiled, and Lorna recalled that he had been there too the first time Malcolm inserted himself into her life. No, 'inserted' was too delicate a description. He had charged in.

Barged in. Knocking down doors, walls and every other type of barrier.

"Okay, well ..." Steven grinned like the Cheshire Cat. "You two enjoy the rest of the evening. And thanks for coming."

"Where's Lisa?" Lorna stalled. "I want to ..."

"No need. I'll tell her you gave your thanks."

"Okay, then ..."

And for the first time, Lorna braved a look directly at Malcolm.

He looked stern, and in the days since she'd last seen him, was growing a little scruff on his jaw and chin, cultivating a beard perhaps, in preparation to look more professorial for his students. She had teased him often about how boyishly handsome he was because he was clean-shaven. *You'll be mistaken for a student yourself,* she said. *And girls will throw themselves at you.* They would only do so more now, because the scruff suited him.

"Let's go," he said.

They walked silently out to the front of the house, only about a foot apart. Lorna felt his body heat, and something like restraint.

"Thank you for the ride," she said, breaking the silence.

"Don't thank me for stupid shit like that," he said, as though he had just been waiting for her to say something, anything, to have a chance to snap at her.

Lorna sighed, feeling a sudden weariness.

"Malcolm. Could we not ...? I don't want to fight with you. I don't want to fight with anyone. I'm just ... I just want to go home and soak in a tub and then sleep."

He looked at her and Lorna forced herself not to look back. If she did, she might cry or something silly like that.

"How've you been?" he asked, his tone gentle now.

"I don't know. I've just ... been." She shrugged.

They got to his car and Malcolm took the opportunity to get her to face him while he held the door for her.

"What's going on?" he asked.

Lorna gave a brief, harsh laugh. "Oh hadn't you heard? I'm being burned at the stake."

She climbed in and leaned her head back against the plush seat. When Malcolm got in on the driver's side, he paused before putting the key in the ignition.

"Talk to me," he said. "You know what I mean. What's going on with you? With Riley? And have you heard any more from the trustees?"

"No, I haven't heard anything from the trustees. And Riley is pissed I didn't tell her all about it right away. But she's also in a honeymoon phase of talking to her father on the phone and planning to meet."

"So, they haven't done that yet?"

"No. I think they're both eager but too scared of scaring the other off to suggest doing it so soon. But they set a date a couple of weeks out."

Lorna felt Malcolm's hand on her thigh, and tears surfaced at the contact. She wanted him to touch her. Had been aching for it. And not just today either. For the last ten days.

"You've got a lot going on," he said.

"Yeah." She laughed again.

"I know it's overwhelming so I didn't mean to ... before, I ..."

"You're used to fighting with me," Lorna said, wryly. "You're used to *me* fighting with you. So why wouldn't you think that's what would happen?"

"No," he said. His voice dropped lower and the hand on her thigh moved to her cheek, and he turned her head to face him. "There's a lot more to us than that." And when he leaned in, Lorna held very still, waiting for him to kiss her. But instead, Malcolm brushed his nose against hers. "A lot more."

Then he pulled back and started the engine, and moments later they were pulling away from the curb. It only took about six minutes to get to her house, and once there, Malcolm stopped at the curb and turned to look at her.

"So if you need anything," he began.

"I need you to come in," Lorna said in a rush.

Malcolm looked taken aback for a second and then quickly recovered, shaking his head. "I don't think that's a good idea," he said.

"Why not?" she asked quietly.

"Because we both know what'll happen."

"And so what if it does?" Lorna asked. "If we both want it."

"That's not what I mean," Malcolm said shaking his head. "What I mean is ... if I come in, I'll fall headfirst into you, Lo. And you'll pull back from me. And then we'll be right back here. Back to ... nothing."

To hear him call it 'nothing' hurt. There it was. The truth. *It hurt.* Even now, with the gulf between them, they weren't nothing. Not to her. Even now. And Malcolm seemed to know what she was thinking, as he often did, because he put a finger at her chin and made her look at him again.

"I know you think this is plenty. Me and you, having the occasional deep conversation, having a few hours of crazy-intense lovemaking ... and I can't pretend it isn't good to me, too. All of that's damn good. But it's not enough. I don't want to fight you. You're right. I want to fight *for* you. Along *with* you. But if you can't offer me that, I don't want anything at all."

"Anything at all." Lorna repeated, forcing the words past the lump in her throat.

"Friendship," Malcolm said.

And her only solace, as she exited the car, was the knowledge that that word was as bitter a pill for him to serve up as it was for her to swallow.

"FALLON, first let me apologize. For being so unavailable. I've had some ... there've been some things I needed to attend to that made it difficult for me to give you the focus you deserve. Both as advisor on your thesis, and as your employer."

"I know," Fallon said, her expression assuming a dolefully sympathetic look that Lorna hated. "I heard."

"Well. It's all being dealt with now, so we can resume your regular hours, and I'm hoping you had some time to absorb the comments I gave you when I came back from ..."

"That's the thing, Professor Terry. I wanted to talk to you about that. I appreciated the comments, but I thought about this and decided to go in an entirely different direction. So, Susan Sontag isn't my thesis subject anymore. I have something else I worked on."

"But I didn't approve a new topic. The process is that I would review it and then ..."

"Yeah, that's one of the reasons I kept calling. Because I was feeling really inspired and started writing, but before I finished, I wanted to talk to you. But now I'm done because I couldn't reach you, so I hoped you could look at the completed paper and give me your feedback on that."

"Fallon ..." Lorna rubbed her temples. "While I appreciate your initiative, two complete theses before your first semester of senior year is ..."

Fallon laughed. "Anal. I know. Sorry." She ran her fingers through her long hair and smiled. "But I just want to show you how serious I am about having a career like yours, so ..."

"You'll have a career like your own, Fallon. Look ... send me the paper you worked on and I'll see whether ..."

"I actually have it right here," she said reaching into the brown leather satchel at her feet.

Of course she did. Lorna sighed and momentarily shut her eyes.

Maybe it was too ambitious of her to believe she was ready to deal with work again, and with students. In a mere two weeks, the campus would be teeming with Fallons, some of them eager freshmen whose clumsy attempts to impress her she would have to humor and smile at. There would be more papers to grade and suffer through. Even with a teaching assistant, she would have limited time and even fewer opportunities for what she craved most right now—peace and quiet.

"Here it is." Fallon handed her a sheaf of papers, clipped together. Fifty pages at least.

"Does this include your source material?" Lorna asked, silently saying a prayer that it did.

"No. Just references," Fallon said, looking proud of herself.

"In the draft of your other thesis, remember what I said about economy of expression? That it's not the word count, but rather the ideas expressed that will be most important?"

"Yes. I definitely took that into consideration," Fallon said nodding. "So you'll read it?"

"Of course. Just give me a few days, alright?" Lorna stood, so Fallon would know their meeting was at a close. "I have a lunch with Professor Hunt, so we'll have to pick up this conversation another time. Hopefully after I've had a chance to read this." She patted the stack that Fallon had given her.

"Great. Thank you so much, Professor Terry. You really inspired me on this one. I even dedicated it to you. It's ..."

"That's lovely, Fallon. So, we'll talk soon then?"

"Yup." Fallon stood and gathered her bag, slinging it over her shoulder and straightening her shirt.

She wore a plaid long-sleeved button-down over a tank top and frayed denim shorts that made her long, golden legs look that much longer. She could easily have chosen a different path, with looks like hers. She could have decided to be one of the "pretty girls", the ones that Lorna sometimes noticed, swanning about on campus, astonishingly attractive, trailed by other girls who were less so, but who might have hoped that some of the glamor would rub off. They were the girls who tried only enough to pass their classes, never going above and beyond. The ones who knew—and had known from a very young age—that their looks granted them entrée into a world of privileges and so working too hard might not be necessary.

Fallon could have been one of those girls if she decided to; if she put a brush to her long, fair, hair. If she wore eyeliner and chose more flattering clothes. If she took off those ridiculous glasses. But she didn't. She instead had chosen a life of the mind. So Lorna decided she would be patient, and generous with her time to reward the girl for opting for a more difficult path. She would read the second thesis, give comments and if it was better than the last showing, help the girl get it to publishable standards.

"Should I come back to work on Monday? Regular hours?" Fallon paused at the door to confirm.

"Yes. You should. See you then."

Lorna waited a reasonable interval until she was assured that the girl would have to have left the building, then she packed up her own things, hesitating before shoving the new thesis into her bag. She would read it tonight, with a glass of merlot in hand to help make her less critical.

She walked across campus to meet Steven, noting how much more activity there already was on the Quad. Some students came earlier to shop for their dorm rooms, get back into the flow of being on campus or to make last-minute pleas to get into certain classes. But special permissions were usually necessary before they could be granted access to student housing before the third week of August, so the number of students around remained relatively few.

Lorna didn't see anyone she recognized as she walked, and was grateful for it. This was the first year within memory that she didn't feel even the slightest bit of excitement to begin the fall semester. Elsewhere on campus, she imagined Malcolm was feeling very much the opposite. He would be teaching for the first time. Lorna still remembered the mix of terror and eagerness, how she had rehearsed the casual amusing references she would use in her first lecture, to get her students and herself at ease. Malcolm likely wouldn't need any of that—he was so effortlessly charming. The way he had been with that couple they had dinner with in Philadelphia had impressed her. She had been proud to be with him that night.

Why had she never said things like that to him out loud? Now, he would never know what he'd meant to her, and how he had changed her.

"Ready to go?"

She found Steven sitting in his office, head down, and even when he lifted it, Lorna noted right away the somberness of his smile and the way he couldn't quite meet her eyes.

"Yes. What're you feeling like eating?"

"Oh. We're going off campus?"

Another bad sign.

"Sure. Why not? Might as well break up the monotony. How's Indian sound?"

"Good."

"I'll drive," he offered.

There was only one Indian place in town, Mumbai Palace. Their lunchtime buffets were inexpensive and delicious, making them a favorite for students and faculty alike. Lorna and Steven took a table near the front, right next to the plate glass window, and put in drink orders before going to load up their plates. Lorna stuck to tandoori chicken and curried chick peas, not wanting to feel too sluggish after eating by overindulging in naan, rice or roti. Lately, her appetite had been almost non-existent, and try though she might, it seemed reluctant to make an appearance, even with the tempting aromas of one of her favorite ethnic foods.

"So how are you?" Steven asked when they were both back at the table. "Back in the office yet?"

"Yes, just this week, in fact. Finally got my research assistant to come back in." Lorna tried a small forkful of chick peas. "She's exhaustingly enthusiastic. But maybe some of her enthusiasm will rub off on me."

"Nothing from Julia then?" he asked, referring to the college president. He sounded tentative. Careful.

"No. Not yet."

Hesitating, he took a mouthful of rice and chewed thoughtfully. When he swallowed, he put his fork down.

"Well. I have heard from her," he said slowly. "And out of friendship, I may as well tell you, even though I guess it won't be too long before ..."

"Just spit it out, Steven," she said, her tone not nearly as forceful as her words. Her stomach had tightened into a hard ball. Not only wasn't she sure she could eat another bite, she might not be able to keep down that which she had already eaten.

"They're suggesting you go on a yearlong sabbatical."

"*Suggesting?*" She barked out a hard laugh.

"That's the wording they're going to use. Seems they checked with the AAUP and with counsel after Williamson pushed for revocation of tenure. And not only is there no precedent for that under circumstances like this, but most of the trustees didn't support that move."

Lorna looked up at that. "Did they vote or something?"

"That I don't know. But seems the clincher was that when the university counsel heard about that little 'informal meeting' they had you go to, he hit the roof. Said that it wasn't appropriate process according to the college's own standards. There should have been a formal Disciplinary Review Committee meeting called ... the whole thing. And by denying you that, they basically poisoned their own ability to proceed with any exclusionary discipline."

Lorna shook her head. "So, I win on a technicality."

"Not a technicality, Lorna," Steven said, putting a hand over hers. "The underlying charge didn't support revocation of tenure. You and I know that. And they know it. But in addition, they messed up on process."

"So instead they're suggesting I take a year off. Effective when? Did Julia say?"

"Effective immediately. With this coming fall."

Lorna leaned back in her seat, pulling her hand from beneath Steven's. She felt numb. Numb, and dumb. She didn't know what to say.

After a few long minutes, during which Steven had the decency not to continue eating though it was obvious he wanted to, she finally thought of something.

"My classes ..."

"Reassigned."

"And my office?"

"It'll still be yours. Locked, I assume."

"So I won't be permitted on campus."

Steven shook his head slowly. "You'll be encouraged not to be on campus for the duration of your time on sabbatical. But because it isn't a formal disciplinary sanction, you'll be on full salary."

Lorna snorted. She didn't care about that. Her salary as a full professor was almost two hundred thousand a year, and she was permitted to keep any honoraria for speaking engagements that she got. But it had never been the most important thing about her job.

Lorna saved most of what she made, having paid off her student loans about five years earlier. And Riley and Shawn had paid off her mortgage as a birthday gift one year. Money wasn't her biggest issue, and had never been something that motivated her.

"Let's finish our lunch," she said quietly.

"Lorna ..."

"It's alright, Steven. I'm alright. I think I'll just eat, go home and wait for the formal axe to fall."

"Was I wrong to tell you?" he asked, his eyes kind.

"No." This time she touched his hand. "You weren't. Thank you for sticking your neck out."

"I didn't," he said, shaking his head. "Not nearly as much as I should have."

"*No*. You *shouldn't* have," she said looking him in the eye. "I wouldn't have stood for that. I wouldn't have wanted it. You've pulled my neck from the noose a million times when I insisted on trying to hang myself." She laughed. "Remember that course title?"

Steven smiled sadly. "That was noth..."

"It wasn't nothing. I've spent so much time thumbing my nose at 'the man' I guess I didn't see how much I was invested in being part of 'the man' myself. Until now, now that it's taken away."

"Lorna it isn't taken away. This is nothing. It doesn't go on your record, there was no formal hearing ... it'll be a blip on the screen of your career."

She looked at him and shrugged. "That's the thing. I've never been one to abide ... blips."

"Then perhaps you ought to be easier on yourself."

TWENTY-SIX

ALL THAT REMAINS

LORNA WASN'T SURE HOW LONG SHE SLEPT. WHEN SHE went home after lunch with Steven, she crawled directly into bed, pausing only to slide off her shoes, and falling into an almost immediate, deep sleep. When she opened her eyes again, it was dark and she avoided looking at the clock. Instead, she went to the kitchen to make herself some tea though hard liquor seemed to be what was called for.

When it was light again, she would reassess, and she would call Riley and focus more fully on what she was going through. Maybe she had been selfish these past few weeks, holing herself up and thinking only about her career when her daughter's life was going through its own sea change. She had a father, after a lifetime of not having one. And Ryan had a wife and two more daughters, so Riley had a stepmother and sisters. The entire landscape of her family had altered overnight, and she must be terrified.

The truth was, Lorna had been depending on the knowl-edge that Shawn was there—as protective a husband as a woman would ever hope for. When Riley was in any state of emotional upset, he was there, shielding her from the source of her discomfort or finding ways to make it better. Maybe that was why Lorna hadn't heard from him much lately—because she was the source of Riley's emotional upset.

Once the tea was made, she wasn't quite sure what to do with herself. She didn't need to prepare for classes any longer, so now what? A list, she decided. She would make a list of the things she needed from her office, and a timeline for getting all of that done by the following week. She would need a system for retrieving messages and snail mail from her department box, and would explore options online for what to do with her time off. There was the book, of course. She could finish it sooner so she could start thinking about contacting publishers. That last idea buoyed her somewhat, because then her sabbatical might later be more easily explained—she had been working on a book, and here it was!

Reaching into her large bag to pull out her planner, Lorna groaned. There was Fallon's thesis. The girl would be assigned a new advisor, so it was someone else's problem now. But still, Fallon was so excited for her to read it, and Lorna hadn't officially been told about her sabbatical. As of tonight, at least, she was still a thesis advisor, and if she read it now, and offered comments now, then at least Fallon could go to her next assigned advisor with a much more polished product.

Sighing, she pulled it out of her bag and clapped it down on the coffee table in front of her, next to her cup of tea. She was wide awake, and unlikely to drift off again anytime soon, so why not dig in now?

Arranging her legs beneath her and covering herself with the afghan, Lorna took a long sip of tea and picked up the document again.

"Okay, Fallon," she said out loud. "I hope you blow me away with this one."

Lorna read the title and froze, then put down her mug, quickly flipping to the first page, which was just the dedication—to her, just like Fallon said—so she flipped to the next page and read the first sentence, and then the second, and another in the middle of the second paragraph, referring to "traditional feminism creating a somewhat constricting view of what is normative for feminists."

Heart pounding, she removed the clip and opened the document to the middle, reading a random passage. By then, a cold sweat had broken out just above her upper lip and Lorna could hear herself breathing.

No, no, no ... This couldn't be. This couldn't ...

Looking around frantically, shoving things aside, she knocked over her tea and quickly righted the mug but not before soaking some of the papers. Still, she didn't stop until she found what she was looking for. Without checking the time, she dialed a number.

Steven's voice, sleepy, groggy and more than a little annoyed, answered. In the background, Lorna heard Lisa's voice, also annoyed.

"Lorna," he said. "What's going on? Is everything ...?"

"Steven, she stole it. She ..." Her words were stumbling, one over the other. She could barely get a sentence out. "My research, for my book. All the notes and ideas ... they're in here, in her ... her ... She wrote all the things I talked to her about writing and it ... It was my ... for the book ..."

"Lorna, it's almost two in the morning. What're you talking about? Have you been drinking?"

"No I haven't been drinking!" she all but screamed. "I'm talking about my book! About Fallon's thesis!"

"What book? I didn't know you had a ..."

"I'm writing it. The proposal anyway. And I have this research. All this research and a thesis that says basically ... it doesn't matter what it says. What matters is that she took it! She took it and used it!"

"*Who* took it? You're not making any sense." It sounded like he was getting up, moving around, probably out of bed and away from his wife who was sure to be livid.

"Fallon ... Fallon ..." Lorna struggled to remember the girl's name and when she couldn't, she looked at the cover page. "Fallon Wright! Wright. She's my research assistant ..."

She tried to slow down her speech, and to sound reasonable. If she sounded reasonable, Steven might listen, and understand how important this was.

"She's helping me with the source material for my book proposal. And I'm her thesis advisor. She gave me her thesis and it's all my ideas, Steven! Everything I discussed with her and had her look up for me. It even uses ..."

"Wait. But her thesis proposal had to have been set a long time ago. You reviewed it. You ..."

"Yes, but it was different," Lorna said impatiently. "That's what I'm telling you. Aren't you *listening*?"

"Yes, I am listening, but you're still not making sense. Your research assistant wrote a whole new thesis based on what? Your book?"

"No, I don't have the book yet! Based on my notes, and the stuff I had her research for the proposal!"

"So, have you shared the book proposal with anyone? Is it complete and she plagiarized from it, or ...?"

"No, it's not complete, but she has access to all my source material and my notes. She put everything into my computer and on a flash drive for me. I've talked to her about ..."

"Lorna." Steven gave a deep, long sigh. "I don't think this is something ..."

"There are standards, Steven. Ethical standards that ..."

"That she obviously doesn't think she broke. Because you said she gave you this thesis to read."

"And even had the nerve to dedicate it to me, the little ..."

"So she doesn't think she did anything wrong. Maybe she thinks she was just inspired by your ideas. Maybe she was. Hell, I haven't read it, so I don't know. The point is, it's late. And you've had an already emotionally upsetting day, so ..."

"Steven, if you dare tell me I'm overreacting ... I know the fucking difference between an idea inspired by someone and one that's been fucking *stolen*! And this is definitely ..."

"*Lorna!*" His tone stopped her. When he continued, his tone was low, serious. "You and I both know your credibility is under a cloud right now. So if you, on the eve of your sabbatical go off on some rant with the administration about some ... *undergrad* stealing your ideas, you ... I don't need to tell you what that'll look like. I don't need to tell you how it'll sound."

Taking a breath, Lorna froze. She could feel her heartbeat speeding up again, her breaths having more difficulty making it through her lungs.

"I don't know whether you're right or not, having not read her paper nor your notes. But even if you're right ... I just ... I don't think this is a battle you need to fight. Not right now."

"This is a completely separate ..."

"Yes. But that won't matter for shit. That's not how it'll get spun. Right now, you should be running for the border. Thinking of how to spend your time off. Not waging a war with some twenty-year old who's younger than the length of your academic career."

Lorna felt like there was ice-water running through her veins. He was right.

"Goodnight, Steven," she said. "I'm sorry to have bothered you so late."

"Lor ..."

She hung up.

IF HE HADN'T BEEN SLEEPING on the sofa, which happened more lately than ever before, Malcolm might never have heard the knocks that gradually turned to pounding on his front door. The bell had shorted out recently, and he hadn't bothered about getting it fixed just yet, because he had no unexpected visitors. At least not usually, and certainly not at this hour.

When his sleep-muddled mind finally deciphered the sound, he sat up suddenly, making him a little woozy. Maybe he'd missed a phone call and something was wrong with his kids? He rushed over to the door and opened it without checking. Stupid, but he was being directed by the sudden rush of fear and adrenaline, rather than common sense.

And outside, standing there in jeans and a rumpled t-shirt, hair askew and face tear-stained was Lorna. She had her car keys in one hand and a pile of papers in the other, held against her chest and in danger of cascading to the ground.

"Lo." He pulled her inside by the shoulder and locked the door behind her. "Baby, what's wrong?"

She began immediately, heaving and gulping, and Malcolm pulled her against his chest, holding her. She shoved back and pushed the papers in her hand at him, telling him between breaths to take it.

"What is this?" He barely glanced down at it. "What's the matter? Is it Riley? What ...?"

"No." She shook her head frantically from side to side. "I have ... I have nothing, Malcolm. Everything I ... I worked ..."

"Look at me, Lo." He set the papers aside. "That's not true.

It isn't. Okay? Calm down. Tell me what's happening? Did you hear from the college?"

Something in her eyes shifted. "Yes. No. But ..."

He led her to the sofa where she took brief note of its state —the blanket, the book, the evidence that he had been spending a lot of time there—and then sat down. She let her keys drop from her fingers onto the rug, and turned to look at him. Malcolm watched her, waiting for her to speak.

Suddenly, a small smile. A sad one. Tears rose in her eyes.

"I missed you so much," she said.

Malcolm tried to offer a smile back.

"And being here," she continued, looking around the room. "I've missed being here with you."

"Baby." Malcolm put a hand at her cheek to re-focus her. It was hot. "What happened? Did the college ...?"

"Sabbatical," she said, her voice emotionless.

"Sabbatical. But no dismissal, no loss of tenure."

"No dismissal, no loss of tenure," she said in that same somnolent voice. She leaned into his touch and closed her eyes.

"Well, that's ... not too bad then, right? How long of a sabbatical?"

"Malcolm, the paper," she said quietly. She had begun to calm herself, but now looked almost like she might faint. "Look at it."

Turning away, he reluctantly removed his hand from her cheek and gathered the pile of papers in front of them that had fanned out on the table in front of the sofa. Arranging them, he read the cover page: *Pop Culture and the 21ˢᵗ Century Feminist Construct.*

Frowning, he read the name beneath it: *Fallon Wright.*

Turning to the first page he skimmed the abstract and then flipped to the main text.

'*A pop star flaunts her chest and buttocks onstage, strutting defiantly away from her audience. Pyrotechnics surround her. She bends over, daringly low. Hints of her sex are exposed. Overhead, in lights, a word appears. It isn't her name, as one might expect. Instead, it reads, 'Feminist'.'*

"Holy ..." Malcolm looked up at Lorna and shook his head. "Wait. But this is ..."

"My idea," she said, nodding. The tears pooled in her eyes spilled over. "For my book."

Dropping the papers, Malcolm gathered her in his arms. She was limp and offered no resistance, but neither did she hug him back. Like she hadn't the strength for either.

"*Baby,*" he said.

And then he couldn't think of anything else to say.

HE TOOK her to his bed, and held her till dawn. And it was only then, when the sun began to rise that she finally fell asleep. Malcolm took much longer.

He watched her for a while, thinking how fragile she looked, how depleted. Her features slackened, as though she wasn't merely asleep, but absent. Her eyelashes were long, and he could see the faint bluish-purple veins on her closed lids. The tiny lines bracketing her naturally-pink mouth were softer, and not as deep, and she breathed quietly, rhythmically and evenly. The feeling he got, looking at her like that, was strong enough to scare him.

He was glad she had come.

No matter the reason, he was glad she had come.

HE WOKE up around one in the afternoon and Lorna was in exactly the same position she had been in when he fell asleep. Malcolm carefully got out of bed, hoping not to disturb her and went in to take a shower.

A sabbatical wasn't so bad. It was far better than many of the other possible outcomes. She still had tenure, and her reputation would recover. But this other thing with the paper presented a real problem. If she wrote her book now, how long would it take before someone, maybe even Fallon herself, claimed that Lorna had been the one to steal the idea. That was the kind of thing an academic career never recovered from.

On the other hand, who would believe it? Lorna Terry was a name in this field, a giant among feminist theoreticians. *Could anyone honestly believe she would plagiarize from an undergraduate?* Although it had been known to happen, and with all the other stuff going on, it would be very easy for people to conflate the two and paint a picture of a woman coming undone.

Shaking his head, and dousing it under the stream of warm water, Malcolm sighed. No one knew better than he that nothing could be further from the truth. If nothing else, Lorna held it all together.

Last night was the first and only time he had ever seen her like that. And he had a feeling he never would again. By the time she woke up, Lorna would have gotten fully and completely ahold of herself. Maybe she would even tell him it had been a mistake to come. She might retreat from him once again, and this time, fortify her defenses even more.

When he was done with his shower, she was still there, and still fully asleep. He dressed without any particular care about being quiet and she didn't stir. Even when he made breakfast for lunch, frying bacon and scrambling eggs, the aroma didn't wake her. So Malcolm ate alone at his table, reading bits and pieces of Fallon's paper as he did. The more he read the angrier he got.

Lorna put her heart into her work. She literally never stopped thinking about ways to refine, challenge and develop ideas. So for some spoiled, opportunistic little twit to come along and simply take them ... Malcolm could only guess at how he would react if someone took his work-in-progress and lifted plot points, characters and themes from it and then called it their own.

A ringtone interrupted his thoughts and he looked around, finally locating the source as Lorna's cell phone. The caller was identified as 'S. Hunt' on the screen, so he answered, more curious about what Steven knew than he was concerned about how it looked that he was answering Lorna's phone.

"Hello?" Steven sounded confused at hearing a male voice.

"It's Malcolm."

"Oh. Yes. Well ..." He seemed at a loss for a moment. "Is Lorna around? I wanted to check in on her. I got a frantic call from her last night and I'm not ... I just wanted to make sure ..."

Malcolm ignored his disappointment that Lorna had called Steven first.

"She's sleeping right now. She's fine."

"Is she? Because ..." Steven stopped, probably not sure how much he should reveal.

"I know what's going on. She told me. About the college. About the paper."

"Oh. Well ... good. I think it all came crashing down. Both things happening at once must have been a shock. So, if you can have her call me when she gets up, I'd ..."

"I don't think I'm going to do that," Malcolm said immediately. "I think I'll let her be. Just for a little while. If she wants to reach out, then you'll hear from her."

"Of course."

"And this thing about the sabbatical ..."

"*That*, I can't talk to you about, Malcolm. I'm sorry. I shared that with her unofficially. Officially, she hasn't been told. I would expect she'll hear something first thing next week."

He spent the balance of the afternoon working, or trying to. Occasionally he checked on Lorna who had changed positions on the bed and now was burrowed under the sheets, the covers over her head. Once or twice, Malcolm lifted them, just to make sure she was still breathing or something. And then felt stupid for doing it. He toyed with the idea of calling Riley, then decided that Lorna would probably want to do it herself, when she was feeling better and wanted to talk.

Around seven o'clock he ducked out to pick up Chinese for dinner and when he returned, heard the sound of the shower running. *Signs of life. Finally.*

Malcolm took the food to the kitchen and was only there a few minutes, before he was joined by Lorna, puffy-faced and wearing one of his shirts, her legs and feet bare, and hair wet. Without speaking, she walked right into him, leaning against his chest, her hair dampening his shirt.

"How're you doin'?" he asked.

"Tired." Her voice was a little hoarse. "Feel like I slept a million years. And could sleep a million more."

"So go do that. After you get something to eat, though."

She pulled away from him and went to investigate what was in the cartons. "Hmm. Rice noodles. Smells great."

Only then did Malcolm notice that she looked a little thinner. Pulling out two plates, he portioned out noodles and rice for them both, along with the Wor Shu Duck that he knew was her favorite. When he handed her the plate, Lorna looked at the food with utter disinterest. Actually, she seemed to look *through* it, like she didn't know what purpose it was supposed to serve.

"C'mon," he said, beginning to feel the first nibbles of real worry tug at the corners of his mind. "Let's go eat at the table."

Lorna followed him without protest and thanked him when he went back to get them glasses of water to have with their meal. But when he started eating, she didn't do the same.

"Lo," he said.

"Hmm?" she looked up at him as if being awakened from a trance.

"You're not eating."

She dug her fork into the noodles and twirled it around a few times then raised the fork to her lips. Malcolm realized he was holding his breath waiting for her to eat it only when she put the fork back down.

"I think what I'd really like is some tea," she said, preparing to stand.

"I'll get the tea. You eat."

"You're treating me like a mental patient," Lorna said in the very first spark of the spirit he was accustomed to from her.

"Because you're acting like one a little bit, if you want to know the truth."

She chuckled a little. "I guess. It's just that ..."

Malcolm waited. "It's just that what?" he finally prompted.

"I feel so strange," she said, her voice taking on the same dreamy quality it had the night before. "So ... light. Not unburdened light. But ..." She shrugged. "Stripped naked. Bare."

"What d'you mean?" Malcolm put down his fork as well, giving her his complete focus.

Lorna looked up and her eyes were almost empty. "Because I have nothing now. Not my work, not my good name ..."

"You have to stop saying that. You're more than your work. And if you're thinking about that paper ..."

"Don't remind me."

"If you're thinking about that paper," Malcolm said more forcefully, "you shouldn't."

"I *shouldn't?*" she demanded.

He shook his head. "You'll have more ideas during the course of this meal than that girl will probably have in her entire adult life. So, she took one of them. Let her have it. You've got plenty more where that came from."

At that, a tiny smile teased the corners of Lorna's beautiful lips.

Malcolm wanted to lean over and kiss her. Not too long ago, he would have, without giving it a second thought. And she would have responded without a second thought. From the very first time they'd been together, their physical relationship had been like that—natural, easy, and effortless. The other things, the emotional things; those took some doing.

"That's nice of you to say."

"No. It's just the truth. Before anything else, I fell in love with that mind of yours. Sharp as a tack. Sharper even than your tongue."

That provoked a full smile. "And for me it was your words," she said.

Trying not to react to that, Malcolm promised himself he wouldn't later obsess over the meaning of that response, whether she was acknowledging falling in love with his words *first*, or just that she loved *only* his words.

"But, the thing about being stripped naked is ..." She looked down, and picked up her fork again, playing with her food. "After that, all that's left, all that remains is the truth. Y'know?"

He shook his head. "No, I don't follow."

"You know, like that biblical reference. About a house built on sand. It can't stand."

"I take you to church one time and you start making biblical references?"

Lorna smiled again, and he saw in her eyes something he wanted to believe mirrored what he felt for her. For all the depth and complication and whiplashing craziness, he loved her. He wouldn't change any of it.

"Don't make jokes right now. I want to tell you something. Some*things*. True things. Truer than anything I've ever told you before. Okay?"

Malcolm nodded.

"Remember when I told you about Claude. The man I thought was my uncle until I was seventeen?"

Feeling a growing sense of dread, Malcolm nodded again.

"The story I told you about him, and about me leaving to come to New York? Most of it is true. But maybe the most important part of it isn't." She paused and licked her lower lip. "It's true that one night I came home from a school play, and that afterward I had been with a boy who liked me. And that nothing happened with that boy except talking and flirting. And when I got home Claude was waiting and he did tell me then, for the first time that I wasn't his niece by blood. It's what happened after that that I lied about."

Sitting forward in his chair, Malcolm felt his anger already beginning to surface. He knew what she was about to say, but just didn't know what he would do when he heard it. Maybe he would throw his plate across the room and shatter it against the wall. Because even the seventeen-year old Lorna felt like his to protect.

"What did he do?" he asked.

"That's the thing," Lorna said. "*He* didn't do anything. It was me."

"What do you mean?"

"I saw how he looked at me. I knew then that he ... he wanted me. I went to bed that night and I thought about how angry he'd been, and how he was the only thing standing between me and the street. I *didn't* have all my credits to graduate just yet. I lied about that too."

Malcolm narrowed his eyes, not understanding.

"I needed to stay there. Or *somewhere*, long enough to get those credits. When I got older, and reflected on that time, I thought about what I could have done. Maybe asked a friend if I could live with them, or gone to a shelter, or ... I don't know. I ... But that's not what I did. Claude saying he wasn't my blood-uncle. It sounded like a threat. Like I could get put out unless ..."

Malcolm's eyes locked with hers.

"Unless I made him *want* me to stay," she finished. "And so I ... made him want me to stay."

"How?"

Lorna's mouth turned downward and she took a breath.

"The next night when he came home, I cooked for him. I waited on him hand-and-foot that evening, like a wife. And when he went in to bed, I followed him. And ... performed all the other duties of a wife."

Malcolm closed his eyes, feeling a sharpness pierce his heart.

"For six weeks, I don't know, maybe it was eight. I was his 'wife' in that way. I made sure he was satisfied. And he continued to give me money, and let me stay. Sometimes I was tired and ... of course I wanted to sleep alone, but I couldn't risk it, getting him upset with me. I felt like I needed to do that, just to be secure for at least those last weeks of school. And as soon as I had the credits I needed ..." She shrugged. "I got on that bus and I left."

"Is that what you've been hiding from me?" he asked incredulous. "Is that why you ...?"

"Not just from you. From the world. From ..."

"Lo, something like that is nobody's business. That when

you were seventeen you did what you thought you had to do *to survive?*"

"Survive." She shook her head. "I would have survived even if I hadn't done it. But it's funny you should use that word." She put a hand up, playing with the curl at her nape. "When I first started studying feminist theory, I learned the term, 'survival sex'. And I *latched* onto it like a lifeline. It validated me. And yet I never felt brave enough to admit that I had done it. Or something like it."

"Why would you have to do that? Why would you have to admit anything to anyone?"

"Because I was standing up there at podiums telling women not to be ashamed of what they sometimes had to do as women, just to survive. And yet I was living with my shame. Hiding from it. Every single day."

Malcolm said nothing. A million tiny things about her were all falling into place.

"But now, all my armor is gone. And I have to face myself. *As* myself. Not as Dr. Lorna Terry, as arrogant as people claim she is brilliant. But just as me, the woman who once screwed a man more than twice her age, just for a place to stay."

"*Lo* ..." Malcolm pushed his chair back from the table. "Come over here."

She hesitated, but finally came. He hugged her about the waist, pressing his face into her stomach.

"Baby, that's *one* truth about you. It's not the *only* truth. You are still the brilliant, *and arrogant* ..." Her stomach rippled against his cheek as she laughed at that. "... Dr. Lorna Terry. That's still true. And you were a *girl*. Just a girl when that happened."

And because he couldn't help it, he ran his hands along her smooth legs, wanting to feel her skin again. They would revisit this conversation, Malcolm had no doubt. It was way too heavy for him to believe she had unloaded as much of it as she would need to.

And it reminded him of what she had shared in North Carolina about her mother's suicide. There was almost certainly more to tell, but he would have to be patient and let Lorna tell it, in her own way and her own time.

"So, was that the 'truth' you wanted to tell me, or was there more?"

"There's more," she confirmed.

"Okay, tell me."

She sat on his knee, and Malcolm looked up at her, but she was staring off to his right. Gently putting two fingers at her chin, he turned her head so they could look at each other.

"You can tell me anything."

"I love you, too," she said in a rush. "I knew it when you first said it to me. I even knew it long before then. That ... that's my other truth. And I don't know why I didn't say it before now."

Malcolm held her closer so she wouldn't see his smile. "That one I'm going to need to hear over and over again," he said.

AFTER EATING A LITTLE—VERY little—Lorna said she was still tired and wanted to go back to sleep. *Do you mind if I stay?* she asked. *I don't want to throw a monkey-wrench in any plans you might have had.*

Malcolm almost didn't know how to answer that. Not because the question was difficult (of course there were no plans more important than being with her right now) but because he didn't know what to make of how she asked it—with uncertainty, and humility. Lorna Terry had been shaken up, and a good bit of her confidence shaken loose. It was tough to see her like that—*Lorna, deconstructed.*

And once she was back in the bedroom, Malcolm thought about what she had told him, about being seventeen and deciding to trade her body for a temporary sense of security after her mother died. There was so much more he wanted to know about the girl she had been then, and about the woman she later became. He could only hope that her saying she loved him meant she would stick around long enough for him to do that. But one never knew with Lorna.

Around nine-thirty, he called his girls, reveling in the sound of Hayley's voice, describing more of her summer trip, and even of Piper's sullen drawl—she was still angry with him about the almost-kiss she had witnessed in her mother's kitchen.

Hearing Lorna's story made him want to hold them even closer, and shield them from a world where girls their age teetered on high heels at rest stops, and for all their suffering only got judgment and the sneering label, "lot lizards."

That could have been me, Lorna had said. *That could have so easily been me.*

For a couple hours more, Malcolm tried to work and even got a few hundred words on the page, but finally, at midnight, he decided to pack it in. Undressing in the dark bedroom, he tried to make as little sound as possible. If rest was what she needed, he wouldn't disturb her. But as soon as he crawled into bed, Lorna turned to him in the dark.

"Malcolm," she whispered.

"Right here, Lo."

She moved closer, and he felt her lips against his.

They stayed like that for a moment, lips pressed together, neither of them moving. When Lorna moved as though to pull away, Malcolm held her by the waist, then searching for the hem of the shirt she was wearing, he pulled it slowly over her head.

As he did, he felt her chest slowly rising and falling. Bowing his head, he kissed her neck and across her clavicle from one shoulder to the other. Beneath his lips, tiny goose-bumps rose on her skin.

Lorna's hands came up and rested lightly atop his head as he moved to the tips of her breasts. The only sounds in the room were her soft labored breaths, and the whisper of skin on sheets. When he kissed her stomach, it rippled and quivered, and her hands fell to his shoulders, not guiding but waiting. It had been so long, Malcolm almost couldn't wait to taste her, and when he did, it was like going home. She was sweetly familiar, silky, soft and slippery under his tongue.

Lorna's trembling and quivering intensified as did his need to dive even deeper into her. Grabbing her behind the knees, he held her captive until she cried out her release and went still beneath him.

Malcolm kissed the insides of her thighs and rested his head on one, feeling the gentle rake of Lorna's fingernails in his low-cut hair. Right about now was when they might speak, one of them teasing the other, engaging in the verbal foreplay that always led to round two—Lorna's mouth on him, his mouth once again on her, tussling, making a mess of the bed. But this time was different.

Wanting to see her face, Malcolm made his way back upward so they were looking at each other again. Lorna's knees fell further apart and with almost no effort on either of their parts, he slipped inside her. She was hot and smooth, like a wet, silken glove. And deep inside, he felt the tiniest of pulses. They lay there, chest to chest, Malcolm's weight resting on his elbows, both of them with open eyes, staring as though trying to read each other's minds.

Lorna's eyes were soft, and a little glazed—with tears, with confusion, and loss. Here, too, for the first time during lovemaking, she was completely stripped bare. This was the Lorna he had been trying to reach all this time—the one who had told all her truths.

But he didn't want her broken. He didn't want her hurt. He didn't want her afraid for her future.

"Look at you," he said. "You're so beautiful."

Lorna attempted a smile, but it was clear she still had a ways to go before the smiles would be genuine once again. Pressing her pelvis upward against his, she signaled that she was ready for him, so Malcolm began to move, slowly, barely pulling out and pushing back in, wanting to keep as much of their connection as he could.

Beneath him, he felt Lorna's quivers begin again, and she grabbed his shoulders, his arms, then his waist, as if trying to find a position that would make the pleasure bearable. She gasped, and panted but still said nothing, her eyes tightly shut now, and head momentarily thrashing from side to side.

Malcolm kissed her, his tongue seeking hers and finding it, biting her lower lip, lightly sucking on the upper. Lorna shuddered in the wake of yet another climax. She had always been able to make herself do that, he knew—disappear in the lovemaking, absenting herself completely from the known world. And he loved that he could bring her that pleasure when she needed it as an escape. But now, he didn't want her to escape; he wanted her with him and in the present moment.

"Baby," Malcolm breathed. "Where are you? I need to hear you."

Lorna opened her eyes and stilled. "I'm here," she said. "I'm here."

TWENTY-SEVEN
RECONSTRUCTION

THE SUN WAS UP AGAIN, BUT LORNA HAD LOST TRACK OF the days. She thought it was probably Tuesday but couldn't be sure. There had been a stream of days and nights, showers, and take-out meals; and the sound of Malcolm's keyboard, clicking and clacking in the next room while she struggled to lift her head from the pillow.

She remembered bits and pieces of the morning, when Malcolm had kissed her on her shoulder and said he was going over to the college, and she moaned in response and turned over onto her stomach, and everything went black again.

The college. There were things there that she needed to do. And there was probably a letter on President Julia Bond's stationary, formalizing her yearlong exile awaiting her in her faculty mailbox. She had to get up. Slinging her legs over the edge of her bed, she felt a slight ache in her thighs, and where she was swollen between them.

Sighing, she recalled the previous evening, her upper body falling partway off the bed, Malcolm's face above her, his arms extended, hands splayed, clawing, and making deep indentations on the bed on either side of her, his face twisted into a tight grimace, and droplets of sweat dripping off his brow. But one could lose oneself in sex for only so long before facing the rest of the world. And she had been hiding out far too long.

Somewhere around here was her phone, she just had no idea where at this point. She didn't even know where the clothes she'd worn over to Malcolm's house were. Finding her pocketbook in the living room, she also spotted the stack of papers that was Fallon's thesis. One more thing she had to face.

Fishing out her phone, Lorna saw that it had been turned off. Malcolm, trying to protect her from the outside world. Once turned on, it immediately started chiming, a staggeringly long list of notifications appearing on the screen. For a second, Lorna had the impulse to shut it off again and go back to the bedroom, crawl under the sheets, and sleep for another twelve hours. But that wouldn't change anything except lengthen the list of notifications awaiting her when she finally woke up again. So, no, she would tackle this now.

Sighing she scrolled to the bottom of the list and slowly made her way up to the most recent. Despite the sheer volume of messages, there were actually only three people trying to reach her—Steven Hunt, Riley and Fallon Wright—and all of them manageable enough. Deciding to begin with the only one she actually wanted to speak to, Lorna dialed Riley's number.

Expecting at least a mild dressing-down, Lorna was surprised at the tenderness in her daughter's voice when she answered the phone.

"I talked to Malcolm," she explained. "He thought he should call me since you were gone from home so long. He thought I might be worried."

"I feel like you two are colluding behind my back," Lorna said half-jokingly. "Whispered phone calls to make sure I'm not a danger to myself, or something."

"You're always a danger to yourself," Riley said dryly.

Lorna rolled her eyes.

"So, are you and Malcolm back together, or ...?"

"I just got booted out of my job and you're worried about whether or not Malcolm and I are back together?"

"Professionally, I'm pretty confident you'll land on your feet. Relationship-wise, I'm not so sure. And anyway, from what Malcolm said, it's not like you were let go. More like a mandatory timeout."

"You enjoy metaphors that tell me I'm acting like a child, don't you?"

"I do." There was a smile in Riley's voice. And then she sighed. "But how are you, really?"

"Much better. I slept for three days, had ridiculous amounts of Asian food and sex, and now I feel like I might be in fighting form again."

Riley laughed. "Yeah. Too much information, but good to hear, I guess. So what's your next move?"

"I'm going to get up, get dressed and tie off the loose ends, whatever they might be, over at the college and then, who knows?"

"Mom, I *am* sorry, y'know. I didn't mean to sound insensitive before. I know how hard this must be for you. Especially that thing with your student."

"She wasn't my student. She was a thesis advisee. An overly eager, ingratiating little snake of a thesis advisee. And my research assistant."

"What are you going to do about her? Plagiarism is grounds for expulsion, isn't it?"

"I don't think there needs to be any more blood on the floor. I'll deal with her in my own way."

Lorna felt a pang, recalling that she wouldn't be teaching classes as planned in a few weeks. Tasks that had once seemed almost burdensome were less so once taken away. And she wouldn't be working on her book either. But if Fallon's betrayal felt like a major calamity when it first happened, now it was more like a medium-sized setback.

"They took me apart, one piece at a time, Riley," she said. "But my mind is clearer now. So I guess I'll get to work putting myself back together."

"I could think of a few things you might do with your time off," Riley said, sounding a little cautious.

"Yeah? Like what? My dance card is completely empty right now, so ..."

"Write for me. My journal. And come stay for a little while. Spend some time with your grandchildren."

Lorna smiled. "I could do that." Which reminded her of something. "What's been happening with Ryan?"

"I'm going up to see him. And his parents."

She still hadn't gotten to the point of comfortably calling them her 'grandparents'. Riley had never had those. Something else, Lorna had robbed her of. She said a silent prayer of thanks that they were still alive.

"That's great, Riley!" And she meant it. "Are you ...?"

"Terrified? Yeah, pretty much. You wouldn't be interested in coming, would you?"

Lorna laughed. "No thank you. I think I've had my butt handed to me plenty to last me a while. I can't imagine either of his parents want to have anything to do with me. And I can't say I blame them."

"I don't know about them, but actually, he says he's been following your career, and that he's very proud of you."

Like the grandparents, Riley still hadn't figured out what to call Ryan other than "my father" and "he". Lorna wondered what she called him when they were speaking.

"Ryan said that?"

Their own conversation had been mercifully brief, with Lorna simply telling him that Riley had asked about him, and that she thought it was time for them to meet. And after that, Ryan had been focused solely on the questions Lorna hoped he would be focused on: *When can I talk to her? When can I meet her? Is she there with you now?*

Later, when he actually met Riley in person and saw all that he had missed, that was when Lorna had no doubt the anger would come.

"He said he thought about reaching out a few times, but wasn't sure how he'd be received."

"Even after you told him about the letter and what I did with it, he wanted to reach out?"

"We didn't talk about that. He didn't ask and I have no plans to bring it up."

"You don't need to protect me, Riley. If it comes up, you should tell him the truth."

There was a pause. "Are you sure?"

"I'd rather he know the truth than think you got the letter and decided to reject him."

"Okay, well ... okay. If it comes up I'll tell him. As long as you're sure."

She sounded like a weight had been lifted. It pained Lorna to think that Riley would be surprised.

"I'm sure."

Had she really been that selfish? And maybe Ryan hadn't said anything because he was protecting her, just as Riley had. It was difficult to consider that of all the players in their little family drama, she was probably the least noble. But making herself look good had, practically overnight, fallen down several notches on the list of her personal priorities.

"You never did answer me about you and Malcolm."

"Didn't I say there'd been lots of sex?"

Riley laughed. "Like that has to mean something to you."

Another pang. "Riley! Of course it means something to me. *Especially* with Malcolm."

There was a prolonged silence.

"*What* did you say?"

"I said ..." Lorna felt her face grow warm. "I said, especially with Malcolm."

"So ... is this ...?"

"I'm not going to dissect it for you, but I ... there are real feelings there. I ..."

Riley laughed. "Just say you love him. Can you give me that tiny satisfaction?"

"I love him," Lorna said.

"There. Now was that so hard?"

Lorna smiled. "No. Actually, it wasn't."

THE LETTER WAS THERE, waiting for her as expected. Lorna fished it out of her mailbox, ignoring the sympathetic glance she got from Inez, the department secretary.

So, the word was out, then. Everyone knew she had been banished. But what they didn't know, and what she was determined they would never find out, was how much it affected her. So before leaving Malcolm's she had found her jeans—which he had considerately laundered—and one of his white shirts, and ironed both. Then she had taken some time to get her hair in order, wetting it and pulling it back into a sleek ponytail.

With all the sleep she had gotten, she actually looked well-rested and relaxed when she checked her reflection in the mirror at his door. No one needed to know that she spent the last several days almost catatonic except for showers and vital bodily functions. She had put on the jeans and her sandals with Malcolm's shirt, which she tied at her waist and buttoned three-quarters of the way up. She looked breezy and casual, like she hadn't a care in the world.

In the refuge of her office, looking down at the letter from Julia Bond's office, Lorna took a deep breath and reached for her desk phone. She arranged to go in to see Julia on the hour, in forty-five minutes. That should be more than enough time to complete the unpleasant task she had immediately ahead of her.

While waiting, she took visual inventory of her office, mentally cataloguing what she would take and what she would leave behind. Keeping a notepad at the ready on her desk lest the mental list become too long, Lorna was surprised to find that there was very little she actually needed to take with her for a prolonged absence.

"Ha," she said aloud, spinning in a circle. All this stuff, and none of it was necessary. Surely, that couldn't be true.

A soft knock on her door interrupted her reflection and she turned.

"Come in," she said.

Fallon entered and Lorna wondered whether she was imagining the slightly defiant tilt of the girl's head, and the way her shoulders were squared back. Maybe she would pretend otherwise for the sake of appearances, but reading her body language alone, Lorna felt sure that Fallon knew precisely what the nature of this conversation would be.

"Take a seat, Fallon."

Fallon did as she was asked, her eyes unreadable. Lorna chose to stand, mindful that the girl was several inches taller than her when standing. Reaching into her satchel, she pulled out the papers she'd brought along from Malcolm's and extended them.

Fallon hesitated before taking them.

"I'm afraid I may have spilled some tea on a few of the pages," Lorna said impassively. "But I'm sure you have it saved electronically."

Fallon nodded, but said nothing. It was only then that Lorna realized she hadn't spoken at all since entering the room.

"I think if you present this thesis to your next advisor, they'll find the ideas to be fresh and interesting. And depending on how well those ideas are fleshed out, they may even consider them to be publishable," Lorna said.

At the corners of Fallon's mouth, there was the barest of twitches. The girl actually wanted to smile!

"But the thing about it is, Fallon," Lorna sat on the edge of her desk. "Those ideas aren't yours. They're all the product of my notes, and conversations I had with you in the context of you being my research assistant."

"You never shared your book proposal with me," Fallon said. "You only told me you were writing something about modern feminists."

"Actually, we spoke very extensively about the thesis of my book proposal. Before I went to North Carolina. And you asked me a few probing questions, which I answered. That's how I remember it."

"It isn't how I remember it," Fallon said. Now the defiance was overt.

"So you intend to move ahead with submitting this as your work," Lorna said.

It wasn't a question. She knew the answer would be a 'yes'. Anyone who was brazen enough to present plagiarized ideas to the original author could do just about anything.

"It is my work," Fallon said. "Inspired by you, Professor Terry. I don't deny that, but ..."

"*The misappropriation of the words, thoughts or ideas of*

another and representing them as one's own original work," Lorna said. "Do you know what that is, Fallon?"

"That's *not* what I did." She sounded almost petulant, and looked like what she was—practically a child. But in this instance, a child who was told that a prize she wanted had not been earned.

"An academic career is difficult," Lorna continued, pretending she hadn't even heard the denial. "If you care about pursuing knowledge, and *creating* knowledge there is nothing that's more bruising to the ego than a career in academia. You'll feel stupid more times than you can count; there'll be people who—no matter your effort—manage to be smarter, sharper and just plain better than you. It humbles you. But you know what's even worse?"

Fallon shook her head. Despite herself, she wanted to know the answer to the question.

"The accolades," Lorna said. "*Those* are worse. Because if you get them too early, or too often, you begin to believe them. And pretty soon, you think you're the smartest person in every room. And if there's a supply of people who confirm that, suddenly the very thing you were most proud of begins to atrophy—your mind shrinks and becomes narrow and prideful, impervious to challenge. Not just in your field of study, but in other areas of your life as well. And I know all of this firsthand. I was the youngest-ever tenured professor at Gilchrist. And the only one of color. There's a lot of pride to be had in that."

"And you have no idea how much I admire that accomplishment, Professor Ter ..."

"So much that you thought you might ... borrow a little of it?"

Fallon swallowed and shook her head. For the first time looking a little uncertain. "I didn't mean to ... I mean, I *didn't* ..."

"The thing about borrowing the wind from someone else's wings, Fallon, is that it might not always be there to keep you aloft. You submit this thesis and pretend they're your ideas, sooner or later you're going to be expected to live up to it."

"Did you read it?"

"I read enough of it to see that you have an enviable and impressive memory. Some of it I might have written myself. I'm not sure I didn't. I did give you all of my notes after all."

"If you thought I stole it, you would report me," Fallon said, sticking her chin out.

"I might have. But as luck would have it, other things happening right now slowed me down, so I've had time to think and reflect on it. I'm not going to report you."

Fallon's shoulders relaxed, and that hint of a smile appeared once again.

"Instead, I want to offer you the choice. To work on your original thesis. With my help."

"But you're not going to be here," Fallon said smugly. "Everyone's been talking about it."

"It would be unofficial help. But I would be happy to do it; if you choose to submit your original work, I'll help you refine your ideas, guide you, support your development in feminist theory."

"Or else?"

Lorna shrugged. "Or else nothing. I said I wouldn't report you."

"But you said I have a choice. What's the other choice?"

"Submit that paper in your hand."

"I don't get ..."

"Fallon, you're free to do whatever you choose. But if you submit that thesis, all I can offer you is a word of advice—that you can't build anything sustainable on a lie. It always comes crumbling down in the end. And when that happens, you're generally on your own, left to face yourself."

Looking slightly bored, Fallon prepared to stand.

"Think it over, Fallon," Lorna said. "Please."

A few beats passed, during which she allowed herself to hope that Fallon would make the right choice. But in the girl's eyes, Lorna saw something she was all too familiar with—the arrogant certainty of youth, and the foolhardy belief that a reckoning would never come.

"Thank you, Professor Terry." This time Fallon did stand, and shoved the thesis into her backpack, avoiding eye contact as she did. "I appreciate you taking the time to read my work."

And then she was gone.

SHE WAS Julia Bond's last appointment of the day.

In fact, just as Lorna arrived, President Bond's secretary, Susan was gathering her things to leave. She smiled and waved Lorna right in, telling her in a cheery voice to have a good evening.

"It's nice to think the place will be flooded with students again not too long from now, isn't it?" she said as she walked through the door.

Lorna smiled back at the elderly woman before turning to head into Julia's inner office.

"Yes. Very nice," she agreed.

Apparently, there was at least one person on campus who hadn't heard of her fate. And ironically, Susan was one of very few people who understandably should have known.

"Lorna, is that you I hear out there?"

Julia Bond appeared at the door. She was wearing dark

blue slacks and a beige blazer. On her feet were bright white tennis shoes that drew Lorna's eyes downward.

"Don't ask," Julia said, ushering her into the office. "My doctor has me walking now. Says I need to get rid of a few extra pounds.'

In the sitting area, Julia had a tea service arranged, along with a plate of mini scones. She took a seat in one of the two armchairs and gestured for Lorna to do the same. When they were facing each other, Julia sighed deeply and audibly.

"You know why we're here," she said. "They have to have their pound of flesh, Lorna."

She was even able to smile, recalling that she had used the identical metaphor. Well, there was no better way to describe it.

"Will it only be a pound?" she asked.

"Barely. More like a pinch. One year sabbatical. Full pay. Full access to resources for research, email, everything. Except physical access to your office and college buildings. And no contact with students whatsoever. Which some might consider a benefit, honestly." Julia began pouring tea into the two teacups on the tray. "And of course, you'll be expected to refrain from discussing any of this with anyone for any purpose whatsoever."

"And there's something I have to sign, I suppose?" Lorna said.

"Of course." Julia's eyes rose to meet hers, and they were for a moment as hard and cold as ice.

Lorna took the teacup when it was offered, declining cream, but accepting two sugars. The entire thing was so civilized. Once she'd settled back into her seat, Julia looked at her again.

"Jesus Christ, Lorna, why the hell did you give them the ammunition?"

"I never would have guessed that was what I was doing when I had a brief ... thing with a thirty-year old man, Julia."

The college president shrugged. "Fair enough. But my god, who would have imagined you were out there living the life you talk about in all your lectures?"

At that, Lorna allowed herself a smile. "It's not all it's cracked up to be."

"And it's been costly. Not just to you," Julia Bond said, her brow knitting.

"I know. With the lawyers, and ..."

"No. Not that kind of expensive. You're one of our brightest stars here at Gilchrist. No one wants to see that sparkle dimmed ..."

"At least one of our trustees wants to see it dimmed."

"Williamson is a small, small man."

"And so was his son," Lorna couldn't help but add.

Julia laughed, almost spluttering tea all over her smart blazer, and stabbed a finger in Lorna's direction.

"You see, it's *that* kind of irreverence that's gotten you in hot water. It didn't sit well with some of them, your lack of humility. I think that tipped the balance. You could just as easily have come out of this completely unscathed if you hadn't come into the meeting with that ... that look you get, of indignant self-righteousness."

"I realize that. But I wasn't about to beg for forgiveness for something that wasn't even a sin."

"I understand. And I wish it could have turned out differently. But you know how it is with men of a certain age. You may as well have showed up with a scythe threatening to cut their balls off." Julia stood and went behind her desk, returning with a folder which she slid across the table.

Lorna opened it and scanned the contents. It was a single-page document in triplicate, describing the terms of her leave of absence from the college.

"You can have your attorney look it over if you wish, and return it later."

"I'm comfortable signing now."

Julia produced a pen—a weighty, expensive Waterman—and Lorna signed all three copies of the document with a flourish.

"One is for your records."

Folding one sheet into a small square, Lorna shoved it into the back pocket of her jeans.

"So that's that," she said.

Waiting for the panic or sadness to come, Lorna was surprised when it didn't. What seemed like it might be the end of the world just weeks ago, had been almost anticlimactic.

"So, what are your plans?"

"For once in ... longer than I can remember, I don't have any," Lorna said musing at how astoundingly good that felt.

"Well, I'm sure that won't remain so for very long," Julia said. "That mind of yours will produce something soon enough I expect."

"I expect so," Lorna agreed.

"Time to finish up the tea and scones? I don't know when I'll see you next."

"Of course. I've nothing but time at this point."

———

"YOU DISAPPEARED like a puff of smoke, Professor Terry."

Malcolm stepped aside when he opened the door. It was just past dark, and Lorna had spent almost two hours with Julia, just shooting the breeze. Finally, the two women had walked together over to the President's mansion where they parted cordially with promises—that neither would keep—to stay in touch during Lorna's sabbatical.

"I left you a note," she said, walking into him, instead of going inside. "Didn't you see it?"

His arms around her, the way she molded into his chest felt perfect, and preordained. It was hard to believe she had once voluntarily deprived herself of it.

"I did. But it didn't say where you were going, for how long, or when you'd be back."

"Because you didn't need all those details," Lorna said into his shirt. "All you needed to know was that I wasn't going to go sailing out the window of a high rise in grief at the mess my life's turned into."

"*Someone's* feeling much better, obviously," Malcolm said, shaking his head. "C'mon inside. I have food."

"You can stop force-feeding me now, Malcolm, I think I'm out of danger of starving myself to ..."

Before she could finish her sentence, he kissed her; hard at first and then with lessening intensity, until finally his lips were just brushing against hers, light as a feather.

"Shut *up*," he said, his lips still on hers.

Lorna smiled.

No kid gloves from Malcolm T. Mitchell. Except when she needed them.

"Is it weird that I get kind of turned on when you speak to me that way?"

It was Malcolm's turn to smile.

"Come tell me all about the adventures you had today."

"Oh, my day was *very* adventurous," Lorna said, leaning against him as they walked together toward the kitchen.

TWENTY-EIGHT

FALL

Hurriedly shutting his laptop, Malcolm slid it easily into the brown calfskin satchel, and snapped it shut with the clasp just beneath the embossed letters, 'MTM'. The bag was a gift from Lorna, for his first day of teaching, several weeks ago. The surprising sentimentality of the gesture, from the least sentimental person he knew, was enough to make a lump form in the back of his throat when she'd given it to him, in an enormous cream-colored gift-box wrapped in a floppy black bow.

It's nothing, Lorna said unconvincingly. *I just want to make sure you look the part of a professor. Nothing is less attractive than a grown man with a sloppy Jansport backpack slung over his shoulder.*

Later, when Riley told him Lorna had gotten it custom-made, Malcolm treasured it even more, but didn't bother telling her he knew the trouble she had gone to. It was an heirloom-quality bag, and something he didn't much like schlepping around on campus, but hell, that was what it was meant for.

The very first signs of the autumnal season were upon them at Gilchrist College. Though it would be November before the leaves completely changed, the Hudson River Valley was beginning to look like fall. But more important to Malcolm at the moment was the fact that midterms loomed and there would be hundreds of pages of freshman essays to grade, around the same time as his publisher's deadline.

Today, though, the cause of his hurrying was something else entirely.

"Professor Mitchell?"

Malcolm looked up and into the doe-eyed stare of one of his students. He still had trouble with most of their names when they weren't in their customary seats in the lecture hall, but this one he remembered.

"Miss Addison," he said, hoping to convey with the briskness of his tone that he had no time to waste. "How can I help you?"

"I hoped you'd have time to go over my last paper with me, because ..."

"How'd you do on it?"

"I got a 'B' but there weren't very many comments in the margins, so I thought maybe if we talked about it ..."

With this one, there was always something. She was the quintessential high school overachiever, who upon entering college, was horrified to learn that suddenly she was among young people just as smart as she. That there were valedictorians and salutatorians aplenty; that she was no longer remarkable.

"Come during office hours," Malcolm said, slinging his bag over his shoulder and beginning to walk toward the exit. "Sign-up sheet's on my door."

"I did. But I just had *one* ..."

"Office hours, Miss Addison. See you in class on Monday!"

He left the building at a trot and kept his head down until he was safely in his vehicle and pulling out of his parking space.

If he was late, Lorna would be antsy and irritable, falling into one of her moods; the moods which were more frequent and unpredictable lately. As it was, he had to twist her arm to be there at all, but this was important enough to make the arm-twisting worthwhile.

Lorna was waiting at his front stoop for him, her face like a storm-cloud, and her weekend bag at her feet.

"Ten more minutes and I would have left," she said.

"The lecture went over by a few minutes and then I got stopped by some kid who thinks a 'B' in Freshman English is the end of the world," he said, kissing her quickly on her tightly pursed mouth. "And they're not even here yet, so it's fine. And we keep forgetting to get you a key ..."

He took her bag from her and dumped it in the master bedroom, coming back out with his jacket shed, and rolling up his shirtsleeves.

"I don't need a key," she said. "And you're sure this is necessary?" Lorna added, for the umpteenth time voicing an objection he'd been hearing for a week now.

"Yeah. You're here almost every night, but so far only on the weekends when the girls *aren't* here. I want Hayley to get used to seeing us here together."

"Sleeping apart every other weekend isn't going to kill either of us, Malcolm."

"Will you stop being so difficult about this? We already agreed ..."

"I know I agreed. I'm just saying ..."

"Don't 'just say' anything, Lorna. Just ... go with the flow. Okay?"

"I *am* going with the flow. I'm here, aren't I? I don't understand what the big deal is. Piper didn't bat an eyelid when we were in North Carolina."

"Piper's older, and that wasn't my house. So it's different. I need my girls to see you being part of my daily life. Especially since you practically live here."

"I *don't* practically live here," Lorna snapped. "I still have my own house ..."

"Yeah, well ..."

"Yeah, well ... what?"

"Nothing. Let's just drop it," Malcolm said, having learned it was best to choose his battles with her. Because if it was up to Lorna, they would fight them *all* to the death; which would only drive him nuts. "But if you don't practically live here, it's weird that when I did laundry a couple days ago, there was more of your stuff than mine."

"I'm going to make some tea. Just let me know when they get here," Lorna said, leaving him alone in the living room.

It was no secret he wanted them to at least live together, but they never talked about it. At least not directly. Instead he hinted, she evaded and then they bickered.

The only reason he hadn't forced the issue was that he knew she was still dealing with a few other difficult adjustments—not only was she not teaching for the first time in over a decade, and without any full-time occupation, but for the first time in even more time than that, she was having to share her daughter.

Riley's in-person reunion with her father had gone more than well; with Riley finding out she was temperamentally more similar to her father and his kin, low-key, mellow people, who had folded her into their family effortlessly. That process had been helped along considerably because though they hadn't known precisely who she was, Riley's two younger sisters had always known of her existence, as had her father's wife.

It was as fairytale an ending as Lorna could have hoped for, but while she was happy for Riley, Malcolm watched Lorna struggle to get comfortable with the new normal of Riley turning her heart and her attention toward people who still wanted little or nothing to do with Lorna herself.

It was only a few minutes later that Malcolm heard the sound of a car pulling up outside, and shortly after that, the sound of his daughters' voices just before that of the doorbell.

He saw Charlotte first when he opened the door. She was wearing white jeans and a frilly, ocean-blue off-the-shoulder top with high-heeled white sandals. Large sunglasses held back her hair.

Smiling at his reaction, she leaned in to kiss him briefly on the cheek.

"I know what you're thinking," she said, stepping past him and into the house. "That I'm a little over-dressed to drop my kids off to spend the weekend with their father. But actually ..."

Her prattle stopped mid-sentence and Malcolm turned to see that Lorna had just come sauntering out of the kitchen, her cup of tea in hand.

"Hi Daddy," Hayley sang.

She breezed past him and toward the guest bedroom that she and Piper had already made their own, pausing to offer Lorna a brief 'hi' and wave. Lorna and Hayley had met now on a handful of occasions, but she had never spent the night with Hayley in the house.

Piper, who hadn't yet spoken at all sauntered in, almost absentmindedly giving Malcolm a hug and then turning her full attention to where Charlotte and Lorna were now facing each other.

Charlotte looked uncomfortable; Lorna merely bemused, as though she was simply observing, rather than participating in the awkward scene.

"Oh. Hello!" Charlotte chirped. "I was just telling Malcolm that I'm all dressed-up for a little thing I'm going to.

One of my firm's partners happens to live about twenty-five minutes from here and he's having a bunch of people over for early cocktails by his pool."

Malcolm saw Lorna's eyebrows lift just a fraction. He could practically read her mind. The phrase "early cocktails by his pool" would strike her as pretentious. She was wondering how he could have married a woman like Charlotte, and what they could possibly have had in common.

"Sounds wonderful," she said, returning Charlotte's smile. "The weather's perfect for it."

"Well, now it is," Charlotte agreed. "But later it's going to be as hot as Hades, so I hope they have a tent set up or something."

Have a tent set up? Charlotte was only making it worse for herself. One more comment like that and she would be dismissed as a twit, forever and for all time by Lorna Terry.

"Anyway, I'd better get going." Charlotte turned and gave Piper a kiss, which she shrank from a little. "Mal, walk me out?"

Only then did Malcolm realize that he, like Piper, had just been standing there, watching the interaction between the two women, like someone in the audience at a tennis match.

"Sure," he said.

"Nice seeing you again, Charlotte," Lorna said as they exited the house.

He couldn't fault her for her anything. She had been friendly, if not warm, and there hadn't been even the slightest trace in her voice or demeanor of the judgments Malcolm knew she must have made about his ex-wife. Although, to be fair, lately Lorna seemed to have no harsh judgments about much of anything or anyone, except herself. Some of her edges had softened.

"Will she be staying?" Charlotte asked, her voice taut, as

they headed down the path toward the street where she was parked.

"Yup."

"Hmm. So it is serious."

"It is," he confirmed.

At her car, Charlotte turned to face him, twisting and playing with the keys in her hand.

"I didn't make a big deal about North Carolina because you had prior plans and I sort of dropped Piper into your lap. And because Piper is, for better or worse, well aware of what happens between a man and a woman. But with Hayley ..."

"That's a justifiable concern," Malcolm said nodding. "But it isn't as though this is a flash-in-the-pan relationship. Lorna's going to be around for ... you know ... the duration, so ..."

Charlotte pursed her lips and studied her hands, for a moment looking as though she might cry. When she looked up at him again, her eyes were filled.

"So ... are you planning to like, *get married* or something?" Her voice rose to a pitch dangerously close to a whine. "You haven't known her that long, Mal. And ..."

"I don't know. I don't know if she wants that."

"But you want it?" Charlotte asked softly.

He nodded, and watched her shoulders sag. She pursed her lips tighter and put the back of a hand to her forehead and shook her head.

"Malcolm, are you sure this isn't just some sort of rebound thing? We just got divorced. We're still getting the girls adjusted to that, and now you're telling me you want them to adjust to ..."

"I'm not talking tomorrow, or next week. And I know they need to adjust. That's why Lorna's here this weekend. And probably will be for a good number of the weekends the girls are with me. She's an important part of my life, and ..."

"So they'll never have you to themselves again? It's a package deal? Is that what you're ...?"

"No, of course not. I'm always going to be there for them in any way they need me to be."

"And what about ... what about me?" Charlotte touched his arm and then just as quickly let her hand drop. "This changes everything between us. You have to see that."

"Charlotte, your affair with Spence changed everything between us. But I don't even blame you for that anymore. I don't even *think* about it anymore. But don't act like I walked out on you when the opposite is true."

"And so this *is* a rebound."

"No. This is where I'm meant to be. It's time you found the same for yourself."

"Well ..." Charlotte unlocked the car and went around to the driver's side, pausing before getting in. "Enjoy your weekend, Malcolm."

"You too."

He watched as she drove away, then headed back up toward the house and was at the door just in time to hear Lorna telling Piper that no, she couldn't have a cup of coffee but she was happy to make her a nice mug of jasmine tea instead. Then Piper saying that she was no fun at all, and Lorna's retort: *yes, so I've been told.*

Malcolm smiled.

IT WAS A MISTAKE, having Malcolm get a television for the bedroom, Lorna thought as she switched it on.

And an even bigger mistake letting him go on his own to buy it. The thing was enormous, and now dominated an entire wall of his bedroom. He had had it professionally mounted, so they could adjust its angle, depending on what part of the room they were in. Lorna could even twist the damn thing around and watch television while she changed in the walk-in closet, which she sometimes did.

She never used to be someone who watched much television at all. Now she had become one of those people who arranged their lives according to her favorite programs. A lot of 'her programs' were embarrassingly mindless, like one called 'The Internet Ruined My Life'.

But there were others that were a revelation, like 'The Rachel Maddow Show'. Now *there* was a woman of consequence. Lorna thought she might even have a little bit of a girl-crush on Rachel. And somewhere in the spectrum in between *Maddow* and the *Internet* nonsense, there were shows like 'Criminal Minds' that managed to be both very intelligent and overly simplistic at the same time.

Anyway, she had a love-hate relationship with the television, and was thinking of asking Malcolm to have it taken out. But maybe all it was, was a convenient scapegoat for why she had done absolutely nothing with herself since her sabbatical began. She hadn't written anything, she had hardly even read anything. And she spent her days on pointless tasks like cleaning out her attic, alphabetizing her books in her study, then changing her mind and arranging them according to subject matter; and then changing her mind again and finally abandoning the project altogether.

The truth was, she was struggling. Riley had invited her down to the city to stay for a while and she went for two days, but felt like an extra in a movie—Shawn and Riley and their kids had full lives and a routine that suited them. And she was left to fill in, and get in where she fit in which was uncomfortable and unfamiliar. For far too long, wherever she went, Lorna had been the main attraction and she was that no longer.

And add to that, being at Riley's only gave her front-row access to the growing love-affair between Riley, and Ryan and his family. His daughters' names were Jane and Ellen, plain, New England traditional names. One was seventeen and the other nineteen, and they were both smitten with Riley and with the notion that their long-lost sister had turned out to be none other than the elegant wife of one of the planet's biggest hip-hop stars. They called constantly, so while she was there, Lorna listened to Riley on the phone with them, chattering excitedly as they learned about uncanny similarities between them.

Ellen wanted to be a writer, Jane was dating a bass guitarist, and they both—like Riley—tended toward the bohemian. When Riley mentioned casually that 'the girls' were coming into the city for a day-trip, Lorna had beat a hasty retreat back upstate. She wasn't emotionally prepared to come face to face with Ryan's other offspring. And besides, she missed Malcolm.

That was another thing—she missed Malcolm.

She missed him not only when she was in the city for a stretch of days, she missed him even when he was at the college for a stretch of *hours*. He was her lifeline to the real world in some ways, because even Shawn and Riley, celebrities that they were, couldn't be said to live in the real "real world."

Missing Malcolm the way she did worried her. It was unhealthy, clingy, and was not who she was. She sometimes feigned busy-ness with him, pretending she had projects and occupations that kept her at home, just to counteract that impulse to cling. But she was fairly certain he wasn't fooled.

So, yes, she was struggling.

"Hey. You coming out to eat with us?"

Lorna looked up at Malcolm in the doorway, in a white t-shirt and cargo shorts, handsomely unshaven. He was growing a bonafide beard now. She loved the way it tickled her neck and her inner thighs, and her sex when he was going down on her. Of all the things she'd lost, at least her libido was intact.

"I'll come grab something in a bit," she said. "Just catching up on ..." She indicated the Sunday morning political program that was on.

"You sure? Piper and Hayley made you bacon," he coaxed. "You know how you love your bacon."

Lorna made herself smile. "Okay, I'll be there in a few."

Malcolm searched her face, and his eyes narrowed. "You okay, baby?"

Lorna felt little pinpricks of tears at the back of her eyes, the way she always did when he called her 'baby'. She still had to get used to this—his unrelenting tenderness, his patience, the way he loved her. It was hard to believe she deserved any of it, especially when she gave—and sometimes continued to give— him such a difficult time.

"I'm fine. I'll be out in a few minutes."

"Okay." He winked at her and was gone.

Who the hell was she now? That was the problem. She wasn't okay, because she didn't know who she was. If not the esteemed professor at Gilchrist College, if not Riley's sole parent, the only star in her universe ... if not those things, who was she? She wasn't even the woman with the many lovers, men falling at her feet anymore. She was a ... housewife.

Staring mindlessly at the television screen, it didn't take too long before Lorna lost all track of time. *What was it? Ten minutes? Fifteen?* She didn't know for sure, but the next time she looked away from it, Piper and Hayley were standing in the doorway, one of them with a tray, the other with a steaming mug.

"We brought you breakfast in bed," Hayley said looking pleased with herself.

Malcolm's younger daughter reminded Lorna of Riley

when she was that age—unerringly sweet, quiet and thoughtful. She looked less like Charlotte than Piper did, except for the auburn ringlets.

"Oh ... girls you didn't have to ..." She sat up, embarrassed suddenly that they were catering to her, rather than she to them.

"Daddy said you're feeling a little sad," Hayley explained, bringing over the mug and handing it to her. "He said you were going to have a bed-a-thon today."

Lorna laughed. "A what?"

"That's when you stay in bed all day and just hang out," Piper said, bringing over the tray, which she set down at the end of the bed. "And watch TV and read magazines, and ..."

"Do your nails," Hayley supplied.

"Lorna doesn't 'do her nails', stupid," Piper said.

"Piper don't call her stupid," Lorna chided, sipping from her mug. "I'd love to do my nails. If one of you would do it for me."

"Really?" Hayley's eyes lit up. "Could I?"

"You'd just mess it up," Piper said. "I should do her nails."

"But it was my idea!" Hayley whined.

"I have two hands, so you can both do my nails. How about that?" Lorna suggested. "But you have to let me eat this great breakfast you brought me first."

"Okay, but we can get some stuff." Piper said. "I always have nail stuff when I go away. Hayley c'mon ..."

"And we have magazines too!" Hayley said, following Piper out of the room.

Just as Lorna was finishing up her second strip of bacon, the girls returned with armfuls of accessories—cotton balls and bottles, nail colors, and little styrofoam toe separators, and a pile of magazines with gleefully grinning teenagers on the cover.

Before Lorna could even react, they had unloaded every-thing on the free side of the bed and crawled in, bickering and arguing with each other as they arranged themselves next to her. Hayley grabbed a magazine and then the remote control.

"What's this?" she asked, grimacing.

It was 'Meet the Press'. Lorna smiled. She could only imagine how boring that must look to a nine-year old.

"I know what Lorna will like," Piper said snatching the remote control from her sister.

"Hey!" Hayley said.

"This." Piper found a channel on the guide and changed it. "Lifetime. It's called 'Television for Women'. Lorna's a Women's Studies professor so this channel is practically invented for people like her."

"Actually ..." Lorna began.

Both girls looked at her.

What she had been about to say that was she'd only recently independently discovered Lifetime during her own channel-surfing and been attracted to it precisely because they billed themselves as television for women. But to her dismay, it seemed to be very much the opposite. Just about every single one of their featured movies seemed to be about women and children being victimized. How the hell that translated to 'tele-vision for women' Lorna had no clue.

But Piper looked so pleased with her choice. And Hayley looked so adorable sitting there with her magazine on her lap, all armed and ready for a bed-a-thon.

So what she did say, was: "That sounds like a great plan. Let's watch some television for women."

Then she 'borrowed' the remote for a moment to make sure the movie on didn't have themes that were too grim, or too adult, and settled back into her pillows to watch.

She wasn't sure when, but she dozed off again and awoke to

her fingers being painted a bright, garish, girly pink, and Malcolm grinning and clearing away her breakfast tray.

And then again later, to the sensation of being too hot, only to find that she was buffeted on either side by Piper and Hayley; Hayley fast asleep herself and Piper lying with her feet practically in Lorna's face, her head at the foot of the bed while she watched what looked like a teen sci-fi movie. Lorna closed her eyes again, not bothering to move, but simply turning her head away from the vaguely cheesy smell of Piper's sooty feet.

———

"WHAT THE HECK is that on your fingers?"

Lorna extended a hand and laughed. "Oh. Chipped nail polish."

Riley leaned in as though she'd heard incorrectly. "*Nail* polish?"

They were in Lorna's backyard, sitting on the ground while Cassidy picked up and studied the crimson and yellow leaves that had fallen and blanketed the grass beneath the large red maple. Before long, it would be way too cold to do this, but it had been an unseasonably warm November, and since Riley was up for the night, it seemed only right to take advantage of it by spending some time outside.

Nearby, Cullen was making piles of leaves, all in a row, and then kicking at and dispersing them once again. He had done so three or four times so far by Lorna's count, and had yet to lose interest in the activity. He looked remarkably like Shawn, but had Riley's disposition. A natural charmer, without even trying.

"Malcolm's girls did it a couple weeks ago. And I don't have the stuff that takes it off, so it's been slowly chipping away. Unsightly, isn't it?" Lorna looked at her nails and smiled.

Riley rolled her eyes. "The 'stuff that takes if off' is called nail polish remover, by the way. We can get some at CVS. I don't think I can stand to look at that all day."

Lorna laughed again. "They had fun putting it on, that's the important thing."

Riley looked down, and idly smoothed Cassidy's hair, a strange look playing about the corners of her mouth.

"Well ... I'm glad you're enjoying them."

Lorna leaned in a little. "Why'd you say it like that?"

"How'd I say it?" Riley shrugged. "I am. I'm glad you're enjoying them. If you didn't I'm sure you'd use it as an excuse to bump Malcolm to the curb or something."

"Riley," Lorna said tiredly. "I think we're well past that, Malcolm and I."

Shaking her head, Riley sighed. "I know you are. Sorry. I ... I just ..."

"Just what?"

Sighing again, Riley looked at her. "It's just ... strange, that's all."

"What's strange? Talk to me."

Cullen wandered over, dropping a few leaves on his sister's head, to her delight. She laughed and he dropped more leaves, crouching next to her and beginning to cover her legs with them as well.

"You talk about his kids a lot. Especially Piper. I can tell you're bonding with them."

"And ...?"

"You never had that much time for me, that's all," Riley said, speaking so quickly that her words tumbled one into the other.

"Riley, that's ..." Lorna stopped herself. *Was* that true?

"We never did nails, for instance," Riley said almost accusingly.

"Because I'm not the doing nails type."

"Well evidently you are, because ..." Riley indicated her hands. "I mean, all I remember is times like you reading me something from Willa Cather and telling me how important her work was to '*the development of notions about how women could undermine gender conventions.*' Jesus ... I think that's even a quote, word for word of what you said. *That's* the kind of thing we did together. We never did *nails*."

Lorna looked at her daughter and felt a surge of love, and of compassion.

She was so used to feeling proud of their relationship, and of how close they were—and they were—but there were enormous fissures there as well. Things she hadn't permitted herself to see because she was too busy being proud, in her heart of hearts taking credit for all her own accomplishments and for Riley's as well—as though she'd 'made' Riley, crafted her with her own hands. When the truth of it was, much of what Riley had become was not at all because of her.

"Did you *want* to do nails?" Lorna asked softly, only half joking.

Riley looked at her. She was smiling but there were tears in her eyes as well. "I wanted to please you. *That's* what I wanted."

"Oh, darling ..." Lorna leaned in and hugged her tight. "You did. You *do*."

Riley was grasping her about the waist, holding on so tight, Lorna could barely take a breath.

"Riley, you are the most amazing unexpected gift of my life. The happiest happenstance ... My first and deepest love. You *know* that."

"It hasn't felt like that lately," Riley said against her shoulder.

Lorna pulled back and looked at her daughter's face. It was tear-stained, crumpled and poised to produce more tears.

"What do you mean?"

"You have all this other stuff going on. None of which has anything to do with me. And I don't even know what you're up to these days. Are you writing a book? Planning a trip to China? I have no idea anymore. And it's ... just ... strange. We never used to be like this."

"I've felt a little bit the same way. You did Thanksgiving with Ryan and his family, and ..."

"Mom, you hate Thanksgiving."

"And so did you at one time."

"I went because they invited us and I knew you wouldn't care about Thanksgiving, so ..."

"I don't." Lorna shook her head. "And I'm glad you went to Ryan's, but I ... Anyway, let's not make this about me. The point I'm making is that both our lives are different and changing. But they're *good* changes. And we're still connected Riley, in ways that no one and nothing could ever compromise. What we're doing is enlarging our circle, that's all. And it's bound to be uncomfortable at first, because we've been so used to it just being us. And then we let in Shawn ... and these babies came along ..."

Lorna looked at Cullen, who by now had all but covered his sister with leaves, like he wanted to disappear her altogether.

"Then, it's not that you like Malcolm's daughters more than you liked me at that age?" Riley asked. And Lorna knew she was only pretending to be joking.

"I don't like anyone more than I like you. At *any* age."

Riley sighed, and looking over, finally realized what Cullen was up to. Laughing, she brushed the leaves away from Cassidy and pointed Cullen back in the direction of his original piles-of-leaves project.

"Looks like I'm not the only one struggling with enlarging their circle," she said dryly.

"MALCOLM."

"Huh."

"*Malcolm.*"

"C'mon, baby, you know I have to be up in like two hours. I got you in the morning, okay?"

Lorna nudged him hard in the side. "That's not why I'm waking you up!"

Next to her Malcolm laughed, turning onto his side and pulling her against him spoon-fashion. "Okay, maybe not, but once I'm up, all bets are off." He slid his hand under her tank and palmed her breast.

"Your hands are cold," she complained half-heartedly, as he started playing with her nipples.

"I know. But we can warm them up ..." He moved it down her stomach and under the waistband of her panties, between her legs.

Lorna moaned quietly, her eyes rolling back into her head as he lazily teased and stroked her, making her almost forget what was on her mind.

"Malcolm ... stop. I want to talk to you about something."

"So talk," he said, ignoring her request to stop. Instead he nudged her legs wider, now using three fingers, sliding them deeper and pulling back, driving her a little out of her mind.

"Do you want babies?"

Malcolm froze. Then he was shifting positions, turning Lorna onto her back and covering her body with his, propped on his elbows.

"What brought this on this time?"

"Just answer the question, Malcolm. You're a young man ..."

"Here we go again with *this* shit. At ..." He glanced at the bedside clock, "... four in the morning."

"It's been on my mind. I want to know. *Do* you?"

"The truth?" he asked.

Lorna's heart began a gradual canter. Depending on what he said, it might reach maximum speed before long.

"Yes. The truth."

Malcolm sighed.

The lights were off, but the window was open. Lorna could see some of his face because the moon was high in the sky, and almost full. When he looked off beyond her, into the middle distance, Lorna took in his strong profile, the new protrusion of his maturing beard. She loved this man. She loved him ... hard. But what he said now had the power to change everything.

"If we could have babies, I would want them," he said. "If you wanted to give them to me, I would celebrate that. I would embrace it."

"I knew it."

"What did you know?"

"That you would want more kids. And Malcolm, that's just not something that ..."

"You weren't *listening* to me, Lo. As usual."

"What did I not hear?"

"If. You didn't hear the word '*if*'. I know we're done with that. But I love you. I love you more than I ... how could I not want the full range of what a man has with a woman, with you? You're right here." He took her hand and placed it over his heart. "You're inside me now. You're part of me. If we could, I would love to see what our babies would look like, what they would be like, the people they would become ... And I regret that we never met sooner. But what we have now? That doesn't feel in any way incomplete. I just want to look ahead. I'm not looking back, Lo. I need you to believe that."

"But you could look ahead to a future that includes children with some ..."

"If you say with someone else, I'm going to lose it. I don't *want* someone else. Can you get that into your thick skull? And I don't *want* babies for the sake of having them with someone else. I want you. *I want us.* More than any hypothetical kid we might have had."

"Okay," she said quietly.

"*Okay?*" he asked, his voice firm. "Can we put this conversation to rest once and for all?"

"Yes," she said. "We can put it to rest."

Reaching down, she cupped him with her hand and was surprised when Malcolm shoved her hand away.

"Nah," he said. "We're not doing that. I'm not in the mood anymore. You pissed me off with this baby nonsense. I mean, hell ... if I want a baby around, we'll borrow one of Riley's." He rolled off her and onto his back once again. "And don't wake me up again. I have an eight a.m. class."

Lorna stared at the dark for a while, listening for Malcolm's breathing to become steady and even again. He was still awake.

"Malcolm?" she whispered.

"What?"

She pulled his arm away from his body, arranging herself against his side and then dragging the arm back around her, since he seemed disinclined to do it himself.

"I love you," she said.

He grunted and then sighed, pulling her closer so her head was on his chest.

"I love you, too," he said finally, and almost grudgingly. "Now shut up and go to sleep."

EPILOGUE

"Are you ready?"

"Almost. Just ..." Lorna typed as quickly as she could, trying to get her thought out, which only resulted in three errors in a single sentence which she then had to go back and change. "Ten more minutes and then ..."

"Lo, I don't have ten minutes. As it is, I'm going to be late if I don't leave now."

"Then leave, Malcolm. I'll meet you over there. I need to do something with my hair anyway."

She glanced over her shoulder at where he was standing near the door of their hotel suite, dressed in dark-blue slacks, brown loafers and a button-down with a sport-coat. The beard was full now, and made him more handsome if that were possible. And today, for the book-signing, the glasses were on.

"If I leave without you, you're not going to come."

"Of course, I'll come. I just need to finish this thought, do my hair and ..."

Malcolm groaned. "The hair alone means you'll miss it."

"Sweetheart, I would never miss your reading," Lorna said.

"And you know I'm not one who fusses over something as meaningless as *hair*. So go ahead. I'm sure the car's downstairs. I'll cab it over and be about twenty minutes behind you. Promise."

He always acquiesced when she called him 'sweetheart'. It was terrible and manipulative, she knew, but Lorna wasn't the emotional, expressive type and Malcolm knew it, so she occasionally could pull out a single word and he folded like a lawn chair.

"Okay. But hurry," he said, turning to leave. Then he came back and kissed her quickly on top of the head while she typed as fast as she could.

Five minutes later, Lorna was staring at her reflection in the hotel mirror. *Ugh*. The lighting in these places, and the mirrors from three angles sure could do a number on a woman.

She quickly arranged her shoulder-length hair into a messy updo and reached for the lip-stain that Riley helped her choose. She only liked colors that heightened, rather than replaced her natural lip-color.

Smoothing her hands over her black pantsuit, she turned to the side, pleased that she didn't see too much of the little pooch she was beginning to develop, and that her arms weren't looking too flabby.

Lately, she had taken to working out with Malcolm twice a week, suddenly aware that good genes could only take a woman so far. Thoughts like this seemed only to come in full force around this time or year. Tomorrow was her forty-seventh birthday, and since Malcolm wanted her to be with him for it, she had traveled to Philadelphia for this, his second stop on his book tour.

His second novel seemed poised to do as well as the first, and so his agent had front-ended all his appearances, but keeping them on the East Coast until the Gilchrist spring semester was over and Malcolm was able to travel farther afield. Lorna knew he was a little apprehensive about the ones out West, because he was under the impression she would make it difficult by refusing to come along.

She'd only been joking when she said she had no intention of traipsing across the country 'following my man'. Of course she would go. She wouldn't enjoy the long separation either, truth be told. He didn't know it, because she had never said as much in words, but she disliked being away from him for any significant length of time. Malcolm kept her in balance, and was the best collaborator and thought-partner she had ever had. Well, that, and she just loved being with him for no other reason than that he was her man, and she his woman.

Besides, she was finding it surprisingly easy to write in the hotel room. There was something about being somewhere else, and out of her element that made the creative juices flow a little freer.

And though she still hadn't thought of a book idea of her own, she was having a great time writing short social commentaries for Riley's journal. All that television-watching had paid off after all, and she had no end of topics for her monthly column. The reality shows alone offered her plenty of material. It wasn't just gender, either; now she was writing about religion pretty regularly, and had a series in progress on the war on Islam, which was provoking lots of attention. Which, she had to admit she had always kind of loved.

Pulling on her lavender pashmina, Lorna glanced one last time at her reflection and bared her teeth to make sure there was no lipstick on them, then grabbed her purse and hurried to meet Malcolm at the bookstore.

HE HAD ALMOST GIVEN up on her.

But just as Malcolm told himself to stop scanning the sea of faces—some of them milling around with his book in hand waiting for the reading to begin, others still on the queue waiting to get their copies signed—he spotted Lorna near the front of the bookstore, chatting with his tour manager, Philberta. Lorna looked pretty with her hair up like that, and was wearing the earrings he'd gotten her for Christmas.

It had taken him a hell of a long time to find the right ones. Feminine yet not too delicate, like the woman they were meant for—they were little gold teardrops from Cartier. On Riley's advice, Malcolm had actually switched them out of the Cartier box into something more modest because she promised him, Lorna would definitely have something to say about how pointless it was for him to have spent so much. The urge to buy her gifts was almost constant now, like he was a kid in the throes of puppy love, ripping daisies out of a neighbor's yard, desperate to bring something to his sweetheart.

"Mr. Mitchell, I just want to say ..." A woman was leaning over the table where he was seated, signing books, her voice a breathy whisper of admiration, her breasts almost spilling out of her snug, yellow dress. "This book, 'Rag & Bone', was the most moving reading experience I've had since ..."

She stopped and giggled.

"Well, since your last book, 'Cadence'. So, I just thought ..."

The rest of her effusive praise was lost on him as he caught Lorna's eyes over the woman's shoulder and she smiled her ironic smile, which he knew was part amusement, part annoyance at the pushy women he met at these things.

He offered her a smile back, which the woman at the table thought was for her.

"Erica," she said. "To Erica."

"Excuse me?" Malcolm said.

"For the inscription?" She pointed a long, tapered nail down at the book in his hand, the pen poised over the fly-leaf.

"Oh, yeah. For Erica," he repeated. "With great appreciation for your support." And then he added his signature.

"Thank you so much," she said. "For all that you do."

Malcolm nodded and smiled, then greeted the next person in line. Across the room, Lorna and Philberta continued their conversation.

She had started working again, often getting up and writing in the wee hours of the morning, or disappearing back to her house, for two or three days at a time. Sometimes she would get so caught up in her ideas and work that she wound up not sleeping at his place for a stretch of as long as a week. What bothered him, though he acted like it didn't, was that she wouldn't even notice until he came to get her—and her laptop, which she never went anywhere without these days—with some ruse like a dinner he wanted to take her to, which would end late.

They still socialized with some of the Gilchrist faculty at off-campus dinners and parties, but Lorna mostly preferred to stay out of that realm and spent more and more time on day-trips into the city to meet with Riley and her team, and to have lunches and dinners and drinks with friends of hers who taught at one of the CUNY colleges or NYU; most of them people Malcolm didn't even know.

The dark period she had gone through right after leaving Gilchrist was definitely over, and while Malcolm was glad she had found new purpose and energy, he couldn't pretend he didn't worry that Lorna's restless spirit—in more ways than one—might rear its head once again.

The book-signing went on another hour, until his hand was cramped, and then there was the reading at the back of the store where he stood behind a podium and tried to look deep and author-like.

Lorna sat in the rear, of the crowd, her gaze trained on his, while he tried to spread his eye contact around the room equally.

When he was done with his passage, which was about the moment his main protagonist walks in on his father making love to his mistress, the small crowd gave him a standing ovation. Lorna stood to applaud as well, the look on her face not just appreciative of what he'd read, but proud of him.

After another half hour or so of glad-handing, he was done for the evening, and as the last of the readers left him, Malcolm and Lorna were free to walk out together into the night. The weather was temperate, and comfortable, so they decided not to take the car that Philberta had on call for him, but instead stroll the twenty or so blocks back to the hotel.

"Your words were beautiful, as always Malcolm T. Mitchell. One of these days I'm going to have to read that book of yours."

Malcolm smiled, recalling that she'd said something similar when they first met. *God, was it a year ago already?* Her quick-witted responses to everything—that had stayed the same, but there was plenty about her that was different as well.

"Read it this weekend," he said. "I want to hear what you think about it."

"I'm sure I'll love it. And that passage you read actually made me more curious. It made me think about Piper."

"Piper? Why?" He glanced at her and she took a breath, then put a hand up to her nape. "What's up?" he prompted.

"Well, remember a long time ago when you said you thought that Piper's acting out was something more than regular pre-teen stuff?"

"Yeah?"

"Well, there was something. Something she let slip while we were talking. I don't know that this is what was bothering her, but I think it could be."

"Okay, well tell me. I'm starting to get worried over here."

"Don't be worried. It's nothing that bad. But remember when she walked in and Charlotte was trying to kiss you? Well it seems that happened before. Except Charlotte wasn't kissing you, she was kissing someone named Mr. Spence, and ..."

"Oh shit. No, not *Mr.* Spence. Just Spence."

Lorna looked at him. "Is that someone you know?"

"Yeah. The guy Charlotte had her affair with. And Piper knows him. And knows his wife and kids too. He's at Charlotte's firm and we used to see their whole family socially, so ..." Malcolm ran a hand over his head. "No wonder Charlotte said she felt like Piper had it in for her sometimes. Maybe she does."

"There's a lot of action in Charlotte's kitchen," Lorna quipped.

Malcolm shook his head. "I'll talk to her."

"Just don't let on that I told you. Otherwise you'll lose your source of valuable insider information. And that's going to be *key* when she turns sixteen, believe me."

"I don't mean Piper. I meant I'm going to talk to Charlotte. I have no idea what I'd say to Piper about something like that." He looked at Lorna. "What'd *you* say to her?"

Lorna shrugged. "That parents are people too, and that when she gets older she'll see her Mom as a person, not just as Mom. But that she should try to do that now, as much as she can, even though it's hard."

"That's pretty good," he said wryly. "Better than what I might have come up with. She loves you, y'know? Her and Hayley."

"They're growing on me as well," she said looking at him

slyly. "And Piper and I understand each other. We're both a little difficult sometimes, but we're worth it."

He brushed the tip of her nose with a finger. "You're not so difficult."

"That's not what you said last week."

"What happened last wee ... *hey*." Malcolm stopped in his tracks. "Remember?"

He pointed at the restaurant across the street where the previous summer they had dined with the couple celebrating their fortieth wedding anniversary.

"Feel like Korean for dinner?"

Lorna nodded. "Yeah, let's do it." She pulled him toward the crosswalk so they could wait for the light to get to the other side. "Who knows? Maybe we'll have our fortieth anniversary there as well."

"Yeah, mayb ..." He turned to look down at her, and she was looking right back up at him, a little smile on her face. "So ... by that you mean, what exactly? That forty years from now, you and I will still be ... in this thing?"

Lorna shook her head. "Not *exactly*."

Malcolm shrugged, swallowing his disappointment and looking away.

"I'm hoping we'll be in a *different* thing," she said. "I'm hoping we'll be ... in a marriage."

"What?"

He leaned in, squinting his eyes as though that would improve his hearing. He'd never mentioned that to her again; not since that one oblique reference way back when they vacationed together in North Carolina. He didn't even let himself *think* it too often in case she smelled it on him or something, and ran for the hills.

But it had always been there, tucked in the back of his heart. That's what he wanted for them. Because Lorna Terry remained, even now, the most elusive woman he had ever met. Even though he had her, often it felt like she was off on her own, someplace far away and just out of reach.

"I want to marry you," she said.

"You want to marry me," he said. "Like ..." He squinted again. "What do you mean by that exactly? Like some kind of new age commitment ceremony with a shaman and candles and chanting, or the real deal with ...?"

"Malcolm, for heaven's sake ... do I have to beg?"

He grinned. "God, I would love it if you did."

"Please." Lorna said, her expression perfectly sober. "Let's get married."

Around them, other pedestrians dodged by, crossing over to the other side when the light changed.

"What about ...?"

"I don't care what anyone thinks," Lorna said, shaking her head. "This is for us. And for you. So you know that I'm here, and in this thing ... for as long as ... as long as you want me. As long as we want each other."

"Forever would have been nice," he teased. "Couldn't you have said for 'forever'?"

Lorna rolled her eyes.

"Okay, fine. That's a little too sappy for you. But let me make sure I have something straight. You're not thinking we'll have one of those modern marriages where the couple lives in separate houses or some crap like that, right? Because I'm not doing that shit. If we do this, it's you and me, under the same roof. Every single day, every single night ..."

Lorna laughed. "Are you trying to talk me out of it? Because if so you're doing a pretty good job."

"No. I'm making sure you know we're having a traditional marriage. Like me, head-of-household, you Jane. That kind of thing."

"Don't push your luck, Malcolm." And after a pause: "So ... do you want to do this or not?"

"Will you change your name to Lorna Mitchell?"

"*No*." She shook her head. She leaned into him when he pulled her against his chest. "But I will introduce you as my husband at parties. *That* I can promise to do."

"And wear a ring and everything?"

"Yes."

"And I get to refer to you as my wife," he said, teasing her lips with his. "*My* wife."

"Yes. *Your* wife. So ... do you want to?"

She was waiting, eager for his answer but not wanting to seem like it, Malcolm realized. She wanted this. She *really* wanted this. Maybe even as much as he did. Every day was a new revelation with this woman.

"Yeah," he said. "If I get around to proposing, maybe we could do that ... yeah."

Lorna smiled and took a breath. This was their way. Always jousting, and jockeying for position. It would probably always be their way—the trading back and forth of power, but neither of them surrendering anything they wouldn't give willingly. This time it was Lorna who gave in, and Malcolm knew it was because she understood that in this decision, as a man, he needed to lead.

"Well, whenever you ask, *if* you ask, my answer would be 'yes'," she said.

She looked up at him and her gaze was unwavering.

"Good to know," he said, straining to sound flippant.

He *would* ask. Soon. Hell, he would ask her *tomorrow*.

Lorna leaned in closer, and Malcolm felt her entire body heave and melt into his. The way it always did, like she belonged there. Because she did.

Before the leaves fell, if he had anything to say about it, her name would be '*Mrs. Lorna Mitchell.*'

Smiling, he pressed his lips to the top of her head.

But that was a battle for another day. And honestly, the outcome didn't even matter, because the hardest fight had already been won.

ALSO BY NIA FORRESTER

The 'Commitment' Novels

The 'Afterwards' Novels

The 'Mistress' Novels

Wife (The 'Mistress' Trilogy Book 2)

Mother (The 'Mistress' Trilogy Book 3)

The 'Acostas' Novels

The Seduction of Dylan Acosta (The Acostas Book 1)

The Education of Miri Acosta (The Acostas Book 2)

The 'Secret' Series

Secret (The 'Secret' Series Book 1)

The Art of Endings (The 'Secret' Series Book 1)

Lifted (The 'Secret' Series Book 3)

The 'Shorts'

Still—The 'Shorts' Book 1

The Coffee Date—The 'Shorts' Book 2

Just Lunch—The 'Shorts' Book 3

Table for Two—The 'Shorts' Book 4

The Wanderer—The 'Shorts' Book 5

À la Carte: A 'Coffee Date' Novella—The 'Shorts' Book 6

Silent Nights—The 'Shorts' Book 7

Not That Kind of Girl—The 'Shorts' Book 8

À la Carte: The Complete 'Coffee Date' Novellas

Standalone Novels

Ivy's League

The Lover

Acceptable Losses

Paid Companion

The Makeover

ABOUT THE AUTHOR

Nia Forrester lives and writes in Philadelphia, Pennsylvania where, by day, she is an attorney working on public policy and by night, she crafts woman-centered fiction that examines the complexities of life, love and the human condition.

She welcomes feedback and email from her readers at authorniaforrester@gmail.com. Or visit with her, at NiaForrester.com